BICYCLE ON THE BEACH

BICYCLE ON THE BEACH

 Peter Viertel

DELACORTE PRESS / NEW YORK

For Deborah

Le roman n'est pas l'autobiographie qui, elle, est du domaine de la mémoire. L'imaginaire, lui, est du merveilleux domaine de l'oublie; le roman le rend, Werther ou David Copperfield, inoubliable. Le roman n'est pas ce qui fut; mais ce qui pourrait être, ce qui aurait pu être.

—ARAGON

PART
I

≫ *one* ≪

YEARS AGO, long before the war, we lived in a house near the sea, in a town named after a Spanish saint. Although it was not as romantic a place as it sounds, I still find myself looking back on that period of my life with hopeless nostalgia, for it seems to me that after I left there the summers were never again as long and as hot, nor the sea as clear and the beaches as uncrowded, nor was I ever again as untroubled by the passing of time. My father was alive then, and although he often went abroad, the reality of final loss had not as yet come into my life, as it did later on when he died.

Money was not as yet a problem either, for despite the Depression, which had just started, my family lived comfortably in the house they owned in friendly partnership with the local bank. It was an enormous improvement over the furnished apartments we had occupied in Vienna and Berlin. California was a paradise in those days before smog and traffic; the sun shone most of the year, and the hills were unscarred by roads or cantilever houses; you could buy six dozen oranges for twenty-five cents, a hot dog cost a nickel, and the beach was free.

The street on which we lived was generously endowed with vacant lots, where we played as boys, delighted to enact our games of cowboys and Indians nearer their true locale. The dry fields covered with stubble made up for the fact that we only had a small backyard. Still, there was a fig tree in one corner of it, and from the back terrace of the house you

3

could see the Pacific Ocean, the part the sun set in. That view of the sea was a source of endless pleasure to my parents, even when the scope of it was somewhat reduced by a small summer house that a neighbor built not more than five yards away from the back fence of our tiny garden. I remember that the architectural style of this annoying structure was Japanese, and that it included false boulders made of wire and cement, which my brother and I scoffed at because they looked like such outrageous fakes.

We went to the public high school a few miles away, and because of our German accents were immediately dubbed Hans and Fritz, although we hardly resembled the Katzenjammer kids; we were still well-brought-up European children at the time. The First World War had ended only fifteen years earlier, and although we were not often persecuted for our nationality, we were nevertheless constantly reminded that our country had lost. If we played at war after school, we were always assigned the roles of the defeated enemy, a role we accepted proudly, and fought as well as we could, although the end result was always the same, preordained, as it was, by history.

When Hitler came to power like the ogre in a German fairy tale, we became more conscious of the difference between Austria and its erstwhile partner in the war that had ended not so long ago. We had not been brought up in any religion, and it was with surprise that I learned from my older brother, Jake, that we were Jews, the new enemies of the German state. It was an unpleasant discovery, and I struggled for a while before accepting it. Why did we have to be special? Wasn't it bad enough that we spoke with an accent and had learned to bow when introduced to an older person? We never went to the synagogue, so why were we Jewish? Because our parents were Jews, my brother explained, which logic put an end to my questions. The only solace he had to offer me was that Christ had been a Jew, too.

It did not change our status with our schoolmates, however. We were still Hans and Fritz, the two little "heinies." Our only ally was a much older boy named Ernie Schaab, the star quarterback of the varsity football team, whose parents had come over from Germany quite a few years before ours. He did not care whether we were Germans or Austrians, but took our side because we spoke his language, which was enough to protect us from the others, for he was an important man on the campus, as well as a tough and skillful fighter whenever the occasion demanded. He became the welterweight champion of the Pacific Fleet and was killed at Pearl Harbor, while serving on an American battleship, the only glory he attained in his brief life.

In those days, however, the tramp of German boots was still a faraway sound, and had, as yet, very little influence on my life. They shut the door on the possibility of a return to Europe, which pleased my brother and me, won over, as we were, by our new environment.

We had arrived in America too late in life to learn to throw a baseball with any great accuracy, so we never tried to join in the games of work-up that the other boys on our street used to play. The ocean made no competitive demands, and it was close at hand. We learned to ride the waves on our bellies, which required no special physical attributes, and was not dangerous. It soon became our main obsession. Like the seals who sometimes visited us out beyond the breakers, we never tired of repeating the same maneuvers, swimming out to where the waves curled before they broke, and then riding them in until our stomachs touched the sand. In the clear water of the early mornings the seals watched with silent approval, waiting patiently for us to come out again, so that they could swim and dive in our proximity, too sensible to join us in the idiocy of our game.

But the summers did not last forever even in those days, although there was always a heat wave late in October when we were already back at school. The temperature would rise to over a hundred, and a warm wind called the Santa Ana would blow throughout the night. We would go to the beach after school, and swim until the orange sun disappeared in the sea. Sometimes my father would join us, and we would walk with him through the foam of the spent waves, our tanned bodies making his skin look even whiter. With his gray hair blowing in the wind, he looked like a prophet from the Old World, flanked by two savages from the New.

I remember returning home one evening and listening to him describe the life of the beach to my mother. The handsomeness of the young Californians had made a deep impression on him, accustomed, as he was, to European resorts and European bodies. "They are like Greeks," he said, "with their muscles and their bronzed skins." Then he executed an awkward dance, his eyes alight with humor. "We are Greeks without brains," he sang. "We are Greeks without brains! That's the song they sing." The joke offended me, as I had already started to identify myself with the people he was making fun of, and I had been secretly ashamed of having a father who looked so different. Only many years later, when I first returned, after a long absence, to the beaches I had been forced to abandon by the war, did I remember his brief song, and found it apt and was not disturbed by it at all.

But not then, not when the jest was made. The United States of America was the strongest country in the world, a place in which tolerance was prescribed by law, which made it doubly strong, I felt, for I was young enough to believe in the invincibility of justice. Without knowing it, I had become a patriot, a patriot with a foreign passport. But as I had been raised by European parents, I was well brought up enough to keep my contradictory opinions to myself.

ᕲᕲ *two* ᕲᕲ

"THERE IS NO AUTUMN, there are no seasons," my father often complained. "Only this endless summer without grass." That was not altogether true. In the canyons at the base of the brush-covered hills, the leaves of the sycamores were already turning brown, and on the high plateaus above the sea, the grass was yellow and dry. Only the date palms, in the public park where I often walked with my father in the evenings, remained untouched by the long hot days and balmy nights.

He had been a painter in his youth, and he longed for the colors of fall in Europe, and the Vienna woods, the vine-covered hillsides of the Wachau. His early work was avant-garde (he was one of the early cubists), and that in turn forced him to take up set designing for the theater and the movies; the deviation from his profession had brought him to America.

Whenever there was no work in the film studios, he helped an old friend of his from Berlin with the decorating business the man had founded, as, unlike my father, he had had the foresight to bring his most valuable possessions with him from Germany. My father brought his knowledge of antique furniture to the enterprise, and together they bought and sold the treasures others wanted to dispose of or to acquire. Pojawlski was a clever businessman, which my father was not, so that he was hesitant to allow him to go off to Europe on the purchasing trip that the shop's diminishing inventory soon made necessary. Yet Pojawlski loved the safe haven he had found, delighted in the mild climate which he said made his arthritis bearable. He had no desire to return to the uncertainty and strife of Europe, not even for a short visit, and armed with an American passport.

So in the end my father had his way. He was the one who would go. There was no danger of war as yet, he maintained. Not that year anyway, and probably not even the next, although he was convinced that it would ultimately come. When I look back now I realize how recent the First World War must have seemed to my parents, for the peace was not even fifteen years old. My father had served for four years in the Austrian cavalry, attached to the service of supply, which fortunate posting had undoubtedly saved his life. My favorite photograph of him was in uniform, with close-cropped black hair and a moustache, both of which styles he had abandoned. He had hated the war, had no pride about his part in it, even in retrospect, which was as unusual a phenomenon then as it is today. Now he wanted to return to Europe before a new wave of destruction began.

My mother protested in the beginning, but as she understood what prompted his restlessness, she ultimately gave in. She even went so far as to support him in his arguments with Pojawlski. My grandmother was still alive, though ailing, and my mother realized that my father wanted to see her before she died. She also realized that he wanted to see Vienna once again, before it, too, was locked away behind the curtain of hate that was already being drawn across part of Europe. Before he left, however, there was one thing she wanted him to do. My brother and I had come to America a few months after our parents, and had been allowed in on visitors' visas, which status my mother insisted be rectified. There were various conferences with lawyers, and a visit to the Federal Building in downtown Los Angeles, and then we all set off for Baja California in the family car, for the law required that we leave the territorial limits of the United States in order to enter the country as bona-fide immigrants. It was an incomprehensible technicality as far as my brother and I were concerned, but as the trip got us excused from school for a week, we went willingly.

Crossing the border at Tijuana brought back unpleasant memories of

Europe. There were policemen and soldiers in foreign uniforms, and we were detained in a stifling room while my father argued endlessly with a group of fat officials behind a glass door. It was reminiscent of all the trips we had taken to Poland and Italy during the European summers, trips I had half-forgotten. Now, like in a bad dream, it was all happening again. Why was the world divided by these arbitrary frontiers that were so difficult and frightening to cross? Why were there so many soldiers and officials questioning us in a language none of us could understand? Why didn't America control the entire continent?

When at last we were free to drive on, I noticed that the countryside changed. The roads were not as wide or as well paved, and the distances were marked off in kilometers instead of miles. I remember that it was hotter in the car than it had been, and when we stopped for a drink there were swarms of flies, and barefoot children begging for pennies. Beggars belonged to the Old World, I felt, to the cold sidewalks of Berlin, which I had not forgotten.

To my amazement, my parents seemed to enjoy the change. My mother said that the countryside reminded her of Poland, and said it with pleasure. There were peasants in the fields again, which she had missed, as there were no peasants in America. Why that was a fault, I could not understand. Nor could I see then that there was color in the disorder and poverty of Mexico. All I noticed was that there were no hamburgers or hot dogs for sale, and when my father said it was probably better that we did not eat the ice cream, I was doubly sure that we had come to a backward country. I remember that I sat quietly in the back of the car and prayed to the God my German nurse had taught me to pray to that nothing would disrupt the plans that had been made, and that we would be able to return as quickly as possible to the house we had left only that morning. Once I was back, I would never leave, I resolved fervently, the first of many resolves I was not to keep.

We arrived at a hotel that stood overlooking a crescent-shaped beach, and once again we were a European family, checking in with our foreign passports. Only my parents' immigration visas protected us from eternal exile in this hot, unfriendly land. The receptionist, in a black coat and striped trousers, stared haughtily down at my brother and myself, for we were dressed in the American way, having immigrated with our hearts and minds long before our papers had been filed. "If the children wish to eat in the dining room, they will have to put on coats and ties," he informed my mother, who replied that it was most unusual for such strict rules to be applied in a seaside resort. The man interrupted her rather rudely, saying that no matter what she thought, the regulations would have to be abided by. My father bristled at the man's unfriendly manner, his violent temper exploding after the long, tiring day. He told the receptionist what he thought of the way guests were received in his hotel, his heavily accented English ringing out across the Spanish tiles of the empty hall.

I was ashamed, when I should have been proud, for the man had been rude to my mother, and had deserved a correction, but to me it seemed that we had once again shown that we were foreigners, as Americans, I was sure, would have taken the situation more calmly. Of course, the manager appeared at once and apologized for the tactlessness of the room clerk. Then he escorted us personally to the *comedor*, to arrange things with the headwaiter. I hung back. I was embarrassed to walk into the dining room, where all eyes were awaiting us, for my father's excited voice had made itself heard throughout the ground floor of the hotel. My mother reprimanded me for my lack of loyalty, and when I was finally led to the table where the others were already seated, my entrance was even more noticeable. My face burned as I stared down at my plate, avoiding my father's eyes, as well as those of the various waiters that were now gathered around us.

But there was worse in store. In the middle of the meal a telegram was delivered to our table, a message from our lawyer in California, telling us that there were further complications in Washington, and that we might well have to wait an additional week in Enseñada. My heart sank as I sat listening to my parents, for I heard my mother ask what my father would do if the government refused to grant us our entry permits. He replied that there was no chance that this would happen, which did not reassure either my brother or myself. I was only thirteen and a half years old, and yet I felt frightened at the thought of losing America forever. My mind raced ahead to imaginary pictures of desperate actions. I would smuggle my way across the border, climb through the dry Mexican hills, until I was back once again where I belonged.

But the gods were kind, and six days later we started back. I had not even been to the lovely beach in front of the hotel, and even the walks we took through the town plaza in the evening did not seem enjoyable to me, for I could not see the charm of the picturesque square. I was homesick for a less romantic landscape, a more familiar stretch of sea.

The border presented only a minor obstacle on our return voyage, as our lawyer was there to meet us, armed with the necessary papers. In less than an hour from the time we left the honky-tonk of Tijuana we were safely back in the United States. The day of our deliverance was clear and warm, and once we arrived at home, I went immediately down to the beach, and when I found the cool water of the sea again, with the gentle surf breaking on the shore, I felt as if I had escaped some awful fate, and that I was safe once again in the land of the free. I had left the danger of foreign lands behind me forever, I thought, and blindly, ignorantly, I resumed my interrupted game with the waves.

ᵉᶻ *three* ᵉᶻ

I USED TO BELIEVE that there was something special about having been born in the year 1920. It was a definite moment in time, the beginning of a new decade. If I had stayed in Europe, I would have belonged to the class of '20 which was due to be called up in five years, and with youthful egotism, I thought of no other class, felt sure that no other year had as unbreakable a rendezvous with fate. My brother, Jake, who had been born in 1918, might even escape the trenches, I thought, which was how I pictured war, having only recently been to see *All Quiet on the Western Front*. That was how a great many generals thought of it too, with or without having been to see the film, as it turned out later.

The day after we returned from Mexico was marked by the brutal assassination of Dollfuss, the Austrian premier, and although the planned takeover of the Austrian state failed, it made those of us who still had close ties with Europe realize that Hitler's announced plan of conquest was not a bluff, but a very real threat. I don't pretend that I was as fully aware of the importance of the event as my parents, but still the conversation at the dinner table that warm July evening disturbed my childish complacency, which had been reinforced by our return home.

The assassination of a figure of no less political significance had been enough to start the World War (it was not classified by a number in those days), only this time, the harvest was not in, which my mother felt was a classic reason for some slight optimism. My father pointed out to her that the harvest had hardly been collected at the beginning of August, 1914, but she merely shrugged her shoulders and said that was the first of the Kaiser's many errors. They sat by the radio until late that night, I remember, waiting for the latest news bulletins, but it was not until the following morning that we learned that the Nazis had been defeated. Some of the murderers had actually been arrested, although most of the conspirators had escaped to Germany. All was not lost yet, and my father decided to keep to his schedule, and to leave for Europe the following week.

I remember the preparations for his departure, the frantic last-minute packing, and the long, tense drive to the railroad station. Of course, we arrived with time to spare, so that there was a long, anticlimactic wait on the platform, with the train standing there as if it never intended to move. My father discovered that he had come away without a hat, for even he had become conditioned to the mild climate of southern California, where it was not necessary to wear a hat until it started to rain late in November. Pojawlski hurried back to his car, and returned with a hat he kept there to protect him against the sun, and there was a brief argument before my father accepted it. "I look like a businessman," he objected, catching his reflection in the window of the Pullman car.

"Perhaps it will help you to remember that you are one," Pojawlski said gently.

Then it was time to board the train. My father kissed each of his sons (among men, Americans didn't exchange kisses, I thought fleetingly), embraced Pojawlski, and while the porter shouted his second warning, took my mother into his arms.

"Take care of yourself," she told him. "And write!" She had tears in her eyes.

My father looked distressed, and crossed nervously to the metal stairs of the Pullman. There were tears in his eyes too, as he turned and waved to us through the open window of the door the stationmaster had closed behind him. He managed to smile only when he saw that I had started running down the quai in order to keep up with the moving train. "Be careful," he called out to me. And then: "Be good!" The train picked up speed. My father raised his hand. I could see his gray hair as the wind caught it, and he was carried off into the bluish haze of the warm evening.

He had forgiven me my lack of family solidarity more easily than I could forgive him for being incurably European. A white-jacketed porter waved to me from the observation platform of the last Pullman as it receded into the distance, a friendly gesture of anonymous farewell. I walked back down the empty platform to where my mother was standing with the others. She was still crying, and Pojawlski was trying to comfort her. "Don't worry . . . nothing will happen to him," I overheard him say. "He's really quite a sensible man." Suddenly it dawned on me that there was an element of risk involved in my father's journey. I was stunned. I had assumed that he would be back in a few months, and that life would go on as it always had. How stupid I had been! The Nazis were as active in Austria as they were in Germany, and my father had always been one of their most outspoken opponents. Why hadn't I been more affectionate with him? Now he was gone. We realize that we have not loved enough only when it is too late, I thought, and felt a little wiser than before.

≥ *four* ≤

I USED TO SAY MY PRAYERS every night before going to sleep; the Lord's Prayer in German (as I had never had a chance to learn it in English), followed by a homemade prayer of my own design. Our housekeeper in Germany (a bossy young woman from Breslau) had always insisted we ask God to take care of our father and mother when we were children, and the habit had remained with me years after its innovator had gone off to marry a Feldwebel in the rapidly expanding Reichswehr. I included my brother on my own initiative, and then when love came into my life I added each successive love's name, for like most children, I was civilized enough not to stop loving one person just because I had started loving another.

A girl who lived a few houses up the street from us was the first on the list. Her name was Helen. She was older than we were, had just finished high school, and was waiting to enter college. On my way home from school I used to catch a glimpse of her seated in a swing on her front lawn. She usually waved as Jake and I went by, which was enough to have a marked effect on me, and I was sad when she left for Stanford without saying good-bye. Fortunately, that winter, I met a girl called Mary Deane at the skating rink where we used to go Saturday afternoon, and although she was a foot taller than I was, and four years older, she consented to skate with me, holding my very unsure arm as we tried to glide rhythmically across the artificial ice.

The music and her blonde hair and the scent she used did not leave me unmoved, and I soon added her name to my nightly list. Then there was a girl whose name I recall, and nothing more. It was Jane. Beyond that my memory fails me, but I know that she existed, for when I fell in love with my music teacher at high school I made up a rhyme so as not to overlook anyone in my nightly plea to God to look after them all. Helen, Mary, Jane, Miss Ruth Payne. I remember the rhyme even though I have forgotten their faces, which is some sort of minor testimony to the lasting power of words. Or perhaps it is merely proof of my innocence, for although I included them in my prayers, they remained idols, untouched idols, except for my hand on my fellow skater's arm. Miss Payne remained as aloof in my daydreams as she was in the classroom where she taught music appreciation, which was why I referred to her as Miss Payne in my special prayers. I remember that she, too, was blonde and slender, and that she appeared often to be quite unhappy, which I imagined to have been caused by some slight or cruelty from one of the male teachers who were pursuing her, and which only made me love her more.

The Irish cook who came to work for us after Christmas was not in the same category as these others, for although I remember desiring her, she was never included in my prayers. Her name was Maureen, and there was something provocative about her figure that had a very definite effect on me. I used to put my arm around her small, aproned waist when I came home from school, and try to look down her gingham shirt front. She made me think of some of the old-fashioned illustrations in the pornographic books my brother, Jake, had found in our library, paintings and drawings of full-figured women in close proximity to their paramours, who were usually fully dressed in tight Edwardian trousers and skirted jackets. Maureen was not unlike these ladies, for her figure was full, and her skin a very perfect, untanned white, especially from her neck down to the more interesting parts of her that were hidden.

She could not have been totally unaware of the meaning of my actions. She never responded overtly to my vague advances, except that I do remember one night when we were alone in the house, my father having taken Jake and my mother to some place I had not wanted to go, and that on that occasion Maureen allowed me to get into her bed. I recall lying there in the darkness while she locked the back door (there was no real danger of being surprised, as the driveway that led to the garage passed by her window), but then when she came to join me in the narrow bed, I found myself seized by a sudden panic. She was wearing a rather voluminous nightdress, that she lifted above her knees as she approached, undoubtedly the habit of a lifetime rather than a provocative gesture.

I sat up in bed. "I'd better go back to my room," I said, sounding as if it were her fault that I was there.

"I'm not stopping you, honey," she replied, lowering her ample body onto the mattress. Her bare arm came briefly into contact with my shoulder. I ducked past her, and fled. I had no clear idea of what was expected of me, which I only realized fully once I was back in the safety of my own room. Jake's explanation of the facts of life had been too theoretical, and not specific enough, which, if anything, I regret more now than I did then.

When I came down for breakfast the following morning, Maureen acted as if nothing had happened. I was grateful to her for her tact, and tried to cover up my embarrassment by pretending that I was late for school, a ruse she must have seen through at once. Still she made no comment. By that time she was obviously aware of the fact that, despite my appearance, I was too young for the more daring side of love, and so that was that. There was never any more physical contact between us. But even though the incident had little effect on Maureen, it caused a considerable change in me.

I had received a bicycle for Christmas, which I treated with all the care a horseman lavishes on his favorite mount, and on it I used to roam the neighborhood after school, not knowing exactly what I was looking for, but feeling myself driven on to a search I did not quite understand. I would ride down the gentle incline of our street, and slowly make my way down to the coast road and the beach. There was little traffic in those days. Trucks would pass at great intervals down the two-lane highway, and passenger cars were a rarity in the winter.

I would ride north, pedaling laboriously over the sandy verge of the road until I was more than two miles away from our neighborhood, and therefore not likely to meet any of the boys I had so often played with during what I then considered to be my childhood. I would cross the highway and walk up the empty beach, leaving my bicycle behind with a lock through its shiny spokes. Once in a while I would meet someone gathering driftwood, an old man or an old woman from the more run-down section of the beach community, and we would pass each other in silence. I was looking for a suitable partner to relieve me of my loneliness.

There was another reason for my solitary expeditions on my bicycle. In our small neighborhood, six miles away from the high school we attended, there was only one group of boys our age, the same group we had played war with earlier that year. Unfortunately, they had come under the domination of a bully named Bruce Macklin, a boy four years older than Jake, the son of an Irish gardener who worked for one of our neighbors. He was strong enough to beat us all up, and so had been able to organize our street into a small dictatorship of his own design. He rode his bike with the agility of a Sioux horseman, and he manufactured powerful slingshots out of inner tubes and the sturdy branches of trees. He would steal lead from the various building sites nearby, pound it into flat strips, out of which he made pellets that could kill birds or even pierce the metal side of a garbage can.

I realize now that he was a budding sadist; he enjoyed sticking straws into the behinds of tadpoles and blowing them up, leaving them to float helplessly on the surface of the neighborhood pond, or he would twist our arms until we cried "uncle," which practice he ultimately combined with a more unpleasant torture, which made us flee his domination forever; he would pin us down onto the ground, and holding us with his knees, would threaten to rub his penis in our faces, which refined torture we did not even dare admit at home, choosing escape as the best way out of our misery.

I can still remember his mean face and his cruel laughter as he enjoyed our desperate squirmings. There was no defense against him, as he would lock one of us up in the garage of the house where he held court while torturing the other. One day my brother and I attacked him after he had released us, and he bloodied our noses in a brief fight in which neither Jake nor I managed to land a blow. "There are Nazis in every country," my mother said when she was told of what had happened.

Jake and I celebrated a year later when our torturer was sent to reform school for stealing cars. But until the day he graduated to practices punishable by the police, he was responsible for our becoming refugees from our own street, Jake returning to our library for sanctuary, and I the beach, where I could wander in relative safety, as Bruce visited that part of our world only when he was overcome by the desire to kill a seagull or a sandpiper.

Late one afternoon, while I was avoiding our tormentor and searching for some more gentle adventure, I came upon a car parked on a rise overlooking the beach, at a place called Castle Rock. It was a Ford roadster, and despite the cold breeze that was blowing in off the sea, the top was down. I abandoned my bike in order to investigate. The car was empty, but near the edge of the water I saw a young woman. She was dressed in gray flannel trousers and a raincoat, and her blonde hair was blowing in the wind. Racing toward her along the white edge of the spent waves was a small black dog with long ears. As I stood watching, she turned and came toward me. She had taken off her shoes in order to walk in the sand, and was carrying them in her right hand. As she approached, the dog rushed past her, snapping at them, as if they were a game they had invented together. After a first failure, he rushed back, encouraged by her shouts, and tried again to snatch the shoes from her grasp.

At last he was successful, and with a sneaker held firmly in his mouth, ran across the beach to where I was standing, and deposited the stolen object at my feet. I picked it up and stood waiting for its owner to arrive. I felt ill at ease, and yet unable to release the prize I had been given, while the dog ran back to try for the other shoe the girl still held in her hand. She was pretty, looked more than pretty to me, as I handed her back the sandy tennis shoe. "He's a devil," she said after thanking me. "This is a new game he's invented." She brushed the dry sand off her feet and slid them back into her sneakers. I hardly noticed her features, saw only that the skin on her feet and legs was still tanned, although there had been little sun that winter. I kept my eyes on the dog, whose name was Tim, and only when she was once again seated behind the wheel of her car did I dare look up. "Can I give you a lift?" she asked. Then, seeing my bike lying on its side on the other side of the car, she added: "Oh . . . you have your bike. I didn't see it."

I would have liked to pretend that the bicycle wasn't mine, that someone else had left it there beside the road, but the lie would have been too obvious, and it would have been too late to come back for it on foot later that afternoon. "No, thank you," I said rather stiffly, which incomplete reply I regretted immediately.

"Perhaps another day," she said, and started the engine of her car. It seemed to me that she spoke with an English accent, but I wasn't sure. She looked behind her to see that the road was clear, warned the dog to behave and not jump out of the seat, and then a moment later she had driven off, her small car disappearing up the coast road. I stood rooted in place, watching her go, and only when she was out of sight did I go to retrieve my bicycle. Then, heedless of the trucks that were passing, I started off in the opposite direction, feeling that I had found and lost what I had been seeking because of my lack of courage. Over and over again I ran through the many things I should have said and didn't, as if by some magic effort of my will I could make the scene recur. Yet, at the same time, I felt certain that I would never see her again.

My father had given me a diary on my last birthday, a small volume bound in red leather with a latch and a key, which I had considered a rather useless present, but that night when I got home I opened it to the day's date and made the first entry, describing briefly what had happened. Then, after resolving to write something in it every night before going to sleep, I turned the key in the small gold lock and put the book away. I felt I had to insure myself against permanent loss. I even put down that the name of the girl's dog was Tim.

five

I WENT BACK to Castle Rock and found the beach deserted. Only the gulls were there to mock at me, as they banked and chandelled above my head. There was a strong wind that carried the sand up onto the road, spreading it over the asphalt like a fine net. I could feel it against my ankles, biting into my skin. I knew that when I got back home I would have to clean the chain and sprocket of my bike, which was still new enough to warrant special attention. But none of that mattered as I stood watching the gray, winter waves break against the base of the huge rock that divided the beach in front of me. I could hardly remember what the girl I was searching for looked like. Her face had already become blurred in my memory, and yet I felt that I must find her again. I had no specific plan of what I would say if I did. I knew that she was much older than I was, so that I nurtured no false hopes of conquest. I presumed that she was lonely, and hoped that we could become friends, nothing more.

Which was why I continued my search throughout the weeks that followed. One day, near a place called Las Tunas, I saw a large La Salle sedan pull up on the other side of the road. Its driver, a man in a gray hat, sat watching me, and when I rode my bike farther up the beach, he followed along slowly. The kidnapping of the Lindbergh baby was still fresh in everyone's mind in those days, and although I did not feel frightened, I was distinctly ill at ease. At last I saw the car start off, only to see it make a U turn and come back toward me on my side of the highway. I rose on my pedals in order to make more speed, when I heard my name called. I stopped, as did the car. A tall man got out.

"Carl! Carl Woolf. . . . It's you, isn't it?"

I recognized my pursuer as he came toward me on foot. It was de Lucca, the real-estate man who had sold my father the house in which we lived. He was a tall, handsome man with graying hair and a thin aquiline face. I remember that he was always well dressed, with an elegance that was unusual in our small town. "What the hell are you doing here?" he asked.

"Just out riding my bike," I lied.

"This highway's not a very good place for it," he said. He was smoking a pipe that fitted neatly into his thin mouth, and nodded his head as he puffed on it, obviously not believing a word of what I had said. "Does your father know you come way up here?"

"He's in Europe."

"What about your ma?"

"I don't think she'd mind."

"She would if she saw these trucks going by." He noticed something on the ground in front of him, and reached down to pick up a screw lying in the dust. "This isn't part of your bike, is it?" he asked.

"I don't think so."

"Well, you'd better put it in your pocket anyway," he said. Then, with a strange smile he added: "It's probably one more screw than you've ever had."

I felt embarrassed, not because I was unused to vulgarity, but because the words had come from the mouth of an adult. I didn't reply, but stared down at the front tire of my bicycle.

"That's right, though, isn't it? You're still a virgin, aren't you, Carl?"

"I guess so," I replied.

"You guess so, eh? How old are you now?"

"I was fourteen last month."

"Well, you've got plenty of time," de Lucca said. "Unless, of course, one of these trucks sideswipes you. So be careful." He got back into his car. "Give my regards to your mother," he called out as he drove off.

That night at dinner I sat waiting for the reprimand I knew to be inevitable, for I felt certain that de Lucca would not keep our meeting on the highway to himself. But I was not prepared for the counter-measure my mother had obviously decided upon long before my wanderings on the beach had been called to her attention. "I've hired a tutor for you," she announced in a calm voice while Maureen was serving the main course.

"A tutor?" Jake's reaction was as violent as mine, only as he was unstained by guilt, he spoke first.

"Yes. A young man who can give you lessons after school. I'm never home in the afternoons, so that I have no idea of what you do with your time."

"We don't need lessons," Jake said. "We both do all our work, and we're not flunking any of our subjects."

"Well, that's not enough," my mother said. "American schools are much too easy. You don't learn anything. Everybody says so." It was an opinion she had formed a few months earlier, the day my father had discovered that neither of us was required to take Latin or Greek.

"The people the schools produce seem to do all right," Jake said. "This country has the best doctors and scientists in the world."

"That may be, but neither one of you is interested in medicine or science. Anyway, I want you to learn French."

"French? What for?" I wanted to know. "I already take Spanish and German."

"You take German because that way you can do nothing for at least one hour a day," my mother said firmly. "Anyway, French is a language that all educated people speak fluently. If you don't learn it now, you never will."

"I don't care," I said.

"I do," she replied. "I don't want you to grow up to be an ignoramus. Sit up straight when you eat." She paused to make certain that she had been obeyed. "The young man I've engaged," she went on, "was brought up in Paris, so you'll learn a good accent. He goes to the university in the morning, and he'll come here in the afternoon."

We groaned in unison, seeing our freedom slipping out of our grasp. "We have quite a lot of homework, you know," Jake said.

"You can do it after dinner. Most boys do it at that time, because they have to help their fathers after school."

"Not in America," Jake said. As usual, she seemed to be talking about another world, the one we had fortunately escaped.

"You're very much mistaken. In any case, you'll have two free days, as the tutor can come only three times a week during the semester. In the summer he'll be able to come every day."

"In the summer? What about our holidays."

"Your entire lives are one long holiday."

"That's not true." We were outraged, although we knew that there was some truth to her statement.

"I've also arranged for you to have tennis lessons every Saturday morning," my mother said, supplying the coup de grace.

"I don't want to learn to play tennis," Jake said angrily. "It's a silly game for the useless rich." His afternoons in the library were already beginning to have a decided effect on his political outlook.

"Don't raise your voice when you speak to me," my mother told him. "I won't stand for it. You're spoiled, both of you. If I had spoken to *my* father that way, I would have been sent out of the room. . . ."

"I'm not going to take any goddamn tennis lessons," Jake said stubbornly.

"You can leave the table and finish your meal in the breakfast room!"

Jake obeyed. I sat in silence, staring across at his empty chair. "I don't know what's the matter with the two of you," my mother said, tears coming to her eyes. "You don't appreciate anything I try to do for you. You're rude and impossible. You should be grateful for the many things you have. Instead, you're sullen and resentful. Do you want to grow up to be like all the other morons out here . . . with bad manners and without culture of any kind?" It was a rhetorical question, and although I recognized it as one, the word "culture" trapped me into making an insolent reply.

"Why do we have to be cultured?" I asked in a low voice, spitting out the hated word.

"Because you're *my* sons," my mother said heatedly, "and I'm not going to let you grow up to be ignorant Nazis, or just bums that hang around the street all day doing nothing. Because I know how you spend your afternoons. People have come to me and told me. . . ."

"De Lucca's a dirty squealer," I said.

"I forbid you to speak disrespectfully about an older person," my mother said, "and to use gangster language at the table."

"Then I'll go and eat with Jake."

"You'll stay where you are until you're excused. And when your father comes back, I'm going to tell him how you behaved while he was gone." She rang for Maureen. "No dessert for the boys," she told the cook.

"But I've made trifle pudding," Maureen said.

"I don't care. They're not to have any." She got up and went into the living room. Maureen stood over me, shaking her head. "American brats," I heard my mother say as she closed the door behind her. I chopped angrily at my cold meatloaf and cursed under my breath. But I knew that the battle had been lost and that I would not be able to continue my search for the girl I had met at Castle Rock.

"How can you be rude to your mother, when she works so hard all day," Maureen said, starting to collect the dishes.

"We weren't rude. She just doesn't realize that we're not kids anymore."

"What are you, then?" Maureen asked, her Belfast accent more pronounced than ever. "Don't be telling me that you're a man!" Our eyes met for a second, like conspirators who have abandoned a useless cause. Then Maureen smiled, a slightly mocking smile, which I knew I had earned. "I'll save some trifle for your breakfast," she said, relenting, or remembering that her behavior had not been above reproach either. "Go in now to your mother and say you're sorry. It won't cost you anything."

But as that would have been a betrayal of Jake, I refused. Before I had finished the food on my plate, however, my mother reappeared, and I went to her and apologized in a voice grown mechanical with long practice. I was already taller than she was at the time, and when she took me in her arms, I stared off into the living room behind her to where Maureen was hovering over the coffee tray. "Don't you love me at all?" she asked. It was not my favorite question.

"Of course I do."

"You don't act like it," she said, releasing me. "Now, go and tell Jake that I want to see him."

I was glad to escape, and thus avoid any further appeals to emotions I preferred to hide. I found Jake in the breakfast room, with a book propped up against a half-finished glass of milk. He was eating a piece of yesterday's chocolate cake, to which he had helped himself in open defiance of "bourgeois authority." He scowled when I delivered my message.

"It's all your fault," he said. "If you'd stay home and read a book once in a while . . ." He crammed the remaining cake into his mouth, and took a swallow of milk to wash it down, thus violating two rules with one gesture, as to help food on its way with liquid was permanently forbidden.

"If you'd gotten your dead arse out of that chair . . ." I replied lamely, but he pushed past me and was gone before I could finish the sentence. He never missed an opportunity to try to impress upon me that the printed page was more beneficial in the long run than my enthusiasm for the beach. His daily sessions with Ortega y Gasset, or Marx and Engels, were at least in the intellectual tradition of our parents, while my actions were those of a mental maverick who looked only for physical gratification. I was equally sure that he was wrong, that he was ruining his eyes and causing his spine permanent damage by sitting for hours in the red chair at the far end of the library.

I stayed in the breakfast room for a while, listening to the raised voices in the parlor, until Maureen pushed her way through the swinging doors and cut short my eavesdropping. "I pray to God that I never have sons like you," she said, to which I replied with a rude gesture. "Your new tutor will put you right . . . the both of you. He'll tan the impertinence out of your young hides," she added malevolently, forgetting, just as I had forgotten, that I had almost bedded down with her a few weeks earlier. Despite her hourglass figure and her Irish good looks, I saw her as one of the enemy at that moment, as she had chosen to take my mother's side against us.

"If you ever do have a kid, I pity him," I told her, a final rudeness that caused her to leave the breakfast room and slam the kitchen door furiously in my face.

PART
II

∼ one ∼

*E*XPERIENCE has taught me that we often live in fear of the wrong thing, feel menaced by an adversary who in the end does us the least harm. Guy Boulard, our new tutor, was the first one to drive that lesson home to me.

Jake and I dreaded the arrival of this young man, who was no more than a foreign-sounding name to us, perhaps because we had had to do with a tutor once before, during the first three months that followed our arrival in the United States. His name had been Schroeder, and he had been hired to teach us enough English so that we could start public school. He was a young German student, with neatly combed blond hair and lean, concave jaws that never showed the faintest trace of a beard. Jake and I decided that he looked like a U-boat commander in mufti. But that was in the days long before the advent of Hitler, so that our parents were as yet less conscious of the true nature of Teutonic methods and Teutonic virtues. Schroeder appeared to them to be nothing more than a typical German medical student, which he might well have been, but he used his ruler on our knuckles to increase the size of our English vocabularies, which made a lasting impression on Jake and me, although we were only eight and six years old at the time. He also had the habit of distributing *Ohrfeigen*, those sharp, open-handed blows to the head that are the basis of all German pedagogy, although Schroeder's *Ohrfeigen* were forthcoming only when the conjugation of an English verb continued repeatedly to escape me.

27

Guy Boulard was as different from his German predecessor as it is possible to be, both in appearance and manner. He was of average height (a few inches taller than I, and about the same size as Jake), with dark brown hair and a pallid, rather handsome face, the most important feature of which, as far as Jake and I were concerned, was a rather frivolous-looking pencil-thin moustache. I will never forget our first meeting, the day he arrived in the book-lined living room of our house, where he was first received by my mother, whose hand he kissed the moment he had come in through the front door. My mother smiled, amused more than pleased, for it had been years since young men had bowed to kiss her hand, a mannerism certainly not in fashion in southern California. "*Mes hommages, madame,*" our new tutor said. Jake and I exchanged glances. It was as if a lion tamer had paused to curtsy at the entrance to the cage.

"These are the boys," my mother said simply. "Jake and Carl."

We stepped forward and shook M. Boulard's strong, bony hand, reverting momentarily to the stiff, hardly noticeable bows we had not used on anyone for a good many years. It was not a mutually planned action, but rather a spontaneous reply in kind, brought on by our hours of reminiscing about Herr Schroeder. The moustache twisted a little painfully, as its owner forced it to join him in a smile. There was an awkward silence; then M. Boulard asked, "Where would Madame like us to work?"

"The boys' room, I think," my mother said. "Their father will be returning from Europe quite soon, and he will need the library."

"Very well, Madame." He sounded frighteningly formal. My mother led the way upstairs, and a few minutes later we found ourselves alone with our new mentor. M. Boulard took off his jacket, hung it neatly on the back of a chair, and turned to face us in a powder-blue pullover which accentuated his bony frame. "My name is Guy," he began. "Not to be pronounced as spelled, please. But Guy, like Guy de Maupassant." He rubbed his hands together as if he had just come in out of the cold, and smiled with satisfaction at his own joke. Then he suggested that we all sit down. We obeyed. "It would be very stupid," he said thoughtfully, "if we could not manage to be friends."

It was enough to win me over, the peace offer that was forthcoming long before the war had started. Jake was more reluctant to drop his guard. He was suspicious of friendship so easily proffered, and did his best to warn me once our new tutor had driven off in his ancient Chevrolet sedan. "It's the oldest trick in the world," he declared. "He just wanted to break down our resistance. He doesn't really want to be friends. He doesn't give a damn about us. It's just a job as far as he's concerned, and he doesn't want any complications."

"Why do you say that?"

"Because it's obvious. Don't be so naïve."

I wasn't sure of the meaning of the word, but I knew that it was not complimentary. But I was in no mood to argue. The nervous, hand-rubbing young Frenchman was so obviously not a reincarnation of Herr Schroeder. All my fears had vanished, and I was even prepared to do my best to learn the language the young man had been hired to teach us.

Jake continued to express his doubts. He had already devised a plan of how we could get rid of M. Boulard, he told me. But I was unwilling to plot against our new tutor, fearing that a worse substitute might easily be found if we did manage to convince him to throw in his hand. In any case, I didn't believe it was possible. "Why make things difficult for the man, when he wants to be friends?" I asked.

"Because I don't trust him," Jake said.

"I do. Anyway, why not give him a chance?"

"You're weak," Jake said disgustedly. "We can give this fellow the business, and he'll quit. I'm sure of it."

"I don't think so," I said stubbornly.

More insults followed, but I chose for once to disregard them. In the past we had exchanged blows over lesser issues, had fought with our fists until Maureen or the Japanese gardener had pulled us apart. I knew that Jake was trying to provoke me into a fight over M. Boulard, but I stood my ground. Guy had not been the one to decide that we had to learn French. It was unfair to take it out on him. If we treated him with respect and friendliness, the time would pass more quickly.

"I tell you he'll quit if we prove to him that we can't learn another language. All we have to do is sit there and look dumb."

"Don't be a jerk. He'll just try harder, that's all."

"No, he won't. He's not the type. He'll quit just to avoid having trouble. Anyway, I think he's a queer."

"What do you mean a 'queer'? How do you know?" I had a vague idea of what the word meant, but I was hardly sophisticated enough to be able to recognize one in the flesh.

"Didn't you see the way he walked? And he kissed Mother's hand!"

"He's a Frenchman!"

"Did you notice how he put his arm around your shoulder when we took him down to the front gate?"

"You're crazy."

"I'm not. You just don't know about those things."

I can still see the room where we lived, my brother and I, and in which most of our arguments and discussions took place. I can remember the view from the windows where our work table stood, with the two beds against the far wall, so that when we awoke on a clear morning we could see our slice of the Pacific Ocean just beyond the green-glass lampshade of the student's lamp mother had bought for us. I proposed a compromise. "Let's give him two weeks," I suggested. "If we decide that he is what you say, we can then go to Mother and tell her, and get rid of him that way."

"One week."

"Ten days," I said. "Be fair."

Jake shrugged. "I think my way is better, but if you insist, it's O.K. with me. Ten days, but that's all."

We both felt ill at ease a day and a half later when the dark green Chevrolet sedan pulled up in front of the house. M. Boulard came into the house humming the tune of an old Maurice Chevalier favorite called "Mimi," which he soon performed for us in the style of the master, complete with protruding lower lip and hat tipped forward. As he was wearing a rather collegiate-looking porkpie instead of a boater, some of the magic of his impersonation was lost, and we found ourselves responding with polite smiles instead of laughter. Guy Boulard was unperturbed, and gave us an extra chorus, before settling down to the business at hand.

He had devised a plan whereby time would pass more quickly. He would take us on singly instead of as a pair, which would reduce the actual torture to three hours a week per man. The one not being taught could read, or study his French vocabulary, or even do his school work if he had already memorized the few French words he was expected to learn each day.

"The main thing is to enjoy ourselves. In two or three weeks we should be able to start reading the Paris newspapers together, and in a few months we'll start in on French literature."

I winced. Boulard looked over at me with surprise. "There are many amusing books written in French," he said, raising his eyebrows slightly. "And some very naughty ones, too."

"My brother's too young for that kind of stuff," Jake said coldly.

"No, I'm not."

"I was not suggesting pornography, boys," Boulard announced with mock propriety, purposely overplaying the part of the very proper young man. "The classics, and *only* the classics, is what I had in mind."

"The classics are usually pretty dull, M. Boulard," Jake replied.

"Guy," Boulard corrected him. "Forget the 'Monsieur.' And the classics are not necessarily dull, I assure you. We will read Voltaire and Anatole France and Stendhal, and I guarantee you will not be bored. Once you've learned a few words, that is, and a vocabulary big enough so that you won't have to ask me to translate every second word. Now, who wants to be first?"

I volunteered somewhat nervously. It was quite apparent that our new tutor was a strange fellow, but that he was a "pansy" seemed most unlikely. His mannerisms were extravagant when compared to the young Americans we knew, and his Maurice Chevalier imitation had been outright embarrassing, but he was not effeminate, which, according to Jake's serious, older-brother explanation of homosexuality, was a fixed prerequisite. Still, I sat well away from him during our first few sessions, and flinched whenever he put his arm affectionately around my shoulders. After a few lessons I noticed that he had become less extravagant with his mannerisms, although the Chevalier imitation remained one of his favorite ways to show he was happy with life as well as his charges. But we got used to that too. He was not a "bad guy," as even Jake was forced to admit.

There was no mention of our pact after ten days, and Jake confessed that we had almost committed a grave injustice. "Christ, can you imagine if we'd gone to Mother and told her that Boulard was a queer? What a terrible crime we would have been guilty of! We might have ruined his life." He was reading about the Sacco and Vanzetti case at the time, which somewhat colored his view of everyday events.

"He would have quit," I agreed, "or Mother would have fired him, and we'd have him on our consciences. . . ."

"You've got to admit, he did *act* like a queer."

"He still does, once in a while. But that doesn't prove he is one." For

Guy still insisted on kissing Mother's hand whenever we returned from work early enough so that their paths crossed. Finally Jake asked him about it, and Guy explained that kissing a lady's hand was a common practice in his country. Even boys our age were taught to do it; boys of a certain class, that is. It was an unhappy choice of words, as any reference to class immediately inflamed Jake's revolutionary sentiments.

"We don't belong to any class," he said testily.

"What do you mean?" Guy replied. "You're a typical upper-middle-class family. This house, and the way you live, prove it." We had completed our lessons, and were walking with Guy to his car to see him off. Mother's Buick was parked behind his ancient Chevrolet, and he pointed to it as added evidence to support his argument.

"The house isn't paid for, nor is the car," Jake told him, somewhat indiscreetly, I thought.

"What difference does that make? Nobody pays cash in this country. You can afford to buy it; that's proof enough. If you prefer, you're middle-class. That is, if you object to being called 'upper'-middle-class."

"We're neither one," Jake told him. "We're classless, because we're bohemians. Even my father says so."

"That's not a class. That's a way of life. There are upper- and lower-class bohemians. In every country. Anyway, why do you object so to being middle-class?"

"Because they're the worst element in any nation. They think only of their material welfare, of their possessions. In Germany, because of their fear of the left, they brought Hitler to power. . . ."

"But in England they've helped maintain a balanced society by keeping the peace between rich and poor, between capital and labor. They're the most important stabilizing element that exists in Europe today, the bourgeoisie!"

"They're the gravediggers of our world," Jake replied with unconcealed hatred. "They prefer war to the redistribution of the wealth, they prefer death to progress, fascism to freedom. . . ." They were off on one of the interminable arguments that made them oblivious to their surroundings, as well as the passage of time; they often wasted more than half of Jake's lesson once they got started, as their violently opposed political opinions had a way of intruding themselves into any subject that might come up.

I would stand listening to them outside the door of our room, impressed with Jake's ability to draw Guy into dispute, when the young Frenchman should have been testing my brother's vocabulary or his knowledge of the regular and irregular verbs. I was convinced at the time that Jake would become an American Lenin, or a Trotsky, for he was incredibly dogged and persuasive in a debate. He seemed to be able to reverse his relationship with his tutor, or at least to bring Guy down to his own level, for once they had locked horns, there was no difference of status between them.

Their violent arguments troubled me, for I was afraid sometimes that they might come to blows. They obviously troubled Guy even more, for he saw his authority over his pupil rapidly fading away. Finally, in order not to be lured into wasting any more time, he decided that they would begin reading Michelet's *History of the Revolution,* which seemed preferable to their translating the old copies of *Paris-Soir.* At least Michelet was writing about a period and issues that were long past, which Guy thought might help avoid the constant fights that the reading of yesterday's newspapers always seemed to involve them in. Jake agreed, for Michelet was one of the few thinkers and historians he was not well acquainted with, and he saw that he could derive a "true intellectual" benefit from his sessions with his "bourgeois" tutor.

I remember feeling that it was unfair that Jake should be allowed to start reading books when his grasp on the language was weaker than my own, and I complained about it. Guy agreed, and one afternoon we searched my father's library for a suitable book in French, but as most of his books were in either German or English, we had great difficulty finding one. Finally we found an illustrated edition of Voltaire's *Candide.* Guy hesitated. "I'm not sure your mother will approve of your reading *Candide,*" he said.

"Why? I'm fourteen and a half. And *Candide'*s a classic, isn't it?"

"Yes, it is. It's a great book. But . . ."

"Then what's wrong with it?"

"Nothing, I suppose. We'll start tomorrow."

It proved to be a slow but thankful task. Instantly Guy Boulard became the syphilitic Professor Panglos, thin and balding and wiry, just as he appeared in the pen-and-ink illustrations, while I saw myself as Candide, complete with knee breeches and staff. Together we began to make our way slowly and painfully through the "best of all possible worlds," which did not seem so different from our own. Soon both Jake and I began to look forward, for different reasons, to the arrival of the squeaking Chevrolet sedan outside the gate of our house.

⇝ *two* ⇜

VOLTAIRE cast his spell, and sitting in the double bedroom overlooking the sea, with the mementos of my childhood still hanging on the walls, I began to think of the world lying in wait outside as an evil, beckoning garden. It was not a deeply disturbing vision, and I was delighted to discover that physical desire was such a commonplace thing. Voltaire made it reappear on almost every page, which was definite proof. Candide found only lust and greed on his travels, plus the machinations of the clergy, and they meant very little to me. Love was something else again.

I felt reassured. I was not the only one who spent most of his waking hours dreaming about the opposite sex. Obviously there was an invisible web called desire that was spread out over all the world and that entangled most of God's creatures from the time they were born to the day they died. There was no escaping it. Like the atmosphere, it was there.

Guy at first pretended that this wasn't so. Seated on my right, close enough so that he could look over my shoulder, he tried constantly to divert my attention to the style of the masterpiece, the purity of the language, and the perfect balance of the syntax. He explained over and over again that the story was a satire, an exaggeration far removed from reality. Hundreds of years ago, he maintained, the world was not as obsessed by sex as it was now. Nor was it as evil and disease-ridden a place as Voltaire had painted it. "He wanted to reform France; that's why he called attention to the abuses of his time by emphasizing their existence," Guy explained.

"Was he successful?"

"In many ways, yes."

It was not what I wanted to hear. "You mean there's less syphilis and gonorrhea nowadays?"

"Much less. But that's not the point." Guy, I had discovered, did not possess a great sense of humor; nor was he one of those Frenchmen who have been converted to cynicism through learning. Thus I realized that Jake was not wholly unjustified in his accusations. Guy was a "hopeless bourgeois," despite all the years he had spent studying in the "colleges of the liberal arts." His mother was still the principal influence in his life—his mother, who was such a good cook, as he never tired of telling us, and who had worked all of her life to educate her son, as she obviously never tired of telling him. "It was quite a struggle for her," he often said, with an overtone of pride in his voice that would have been more touching if he had not sounded so smug.

His pride in his mother's sacrifice infuriated Jake and bored me. "That's why I thought he was a pansy at first," Jake informed me from his corner of our room. We were discussing the events of the day, as we often did late at night, after the lights had been turned out. "He's a mother's boy. That's why nothing he's learned has sunk in. All the facts, all the knowledge he's acquired—none of it has made him change any of his opinions."

"Everybody who goes to the university doesn't become a red," I said bitingly.

"You sound like a fascist."

"Anybody who disagrees with you is a fascist."

"That's not true. I never said Boulard was a fascist. He's a typical liberal. Weak, half-convinced, ready to compromise. He still thinks that Kerensky was the correct solution for the Russian people. . . ."

"Well, maybe he's right. Just because you don't agree with him doesn't make him wrong. Anyway, I think we should go to sleep." I knew that I was not equipped to argue politics with Jake.

"O.K., but I'll tell you one thing . . . Guy will never become an important professor, or even a good teacher. His opinions are too wishy-washy. You have to doubt what they teach you, not merely parrot what you've learned. That doesn't mean I dislike Guy. I just feel he's doomed to being a second-rater, a nonentity. . . ."

Probably because Jake was hostile to him, Guy decided to make me his friend. I noticed that he began to talk about himself during our brief rest periods. I learned that his father had gone to St. Cyr, and had been commissioned in the regular French Army in 1913. It was not a good time to begin a military career, Guy maintained sadly. The war started, and after marrying his childhood sweetheart on a brief leave, he had gone out to die anonymously in one of the first German attacks across the Meuse River. Guy's mother never recovered from the initial blow of her husband's early death. She decided then and there that, whatever might happen, she would not allow her son's life to be wasted in a similar manner. As soon as the war was over, she left France and went to live in England, thinking that Guy could thus be able to avoid military service when he came of age.

"The smell of mutton grease and the endless rain drove her back to Paris, my mother always says," Guy explained. The remark was obviously one of her *bons mots,* for her son managed to work it in whenever there was any mention of England. I thought it more probable that their anglophobia stemmed from some social slight the young widow Boulard had received while attempting to escape her own country's conscription laws, for the smell of cooking and the weather were hardly enough to make such a strong impression in so short a time. Or perhaps Guy's mother held the English responsible for the First World War, and therefore the death of her husband. In any case, she was emotionally an enemy of the crown. "*Ah, les Anglais,*" she said despairingly almost the first moment I met her. "It is the only thing I do not like about thees country. The language the English have imposed on the people."

"*C'est une belle langue quand-même, Maman,*" Guy replied, a little embarrassed by his mother's fanaticism. He had taken me with him to introduce me to her, and to show off her fine cooking. Obviously he found it embarrassing to have his mother begin propagandizing me even before the meal had been served. We were standing in the small dining room of their apartment, just the three of us, for Jake had turned down the invitation, saying that he had too much homework that night.

It was an excellent dinner, as promised, the first truly French meal I had ever had. The wiry old lady had prepared it with loving care. We ate civet de lièvre with boiled potatoes, and drank red wine. There was a Camembert with the salad, and a chocolate soufflé that had been made in my honor. The conversation throughout dinner was about food, and as it was in French, I was limited to brief replies, which I hoped were correct, for reading *Candide* had not prepared me for all this talk of the kitchen. After coffee Guy lit a pipe and sat for a few minutes in a faded red armchair with his feet stuck in his slippers before proposing that we start back home.

I thanked my hostess in my halting French, and was glad to be off, for I had found the atmosphere depressing. Guy was not just a son, it seemed to me. He also played the role of the father of the family. Once we were in the street he discovered that he had left the keys to his car upstairs, and as I stood alone on the sidewalk waiting for him to return, I suddenly understood why Jake was so adamant about not being middle-class. I looked over at the street sign on the corner and realized that I was on Fourth Street, only four blocks from Ocean Avenue, which was the street that ran along the top of the palisades below which we lived.

"I can walk home, you know," I told Guy once he had reappeared with the keys. "It's only nine o'clock."

"I'd better drive you," he said. "Anyway, my mother prefers me to finish my pipe out of doors."

We got in the car. "What do you do in the afternoons you don't teach us?" I asked, trying to make conversation.

"I give lessons to a young English girl who lives farther up the beach," Guy replied. "I'll take you with me one day if you like."

"Sure, anytime," I said, not wishing to offend him.

"This Saturday, perhaps."

"I'll have to ask my mother."

"I'm sure she won't mind. The girl's parents are very well-to-do. They have a swimming pool and a tennis court. If you get to know them, they might invite you for a swim in the summer."

"I prefer the ocean," I said. I was not eager to go on another outing with him. I was beginning to realize that he was not Professor Panglos after all.

⇜ three ⇝

THERE WAS NOT A CLOUD in the sky. The breeze off the sea was mild, almost warm, and although it had been cool in the garden, it was hot and stuffy inside the car. My gray flannel trousers and the new suede jacket that had been my main Christmas present (and which I still wore

only for special occasions) clung to the brown imitation-velvet upholstery of the Chevrolet sedan. But I did not dare open the window for
fear of mussing my carefully combed hair. I looked over at Guy. He, too,
I noticed, was dressed more elegantly than usual, for instead of his customary gray tweed jacket he had on a brown gabardine suit with a yellow
waistcoat, from the slit pocket of which hung the Phi Beta Kappa key he
was never without.

"I'm glad you decided to come," he said, manipulating the spark and
choke levers, until the engine under the rounded hood seemed to be
firing with an almost regular beat.

"It wasn't only up to me," I replied, not quite truthfully.

He said nothing. We had come to the end of our block, and after
turning right, we drove parallel with the ocean down the continuation of
our street. We turned right again, onto a section of our road called Costa
Mesa Road. It led to the bottom of the canyon, where a sharp left turn
brought us back to the coast highway. Guy stopped for the light, and
when it had changed we started north in the direction of Castle Rock.

"I'm glad you *could* come," Guy said, dwelling slightly on the modi-
fication of his initial opening phrase, "because today you'll meet one of
the most charming girls you will ever know. She's much too old for you,"
he added with a sly smile, "but she's not too old for me."

"Is that the girl you're teaching?" I asked.

"No," he said. "It's her aunt. That sounds funny, doesn't it? You
think of somebody's aunt as being an old goat, but that is not the case
this time, I assure you. . . ."

"Is this 'aunt' your fiancée?" I asked.

"No, she's not my fiancée," Guy said wistfully. "I wish she were, but
she's not. Maybe someday, if I make a fortune, I'll make a pitch for her.
But the way things are now, she's only a friend."

"What does making a fortune have to do with it?"

"You'll see for yourself," he said mysteriously. "Once you've met her,
you'll understand that a poor French teacher hasn't got much of a
chance." We were driving at a greater speed than I had thought possible
in the old Chevrolet, as if the thought of this marvelous girl had affected
even the engine of the ancient car. I noticed a look of elation on the
pale, rectangular face of my tutor. "I'll tell you a secret," he went on,
"and that is that after meeting her I began to think seriously of robbing
a bank, or stealing a diamond necklace, anything to get rich . . . so that

I could sell this old car, and buy a big Packard and new clothes, and be a different person." He touched the brakes, and we swerved dangerously inside the confines of our narrow lane. Putting out his hand to signal a right turn, he broke away from the highway and started up a long, smoothly paved street that led up into the brush-covered hills behind the beach. I caught a glimpse of a sign that said "Portofino Road," and sat watching the speed of the car decrease as we climbed.

"I always have to take a run at this hill," he said. "Otherwise my Rosinante would never make it."

He shifted into second, and we ground on at an infinitely slower speed, the daring abandon of the approach all used up by the time we were halfway up the hill. "Poor old girl," Guy said. "Her heart's still there, but her legs are gone." We arrived at a large plateau that was hidden from the coast highway by the steepness of its approaches, which was obviously why the road we had turned off was called Escondido Drive. A Romanesque villa with marble columns stood near the intersection of the two streets, its formal garden complete with clipped hedges hanging out over the abyss. It was very much like the spot in which Magellan stood in the illustration in my high-school history book, with the sun reflected in the sea just beyond his steel breastplate. "Is that the house?" I asked Guy.

"No, that monstrosity belongs to some oil millionaire. We still have a little way to go."

We drove on, following the curve of the road that led us away from the ocean. On our left was a dense grove of eucalyptus trees, on our right a brush-covered hillside. Suddenly the eucalyptus trees ended, and a neat orange grove began. There was a large white plaster gateway on which was hung a sign that read "Las Golondrinas." We turned down an asphalt drive that was lined on both sides by flowerbeds. There were banks of red and white geraniums, bordering a rectangular rose garden beyond which stood a forest of fruit trees—avocado and loquat and citrus of all kinds. The perfume of their blossoms filled the car. After a hundred yards or so we came to the house, lying at the bottom of a mild incline, its red-tiled roof and white plaster walls visible behind vines of bougainvillea and honeysuckle. Guy parked beyond the wrought-iron gate that was apparently the main entrance, and I got out hesitantly, waiting for him to lead the way. A dog was barking inside the house, and I could see a white-jacketed servant walking across the patio toward me.

He opened the gate and smiled, the happy smile of an emancipated slave, and said: "Oh . . . it's Mr. Boulard. Come right on in."

"This is Master Woolf," Guy said, using a title no one had ever attached to my name. "This is James."

"Glad to know you," the butler said with an informal nod. "Just follow me, if you will, please."

We crossed the small patio to a covered terrace, where another iron gate (this one set in glass) was opened for us, and we found ourselves in an entrance hall with a dark wooden ceiling. James paused momentarily, and then, realizing that we had no coats or hats to add to the large collection hanging from metal hooks on the walls, he proceeded to lead us into an adjoining room that was obviously a library, for there were bookshelves and leather chairs and reading lamps. This room was almost as dark as the entrance hall, in keeping with the formal Spanish style of the house.

"Keep on going," James crooned softly, and led us on through yet another door, and we found ourselves in what would have been called the "parlor" in a more modest house. There was a wall made up entirely of windows and French doors facing me, through which I could see the swimming pool, set like a huge rectangular sapphire in a long sweep of lawn. I know I was staring at it with childish awe when Guy said my name, calling me to attention the way one calls a dog to heel, and I turned and realized the reason for his sharp tone of command. We were not alone in the living room. An elderly gentleman with gray hair and glasses was seated in an armchair near the French windows.

"Good afternoon, Count Tucci," Guy said nervously.

The old gentleman lowered the newspaper he was reading, and stared at us over his glasses, the expression on his face unaltered. He didn't answer Guy's salutation. He merely nodded, and when Guy introduced me by name, he nodded curtly again. We filed past him out into the garden, with James still leading the way. "Lovely afternoon, isn't it, sir?" Guy said as we stepped out onto the well-mowed lawn.

"Yes, lovely," the Count answered sourly.

Guy closed the French door with as little noise as possible, and we continued on in single file past the pool. In the distance I could hear the sound of a tennis ball being hit at regular intervals, and as we drew nearer the court I could make out what sounded like a deep female voice repeating a chant that was just audible as we drew closer. The words of the chant varied very little, I discovered. "Get your racket back, eye on the ball, stroke . . . that's it. Racket back, eye on the ball, stroke . . ." The court was still not visible, although the sounds of the game were close now, and then suddenly I caught a glimpse of the green concrete playing surface at least twenty feet below the level of the lawn.

We went down some concrete steps and ended up in a small pavilion that faced the court like a miniature grandstand. My nervousness had increased during the last few minutes of the walk through the garden, and I could feel the palms of my hands getting moist the way they always did when I knew that I was about to meet a person I would have to shake hands with. I asked myself: "What are you doing here? Why did you come?" Then I looked up from the straw carpet under my feet, past the back of Guy's head, and there at the far end of the court, running to return a low backhand, was the blonde girl I had fallen in love with that afternoon long ago on the beach at Castle Rock.

Strangely enough, I experienced very little surprise at seeing her there, for the moment Guy had started telling me about the girl that he had been tempted to rob a bank for, I had begun to suspect that he was talking about the girl with the dog I had met on the beach. But I had invented so many dream meetings between the two of us that I did not dare admit my premonition to myself for fear of the inevitable disappointment that would follow if it turned out not to be true. So I stood and stared, grateful for the concealment Guy and the butler were providing, not sure in my own mind that all of it—the house and the girl and the brilliant afternoon sunshine—were not just another daydream.

In order to check on my senses, I looked over to the other side of the net and saw a plump, elderly woman with curly gray hair, whose face was hidden by a white tennis visor. Her legs below her white skirt were tanned and sturdy, and she moved with surprising agility as she ran to return her pupil's rather wild shots, volleying and half-volleying effortlessly. The chant which accompanied her movements had continued throughout our entrance, but it was interrupted now as she bent over a basket full of tennis balls near her feet in order to replenish the supply she held in her hand. James used the pause to intervene on our behalf. "Miss Edwina," he said, his melodious voice ringing out across the court, "Mr. Boulard is here for Karen's lesson. . . ."

So it was not a dream. The girl turned and came toward us, putting her racket under her arm to tidy her disarranged hair, and smiling briefly,

called out to the tennis teacher: "I'm sorry, Ethel. I won't be long."
Then she ran up the stone steps to greet us, and I found myself thinking: "She's more beautiful than I remember her." And more unattainable—of that I was even more conscious than of her beauty. I understood what Guy had meant earlier in the car about somehow making a
fortune in order to be able to declare his intentions. But I also knew that
his cause was as hopeless as my own.

"I hope you won't mind," he was saying haltingly, "but I've brought
along a young friend of mine, Carl Woolf. I wanted him to see the
house—"

"Of course I don't mind," the girl interrupted. She put out her hand,
and I was relieved to find that she had been perspiring, and would therefore not notice my own damp palm. "I'm Edwina Gordon," she said,
with not even the slightest flicker of recognition in her eyes. "I'm so glad
you could come."

≥≥ *four* ≥≥

TIM, THE BLACK SPANIEL, had been lying out of sight under a table,
and he rose now and came over to me to be patted, trying to prove,
perhaps, that his memory was better than that of his mistress. I bent
down and scratched him behind the ears and said: "Hya, Tim. How are
you, boy?" It had the desired effect. Edwina Gordon frowned and
looked puzzled.

"Have you met Tim before?" she asked.

"Yes, a couple of months ago, on the beach," I replied.

"That's strange," she said, "because he never goes out without me.
James takes him for a walk once in a while, but never as far as the
beach."

James had already started up the pavilion stairway and was out of
earshot, so I let the matter rest. Nor did Edwina seem to attach much
importance to the mystery of where Tim and I had met. She merely
smiled her dazzling smile and turned to introduce Ethel Wilson, the

tennis teacher. She had already forgotten my name, which didn't matter, for Guy came to her rescue, so that her second lapse of memory passed as unnoticed as the first. It turned out that she was embarrassed enough anyway. Karen, Guy's pupil, had been invited to a luncheon party that day, and her mother had asked Edwina to call Guy and find out if he could come later in the afternoon. "Of course I forgot," she said. "And now she's not back. That's why James brought you down here, I suppose. Because he knew it was my fault."

"That's perfectly all right," Guy said with an adoring smile. "I'm sure she'll be back soon."

"I hope so. But perhaps we'd better go up to the house and telephone. Ethel can hit a few balls with your friend while we're gone." She picked up a sweater, and pulling it on over her bare arms, started up the concrete steps. But before she had gone very far, she turned back again (a little too theatrically, I thought) and called out to the tennis teacher: "You don't mind, Ethel, do you? Just rally a little with . . ."

" 'Carl,' " Guy said, forced to come to her rescue again.

" 'Carl,' of course. It's such a simple name. I don't know why I can't remember it. Maybe it's because you don't look like a 'Carl' to me. I'll have to find some other name for you," she said, and she was gone, with Guy trotting after her, and Tim bringing up the rear.

I felt something change inside me at that moment. It wasn't because she had forgotten my name a second time, or because of her highhanded treatment of the elderly lady with the sunburned, wrinkled face. None of that endeared her to me, of course, but it was hardly enough to influence my feelings. I suppose it was her manner, the extreme confidence with which she moved, as if she felt certain that she was the center of all attention, the darling of all present, as if a spotlight had been trained on her by God right from birth, a spotlight that followed her everywhere. Or perhaps it was simply because she was affected, although at the time I was unable to nail it down so neatly. All I felt was an irrevocable change inside me, and I knew I had been liberated from an illusion I had kept alive for quite a long time.

"Would you like to try to hit a few?" a voice behind me asked, and I turned, remembering that Mrs. Wilson was still there waiting to continue with her job.

"I've never played tennis," I said. "I wouldn't be able to get the ball back. It'd be a bore for you."

"Not at all. Come on, have a go." She was obviously British too, although her accent was not so pronounced as Edwina's. I took off my suede jacket and rolled up my sleeves. Mrs. Wilson inspected the soles of my shoes, and found, to her satisfaction, that they were made of smooth rubber. Then I walked out onto the court. I was shown the correct grip, and where to stand, and the first ball came at me from across the net. I sent it flying over the fence with a full baseball swing. I started after it.

"Don't bother," Mrs. Wilson said. "We'll find it later. And call me Ethel, dear. Everyone does. Now, come over here a minute, Carl, and I'll explain the forehand stroke to you."

I crossed to her side of the net, and she stood behind me, and covering my hand with hers, she forced me to follow the movement she prescribed. "You hit with your arm, and your body makes you follow through. It's a stroke, not a blow. You stroke the ball." She repeated the movement again, forcing me to imitate her. Then she made me try it alone. "Your hips pivot as you stroke," she said, placing her strong hands on either side of my body and turning me forcibly as I pretended to swing at the ball. "Now we'll try again," she said.

I repeated the movement, and missed. "Never mind, the stroke was much better," she assured me. "Now try to keep your eye on the ball. That's it. Racket back, watch the ball, stroke." She had started the chant again, and I found myself responding to it, discovering at the same time that to connect with the tightly strung racket was an amazingly pleasant sensation. "Tennis is a game of control and restraint," Mrs. Wilson said. "And putting the ball where the other guy ain't."

I laughed politely, although I had heard the old joke before. Still, I was enjoying myself. My disillusionment was vanishing. I had no real reason to feel bitter, I told myself. I had invented a girl, so I could hardly blame Edwina Gordon for being so totally different. Anyway, why should she have remembered me? Two months was a long time. If I had met her a week later, and in the same place, things might have been different.

Mrs. Wilson had finished collecting the balls I had hit to every corner of the court, and with her basket full again was returning to her place at the net. Edwina had not come back, so there was nothing left to do but go on with the lesson. Perhaps she had forgotten that her tennis teacher was waiting. She was not a girl with a very good memory. Mrs. Wilson brought me to the net again and explained the movements of the backhand to me. As she was showing me how to change my grip, I saw an elderly man in a navy blue blazer and white flannels come down the stairs into the pavilion.

"I'm here, Ethel," the newcomer said in a low voice, as if he were anxious not to disturb. He was holding a tennis racket in his right hand, and once he had stopped, he stood leaning on it, as if it were a cane.

"Oh, hello, darling," Ethel Wilson said. "I've got a young natural here." She nodded her head in the direction of the elderly gentleman. "Carl, this is Bert, my husband."

"How do you do," Wilson said, raising his racket by way of a brief greeting. He was almost completely bald, but his face and forehead were so deeply tanned that at first glance one was not conscious of any absence of hair. He was quite short, and bent over with age, or perhaps his posture had been conditioned by the many years of standing hunched over in the position his wife had told me was the correct one when waiting to return any given shot. He watched us for a while before he came down onto the playing surface with slow careful steps and began to retrieve the balls that had again accumulated against the fence on the far side of the court. I was worried that I might hit him with one of my wild swings, and began to pull my shots.

"Don't worry about Bert," Ethel Wilson said. "He's very good at ducking." And she continued to send me more of the low, accurate shots I was doing my best to return. Bert Wilson slowly collected a racket full of tennis balls, which he replaced in the wicker basket before joining his wife at the net.

"He seems to have a good eye," he remarked.

"And excellent footwork. He's never held a racket in his hand before this afternoon, you know."

"That is remarkable. Hit a few to his forehand now, my dear," the old boy suggested.

Ethel Wilson obliged her husband, and I was able to show off my abilities to even greater advantage, not realizing at the time, of course, that the greater ease with which I was able to hit the ball off my right side would ultimately condemn me to a lifetime of playing nothing more than social tennis. But I was unconscious of any possible limitations that bright March afternoon. I continued to chase after the balls Ethel Wilson sent across the net with a growing enthusiasm, intoxicated by my own speed and dexterity.

To have discovered this marvelous game more than made up for Edwina Gordon's short memory, or for any of the other faults I had attributed to her because I had felt slighted. I didn't even think about her anymore. If the perpetually smiling James, who had appeared at the top of the stairs once again, had announced that she had run off with my tutor, I would hardly have paused to listen to him, so intent was I on obeying the instructions the Wilsons were calling out to me from across the net. They were like a musical aunt and uncle who have discovered that their nephew has absolute pitch. Again and again they put me through my paces, as if to verify their natural findings, while even James paused to watch with mild interest. "Say, he's pretty good, this boy," he allowed after a while. Then he added: "Miss Edwina says you all should come up to the house for tea."

"Thank you. We'll be there in a few minutes," Mrs. Wilson replied. "Just a few more backhands, and a good forehand to finish up."

I was reluctant to stop. I could have gone on for hours. And only when I started to help collect the tennis balls that were strewn all over the court did I realize that my clean shirt was soaked with sweat, as were my best gray flannel trousers. Wilson advised me to take a shower, and led me to the dressing-room door at the back of the pavilion. "I haven't got a clean shirt to change into," I told him, horrified at the prospect of appearing red-faced and sweating in Edwina Gordon's elegant living room.

"That doesn't matter. Just put your jacket on over the shirt you have on," Wilson counseled.

Ethel Wilson was more sympathetic to my problem. "He can't do that," she said. She was drying her face and hands in the yellow towel she carried wrapped around the handle of the wicker basket. "We'll go up to the house and send him down one of Richard's. He won't mind."

I had no idea who Richard was, but as I was in no position to be difficult, I accepted. I took off my wet clothes and stood under a hot shower until I had stopped sweating. I was drying myself in one of the huge bath towels initialed with a G that I had found hanging nearby, when there was a brief knock on the dressing-room door, and a man appeared in front of me. He was tall and thin, with a narrow, handsome face that looked vaguely familiar to me, and as he came toward me he held out a blue sport shirt that was neatly pressed and folded. "I'm Richard Gordon," he said in a deep British voice. "I believe that you're in need of a clean shirt."

It was his dark, curly hair that made me uncertain. An instant later I realized that he was Edwina's older brother. The full, heart-shaped mouth and the clear blue eyes were identical. Only his nose was more prominent in his face. And yet, as I stood facing him, still holding the bath towel around my waist with my left hand, I realized that there was another reason why his face looked familiar to me. He was an actor, a well-known English actor whose picture I had quite recently seen in the theatrical section of the Sunday paper. He had come to America to play a part in some important movie, and the photograph I had glanced at had shown him in the costume of a nineteenth-century English country squire. Remembering everything I had read about him made me no less shy, especially since I was standing in front of him now in my hairless nakedness, about to borrow a much more elegant shirt than I had ever worn. "Are you sure you don't mind, Mr. Gordon?" I said, hearing my own high voice, as if it were a record that was being played a little too fast.

"I presume I'll get it back," he said with an ironic smile. "If I were sure that I would never see it again, I might mind a little." He dropped the shirt carelessly on a nearby chair and started toward the door. "You'd better hurry, or my greedy sister will eat all the crumpets," he said over his shoulder, and was gone.

I dropped the towel and crossed to the brass hook on which I had hung my clothes. My underpants were as moist with sweat as my shirt, so there was nothing to do but pull my flannel slacks on over my bare behind. Richard Gordon's shirt hung loosely from my thin shoulders, and yet it looked just as presentable as the one in which I had arrived. I pulled on my socks and shoes and inspected myself in the mirror. Not too displeased by what I saw, I put a fresh hand towel around my neck and combed my wet hair. My suede jacket hid the flapping sleeves that were much too big for my thin arms. Only then did I realize that the wet underwear I had abandoned presented quite a difficult problem. I couldn't roll it up and put it into a pocket of my jacket, as it would undoubtedly stain the suede. Nor did I feel like leaving it behind in the neat dressing room. There was only one thing to do. Folding it up until it fit neatly into my right hand, I left the dressing room.

The pavilion was deserted. The light green concrete playing surface of the tennis court lay in the deep shadow of the late-March afternoon. I went up the stairs, stopping once to look back at the neat white lines that had taken on such a new significance to me. If I could only learn to keep the lively ball within their strict confines, I thought as I walked slowly along the edge of the moist lawn. The last rays of the sun were still touching the tops of the avocado and loquat trees as I approached them. The flat, undisturbed surface of the swimming pool lay behind me to my left. Making sure that I was not in full view of the living-room windows, I threw my wet underpants as far as I could into the thickest part of the orchard. I could not see where they landed. That in itself was reassuring. Then, turning once again to face the pool, I started off in the direction of the house and the tea party to which I had been invited.

five

I CAUGHT A GLIMPSE of the room behind the glass panes of the French doors and quickly turned away. There were too many people inside, a crowd of strangers, all of them adults. Guy was nowhere in sight. The only face I recognized was that of the Count, staring coldly at me from in front of the fireplace. I would wait in the car, I decided, or walk around the house and come in by the front door. That way I would at least have James to keep me company. But it was too late. I heard the door I was walking hurriedly away from open, and a woman's voice call out: "This way, Carl, where are you going?" I retraced my steps, feeling the blood rush to my face.

"I wasn't sure," I lied. "I was just going around to the front door."

"You'd have had a long walk for nothing," the young woman said, holding out her hand. "I'm Pamela Gordon. I don't believe we've met."

I will never forget the failing light, and the way she stood there at the edge of the lawn in a dark-blue jersey skirt and a white blouse, her hair, darker than Edwina's, neatly curled back on itself in the style of the day, her face with its Grecian-coin beauty smiling at me, trying to make things easier, as if she had guessed the reason for my sudden flight and was trying to help me overcome my shyness. I see myself too, in the borrowed shirt that was too big for me, as if I were some other person, a gangling, skinny kid with curly hair that refused to stay combed as it dried, taking her hand hesitantly and letting myself be led into the room I had been afraid to enter alone.

"I've heard a lot about you from M. Boulard," Pamela Gordon said, resting her hand gently on my shoulder as we went in through the door. "He says that you're by far his best pupil, much better than my daughter, Karen . . . and from Ethel Wilson just now, who claims that you're going to turn out to be a jolly good tennis player, and beat us all. . . ." She was steering me toward the fireplace and the Count, who turned out to be much shorter than I would have guessed from having seen him in the armchair near the window, and who was staring vacantly across the room with his heavily ringed, sagging eyes. "Now, where shall we start?" she asked, her hand still resting on my shoulder. "Whom haven't you met? Count Tucci, my father-in-law, stepfather-in-law, actually. This is Carl Woolf."

The Count nodded, just as he had done when he had first been introduced, only this time he held out his thick, lifeless hand, which I shook, grateful that the tennis and the shower had made my palms drier than they were apt to be at moments like these. I said: "How do you do, sir?" rather hesitantly, not expecting an answer, and none was forthcoming.

"And this is Paul . . . Paul Hévesey," my hostess was saying as she turned me to face a tall, dark-skinned man whose black, lacquered hair was combed straight back from his forehead. He wore a white turtleneck sweater and a blue blazer with golden buttons, and I noticed that he looked at the young woman behind me with a conspiratorial look that made me dislike him at once.

"*Alors, tu t'intéresses à la jeunesse maintenant?*" he asked Pamela as he shook my hand.

"*Je t'en prie,*" she said, laughing. "He's a fool," she added for my benefit. "Don't pay any attention to him."

"Not a fool. Just a Hungarian." Hévesey grinned. "And I'm delighted to meet you. We need new blood in this house. We're all getting old and tired waiting for Pam to relent."

She shook her head and pushed me on past him. "*C'est vrai, ma beauté,*" he called after her, but she didn't look back.

"You know Richard, don't you . . . my husband."

"Yes, he loaned me this shirt."

She smiled, and she said, "Then we won't bother with him. Anyway, he's talking to a young lady whose name I've forgotten, and you probably want a cup of tea more than anything. So why don't you come along with me?" She led me into the library, where tea was laid out on a large table. There were crumpets and cucumber sandwiches, and a cake with a frosting of honey and nuts that she promised was as delicious as it looked. "Now, how do you like your tea?" she asked.

It was a beverage that was as foreign to me as whiskey. At breakfast we were sometimes allowed a little coffee in a cup of hot milk, but in the late afternoon we drank apple cider or Coca-Cola, but never tea. "You prefer it with milk or with lemon?"

"With lemon," I answered bravely, thinking that with milk was probably the way children took it. Through the open library door I could see the Wilsons standing near the Count; and Richard Gordon, who was talking to the girl whose name his wife had forgotten, a girl with long dark wavy hair who looked Hawaiian and was very beautiful in an exotic way. It was a strange household, I thought, so totally different from ours. Jake would probably describe them as the "decadent rich," which thought made me feel just as glad that he had decided not to come along.

Mrs. Gordon was handing me my tea, but she thought better of it and put it down on the edge of the table. "We can sit here," she said. "It's easier than balancing a cup in one hand and a plate in another. And I'm sure you want something to eat."

She was right, but I didn't dare to express all of my wishes, and allowed her to put only two small sandwiches on a plate, plus a piece of the cake she had recommended. "Are you sure that's all you want? Growing boys are supposed to be ravenously hungry all day long. You're not an exception to the rule, are you?"

"I'm not very hungry," I said. I could easily have eaten the entire trayful of sandwiches, plus a big piece of each cake, but I preferred to starve rather than act like a "growing boy."

She poured a cup of tea for herself, and I had a chance to look more closely at her face. She had a wide mouth with full lips that stood out in contrast to her pale skin. Her eyes were grayish-blue (not the bright blue that was obviously a Gordon-family trait), and they were almond-shaped rather than round. "Are you English?" I asked, realizing as I said it that I was being too inquisitive.

She smiled and said, "What do you think?"

"You sound as if you were English. . . ."

"But I don't look English. Is that what you mean? Well, I'm not," she added. "I'm half-Scottish and half-French. I should have held on to my burr, I suppose, but my mother and father wanted me to get rid of it, and . . . well, I finally did. What nationality are you?"

"Austrian . . . at least I've an Austrian passport. My mother is half-Russian."

"You sound like an American." It was the highest compliment she could have paid me. "Guy tells me that your father lives in Europe. . . ."

"He's away on a trip, that's all. He'll be home soon."

"You must ask him if you can take tennis lessons when he gets back," she said. "Then you can come up here with Guy and learn to play."

"That's very kind of you, but . . ."

"Don't be silly, we'd love to have you. During the week the court's empty, and Ethel is a wonderful teacher. My daughter, Karen, says she doesn't want to learn, but perhaps if she saw you taking lessons she'd change her mind."

It was almost as if she were asking me to come and play with the children. She must have realized what I was thinking, for she added: "I know Karen's much younger than you are, but I need a partner too. . . ."

I said: "I'm not good enough to play with anyone," and she laughed nervously the same way she had done when Hévesey had asked her if she were interested in the young now.

"We're all fairly hopeless," she said, "so you needn't worry. And if you don't want to play tennis, there's always the pool."

She was being kind, too kind, it seemed to me, as if she were trying to make up for the others, the Count and Edwina, and her own husband, who had hardly seemed to notice that I was alive. A small girl with a tooth missing in the front of her mouth came running into the room, and I realized that this was Karen, the truant from the French lesson. "Look, it's gone, it's gone," she cried, pointing to the gap in her teeth. "I bit into a piece of cake, and that was the last I saw of it."

She was corrected for not saying hello, which almost spoiled her joke, for she had found the tooth, of course, and was keeping it hidden in the pocket of her gray cardigan. Guy and Edwina appeared in time to share in the producing of the missing incisor, Guy looking pleased and slightly smug, I thought, probably because he had spent almost an hour alone with the girl he so admired.

He had collected the evening papers from the driveway, the *Herald* with its green outside page, and the *Evening Outlook*. He unfolded them both on the table, and stood looking down at the headlines with a professorial air, shaking his head as if he was the only one who was at all concerned with the troubled condition of the world. He said: "The news is a little worse than usual tonight, I hate to tell you. . . ."

Richard Gordon had come into the library to greet his daughter. He was followed by the Count and Paul Hévesey, I remember, and with Karen's tooth lying in the palm of his hand, he turned to Guy and asked: "Why? What's happened? What's the little man with the moustache up to now?"

In reply to his question, Guy read the headline out loud, making the most of his small moment of importance, enjoying his role of the bearer of bad tidings, or so it seemed to me. "Hitler scraps Versailles Treaty," he read, adding: "As Reichs-chancellor he's decreed a law bringing back compulsory military service. In a year's time Germany will have an army of half a million men, unless England and France intervene."

"What do you expect them to do?" Richard Gordon asked. "March into the Rhineland? Of course, they'll protest to the League of Nations, and a fat lot of good it will do them."

"If it were up to the French, they would do more than protest," Guy replied.

The Count had taken the *Evening Outlook* and had gone over to the window to study the front page. "A German army is not necessarily a threat to France," he said slowly. "Their main enemy lies to the east. Our enemy, too," he added ominously.

Gordon laughed and said: "Andrea is more worried about the Bolshevik menace than the Nazis," which remark caused the old man to turn and stare angrily at his stepson.

"They are not a menace in my country," the Count replied. "But they are everywhere else. Even here. That is why I am not alarmed by the reappearance of a strong Germany. I believe it's a good thing, even. . . ."

"You mean to say that you approve of Hitler and the Nazis?" Pamela Gordon asked. "You can't be serious, Andrea."

I noticed that the lines in the Count's face seemed suddenly to have grown deeper, and that he rolled up the newspaper he was holding with a nervous movement of his big hands. "You are all too much under the influence of your Jewish friends," he said angrily. "That's why you make fun of this man Hitler. But he's right when he says that the main danger to peace lies in the East, that the Slav and his ideas are more to be feared than anyone else in this world. . . ."

"Marxism is hardly a Slavic idea," Gordon said. He was smiling, apparently enjoying himself.

"Jew or Slav, there is very little difference," the Count replied. "You will see. England will be grateful once Germany is strong again. . . ."

"But not Scotland!" Gordon shouted, laughing. "You always forget that we're not English, Andrea."

"Scotland and England, Austria and Germany—they are all one. It is our world against theirs. . . ."

"That's ridiculous, Andrea," Pamela Gordon said heatedly. "Why, all the Germans we know are in despair about the Nazis and their leader. They can't stand the sight of him. And the Austrians even more so. Ask Carl here. . . ." She turned to me. "What does your father think about the Nazis?" she asked. "What does *he* say about them?"

It seemed to me that a silence had fallen over the entire room. I could see the Count staring at me from his place near the window, his sagging eyes studying my face, as if he knew that my answer could be easily foretold after a brief study of my features. "My father is a Jew," I said in a voice I intended to sound calm and controlled, but which quavered slightly. "He hates the Nazis."

There was another silence, and then Richard Gordon said calmly, "Well, I agree with him." But it was as if the Count had won the argument.

"It's a mistake to argue about politics," Guy said.

"I don't agree," Pamela Gordon said quietly. "You find out what people are by arguing with them."

Richard Gordon raised his hand and said, "Sssh," as if he was afraid of what his wife might say next. "My stepfather is not really a fascist," he added for Guy's and my benefit. "He's a conservative old gentleman, and an Italian, and, well . . . he's not as bad as he sounds. In most matters he agrees entirely with us."

I did not dare to ask what those matters were. The Wilsons had come to say good-bye, and Guy added that we, too, must leave. It was getting late.

"I'll walk out to your car with you," Pamela Gordon said.

It was cold in the garden. The purple hills behind the orchard stood out darkly against the sky. The darkness had come quickly, as it always did in the spring and the fall. I could smell the citrus trees on the moist air. "I'll send the shirt back with Guy," I said politely after having said thank you and good-bye.

"Don't send it back. Bring it yourself," she replied. "I'm always at home in the afternoon." She waved as we drove off. I watched her through the rear window of the car. She was walking slowly down the drive, as if she wanted to put off going back into the house for as long as possible.

PART

III

≈ one ≈

I WANTED TO LEARN to play the game of tennis; that was why I went back to Las Golondrinas, without premeditation or malice aforethought. No, that's not quite true. If it hadn't been for Pamela Gordon, I never would have accompanied Guy on another of his visits. One encounter with Count Tucci had been quite enough for me. He was the first adult person I had met up to that time whose views coincided with those of the enemy, and I was not anxious to cross swords with him again. Guy argued with me, telling me that I had taken the old man too literally, that he was not a fascist, but merely homesick for Italy, and a little too chauvinistic perhaps because he was forced to live in a foreign land.

"But why doesn't he go back, if he doesn't like it here?" I asked, using the same phrase I was to resent when I heard others use it later on in life.

"He can't go back, because he has no money, and because he's alone. Edwina and Richard are the only family he has left, and *they're* not his real children. He truly has nothing to go back to. But the idea of going home, of being able to die at home, is virtually all he thinks about now. That's the reason he has a kind of gaga old man's sympathy for Mussolini. Because he still thinks of Italy as his country. . . ."

"Is that what makes him an anti-Semite?"

"He's not an anti-Semite. You must learn not to take all that too seriously. People say these things, but they don't really mean them. In any event, the Gordons are not like that."

I was not entirely convinced about what the Count meant, or didn't mean, but in the end I allowed myself to be persuaded that it would be foolish to take offense because of an old man's ill-considered remarks. It was not his house I had been invited to, and if I returned, it would not be as *his* guest.

At first I went only on Saturdays, driving over with Guy after lunch. Then, as we were usually early, I would watch the others play, occasionally keeping score, as well as retrieving the balls that were knocked over the fence onto the lawn behind the pavilion. Paul Hévesey, I noted, had a powerful service and a good forehand, but he ran around every backhand shot that came his way, while Edwina, despite all of the coaching she had received, seemed to dance across the court, more concerned with her form than the results of her graceful strokes. As Richard Gordon seldom returned home from the studio in time to take part, Ethel Wilson usually made up the fourth. She must have been in her late fifties at the time, but she was as lithe and quick as any woman half her age. She had been a champion once, and she still hit the ball with astounding accuracy and speed, winning any point she really wanted to win. Apart from her, Pamela Gordon was the only one who had any real notion of the game, although she didn't serve very well.

So that the sides might be even, Hévesey was always her partner, for Edwina was by far the weakest player. Whenever there was a long rally, Hévesey would begin to shout excitedly, and when his side won the point, he would run over to his partner and take her in his arms and kiss her delightedly. Sometimes he would jump over the net in order to console Edwina, who would push him away when he tried to kiss her, for she did not like losing or being consoled when she had missed a crucial last return.

Ethel Wilson disapproved of his behavior, and protested that it was unfair of him to yell while the ball was still in play. I agreed with her secretly, but for a different reason. It disturbed me to see him kissing Pamela, and it irritated me even more when she would laughingly return his embrace to celebrate one of their brief moments of triumph. "Darling Pam," he would say, clinging to her. "Why did I not meet you before Richard did? Why? Can you tell me? And now it is too late! Much too late! How can I betray the man on whose tennis court I play, and whose liquor I drink? It's impossible. Even for a Hungarian!"

"Play shall be continuous," Ethel Wilson always reminded him on these occasions. "That's one of the basic rules of the game, Paul."

Reluctantly he would release his partner and return to his side of the court, saying: "We are not at Wimbledon, Ethel. We are in California. A country with a warm climate. Not your cold England with all its strict rules. Serve him up, darling."

"It's *your* serve, Paul."

"Ah, I forget everything. It is the fault of this woman, this blonde goddess. Forgive me, Ethel. I will serve. With Hungarian top spin! Are you ready? Now, for blood!"

I didn't like him, because I was jealous. I realized that he was Edwina's suitor and not Pamela's, and yet I suspected that he might well change his mind if the opportunity presented itself. Also, I resented the ease with which he treated all women, his good looks, and his humor (for they did laugh at him, even Ethel Wilson), and more than anything else, I resented the fact that he was older, a man, while I was still a boy. He was free to do as he pleased, to stay on to dinner if he was invited, or to leave, to drive off in his black Packard convertible, wrapped in a polo coat, with a silk scarf tied in a perfect knot inside the unbuttoned collar of his shirt. While I had to go home to dinner with my brother, and do my homework before going to bed. I think I hated him.

I blackened his eye once. It was early in the summer of 1935, more than six months after I had first met the Gordons. My initial series of twelve half-hour lessons had been concluded long ago, but I still went back every Saturday afternoon to Las Golondrinas. Out of kindness, Pamela would often rally with me before or after a match. Needless to say, I was ecstatically happy during these brief intervals, although I seldom played my best games when she was on the other side of the net.

Because Pamela was kind to me, Hévesey followed suit. He, too, used to rally with me, correcting my swing and giving me complicated advice on strategy, "the Hungarian method of instruction," as he called it. I always played well against him, trying desperately to hit the ball to his backhand, which I knew to be his greatest weakness. They would never last very long, these practice sessions, for the other players who were to make up the foursome would arrive, and I would be forced to return to my anything but impartial place on the umpire's chair.

On this particular afternoon James appeared as I was rallying with Paul, to inform us that Mrs. Wilson had called and had asked him to transmit the message that she would be a little late. "Why not let Carl play until she arrives?" Edwina suggested, possibly because she was delighted with the prospect of not being the weakest player for once. Pamela agreed, as did Hévesey. "Of course, the sides will have to be rearranged," he said. "I'll play with Carl against the two of you. The men against the women. A blood match at last."

But Edwina didn't agree. "That doesn't sound as if it would be any fun," she said. "Anyway, I don't like playing 'for blood,' as you call it. Carl should play with Pam against the two of us. That makes much more sense."

I said nothing, for I felt I was lucky to be allowed to take part at all. Pamela appeared to be agreeable to any solution, and so the match was decided upon. Nervously, I made my way to her side of the court. It was my first real set, and I was apprehensive about how I would perform. Playing with the others was bad enough, but to be asked to hold up my side with Pamela as a partner was an additional strain. She smiled at me as I approached, and swung her racket fiercely at an imaginary ball. "We've got to beat them," she said, "or we'll never hear the end of it."

I nodded and took my place. The next twenty minutes were almost enough to convince me to give up the game forever. All of Ethel Wilson's careful coaching seemed to leave me, as Hévesey began to serve. I had no control over my muscles, and my breath seemed in short supply. I ran as if my life depended on my legs, but the only time my running had any effect was when I rushed off to retrieve the balls when it was Pamela's turn to serve. The rest of the match I spent getting in her way or sending my shots well out of court.

Needless to say, we lost. The score was six-love, and Paul executed a brief victory dance, with Edwina in his arms. Then he leaped over the net and came running to console Pamela, who was demanding a return engagement. He tried to embrace her, but she pulled away from him. "Go back to where you belong," she told him, laughing. "Get out of here. You're the enemy."

"But, darling, beating you was much worse for me than it was for you," he said, locking her tightly in his arms.

It seemed to me that she called for help, and I sprang forward to free her. Hévesey pushed me away, not quite as roughly at first, as I pulled at him. Unable to untangle his left arm from my grasp, he slapped at me with his right hand, lightly hitting the side of my face. As if it were a trained reflex, I lashed out at him, recalling my old friend Ernie Schaab's instructions far more easily than all of Ethel Wilson's coaching. A straight left jab, the future welterweight champion of the Pacific Fleet had told me, was the best way to repel any attack. I followed his never-quite-forgotten advice blindly, and felt my fist make solid contact with Paul Hévesey's head.

He shouted an unintelligible Hungarian curse and released Pamela. Then with both hands covering his left eye, he started to jump around the base line as if he had been permanently blinded. Edwina was there at once to console him, while I stood off at a distance, horrified at what I had done. Ethel Wilson appeared at that moment on the stairs leading down into the pavilion, and as she had not seen me strike the blow, she assumed the damage had been done by a hard-hit ball. "Put some cold water on a towel," she said, "and dab his eye with it."

I followed my wounded opponent to the couch in the pavilion, where he lay down to be fussed over by Ethel and Edwina. "I didn't mean to hit you so hard," I said over and over again.

He didn't answer, he was that angry. And yet the whole incident was so ridiculous that he could not quite show the irritation he felt. After a while he mumbled something about my "taking up boxing, instead of tennis," which was as close as he came to accepting my apologies. "He didn't mean to sock you in the eye," Pamela said, trying hard to keep a straight face. "And anyway, you slapped him."

"I gave him a mild love tap, and he hit me with his fist!"

"He was defending a lady's honor. . . ."

Paul cursed again in Hungarian and said: "Well, as long as I don't wind up with a black eye . . . I'm going to an opening tonight."

"He wasn't hit by a ball, then?" Ethel Wilson asked. The incident was explained to her, and she chuckled, and turning to Hévesey, said: "Well, that will teach you, Paul. It's a mistake to mix love with tennis."

"You mean it's a mistake to play with children," he replied bitterly, a remark he repeated again later on, when we were all at tea.

It was the most effective way he could have found to strike back at me, and I sat in stern silence, not regretting my actions, but feeling vindicated instead. Across the room I could see Hévesey, in a chair next to the fire, holding an ice bag in one hand, that from time to time he would press against his left eye. I remember glancing over at Count Tucci, and to my surprise I discovered that the old man was smiling.

"I am sure that Carl didn't mean to hurt you," he said. It was the

first time he had ever used my christian name, and I sensed that somehow, quite mysteriously, he had become my friend.

≫ two ≪

"IT'S A MISTAKE to play with children. . . ."

The words rang in my ears, although I knew that the remark was
merely another of Paul Hévesey's wisecracks, that sounded more amusing than it was because of his thick Hungarian accent and the painful
grimace that went with it. But I was not a child, although I had behaved
like one. Of course, I had been provoked. He had pushed me away and
slapped at me, as one does with a jealous dog, and I had lashed out at
him because I resented the insinuation that I had no right to interfere.
Still, I realized that I was in the wrong, and agreed reluctantly to accompany Guy on the following Tuesday afternoon and apologize to Mrs.
Gordon, at whose house I had misbehaved.

"But you needn't have come all this way just for that," she said once
we had found her. She was standing on a ladder in the kitchen patio,
cutting the roses that grew along the iron grillwork outside the windows.
Karen was crouched on the floor, collecting the flowers in a straw basket.
"Anyway, it's all over and done with," Pamela went on. "And Paul
should have had enough sense not to crow about beating us. He wasn't
being very sporting. Although, of course, it's a mistake to hit anyone."

"I agree with you," Guy said pompously. "It was an unfortunate
incident."

"Well, I shouldn't worry," she said. "Paul called this morning and
said that his eye was a lovely color. He's telling everyone that he was in a
fight, and getting all kinds of sympathy."

"I want Carl to write him a letter," Guy said.

She laughed and said: "Oh, what for?" and came down the ladder to
join us. "That would be making too much of it."

"Shall I go sweep the leaves off the court?" I asked. Guy, it seemed to me, was being ridiculous, and I was eager to leave, so as not to be a part of his false solicitude.

"I shouldn't bother," Pamela said. "I can't play today, because I have to do the shopping . . . and Edwina's in town." She must have noticed the change of expression on my face, for she added: "If you like, you can come with me to the market . . . if that's not too much of a bore."

"Can I come too?" Karen asked, swinging the basket full of flowers in nervous anticipation.

"No, darling. You have your lesson today. . . ."

"But why, Mummy? None of the other kids have lessons after school."

"You know why, Karen. Because I want you to learn to speak French, and so does your father. Now, go along with Monsieur Boulard, and I'll see you at tea."

"But do I have to? I hate French," Karen said.

The words of complaint sounded familiar, and I felt like a traitor standing there without coming to her aid. But she was six years younger than I was, only nine, and was still truly a child. Looking back now, I see that she was more a contemporary of mine than anyone else in the entire household. But at the time I thought of her as a creature with whom it was impossible to have any civilized contact, which no doubt was how I appeared in Paul Hévesey's eyes. I was relieved to see her go off with Guy, dragging her scuffed moccasins across the tiles, looking back as she went, still hoping for a last-minute reprieve. "Do I *really* have to, Mummy?" she asked plaintively from the doorway that led into the back of the house.

"Yes, you have to. Carl takes lessons, too."

"I don't care. He's older than I am!"

"Don't be bad-tempered, Karen!" That was her mother's final warning. Then, turning to me, she added: "If you'll wait just a minute, I'll change my clothes and we'll go." She was wearing an off-white silk shirt and a pair of black corduroy shorts, which she felt were "improper," because of their brevity. I noticed that the initials *P.H.* were monogrammed on the breast pocket, which had made me feel a moment of doubt and jealousy, but as Guy had lectured endlessly to me on the day before about not asking personal questions, I controlled my curiosity.

I went through the living room and started out into the garden, in order to wait for her at the side of the pool. But the Count was there, seated in a wooden armchair. He caught sight of me before I had time to step back into the house, and called my name. "Are you looking for Ethel?" he asked. "Because I don't think she's here."

"No, I'm waiting for Mrs. Gordon," I replied. "She's going to give me a ride home." I don't know why I thought it necessary to lie. What difference did it make to him if I accompanied Pamela on her errands?

"You're leaving?" he asked. "But you've just arrived! Why not stay and have tea. There won't be anyone else coming today." He sounded as if he were lonely.

"I have a lot of homework to do. I just came over for a few minutes with Guy. . . ."

He chuckled. "Looking for your enemy?" he asked.

"No, sir. And I'm sorry about what happened."

"You needn't be, as far as I'm concerned. I can't stomach that fellow Hévesey. I don't understand what they all see in him. He's a cad. If I were Richard, I wouldn't have him around the place. He's always pawing everyone."

Pamela came out onto the terrace. "Are you ready?" she asked. I noticed that she was still wearing the silk shirt with the monogram. She had put on a tweed skirt and a coat.

"I've invited Carl to stay for tea, but he tells me that he has a lot of work to do," the Count said.

"Oh, he might change his mind." She turned to me. "Shall we go?" she asked.

I followed her around the side of the house to the garage. The gardener's pickup truck was parked on the asphalt apron outside one of the three wooden garage doors. "We have to take Edwina's car," Pamela said. "She took mine because the gardener's truck was blocking the way." She opened the door nearest her and glanced inside. Except for the small Ford roadster, the garage was empty. The truck was parked directly in front of the door through which we had hoped to leave.

"I'll move it," I said. "That is, if he's left the key."

"D'you know how to drive?" She sounded surprised.

"Sure . . . I'm going to get my license this summer."

"But you're only fifteen. . . ."

"You can get a license to drive in the daytime when you're fourteen," I said casually. "With your parents' permission, that is." I helped her open the door, then got into the cab of the truck. The key was there. I stepped on the starter, and the truck jerked forward. The gardener had left it in gear.

"Be careful!"

I felt the blood rush to my face. I stepped on the clutch pedal, and put the truck into neutral. The engine started with a good deal of noise. She was watching me, smiling a little, and yet she said nothing about my carelessness. I backed down the drive, pulled the truck off to one side, and left it in gear as I had found it. Then I got into the roadster beside Pamela. She had put a scarf around her head and turned up the collar of her coat.

"Will you be warm enough?"

"It's not cold."

It was the first time we were alone together. I wanted to ask her to let me drive (I had a learner's permit, which meant I was allowed to take the wheel when accompanied by a licensed driver), but I didn't dare. Sitting beside her in the open car made me feel inadequate, a child that is taken from one place to another.

"Do you really have a lot of homework to do?" she asked. We were making our way down the long, steeply inclined road that led to the beach.

"I can do it after dinner."

She seemed puzzled. "But then why did you tell Andrea . . ."

"I didn't know if you wanted me to come back to tea."

She didn't answer at once, for she was concentrating on pulling out onto the coast highway. "You're always invited, you know that," she said once we were safely on the main road. The wind was blowing in strong gusts from the sea. She reached up to adjust her scarf. "Would you hold the wheel for a second?" she asked. I was delighted to comply with her request. She raised both arms, but the wind caught in the navy-blue silk, making it flutter and snap behind her head like a piece of bunting. "We'd better stop," she said.

I steered the car onto the sandy verge of the road. In the distance I could see Castle Rock. I looked over at her shyly. She had taken a comb out of her purse and was trying to rectify the damage that had been done to her hair. Her coat fell open, and again I saw the letters P.H. below her breast. It was as if someone had put them there to taunt me. "It's a mistake to play with children," they seemed to say.

She must have become aware of the change in my mood, for she asked: "What's the matter?" after she had finished tying the scarf tightly around her head.

"Nothing."

"Yes, there is. I can tell."

Guy Boulard was far away, and so I decided to blatantly disregard his last lecture. "Why do you wear that shirt?" I asked. "It's Paul's, isn't it."

She laughed with surprise. "You sound like my husband."

"I'm sorry."

"But I don't mind," she said gaily. "The answer is simple enough. The cuffs were frayed, and Paul was going to throw it away, so I asked if I could have it. I love men's shirts. You don't approve, do you?"

"No, I just wondered. . . ."

"You really don't like him, do you? Now, why? It's too silly. I know he acts the fool now and then, but he's really a very nice man. And he's talented, too. If he hadn't become involved in the movies, he would have been a fine painter. There's no reason for you to dislike him."

"He's always pawing everyone," I said, borrowing the Count's phrase.

"But it's all in fun. He's in love with Edwina, anyway, and has been for almost a year. I'm just his tennis partner." She glanced over at me. "Or is that the reason for your disapproval? Do you fancy Edwina, too? Because she's much too old for you." She put the car into gear, and started to drive on.

"It's not that," I said, both relieved and wounded by her remarks.

"Then what else could it be? He's nice to you, and he likes you, so there's no reason to bear him a grudge."

"Never mind. Let's forget it."

"No, I'm interested. Don't brood, Carl. Get it off your chest."

"He treats me like a child. . . ." The words were out before I could test how they would sound.

She laughed. "But you are really a child, aren't you?" she said, and stopped. "I'm sorry. You know what I mean. You're not like Karen, but you're very young. It's wonderful to be just fifteen years old. I wish *I* were that age again."

"Do you?"

"Yes, of course I do. To be fifteen, and start all over again . . . I wouldn't mind at all. I'm twenty-seven, nearly twenty-eight. That makes twelve years you still have to live before you're my age. That's a long time, Carl. Everything still lies ahead of you. You mustn't be in a hurry. Enjoy being young. I know that sounds silly, and that no one ever does . . . but take an old lady's advice. Don't be in a hurry to grow up. And if Paul treats you like a child, let him." She put out her hand, and turned off into the parking place of the small beach market that was only a few blocks away from our street. "Will you help me do the shopping, or would you prefer I took you home? You live quite near here, don't you?"

"I'll help you for a while, and then I'll walk back," I said. I was not in a particularly happy mood.

"Don't be silly. I'll take you. That is, if you really don't want to have tea with us . . . ?"

I was weak. I knew that it would perhaps make a more grown-up impression if I didn't hang around her like a child, but I enjoyed being with her no matter what. So I carried her parcels from counter to counter for her, and helped load them into the rumble seat of the roadster, and drove back with her again to Las Golondrinas, and had tea by the fire, and ate the honeycomb tart she had promised Karen she would buy, and felt myself falling more and more in love with her, unattainable as she was.

≥ *three* ≤

TOWARD THE END of that summer my father returned from Europe. Although he had been away for only a little more than a year, it was as if he had been gone for a much longer period of time. So much had happened that I felt I was a different person from the boy who had run down the platform trying to keep up with the train that was taking him away. My father had changed too, I thought when I saw him again, but that was perhaps due to the photograph I kept on my night table, the small sepia-colored portrait he had had taken in 1918, when he was still in uniform. I realized that the photograph had influenced my memory, so that I almost expected him to look the way he had long before I had ever seen him, with close-cropped black hair, smooth skin, and dark, piercing eyes.

Now his face was gray, and heavily lined, and although his eyes had not lost their fierceness, there were always large circles under them, as if he were plagued by a constant lack of sleep. (I see the same circles under my eyes today, and I know that sleeplessness is not the cause.) I suddenly realized that he would die one day, which thought was deeply upsetting to me. Up to that time I had not really thought of death as a personal threat to anyone I loved. I had had no close contact with old age, as what grandparents I had left still lived in Vienna, so that I had not seen them since I was four or five years old.

Once, during the winter while my father was away, his photograph had been knocked over by the evening breeze, and coming back into my room, I had seen the leather frame lying face down on the small table next to my bed; I had experienced a moment of panic at the time, thinking something had happened to him, and that this was God's way of notifying me. But any portent of his death became even stronger when I saw his hand shake while holding a match or trying to insert a collar button into a freshly starched shirt. He had not been as nervous before he left, so I began to blame Europe for his physical deterioration, Europe and its endless strife. And despite the fact that I loved him, I began to think that, like some person who has been exposed to a contagious disease, he needed a period of quarantine before he would once again be permanently out of danger.

But in believing that this was remotely possible, I underestimated the size of the epidemic and the virulence of the germ, as did everyone else who lived in the *Schlaraffenland* we inhabited (which was what my father called it, using the German word that means "the land of indolence and plenty"), the never-never land of southern California, that was so blissfully unconscious of what was going on in the rest of the world. And he was not a little dismayed to find that his youngest son was so completely acclimatized to his surroundings, I discovered, for once when I went to say good-bye to him in his room before going out to play tennis he remarked how amazing it was that one of his sons should have turned out to be an athlete.

"I'm just going out to play for a couple of hours," I told him.

"I don't disapprove, Carl. Don't misunderstand me. I wish I'd learned to play a game that would take me away from this table and these letters. Unfortunately, I never did."

"We can go to the beach for a swim when I get back," I said.

"Yes, we'll do that. But don't be too late. The air cools off in the evening, and I'm not a Spartan, as you probably remember."

I asked Guy to take me home before tea was served at the Gordons that afternoon, but when I got home I found my father having coffee on the terrace with a small man in a crumpled-looking gray suit who had never been to our house before. My father introduced me as his "American son" and apologized for not being able to go swimming with me. "Mr. Gutchen can only stay for another hour, and I have to talk to him," he explained.

"Go with your son, Friedrich," the man said. "I can come back next week sometime." The young German-shepherd dog my father had given us as a homecoming present was playing with a ball in the garden, and he appeared now on the terrace, looking hopeful, as if he knew that we might take him for a walk on the beach. "You have a house and a son and a dog," Mr. Gutchen said in his soft Viennese German. "Enjoy them while you can."

"I'll go with you tomorrow," my father said to me in English. "Take Prince with you. He'll keep you company."

"There's no place to tie him up at the beach," I complained; "anyway, if you don't go, I'll take my bike."

"All right, then, leave the dog here."

I knew that he was annoyed with me for not wanting to take Prince, as the hopeful face with the pointed ears was always difficult for him to resist. He got up from the table, turned to Gutchen, and said: "Just walk with me a little in the garden so that the dog won't be too unhappy, Heinz. Or don't you feel well enough?"

"I think I can walk as far as the fig tree," Heinz Gutchen said with a sad, toothless smile. I went over to him and we shook hands. "You can have your father back tomorrow," he told me. He sounded slightly ironic. "Good-bye, my young American friend," he added as I ran down the terrace steps on my way to the garage. "Enjoy yourself."

That night at dinner my father told us about Gutchen, assuring us that he had never met a better or a kinder man. He was one of the greatest living experts on ancient Chinese art, and certainly the outstanding man in Germany in that field. Although an Austrian by birth, he had lived all of his life in Berlin, lecturing at the university and occupying a position of respect among art dealers and students of Chinese civilization. He was not a Jew. The Nazis had arrested him because he was a member of the Socialist party, and had beaten him almost to death in one of their halls of torture. Then, because he had an Austrian passport, and because someone from the embassy had intervened on his behalf, they had released him, but not until they had smashed whatever art treasures he had in his possession in the small apartment where he lived.

He had borrowed enough money to pay for his passage to Mexico, and after months of waiting in Tampico, had at last been admitted to the United States. He now lived in Chinatown, where he made a meager living gambling on Chinese roulette and the other Chinese games of chance he was familiar with because of his life-long studies. Physically he was only half a man. The Nazis had left their mark on his frail body, had almost destroyed his kidneys with their rubber truncheons, and had knocked out most of his teeth, which explained his toothless smile.

"The next time he wins at roulette, he should go to the dentist," my mother said. She did not mean it unkindly; it was merely a bad joke. My father bristled, his eyes concentrating on the calm face across the table from him.

"His appearance is not important," he said icily. "Not to him, and not to me."

"I wasn't thinking of his appearance. I was thinking of his health."

"Every dollar he makes goes to the doctors, as it is."

"Then perhaps we should help him." At times she seemed willfully to misunderstand his moods. She was certainly not any less concerned about the victims of Nazism. During my father's absence she had listened every day to the radio, and was fully aware of what was happening in Germany. However, since his return she appeared to be taking a calmer view, as if she had recognized the uselessness of living in a state of unrelieved anxiety.

"Are you suggesting I go to Heinz and say: 'Here's some money, buy yourself some new teeth?'" my father asked angrily. "Because then I would really deserve his contempt. Thousands of people are trying to escape with their lives. Whatever money we have to spare must go to helping them. You don't realize what it means to be trapped in Germany, else you wouldn't say things like that. . . ."

"I realize just as well as you do," she replied fiercely. "I'm not a child, and I don't live in a dream world. I have my family to support, but aside from that, all the money I can spare goes to our friends."

"I don't want to continue this discussion at the dinner table," my father said. He put down his napkin and went into the living room.

"Don't be so dramatic, Friedrich," my mother called after him. It was not the right thing to say, not if she wanted to avoid a quarrel. Any insinuation that one of my father's moods or statements was not genuine was, in the words of the newscasters of that day, tantamount to a declaration of war. We heard the front door slam and knew that he had left the house in a rage.

My mother acted as if nothing had happened. When we had finished eating the main course, she rang for the dessert. There had been no conversation following my father's departure, so that Maureen was the first one to break the silence. "Isn't Mr. Woolf feeling well?" she asked, with false innocence.

"He's gone for a walk," my mother said calmly.

"Shall I keep his food warm for him?"

"I don't think that will be necessary. Give it to Prince."

Maureen raised her eyebrows slightly and picked up the plate of unfinished food. "Will I serve the strawberry shortcake now?"

"Please."

My mother was always very controlled in moments of crisis, although she too had a violent temper. She sat very straight now as the dessert was served, her face composed and calm, except for her tightly closed mouth. She was of medium height, and delicately made, with straight blonde hair that she wore short and close to her head, like a close-fitting blond helmet, more in the style of the twenties than the thirties.

When next my Father left, it became necessary for her to take his place in Pojawlski's decorating shop. Perhaps because of this she had changed her appearance somewhat and started favoring an almost mannish style of dress. Fortunately it was most becoming to her, because she was a thoroughly feminine woman, and her femininity was made more apparent by her severe style of dress.

I don't believe I ever had any preference for either of my parents, not consciously, in any case, but at that moment in my life I undoubtedly felt closer to my mother. Aware of the threats of the outside world, she believed that the most important thing was for the family to survive. She knew that there was nothing she could do about Hitler, and so she tried to push all political problems temporarily out of her mind.

Jake was more in sympathy with my father, although he had already formed his own views by that time. The class struggle was all that mattered. The family was a bourgeois institution that really did not deserve to survive. If it could adapt itself to the new and better world, all right; if not, it wasn't worth saving, not even his own family.

We both sat in silence and ate our favorite dessert, hardly able to taste its rich flavor. "Do you have any homework to do tonight?" my mother asked once we had finished.

"A little," Jake said.

"What about you, Carl?"

I said that I had some irregular verbs to learn for Guy, which was not quite the truth. But I was just as eager to escape as Jake, knowing that my father would ultimately return and that a quarrel was certain to follow.

Jake closed the door of our room and locked it, which we had seldom done before, and never against either one of our parents. The length of the silence downstairs that followed was disturbing. Obviously my father had taken a longer walk than was his habit on such occasions. We found ourselves getting sleepy, and there was still no indication that a battle was about to begin. Jake unlocked the door, tiptoed down the stairs, and returned to report that "Mother was reading, and Father was not around."

"Do you think he's gone for good?" I asked, awed.

"Don't be silly. He'll be back."

Jake had a powerful flashlight, by which he read late into the night. He was trying to finish Malraux's *Man's Fate* so that he could write a paper on it in French for Guy, while I was making my way slowly through *The Charterhouse of Parma*. However, I was too tired for Stendhal that night. I was awakened a few hours later by the sound of voices coming from downstairs. I looked over to Jake's bed and saw that he had fallen asleep with the flashlight next to his head, its white beam focused on the wall behind him. I could hear my father's voice shouting angrily now, sounding even fiercer than he had that day in Mexico, when he had felt called upon to defend my mother against the room clerk's impudence. I got out of bed and went to the door. It was not that I wanted to eavesdrop on my parents' conversation. I had some vague idea of appearing in case the fight got out of control, although I knew that my father was incapable of physical violence.

Jake stirred restlessly. A moment later the flashlight was focused on my face. "What the hell are you doing?"

"I was just going to the bathroom," I lied.

There was a long silence, while he, too, listened. Then he asked, "How long has that been going on?"

"I don't know."

He joined me at the door. We could not quite make out what was being said in the living room, for my father's voice had subsided, and my mother was speaking. Jake opened the door, and we tiptoed out into the hallway. At that moment my father's voice seemed to explode from directly below us. "I suffocate here," he shouted. "Is that what you want? To strangle me? To ruin my life?"

"How can you even say a thing like that?" my mother replied.

"Because that's what this place does to me. I feel it shutting off my breath, a little more each day. . . ." He was obviously pacing the floor, for his voice had grown a little fainter. "I don't belong here," he went on. "I even feel that I'm a stranger in my own house. My wife has no need for me, and neither do my sons."

"Don't be absurd, Friedrich. You have your own reasons for feeling restless, and they have nothing to do with any of us. All I ask is that you be honest with me. After all these years, you could at least tell me the truth."

The wooden floor was cold under our feet. Jake crossed to the carpeted landing. A board creaked. An instant later my mother appeared at the foot of the stairs.

"What are you doing, boys?" she asked. She had been crying, but when she saw us, she managed to gain control of herself. She wiped her eyes with a handkerchief and started slowly toward us. She said: "It's late. You should be asleep."

My father came to the foot of the stairs an instant later. He stared up at us, the expression of anger leaving his face the moment he saw us. "Go to bed, both of you," he said impatiently. Then in a kinder tone of voice, he added: "Your mother and I are discussing something that doesn't concern you. Else we would have asked you to join us. . . ."

My mother was shaking her head as she approached, as if she were amazed that he could not have found anything better to tell us at that moment. "There's nothing to worry about," she said, putting her hand on my shoulder. "Go to sleep. Everything will be all right in the morning."

⤛ *four* ⤜

"I'LL BE GOING away again soon, Carl," my father said. We had gone for a walk on the beach, just as if nothing had happened the night before. Jake was far ahead of us, running across the wet sand with Prince, the waves coming up to churn around their legs. "I'll be back, of course. . . ."

"Does Jake know?"

"Yes, Jake knows. I had a talk with him earlier this afternoon while you were off playing tennis. . . ."

I thought I could detect a note of criticism in his voice. I was the one who was never at home, while Jake was always there. "How long will you be gone?" I asked.

He frowned. "I'm not sure," he said. "Six months, maybe less. . . ." The sun was a large orange ball hanging over the end of the sea. We were moving toward it, our eyes squinting against the mild glare. A wave caught us by surprise, wetting us to our knees and dragging at our legs as it receded. My father put his hand on my shoulder to steady himself.

"I thought you might be leaving," I said.

"You did? Why?"

I hesitated. "Because I know that you've never really liked it here."

He tried to light a cigarette in the breeze. I stood in front of him to shelter the flame. "That's not quite true," he said, putting the matches back in the pocket of his toweled bathrobe. "I like the countryside, and the ocean . . . and I like our house and our friends. But that isn't enough. I have to work. And I can't suddenly become a shopkeeper at the age of fifty. There's no theater here, no opera. We live in a cultural swamp." He stopped to catch his breath. Indicating the sunset, he remarked: "It's quite beautiful, you know." It was merely an aside, for he continued where he had left off: "Your mother doesn't mind so much. She has the house, and her sons, and the shop. A complete life. And she adjusts better than I do. There's no doubt about it. She's efficient by nature. That enables her to enjoy her work at Pojawlski's, while I feel out of place, an old Jew who doesn't know how to sell anything to anybody. Then I miss the *Kaffeehaus*, and the friends, and the gossip of the theater. I know that kind of life probably exists here too, around the film studios. But they're far away, and I've never learned to drive. It's too late for that, too, it seems. So I feel like a man without legs, a cripple. Can you understand that? I need to live in a city, not in this lovely, meaningless oasis. I say 'meaningless' because it doesn't really save anybody from the desert. It keeps us alive and prisoners at the same time. And what do all prisoners ultimately do? They quarrel. The ones who hate their prison most begin to hate those who've learned to accept its walls." His cigarette had gone out, and he threw it away. "Like last night," he continued. "It was my fault, I know. But recognition is never a cure."

I felt relieved because he had mentioned their quarrel. It was impossible to go on pretending that I'd forgotten all about it. "You said you felt like a stranger in your own house," I said.

"Did I? Did I really say that? I don't remember. In any case, people always say things they don't mean when they quarrel. That's one of the reasons why it's so stupid. How could I feel like a stranger with all of you here? If I said it, I didn't mean the house, I meant this place, that dries out people's brains and makes them old and senile before their time. I wake up sweating at night, feeling trapped, thinking I'm going to die here and never get back to my work and the world I belong to. It's pure hysteria, I know, as your mother points out. But a man's work *is* the most important thing in his life. You'll learn that too, someday. Work and friends. And both are missing here."

"But you used to work in the studios. You designed sets just as you did in Berlin."

"Yes, I did. But not often. Only when the great Jewish princes who reign there decided to give me a crust of bread, a crumb. But they don't really want me. I'm an intruder. I belong on another continent . . . they resent me. I'm a man with an accent from a place they've never heard of, or, in any case, would like to forget. That's why I've decided to go and live in New York. It's not so far away from Europe. I know there are still three thousand miles of water to cross, but that somehow doesn't matter. The city is not as foreign, and I can always come back here when that blessed thing known as a job appears. The rest of the time I can work in the theater. Or try to. For even the theater is a strange institution in America. A racket, they call it." He imitated an American accent. " 'What's your racket, Friedrich?' 'I'm a set designer. . . .' 'A what?' 'A set designer!' At last they understand, even though they're more used to people with accents there." He paused. "We'll keep the house, and come back in the summers, if all goes well. . . ."

So we were all included in his plan. "When do you think we'll be leaving?" I asked in a low voice.

"You and Jake and Mother? Oh . . . not for a while. I have to find a place for us to live first, an apartment—a house is too expensive in the city. Jake will be going to university this winter, and he says he wants to come east, too."

"He can't start college until September of next year," I said. Jake did not have the credits that were required. Although he was brilliant in some subjects, he was on the whole only a fair student.

"Well, then, he'll come to New York in a year. You'll be just about ready to come then too, won't you?"

"I still have another two years of high school."

"Well, you could transfer to New York."

"That would be difficult."

"Why? It's the same country."

"I don't want to leave here," I said. "I want to stay in California."

"You mean always?"

"As long as I live. . . ."

He looked over at me, not angrily, but with that fierce look in his eyes that often presaged anger. "That's absurd, Carl. How can you be sure of that now? You'll change your mind a dozen times about where you want to live before you're twenty. . . ."

"No, I won't."

"But you're only a child. You don't know anything about the rest of the world. You have no idea what you want to study, or the kind of work you want to do. And if the family moves . . ."

"I'd still rather stay."

"I really don't understand you." I knew that I was exasperating him with my willfulness, but I couldn't explain that there was a person here who mattered more to me than anyone else in the world. I sensed that he felt I was getting ready to betray the family again, as I had in Mexico.

"I don't want to live in an apartment in a city," I said. "And as we're going to keep the house anyway, I'd rather stay here and wait for you to come back in the summers."

"But we may find that we can't always afford to come. The train is expensive. . . ." He shook his head. "Carl, you must learn that the place you live is not that important. Something happens, and you have to give it up. It's already occurred once in our lives. If I hadn't felt that it was time to go, we'd all be trapped there now, like so many people. They clung to their houses and their furniture and their jobs, yes, and their country, and now it's costing them their freedom and their lives. You have to learn that the only thing that's important is who you are, and what you believe in. Nothing else matters finally. That's why you have to try to be more elastic, less stubborn. I know you like it here, and you have every reason to. You have the sun, the sea, and your friends . . . but that can all change. So you mustn't be so dogmatic about your opinions. Especially at your age. At fifteen or sixteen you can't say: 'I'm going to live in this one town until I die. . . .'"

"We're not in Germany," I said. "That kind of thing will never happen here. People would fight. . . ."

"I don't think it will, either. But still you can't attach yourself to one place, and hope to live there forever."

"Why? Because I'm a Jew . . . ?"

"No, not because of that. But because the world has grown too big for provincialism, or patriotism, or whatever you want to call it. The world should be your country, the whole world, not any one city or country. . . . We owe complete loyalty only to what we believe in, and to the people we love. Nothing else. No flag, no bit of land. You don't agree with me, do you?"

I shook my head. He sighed deeply and fell silent. I went on walking beside him across the moist sand. I could see Jake approaching, swinging his arms as he ran, practicing his miler's gait, while Prince followed close behind him, snapping at his heels. "We won't talk about it any more now," my father said. "Nothing will be decided for at least another six months or so. But think about what I've said." He walked up onto the higher part of the beach and stood with his hands on his hips, looking off into the distance. I knew that I had upset him with my stubbornness, but I did not know how to go about putting things right between us.

When Jake was only fifteen yards or so away, my father took off his bathrobe and started toward the ocean. He wet his wrists and splashed a little water across his chest, "to prepare his heart for the Pacific Ocean," as he had a habit of saying on such occasions. Then Prince came galloping up to him, snapping at his arms and ankles, which appeared to improve my father's mood a little.

He walked through the shore break and began to swim out to sea, his head with its gray hair staying well above the water, his body moving steadily off in the direction of the setting sun. Jake plunged in and soon caught up with him, while Prince ran excitedly along the shore, barking. I called the dog, and he came reluctantly over to me and sat down on the sand, his eyes never leaving my father's head, occasionally emitting halfhearted yelps of warning, as if he knew that both swimmers were well out of the reach of his dog's voice.

A quarter of an hour later my father and Jake returned. "That was pleasant," he said. "We should do that every evening." He put an affectionate hand on my shoulder. "You see, I do appreciate the good qualities of your dear California, although I don't love it quite as passionately as you do."

We walked home in silence, Jake and I on each side of him, sharing our father all the way to the corner of Seaview Lane, where we noticed a solitary figure in a gray suit moving slowly down the sidewalk toward us. It was Herr Gutchen. He nodded gravely as we shook hands with him.

"I didn't know you were coming today, Heinz," my father said a little testily. He never liked being surprised by visitors.

"I wrote you a card," Gutchen said. "Perhaps you didn't get it."

"A card . . . a card? Oh, my God, yes. I did get it, but then forgot. You must learn to call instead of writing, Heinz. . . . Be more American." Prince was sniffing at Gutchen's trouser leg. The small man made a nervous gesture of retreat and fear. "Don't be afraid! He's only a puppy. . . ."

Gutchen shook his head. "I hate that kind of dog," he said. "Can't you put him on a leash?"

"You hate him? But that's ridiculous," my father said. "He hasn't done anything to you."

"You have nothing to tie him up with?" Gutchen asked. He was visibly frightened. I grabbed Prince by the collar and pulled him away. I could see that my father was annoyed.

"I prefer this dog to most of the people I know," he said, "and certainly to your cats that meow and scratch and smell bad."

Gutchen turned away, as if he were going to walk off in the opposite direction. "I knew that I shouldn't have come today," he said. "I knew it when I saw your face. You don't want to see me, Friedrich. Why . . . I don't know. But what I do know is that the dogs they had guarding the camp where I was kept were like this one, and they loved their German masters, just as much as they hated us."

My father grabbed Gutchen by the arm. "Don't be a fool," he said in a milder tone of voice. "Because some men are beasts, you can't hate all mankind, just as if certain dogs . . ." He stopped short. "I'm sorry," he went on in a contrite voice. "Of course, I wasn't there, and you were, my dear Heinz, you were. . . ." Gently he steered Gutchen up the sidewalk, in the direction of our house, apologizing again for his bad temper.

I knew then that there was no escaping the past, but as I was still a child, I disregarded my intuition and went on believing that some miracle would put an end to all of our problems, so that I could go on living in the place I still hoped I would never be forced to leave. "Why doesn't somebody kill Hitler?" I wrote in my diary, in which I confided my most secret thoughts. It was not altogether a childish question.

Herr Gutchen never returned to visit my father at our house, preferring instead to meet him in town. At the end of the summer he moved to San Francisco, where the climate was less agreeable but where his services were more in demand. He died there during the following winter, of pneumonia, one of the first victims of National Socialism. I remember my mother saying that he was only thirty-eight years old when he died, which didn't seem as young to me then as it does now.

five

THE FOLLOWING SATURDAY Guy appeared after lunch in order to provide me with transportation to the Gordons', "my real family," as my father had started calling them. Not that anything he might have said would have mattered at that moment; I would have gone even if he had forbidden me to leave the house that afternoon. He didn't, of course. He was much too intelligent a man to interfere in any human relationship that he sensed was important, and he knew that it was more than a game of tennis that was making me give up the beach on a hot summer afternoon.

That year the heat had started late in the season, and now, at the end of August, it beat down on the dry hills out of a cloudless sky, melting the tar patches on the recently repaved road. There was no breeze. The eucalyptus trees that lined Escondido Drive stood like sleeping sentinels under the clear sky. We drove through the familiar gateway and were astonished to find the parking area in front of the garage filled with cars. It was apparent that there was a luncheon party in progress, and both Guy and I felt hesitant about going into the house. To kill the time we strolled for a few minutes among the parked vehicles, trying to guess the identity of their owners.

"Your enemy is here," Guy said with a false smile, indicating Hévesey's black Packard.

"Your rival, you mean," I replied.

"Not anymore," Guy said. "I've decided to quit the game. I'm a realist, Carl. The grail is not in the search, but in the finding, as far as I'm concerned. I shall look for a nice, middle-class French girl . . . someone with my own background. There's no use crying for the moon!"

It sounded to me as if he were parroting the words of his mother, but I refrained from saying so. Poor Professor Panglos. He had changed a lot during that summer, had become sad and resigned. Even Jake had noticed the change in him and had started treating him a little better. "A French girl will be hard to find here," I said cautiously.

"Well, I'll probably go back to France in a few years anyway," he said. "If there's a war, I'll have to, for they're sure to call my class."

So all of his mother's scheming had been for nothing, I thought to myself. I said: "If there's a war, the Americans will be in it too sooner or later. So you might as well go with them."

He shrugged. "I'm not too sure," he said. "They might stay neutral this time. There are a lot of people here who feel that we should let Europe settle its own problems. . . ."

"I don't know anyone who thinks that way."

"That's because you live in a special environment. I'm sure a lot of your classmates feel that this country shouldn't get involved."

"Not the ones I like," I said.

He laughed. "The world is not made up of friends," he said. *"Plutôt des ennemis . . ."*

We wandered on down the drive. I could recognize the cars of a few other people who had become regular guests at the Gordons' that summer. There was Bill Lovat's open MG, its tarpaulin seat cover stretched tightly over the cockpit to protect the upholstery from the sun. Lovat was a young Scottish journalist who wrote about Hollywood for an English newspaper and who was certainly more of a rival of mine than of Guy's. But as his admiration of Pamela was always expressed in a bantering tone of voice, I did not resent him the way I did Paul Hévesey. Furthermore, he was not the type of young man who could be taken seriously as a suitor. He was like a character out of Wodehouse, a sort of Bertie Wooster with a cherub's face and the inevitable double-breasted gray flannel suit that was never pressed. I was always glad to see him arrive on the tennis court on a Saturday afternoon, for apart from liking him, I enjoyed riding in his small open car.

Beside the MG stood a dark green Chrysler coupé, belonging to Charlie Bennett, a middle-aged character actor who was an old friend of Richard Gordon's and who had only recently arrived from England to play a part in a film about a famous British cavalry regiment. The action of the picture took place in India, and was therefore being shot out in the desert, which accounted for Bennett's perpetually sunburned face, which was a constant bright red, right up to the roots of his sandy hair. He was married to a tall, lanky Welsh girl who had often been my tennis partner in recent weeks. Her name was Wendy, and she had long straight legs which looked to be completely unmuscled but which carried her surprisingly quickly around the tennis court. There was also the Wilsons' battered Ford, its rumble seat full of Ethel's tennis equipment: her spare rackets, as well as the wicker basket full of practice balls that I had already outgrown, as I had been promoted to playing in the regular matches. Most of the other cars were unknown to us, and remained a mystery, even after we had read their names off the registration cards on the steering columns.

"I don't think Karen will be in the mood for her lesson today," Guy said. "Maybe we should leave a note in the pavilion and join Jake at the beach."

"But they're expecting you, aren't they?"

"I suppose so. Still, I don't think it would matter if I didn't appear."

I had never known him to propose a subterfuge in order to avoid having to do his job, and I looked over at him with surprise. I realized that he felt out of place, and I was sorry for him, but not sorry enough to agree to our leaving. Despite the many guests, I was quite determined to stay. It was not that I had any false illusions about the ultimate outcome of the pursuit of my affections; if anything, I was even more resigned than he was to playing the part of the unrequited lover. I wanted to stay, because I enjoyed life at the Gordons' house. There was no Herr Gutchen to appear at unexpected moments and remind the sunbathers around the pool or the tennis players on the clean court that somewhere people were being beaten to death or were trying to escape the country in which they had so unfortunately been born.

"Let's go around to the kitchen," I suggested. "James will tell us what's going on." There was an ulterior motive behind my suggestion, for I knew that if anyone from the household saw us, they would insist on our staying on.

Guy hesitated. "They'll be having coffee now," he said. "It'll be hours before they start playing tennis."

But I was determined not to be dissuaded, and led the way across the patio into the butler's pantry, where we ran into Richard and Pamela Gordon standing in front of the open liquor closet. My plan had worked perfectly. Guy suggested that we should come back another day, which idea Gordon rejected immediately. "Good God, you're not suddenly going to start acting shy, are you?" he said, his resonant actor's voice filling the small room. "We're in need of friends today. The entire company's here for the afternoon, so we want all the help we can get. If we don't get them out on the tennis court soon, they'll be rolling around the lawn dead drunk before it's even time for tea!"

"I doubt that," Pam said caustically. "There isn't that much to drink in the house."

"Well, we'd better get more in, luv," Gordon said, patting his wife on the behind, a comic gesture that was meant to go with his assumed cockney accent. "They won't 'arf be thirsty in this 'eat."

I noticed that she pushed his hand away irritably and that her face was flushed as she straightened. "I'd better run down to the store, then," she said. "If you'll give me some money, that is. . . ."

"Why not send James?" Gordon asked, reaching into his pocket for his money clip.

"He has to serve coffee and help with the dishes," she replied. "I won't be a minute. I'll take Carl with me to help carry the bottles. And we need more tennis balls. . . ."

"Just as you like." Gordon did not appear to be in the least aware of his wife's irritation. He took Guy by the arm. "M. Boulard and I will entertain the guests while you're gone. But for God's sake don't be long. My repertoire of dirty stories is not unlimited. . . ." He thrust his hand into the pocket of his blazer. "Take my car. You'll never get yours out of the garage," he added, tossing her his key ring.

She reacted too late, and the keys fell to the tile floor. There was the sound of breaking glass, and I noticed that a small gold and crystal heart that was attached to the ring had shattered. Gordon cursed. "You're not yourself today, darling," he said. "Now the damn thing's broken, and it's the only good-luck charm you ever gave me."

She had picked up the key ring and was holding it in the palm of her hand. The golden lacing of the heart was still intact, but the glass with the four-leaf clover pressed inside it was broken. "Perhaps it can be repaired," she said.

Gordon laughed. "It's a good job I'm not superstitious," he said. "Or how many years' bad luck would I be in for? Seven, is it? Or is it more?"

"That's if you break a mirror," Guy put in diplomatically. "Breaking glass has no meaning at all."

"And a shattered heart is easily mended," Gordon said. "I know. Well, it's back to the fray, now." Still hanging on to Guy's arm, he pushed against the swinging door, and together they went off into the dining room. I caught a glimpse of the large table filled with used dishes, which James and one of the maids were clearing at that moment. The guests were already in the living room beyond.

"Come on, we'll have to be quick," Pamela said. "Unless you want to stay?" It was not a question worth answering. I followed her out through the kitchen, where the colored cook, Bessie, was preparing the coffee trays. "We'll be back in a few minutes," Pamela told her.

"I see you got your helper with you," Bessie said. She was a stockily built woman with thin, knock-kneed legs, who, unlike Maureen, was never in a bad mood. "You're right, honey. Put 'em to work, I always say," she called after us.

Pamela laughed, and we went out the back door. After the heat of the kitchen, it seemed almost cool outside. We walked up the drive and found Richard's car parked at the curb just outside the gate. He drove a black Buick convertible, disdaining the huge Cadillacs and Packards most other actors owned. "We haven't got time to put the hood down," Pamela said, getting in behind the wheel. "I love this heat, don't you? It's the only time I really feel alive . . . in the summer. I suppose I'll wind up as an old lady, living in some villa near Florence."

"Not here?" I asked. The people we knew wouldn't even travel on Italian boats.

"Here? No, I don't think so. At least, I never see myself getting old in California. I don't know why . . . I suppose because I'm a European. But you never can tell. If the Italians go on being friends with the Germans, none of us will ever be able to go there again. But it's beautiful, Tuscany. Florence and Lucca . . . and all the little villages standing among the terraced hills. The sea is calm there in the summer, and the evenings aren't cold and moist the way they are here. Have you never been there?"

"Only once," I replied. "When I was a little boy. We went to a place called Portorose, for the summer. It's on the Adriatic. All I can remember is that there were a lot of Italian officers, and one of them let Jake and me sit in the cockpit of his plane."

"Probably because he was flirting with your mother," she said, laughing. "I know the Italians." We had reached the coast highway and were driving along the ocean. A mist was gathering far out at sea, hanging low over the shimmering water. "It's not like this," she went on. "The sky is bluer, somehow, and the hills are not as dry as these hills. And then, there's Amalfi and Sorrento."

I sat in silence looking out at the road. Why was everyone always wanting to leave this place, I thought. And why did they complain about the cool nights? Wasn't it better that the heat subsided at the end of the day? And why was a calm sea preferable to the ocean? "I like it here," I said, and realized that I sounded as stubborn and as truculent as I had when talking to my father on the previous day.

"I do too," Pamela replied. "I love it, even. But it's still not the same thing." She looked over at me. "You're not in a good mood today, are you, Carl?" she asked.

"Yes, I am."

"No . . . you seem a little glum. It's not like you. What's the matter?"

"My father says we're going to leave here," I said. There was no use pretending everything was all right. "He feels the way you do about California. He says we're going to move east and live in a city."

"Really? When?" She actually sounded alarmed, and I almost forgave her her preference for Italy.

"In a year or so," I said. "But I'm not going. We're going to keep the house, and the rest of the family will be coming back in the summers anyway. So if they let me, I'm going to live here and wait for them. I don't want to go to New York."

"But that's ridiculous, Carl. You can't do that. You can't stay here by yourself. You'd miss a lot. Anyway, why are you so set against going?" I shook my head. How could she *not* know why I did not want to leave? She looked quickly into the rear-view mirror. "You don't want to tell me, do you?" she said, and steered the car out into the center of the road. I didn't answer her.

"But why is it such a secret," she asked. "Does it have something to do with your family?"

"No, it hasn't."

"Then why can't you tell me?" She put out her white-gloved hand and turned into the market parking lot.

"Forget it," I said, as we stopped.

She set the hand brake and switched off the ignition. Then she turned slightly to face me. "I'd like to know," she said.

I shook my head again, regretting that I had brought it up. "I don't want to leave California," I said, "because I don't want to leave you." She had forced me to tell her, and still I could see by the look of surprise on her face that she was taken aback.

"You don't want to leave me . . . ?" she repeated. "But dear darling Carl . . . I don't know what to say. . . . Of course, I'm flattered that you like me, and that being with me is important to you. But I can't be as important to you as your family. Friends are a necessity for us all, but they're not like the people we belong to." She took my hand and held it in both of hers.

"That's not the way I feel," I said. "It doesn't make any difference if you believe me or not," I told her, unable to look into her face. "It won't change anything."

She glanced quickly at her wristwatch, moving my hand with hers in order to do so. Then she pulled my hand a little, as if to attract my attention. "Listen to me, Carl," she began, lowering her voice as if she did not want to be overheard. "I'm your friend, and I always will be. I'm much older than you are, but that doesn't matter in a friendship. It's not even very important. What does matter is that each of us is obligated to other people as well, you to your family, and I to my husband and to my child. Of course, you know all that, but I have to say it anyway, so you'll understand what I'm trying to tell you. You mustn't try to alter the plans your father and mother have for you. Because I'd feel terrible if I thought I was having some sort of unsettling influence on you. No, don't look away. Listen to me. I like you, and I'm always happy to see you, and play tennis with you. But life is full of uncertainties, and we can't really control what happens to any of us as much as we'd like to. . . ."

"I know that," I said. "But there are some things we can control. Or we can try to, right?" I asked, half-wishing I had never said anything at all to her about my having to go away. "For instance, if my mother and father agree that I can stay here, then it would be all right, wouldn't it?" I asked.

"Yes. Of course," she said. "But I don't want you to stay because of me."

"Why not? What difference does that make?"

"Because, can't you understand, things are uncertain in my family, too. Richard's going back to England in a little while to act in a play, and we'll probably stay there for six months, or a year, or perhaps even longer. We'll come back, of course, but exactly when that will be is uncertain."

The heat in the car had suddenly become unbearable. I could feel beads of sweat breaking out on my face, although my hands were ice cold. "When are you leaving?" I asked in a choked voice.

"In two or three weeks. The exact date hasn't been decided on as yet." It was as if God had decided to play a dirty trick on me. I couldn't speak. "I'll write you," she went on quickly, "and you can write me, of course, and tell me what you're doing, and if you do go to live in New York, I'll come to see you on the way back."

I felt trapped by life, by my age, and by the feeling of complete helplessness that went with it, that was the most important part of being only fifteen years old at that moment. "I'll never see you again," I said.

"Of course you will," she replied. "Don't be so silly, Carl, I'll be back, I promise you. . . ."

But I didn't believe her. No matter what she said. Even as she held my hand tightly in hers, I knew I was losing her, could already feel her drawing away. A week or two was all there was left. It might as well end now, I thought; I wanted to get out of the car and go off by myself. But I didn't. Instead I sat staring at our clasped hands, until she relaxed her grip and my cold hand fell limply onto the warm leather of the seat.

"We have to go and shop," she said, and I nodded and followed her into the market. Then, as I stood facing the shelves of multicolored bottles, I remembered the charm that had shattered on the pantry floor, and remembered also that I had been secretly pleased, because it was a present she had given Gordon. Yet the first person to have bad luck was me.

I began to pray that something would happen to make Richard Gordon change his plans. But I knew that it was hopeless, that even if there was a God He wasn't there to be used for such requests. Nor would He listen to me after so many years of neglect. There was nothing I could do. I had lost her.

⇛ Six ⇚

I CAN STILL SEE the setting for the scene of farewell, the cars parked in the drive, and the neat row of suitcases James had assembled outside the patio gate, with the purple bougainvillea hanging next to it, all of it, the drive and the house bathed in the fading sunlight of the late-summer afternoon. The "regular" guests were all there: the Wilsons, Paul Hévesey, Billy Lovat, the Bennetts, and Guy and I, who were not really guests, but "staff" rather. Although it was nearly six o'clock, the heat of the day was still lingering on, as if to repudiate all of Pamela's complaints about cold nights with a final evening of "Italian climate," which I made a mental note to call to her attention.

But the opportunity never presented itself, for she made her appearance only minutes before it was time to go; and so, that and a great many other things I had planned to say to her remained unsaid. She came into the living room, where everyone was waiting, wearing a gray-and-lilac tweed skirt, with a paler violet blouse to match, and a coat of the same luminous tweed over one arm, already prepared for a colder climate. She had on a hat, which made her look like a stranger at first glance, but when she smiled at me from across the room, I experienced a feeling of pain no stranger could have evoked, for she looked more beautiful than ever, as if she had planned to engrave her face on my memory, which in any event was an unnecessary precaution.

There was only time for her to sip her champagne, and already Richard was warning her that they would miss the train. Karen seemed to have disappeared, and there was a brief frantic search, until quite by accident Guy discovered her seated in the back of the Packard into which James was carefully loading the matched leather luggage. By the time Guy had found his former pupil, the departure was already many minutes overdue. Edwina and the Count, who were going along to the station, got into the back of the car with Karen, while Richard shook hands hurriedly with each of us, a little like a prince who has been forced to leave his castle for a brief journey.

As I stood waiting, I watched Pamela saying her good-byes, sad that my last meeting with her should turn out to be such a public occasion. She embraced the Wilsons, kissed Lovat and the Bennetts in a more hurriedly cool British way, and shook the reticent Guy by the hand, who appeared to draw back, as if he felt obliged to indicate to her that she did not really have to kiss him too. Then, as she arrived in front of me, she suddenly realized that she still held the empty champagne glass in her left hand, having carried it out of the house during the excitement of the search for her daughter. "Good Lord, look what I've done," she said. "Carl, be an angel, and take this back for me."

I took the glass and started numbly off in the direction of the front door, and she called after me: "Not now, silly. . . . Let me kiss you good-bye first!" So I went back to her, and everyone laughed as she took me in her arms and kissed me on both cheeks, laughing with the others as she released me, and yet I noticed that there were tears in her eyes, brought on, no doubt, by the haste and tension of the moment. "Work hard, and write me when you can," she said, her perfume and her brief nearness obliterating all else for an instant. "And don't forget to come and visit Edwina and the Count once in a while."

She stepped past James, who was holding the car door open for her, and I saw Karen pull away from Edwina and move quickly onto her mother's knees. Richard called out from the front seat, telling James to hurry, for he had stopped to say something to Bessie, who was standing off to one side with the maid, anxious not to miss the last moment. I raised my hand and waved, and the car started up the drive, slowed for a moment at the white gates, and was gone from view, leaving us all standing there as if we had just finished posing for a photograph.

I felt someone's hands gripping my shoulders, and turned to see that they belonged to Hévesey. "Let's go back into the house and finish the champagne," he said cheerfully. "It's an old Hungarian custom." Which we did rather solemnly, opening a second bottle despite Guy's look of disapproval, for there was not enough left in the original one to go around. When it came my turn to be served by Billy Lovat, I held out Pamela's glass, and turning it so that the rim that still bore the traces of her lipstick would touch my lips, I drank the contents down with one gulp.

The heat and the two glasses of wine were enough to make me feel light-headed. It was a welcome sensation, the vagueness that took hold of my mind and body. "Only wine can console us now, my friend," Hévesey was saying over and over again, while the dimly lit room seemed to come in and out of focus, like the optic effect in an old-fashioned film.

Guy would not permit them to refill my glass again. He took me firmly by the arm, led me out of the house, and told me to get into his car. Once we had reached the coast highway, he stopped, and reaching across me, pushed open the door. "If you feel sick, get out here for a minute," he said sternly. "I don't want you throwing up on the seats."

"I don't feel sick," I told him.

"Well, take a little stroll, anyway. The fresh air will do you good."

I walked along the embankment above the beach, making a great effort to move in a straight line, for I knew that he was watching me. For the first time the curve of the coastline ahead looked dry and dirty to me. Perhaps my father and Pamela were right, I thought. There were probably a good many places in the world more beautiful than this.

There was the sound of Guy's croaking horn, and he pulled up alongside of me. "You're not going to walk all the way home, are you?"

"Not unless you want me to."

"Get in. God knows where you'll wind up if I leave you on your own."

"I'm not drunk!" I shouted, the first time I had ever dared raise my voice to him.

"Don't yell at me."

"I'm not yelling at you." Reluctantly I got back into the Chevrolet. Guy shook his head. "I don't know what's come over you," he said. "Rather, I do know." He pulled cautiously out onto the highway. "I've never seen you take a glass of wine before . . . not in all the times we've been invited to the Gordons'. If it happens again, I'll have to speak to your father."

"I don't give a good goddamn if you do!" I said. I was tired of being treated like a child. In any case, my father was hardly the person to threaten me with, as he rarely intervened in matters of discipline. He had other things on his mind. I had a sudden moment of appreciation for the way he had always treated me. Even when I had contradicted him, or disagreed out of stubborn ignorance, he had never talked down to me, never demanded respect or obedience because of his age, or because he was my father.

"I think you might show me a little respect," Guy said, pursing his thin lips. "I'm not one of your pals from down the street."

"I apologize," I said mechanically. I didn't care. I would have said anything in order to put an end to the conversation. My mind had left the car and Guy long ago, was racing ahead. My father had been right. The place didn't matter. Only the people in it counted. How stupid I had been. I had disregarded what he had said, had listened to him with one ear, believing him to be prejudiced because he had lost his own country. But he was right. "The world should be your country," he had said.

I was miserable, and yet I found that my sense of loss was an almost enjoyable feeling. Guy stopped in front of the wire gate outside our house, and I realized that my mind was not so clear anymore. I went upstairs. The door to my father's room was open, and I caught a glimpse of him seated at his writing table. I didn't want to disturb him, but he called out to me, and I retraced my steps, and stood in the doorway of his room. "Come on in, Carl," he said, looking up over the rim of his glasses. "Or are you in a hurry?"

"No, I was just going to get ready for dinner. . . ."

"Then perhaps you have time for me." Despite his sarcasm, I knew that he was in a good mood. "I've been reading Santayana," he said. "D'you know who that is?"

"No, I don't think so," I said. Once again I felt I was the less intelligent of his two sons.

"You should, you know," he told me. "He's an American philosopher, and a good one. You must read some of his essays."

"I will," I promised, although to this day, I regret to say, I have failed to do so.

"He shares some of your sentiments," my father continued. He picked up the book in front of him and began leafing through it. I couldn't imagine what he was referring to. After a while he put the book down again. "I can't seem to find the place right now," he said, taking a cigarette from the crumpled pack on the table in front of him. "It doesn't matter. There's a wonderful essay on patriotism here that I came upon late last night, and that made me think of you." I felt relieved. I had thought that he was going to make some reference to Pamela, although he had never mentioned her, had never admitted that he knew of her existence.

"He doesn't disapprove of patriotism, then?" I asked, trying not to sound too stupid.

"No, not as much as I do, anyway," my father said, smiling. "Perhaps he doesn't feel that it's done quite as much harm in the world. . . . I can't put it as well as he does, of course, but he writes that the truest form of patriotism is the feeling that is based on a man's love for the countryside in which he lives, the meadows behind his house, the brook he crosses on his way to work, the hills that form his horizon. It's natural that he is willing to defend this terrain, and so on. He says that this kind of love of country is a noble sentiment, an integral part of man, and despite what I said to you the other day, I can see that there's some truth in this." He paused briefly, to ask if I didn't want to sit down.

"No, I'm all right this way," I said. I was leaning against the bookshelves nearest the window. I had not completely recovered from the champagne.

"I know that I always long for the fields and the woods of the Wachau . . . the wine country near Vienna. We lived in the city, but I can remember that in the spring we went there every Sunday. My father would take us on an excursion boat up the river to see the trees in bloom and the vineyards behind the old castles. We would have lunch in an inn, and then take a walk through the countryside before catching the steamer back to the city. Reading Santayana last night, I suddenly found myself remembering our excursions, although I went along reluctantly as a child. I would have preferred to play football on the *Schmeltz*, the meadow on which our club used to meet on Sunday afternoon. But when the weather was fine, the old man insisted on his *Sonntag's Ausflug*, and in those days to say no to one's father wasn't possible." He smiled. "That's not by way of a complaint. I said no to the old man a little later in life, that's all. . . . But on Sundays in spring I always went along. I'm glad I did now, and not only because it gave my parents pleasure." He sighed and leaned back in his chair so that he could look out of the window on the other side of his writing table. "These dry mountains and this ocean are your Danube and your Wachau. I realized that late last night. That's why you don't want to give them up."

"I guess I'll have to someday," I said.

He looked at me with surprise. "You haven't changed your mind, have you?" he asked suspiciously.

"I mean, when I go to college. . . ."

"I thought you planned to go somewhere around here?"

"It depends on where I can get in."

"But there are a lot of colleges in California. Certainly one of them will accept you."

"I don't really care that much," I said.

"But you were so adamant the other day." He looked closely at me, his eyes under their bushy eyebrows concentrating on my face. "It couldn't have been anything I said, because nobody ever listens to their own father. I didn't either, you know. He wanted me to be a lawyer. Lawyers never starve, he used to say. . . . Another doubtful maxim. . . ." He paused to put out his partially smoked cigarette. "What was it, Carl, that convinced you that it was possible one day to leave this paradise?"

"I guess I finally realized that I was being childish and stubborn," I said.

He got up and started to walk slowly around the room, stopping beside the small table next to his bed to rearrange the various objects that stood on it, the alarm clock in its leather case, the notebook and pencil he always kept there, and the photograph of all of us, Jake and Mother and me. "The Gordons left today, didn't they?" he asked after a while.

"Yes. . . ."

"Is there any chance that that had something to do with your changed attitude?" he asked slowly.

"It's not the only reason."

He went back to his chair, and as he passed, he rested his hand for a second on my shoulder. "I can't help it if I'm curious about what you think and feel," he said. "We're very much alike, you know. We both follow the voices of our hearts too much. It's not a thing we can change, though. It's the way we're made." He paused, waiting for me to answer, but I had nothing to say. "You look very serious this evening, Carl. I'm not sure it suits you." He raised his eyebrows to make a face, as he had often done when we were children, clowning for us, which he could do so well when he felt like it. "You're supposed to be the lighthearted one of the family. The American! What's happened to you?"

"The European part is asserting itself, I guess," I told him.

He shook his head. "Struggle against it," he said. "And remember that most people who leave you come back. It's one of the world's better tricks. . . . As it's round, it brings all of us in contact with each other again. While we're lucky enough to be alive," he added. "Now, go and take your bath so you won't be late for dinner."

I nodded and started to leave the room. For a moment we had almost managed to break the wall between us. Years later I realized that he had come as close to breaking down his side of it as was possible under the circumstances. Only his good sense had made him stop short of a confession. I had already guessed the direction in which the conversation was carrying him, and was grateful for his tact. I did not want to know any more than what he had already told me. All that mattered to me was that he had forgiven me for "acting like a stranger." I recrossed the room, and he took me in his arms without saying a word. For once I forgot that men were not supposed to embrace in America.

And when, at the end of that week, we drove him to the railroad station, I sat in silence in the back of the car, wishing that I could have smuggled my way into one of his suitcases. I had become reconciled to leaving California. Only an ocean separated New York from London, and I could thus have joined him in following the "voice of his heart," which I had guessed was the basic reason for his journey. The drawn look on my mother's face made matters doubly clear. I remember that she didn't cry as the train began slowly to move, but stood quietly on the quai, her arm raised in a resigned gesture of farewell, the palm of her hand turned inward, which was how Europeans waved, the movement of the hand designed to mean "Come back someday" or "Come back soon." I also remember that from that moment on there was no more talk of leaving our house by the sea. . . .

PART
IV

≈ one ≈

"T HE PLAY will be closing at the end of summer," she wrote, "so we will be home soon. I say 'home' not only to please you, but because it's the way I really feel at this moment. I long so for the sun and the beach, and the sensation one has out there of being far away from everything, that I'm actually beginning to believe that I belong in those dry hills of yours, at least more than I do in the green squares and gray streets of this city. Everything is too close here, the strife and the tensions that appear to begin on the other side of the channel but that finally always affect this island and one's friends and one's life. A lot of the young men we know are talking about going to Spain to fight, and one or two have even left England in order to do so. It's commendable and brave, I suppose, but it only seems like the other day that the World War came grinding to a close (I was ten years old, remember, although you were not even born), and one can't help feeling that the same kind of madness is about to start all over again. And there is nothing one can do about it! What a terrifying world we live in! I'm sure that in California you are not as conscious of all this as we are, but here the papers are full of it, and people talk of little else. I know it's wrong to want to escape, but I can't help it. Enough of my complaining! All I really wanted to tell you is that we'll be back before very long—in two or three weeks, or a month at the most.

"I wonder if I'll be able to recognize you when I see you again? Have

97

you changed much? You sound very grown up in your letters. How is your tennis? I only get to play on weekends—when it isn't raining, that is! Edwina writes that you never come to the house anymore. I hope that's not because of Andrea and his political opinions. Actually, I think he's very upset about everything that's happening. He wrote to say that he was glad that the war in Ethiopia was over, that the killing had finally come to an end. *Go and see them, please!* Otherwise they'll think that you're my friend only!

"If you have time to answer this letter, don't forget to put your return address on the envelope, as we may have left London by the time it arrives, and I shouldn't like to think of one of your long epistles floating around in limbo, or worse yet, falling into the hands of our snoopy landlady. I look forward to seeing you again."

She had signed with her initial, and had added a P.S. that followed the irregular margin left by her handwriting, something about wearing a red carnation in my lapel so that she would be able to recognize me. I folded the two sheets of heavy blue paper, slid them back into the envelope in which they had arrived, and went over to the mirror in the bathroom door to inspect myself. Love encourages vanity, although I don't think I was excessively vain. But I *was* concerned with how I would appear in the eyes of Pamela Gordon now that I knew she was about to return.

I hadn't changed much, certainly not to my own eyes. I was still plagued by the same unruly hair that had a tendency to curl tightly when not plastered down with brilliantine, and I was just as knock-kneed as before, which inherent fault in my conformation I had spent many hours trying to cure by standing with my clasped hands jammed between my straightened knees. My bones had resisted this treatment; nor was the shape of my nose to be altered by pushing up against its rounded end with my forefinger.

On the credit side was the fact that I had grown an inch in the year that had passed since the Gordons' departure, and that I was already having to shave three times a week, a chore I did not find too unpleasant, mainly because it was proof of approaching manhood. I was, of course, constantly being subjected to remarks about the change in my appearance, for almost everyone who came to our house in those days seemed to have known me years ago in Berlin or Vienna. "*Ist das der kleine Karl?*" they would exclaim, clasping their hands in astonishment. "You don't recognize me, do you? I'm Tante Hilda! I knew you when you were a little boy. You were such a darling!"

I can still remember how difficult it was to reply to these voices out of the past. I would shake my head and look embarrassed, just as my own children do today when they are confronted with an old friend of the family's, struck dumb because they don't want to offend with too truthful an answer, or appear impertinent by demanding: "If I looked like such a darling then, what the hell do I look like now?" Although I recall that I quite enjoyed the look of surprise on the faces of these self-proclaimed aunts and uncles, as they never failed to add some remark about my "looking so American." "*Unglaublich! Ein richtiger Amerikaner*," they would say to my mother, which at the time I considered to be the highest possible compliment.

I can remember that I was even in a hurry to grow old. The days and weeks seemed interminable, while the months and years race past now, bringing to mind a calendar in a passé movie montage, in which the numbered sheets of paper are carried off by a mysterious wind. Time stood still then because I disliked being treated like a child, resented being sent to bed, or having to ask permission to go anywhere outside my regular beat of school or beach or the local movie theater on Friday night. I was impatient to be "free," and I felt the day would never come when I would have a job to go to every morning in a car of my own. That was the desirable goal then—a car, a job, and a small rented house hidden away in one of the many canyons that seemed to have been created as a natural redoubt against the already mushrooming town. It was a goal, however, that I was not certain that I would ever achieve. For the year 1936 was not a good year, even by the standards of our present decade.

Almost every week the headlines came screaming into our lives, increasing our fears and apprehensions. Early in March the Germans had marched into the demilitarized zone of the Rhineland, violating the Treaty of Versailles, which, curiously enough, was still considered to be some sort of safeguard against a European war. The newspapers were full of photographs of steel-helmeted troops goose-stepping across cobblestoned streets, while blonde girls in braided pigtails cheered and threw flowers.

A few weeks later the German electorate placed its stamp of approval on the actions of their leaders by voting almost unanimously for the

Nazi-party candidates, putting an end to the dream that many of my parents' acquaintances still clung to, the naïve dream of a political reversal inside Germany, caused by the asserting of the anti-Nazi spirit of the "freedom-loving majority." That spirit did not exist; we knew that for certain once the votes had been counted. Germany was lost forever. Nor was there much hope for Austria, where my father had gone to visit his family. "Despite Schuschnigg's Fatherland Front," he wrote, "the Nazis are getting more numerous every day, especially in the Tirol and in Linz." And there was certainly no sign, he added, that the trend would reverse itself. "The poison is spreading," was how he put it; "the epidemic is almost out of hand."

My mother was spending all of her spare time and money trying to help people who wanted to escape. But there was no place to go. The frontiers of nearly all European countries were closed. Mexico and the Americas were the only chance that most of the refugees had. Money was needed, and affidavits, and the promise of jobs. Well-to-do women my mother had known in Berlin were hiring themselves out as cooks and maids. In Vienna the current joke was about how a Jew in a travel agency, when presented with a map of the world, had asked the man behind the counter "if he didn't have something else."

Then in May the news came of the fall of Addis Ababa. In the Sunday supplement there were pictures of Mussolini's soldiers riding as conquerors among the black, barefooted conquered, another victory for Hitler's theory of the master race. I remember how sad the King looked in the photographs (the papers referred to him as the Lion of Judah), even though he had managed to escape with his gold. There were newsreel shots (people hissed and booed in the theater, I remember) showing Italian aviators laughing as they climbed out of their planes after having bombed armed tribesmen with spears and shields, the "enemy" who needed to be subdued. Americans were shocked then by a modern war machine being used to strike down a backward people.

But it was in the summer that the crises reached their high point, for in the dry heat of a Californian July the news came that the generals Mola and Franco had started an insurrection; that, airlifted in German Junkers, they had landed on the mainland of Spain, where Seville and Badajoz were soon in their hands. Steel-helmeted soldiers with darker faces were marching with their right arms raised in salute, and their victories were Hitler's victories, the twisted man of hate whose feminine gestures my schoolfriends imitated, holding a comb above their mouths. He was a comical figure to them. They laughed at the film that showed him entering the jammed Berlin stadium where he opened the Olympic Games (at which the only victories that counted for our side were the victories the Negro athletes from the USA won for their politically dormant country). He was a joke to them, because they had no relatives or friends in Germany, and because they discounted what they read in the papers about Nazi brutalities, and so they went quite happily to Berlin for the Games, parroting the absurd cliché that "sport is a messenger of peace and understanding." "He's done a lot for Germany" was the phrase we learned to accept, even from those who disapproved of "what's happened to the Jews."

"What's happened to the Jews . . ." It sounded as if it were an act of God. But we knew that it was an act of man, or of many men, who went into people's houses and apartments late at night to arrest them without a warrant, and closed their shops and publishing houses. There were photographs of storm troopers herding whole families into police vans to substantiate the reports in the papers, but that hardly affected most of the Americans we knew. Germany was thousands of miles away.

I used to think about what I would have done had I been there. I was still a child, and the proof of it is that I honestly believed that I would have fought and struggled, bought a gun or a knife with which to defend myself. "Why doesn't anyone resist?" I asked my mother, not believing the obvious answer that no one can resist a private army operating with the consent of the police, nobody thinks of fighting when the rest of the nation looks on without protest and when the victims themselves still hope that the law of the country they have loved all of their lives will protect them.

But in Spain they were fighting, I couldn't help thinking; in Spain they were willing to die to resist fascism, and that country and its people took on an aura of heroism.

I can still remember how we used to sit in the living room after dinner, in front of the polished mahogany box that housed our radio, and listen to all the reports of defeat and surrender that were invariably assembled for a final evening parade across our carpet, as if reading the daily newspapers wasn't torture enough. Still, I never gave up hope, felt certain that someday the tide would turn, that somehow the free nations of the world would get together to make their stand and save Spain, and along with Spain, the world. Needless to say, it didn't work out that way. When the democracies finally did get together, it was only to sign a nonintervention pact, which we knew at once was a death sentence for the Spanish republic. But that was later, my almanac tells me now, in December, although that autumn Jake was already pessimistic about the final outcome of the civil war, despite all the Russian planes and tanks that were beginning to appear in the newspaper photographs.

He had become disillusioned with the Communists by that time, had slipped still further left into a stubborn Trotskyism, which political position enraged me even more, for he and his friends seemed to want the worst to happen, prophesying that only when all was lost would it be possible to save mankind again. He had fallen in love with a girl called Marcia, a thin dark-haired hawk of a girl who was fiercer in her arguments and her convictions than he was, and who seemed to delight in making black predictions about the destruction of the bourgeoisie in the coming holocaust, as if she wanted even our book-lined living room to be engulfed by the flames. Spain was doomed, Marcia used to declare with a smug look of superiority. The Russians wanted only to prolong the war, were not interested in winning it, which was why they had turned their guns on their own comrades in arms, the anarchists and socialists, while the rulers of England and France preferred a victory for Franco to the survival of the popular-front government. All their expressed sympathy was lip service, an emotional sop for the middle-class intellectuals who were "bleeding so far away from the barricades." Those who went to die there were fools, victims of a propaganda machine that liked to extoll the virtues of a gallant defeat.

I used to argue with her, but with little success. She was better informed than I was, and she had a superior manner when she spoke that would soon provoke me into making the wildest kind of statements. Then, once on shaky ground, I would become personal, thus weakening my position even more. "Carl has always had fascist tendencies," Jake would declare on these occasions, which familiar remark had the effect of a well-placed pair of *banderillas* on me. I would charge wildly at my opponents, increasing the slanderous quality of my insults, until even my mother and Guy Boulard would find it difficult to agree with me.

"Maybe Franco is right," I recall shouting on one occasion, "because there's certainly no hope for a country where people like you and Marcia are allowed to have a say."

"Sure, and so is Hitler," was Jake's calm reply.

"And Mussolini and Stalin," Marcia added. "All the murderers together. They're right because they know how to take care of the dissenters in their country."

"And what would you do if *your* party came to power? Would you be tolerant? Would you give your enemies a chance to destroy you?"

"We would take all measures necessary to safeguard the continuing welfare of the true dictatorship of the proletariat," Marcia replied calmly, as if she were Rosa Luxembourg speaking in front of the Reichstag, or La Pasionara addressing the International Brigades. "All measures," she underlined significantly. She wore a fringe that hung like a dark curtain across her well-shaped forehead, and when she spoke, her fierce black eyes glared in defiance at the rest of us.

"Even if these measures were to destroy your family and your friends?"

"Even then," she declared resolutely. "Because my friends think as I do." She was all the more infuriating because she so often came close to the truth. Yet without the "middle-class liberals" and their constant agitation for the right of free speech, she and her comrades would be lost, I would remind her at least once during every one of our arguments. Without "our Roosevelt," whom she seemed to hate as much as Hitler and Mussolini, they would all be in jail, those of them the local Red Squad hadn't beaten to a pulp with their nightsticks.

It was apparent to me that people like Marcia could exist only in the tolerant America they wanted to destroy, but that was something I could not make either her or Jake understand. Certainly in Russia the opposition had no voice, I would argue. The "dissenters" there were treated with equal harshness as in Germany, and that was the beloved socialist homeland which they defended despite their disenchantment with Stalin. That line of reasoning would make Marcia sneer and look with a shrug of her thin shoulders over at Jake, as if she needed an endorsement of her low opinion of me.

Only the hysterical voice of Hitler, shouting his frenzied slogans of hate, could restore some sort of political unity to our household, a unity from which Marcia was temporarily excluded, for she alone among us was dependent on the watered-down translations that the network's Berlin correspondent was in the habit of sending back across the airwaves. The rest of us—Jake, my mother, and I, and even Guy Boulard, who was studying German—could understand the Reich Chancellor's original words. And while the roar of the *Sieg Heils* of his followers would come pulsating across the airwaves, we would sit in gloomy silence in front of the radio, rediscovering the solidarity that we had temporarily lost.

For Hitler simplified all the issues, gave all of our lives a single direction, one driving hope we could not help sharing: to live long enough to see him dead. So that finally the arguments and disputes were forgotten, and I would lie in my room in the darkness (Jake had been moved temporarily into my father's study) and pray that Spain would turn out to be the flint, the spark that would ignite the powder barrel, that contrary to Pamela's hopes, and Marcia's predictions, the big war would start that would put an end to Nazi Germany. There were times when I would fall asleep and dream that I was already caught up in the battle, and invariably the scenes in my dreams were those of cratered mud and shell-torn villages, images my mind had retained from the war films I had seen, and I would tense in my sleep as the shells screamed over my head, and machine guns chattered above the sound of the waves to which I usually awoke. "I'm not too young to go and fight," I wrote in my diary, seated alone at my desk at the end of a warm autumn day, safe and healthy, with the battle I knew so little about five thousand miles away.

≈ *two* ≈

I DID AS I HAD BEEN TOLD. On the Saturday following the arrival of Pamela's letter, I borrowed my mother's car and started up the coast highway. A warm south wind had been blowing since early morning, bringing with it a smell of petroleum and desert. Even in the hills above the sea the air had been tainted by the wind, and as I drove up Portofino Road I saw the smoke from a brush fire farther up the coast that was spreading a thin haze across the sky. A man on a gray horse was making his way down the ridgeline on my left, the horse's rear legs lost in a cloud of dust as the animal braced itself to keep from sliding too quickly down the steeper parts of the slope.

The man on the horse silhouetted against the arid hills made me think of Spain, and for a few seconds I allowed my mind to wander, and I imagined that I was driving an ambulance to the front near Madrid. In those days I was always an ambulance driver in my reveries, partly because I had recently finished reading A Farewell to Arms, and partly because driving a car was the only skill I had to offer "the cause." But the weather was not right for my daydreams, for I knew from the latest newsreels that the first cold of November had come to the war in Castile, while here in "New Spain" it was still summer, still hot and muggy, with no enemy in sight.

At least no enemy with a weapon in his hands, I thought as I turned into the gateway of Las Golondrinas, reluctantly abandoning my heroic image as I shifted my mother's car into second gear. It was the first time I had been back to the Gordons' house since the start of the summer, and I felt ill at ease. It would probably have been better to have called, I thought as I crossed the patio to the front door and rang the bell. The flowers in the small rectangular garden around the stone fountain were still blooming, although the roses were beginning to lose their petals. Once again I was struck by the size and elegance of the old house, and I realized that I had never arrived there alone. The few times I had gone to play tennis after Pamela's departure, Guy had always brought me, but as he had long ago lost his pupil, there was now no reason for him to make an appearance without having been invited. I had received my driver's license late in August, which important event had finally made me independent, at least on Saturdays, when I could borrow the car.

The door opened, and I stood facing a strange man in a white coat, not James, who was a friend, but a rather forbidding-looking man with dark wavy hair and a broad, pale forehead that was moist with perspiration. He said, "Good afternoon, sir," with a strange accent, but made no move to allow me to enter.

"Is Miss Edwina in?" I asked hesitantly.

"Miss Gordon? I believe so. Who should I say is calling?"

"Carl Woolf," I replied, although I was tempted to say "Mr. Woolf" in an equally austere voice. He half-closed the door, and disappeared. Where was James, I stood wondering. Had he been fired, or had he given notice? I couldn't conceive of anyone voluntarily replacing his friendly brown face with the face of this forbidding-looking Pole, or whatever the man was. After a while I heard Edwina's voice, calling from upstairs. The new butler returned, and opening the door wider, motioned for me to pass.

"Is that you, Carl?" Edwina asked. "What on earth are you doing ringing the bell? Or have you forgotten the way?"

"Yes, it's me," I answered.

"Well, then, come upstairs, silly. I've just washed my hair, and it's still wringing wet. . . ."

She was sitting in front of the mirror in a pale blue dressing gown, her head wrapped in a turban made of a bath towel; she got up as I came through the open door, and offered her scrubbed cheeks to be kissed. "Why didn't you call if you wanted to come and play tennis?" she said. "I could have washed my hair later. . . ." She sat down again and continued the inspection of herself in the mirror, looking me over at the same time. It made talking to her difficult, as I was forced to address either her back or the looking glass.

"I haven't come to play tennis," I confessed. "It's much too hot, and too windy."

"You mean you've come to see me? Why, Carl . . . what a surprise. And I thought you were either here to use the court, or after news of Pam."

I flushed and said: "I came to see if you were all right. . . . Is that so amazing?"

"You did? Oh, darling, you *are* kind." She laughed falsely. "Well, as you can see, I'm fine. . . . I'm about to go to work in a film, believe it or not, and apart from that, I play tennis whenever anyone bothers to come up here . . . and I look after the house and Andrea, and what else have I been doing, let me think? Oh, yes, I take singing lessons, and go riding with Paul . . . and what else? Nothing, I suppose. Now, what about you? Did you get a job this summer? You were going to, when I last talked to you. Did you succeed?"

"No, not really," I said. "I could have gotten a job in a real-estate office, but my mother didn't like the idea. She thought it wouldn't be good for me to spend the entire summer indoors."

"Well, I agree with her," Edwina said, getting up to search for a cigarette. "What on earth do you want to waste your time being an office boy for?"

"I'd have liked to make some money. I want to buy a car. . . ."

"But you can do that next year, or when you finish school."

"Next year? I wonder . . ."

"What do you mean by that? You sound so ominous. You think the world's coming to an end?"

"Well, there might be a war."

"Oh, don't be ridiculous!" she said impatiently, blowing a cloud of smoke up toward the ceiling. "There's not going to be a real war for quite some time. Anyway, you're not nearly old enough to have to go." She opened the window, and then closed it again quickly. "It *is* hot outside," she said with amazement. "I hadn't noticed, because I haven't left the house all day." She turned to look at me, and something about the way she did it made me think that it was all part of a well-rehearsed act, a role she had suddenly invented and decided to play. "In any case, you look much better for having been out in the sun a little," she said, getting up and crossing to the edge of the bed on which I was seated. "Look at me, I'm all pale." She pulled back her sleeve, and opened the slit of her robe to show me her naked leg, as if her arm were not proof enough. "I might as well have spent the summer in England," she said, "although I am happy with what I've accomplished. I love acting. Imagine not having to be yourself all of the time. It's such a relief." She stopped suddenly. "Would you like some tea?" she asked, going back to the dressing table. "We could have it up here. I think there's some of the honey-and-nut cake that Pam used to buy for you. They keep getting it. I don't know why. Probably because they like it too. . . ."

"If you're going to have some," I said, answering the question she had already left far behind.

"Good. I'll ring down for it. But perhaps I'd better get dressed first. . . ."

"I'll wait downstairs," I said politely.

"You don't have to. I'll only be a second," she said, disappearing into the bathroom, but leaving the door open behind her. I felt ill at ease. She was being so much more friendly than she had ever been before. And why did we have to have tea upstairs? The servants were bound to think it strange.

"What happened to James?" I asked.

"Oh, he got to be quite tiresome, and I had to let him go," she said lightly from inside the bathroom. "He never really was a good butler. He used to refer to all of us by our first names, and he couldn't stop treating me like a child."

"What about Bessie, the cook?" I asked.

"She's still here, although I don't know for how long. I think she was having a thing with James, which she wouldn't admit, of course. She almost left, but in the end she decided to stay. They're strange people, you know." She reappeared, the front of her in a green summer dress, the top of which she held in place with one hand. "Would you button me up the back, please?"

My hands were suddenly cold and clumsy. The buttonholes seemed to have been made much too small for the cloth buttons. "Have you written Pam?" I asked, while trying to concentrate on my task. "About James leaving, and all that. . . ."

"Oh, Pam, Pam . . ." she said irritably, turning so that the dress was pulled out of my grasp. "This house is as much mine as it is hers. Of course, you were so mad about her that you didn't even notice I existed. Why, I'll never know. She's almost twice your age, and married to boot . . . although I suppose a married woman's just the thing for an innocent young man. . . . At least, that's what they say," she added flippantly. I blushed, and she laughed and took me by the hand. "Have I shocked you, Carl? I *am* sorry. But I never did understand why you were so mad about her. I was even quite hurt for a while, believe it or not."

"You have enough admirers," I said, realizing it was a mistake even as I said it.

"Oh, is that why you chose my sister-in-law?" she said quickly. "Because she was fairer game? That's not very flattering, you know," she added, finding a pair of shoes to step into with her naked feet. "Anyway, you made a mistake. I was quite intrigued for a while. But then you were terribly young, a child, really. . . . A very serious child, in love with my sister-in-law and tennis, or tennis and my sister-in-law, I don't know which came first. Are you all over that now? Has some young thing at school finally snatched you away? Or are you still faithful?" She turned her back to me again. "Finish buttoning me up now, and tell me the truth," she said cheerfully.

"There isn't anything to tell," I said, more embarrassed than ever.

"Are you sure? Well, I'm not the one to pry. Keep your secrets, it's much better that way, and I shall keep mine."

"Fair enough," I said. I locked the last button in place. "You're dressed now, madame. . . ."

She turned, and kissed me lightly on the cheek. "You *are* silly, you know," she said. "And to think I met you first. . . ."

"You didn't remember it at the time," I said. Undoubtedly Pamela had told her of our first meeting at Castle Rock.

"Did I not! What makes you think that? I just didn't want to admit it. I wasn't supposed to be on the beach that day. I'd lied to my brother, because I wasn't allowed to take the car out by myself. I had one of those temporary licenses, and Richard was being stuffy, abiding by the letter of the law and all that, and I was alone in the house that afternoon, and bored, just as I was today before you came, and so I took the car and Tim and drove down to the beach, and there you were on your bicycle, probably as bored and lonely as I was. I offered to give you a lift, but you refused." She laughed delightedly. "You thought I'd forgotten! Well, I hadn't. Then, a few months later, you came to tea with that wet young man Guy Boulard," she said. She linked her arm in mine and led me across the room to the closed bedroom door, which she opened very slowly and meaningfully, and we went out into the hallway together. "We'll have tea in the library, which is better anyway, in case Andrea comes home, and I'll tell you everything you came here to find out—exactly when and how your darling Pamela will arrive, the date and the hour, and everything else. Don't pretend you don't care, because I know better. . . . When someone is being nice to you, the least you can do is not lie."

"I don't lie," I said. "I'm much more honest than you are. You think I swallowed all that about your not being allowed to take the car that afternoon? You made it up, the whole story. Not that it matters. . . ."

"Well, you can think what you like," she said. "Because you're right, it really doesn't matter anymore now." She was smiling to herself as we went down the stairs together, and on through the empty house, hand in hand, into the library, where she rang for Guido, the new butler, while I stood there wondering whether I had been a fool. What would she have done if I had grabbed her while she stood with her dress half-open, and had turned her around and had kissed her? Not that she was taking very much of a chance. Whatever daring thing I might have done would not have been particularly dangerous, for I knew less about kissing than most boys my age, and even less about the rest. The truth is that I was frightened. I was in love with someone else, and although I found Edwina desirable, it was only in theory that I thought of her in that way.

My instinct to avoid temptation was a sound one. I did not trust her, and trust, I sensed even then, was an important part of loving. Edwina was the kind of woman who enjoyed the adoration of as many men as she could attract, which she proved in the years that followed. And her success as an actress had little to do with it. She enjoyed the act of seduction, off and on the screen, felt that she always had to be desired, something I had noticed when I had first seen her prancing gracefully around the tennis court.

So I was saved a little early torment by my loyalty, and by the arrival of the Count just as tea was being served. Perhaps if he had not arrived until dinnertime things might yet have been different, for her performance was beginning to have an effect on me as we sat there waiting for Guido to serve the promised honeycomb tart. She seemed gentler and more romantic than ever before, even if she pretended to be only concerned with my feelings for her sister-in-law, who was, at that moment, she said, getting ready to board the liner that was to bring her back to California.

She was coming alone with Karen, while Richard was staying on for a month or so more. She had no idea why Pamela was preceding her husband, she said. Perhaps things were not going well between them. Life was so complicated at times, she added with a sigh. She was worried that her brother was unhappy, and had been for some time. "I'm afraid your Pamela is not really the person she appears to be," she said. "I'm scared to death at the idea of living alone with her here. We're friendly, of course, but we've never been close. . . . She's always made herself unapproachable, austere. I've often felt that she really doesn't like me. I don't know why I'm telling you all this, except that I find it easy to talk to you. Probably because we're so nearly the same age. I'm a few years older, but not all that many, and you're very precocious, in some ways. In any case, it would have been much better for all concerned if you'd fallen in love with *me*, dear heart!"

At which moment the Count had appeared, immaculately dressed, as always, in a gray flannel suit, the jacket of which he wore like a cape over his shoulders, his silk shirt with the crested monogram as uncreased as if he had just put it on.

"Ah, Carl . . . you're here," he said, shaking my hand. "I couldn't recognize the car in the drive. I thought Edwina had found a new suitor. . . ."

"An old one," Edwina said with a mischievous smile. "An old suitor I lost a long time ago. . . ."

⇜ *three* ⇝

THE WEATHER CHANGED, grew colder. Clouds gathered in the windswept sky, and it began to rain. Soon the brush fires in the hills were reduced to smoldering scars. Then after the second day of rain the floods and land-slides began. It was the same every year, with occasionally more memorable disasters, such as earthquakes. But mostly there were only brush fires. Ultimately the rains would always come, flooding the principal boulevards and causing hundreds of cars to stall at the same intersections as the year before. The newspapers would print photographs of the flooded streets and the houses that the mud slides had damaged, as if nothing like it had happened in at least a decade.

My father had always maintained that the entire community was meant to be a temporary settlement (a gold town no one had intended to live in once the lode had been exhausted) and that ultimately a less controllable fire would reduce the entire place to ashes. Then a flood would wash whatever wreckage remained out to sea, at which moment the Indians would return, and soon life would revert to the peaceful normalcy of fishing and pottery-making, which, in his opinion, was as much culture as that part of the world was capable of maintaining.

I thought of his bitterly humorous prophecy again that year as the rain came down without respite and the number of local disasters multiplied. I missed him, and began to wonder when he would be coming home. Then I thought of Pamela, hurrying back in search of fair weather, and arriving to find English skies, with water everywhere, covering the lawns and pavements, and soaking the fronds of the palm trees that lined the principal boulevards. Even the edge of the ocean was brown, I noticed as I hurried through the park where the bus had deposited me that evening, although just above the horizon there was an orange streak of sky that might mean better weather for the following day.

I remember the brown sea and the sad palms, because that was the evening she called. We were at dinner when the telephone rang, and Maureen came in from the kitchen to announce that there was "a lady calling for Carl." I felt my face getting red, and excused myself, getting up to go into the breakfast room to answer the telephone. Maureen lingered on nearby, "getting out the dessert plates," as she explained in a grumbling voice. Not that it made much difference. I would have been equally ill at ease had I been left alone. For suddenly it seemed that Pamela had been away for such a long time that she was no longer the same person. Her voice sounded different to me, her accent more markedly British than before, and I stumbled over my words, not knowing what to say, finally asking her how she was, as if I had seen her on the previous evening.

I had planned to tell her how much I had missed her and how nothing had been the same since the day of her departure, things I had written often enough in my letters but which I was longing to say. Instead I heard myself asking her about her trip, and if she were tired, until at last she laughed and said: "You sound so formal, Carl. What's happened to you?"

"Nothing. Nothing's happened."

"But you sound different. . . ."

"You do too. You've got more of an accent."

"Oh, I can't help that," she said. "The English always do that to me when I live among them for a while."

"I see," I said. There was a long pause. After all of the months of imaginary dialogues, I found that I had run out of words.

Finally she said: "If it's a nice day tomorrow, why don't we play tennis? I'll pick you up at four. And if it's raining, I'll come the next day."

I collected my wits enough to tell her that I was sorry about the weather, and she laughed and told me that she couldn't really hold me responsible for that. For sounding like a stranger, yes, but not for the rain.

"I'm sorry," I said, nettled. "I don't mean to sound like one."

"All right, then I'll forgive you," she answered gaily. "I'll see you tomorrow."

But the weather didn't improve. The orange streak of sky had only meant a lull in the storm, and two more days of heavy rain followed.

Then she called again to tell me that on the following day Edwina was going to an opening, and that she didn't feel like joining her, so that we would go to the movies, if I had nothing better to do.

I agreed without knowing whether I would be permitted to go, but as it was Friday, I had my way in the end, although my mother said she would have preferred me to go to the movies with Jake and Marcia. For once Jake was on my side, and I on his, so that in the end my mother shrugged her shoulders and agreed. She was going to the Pojawlskis' that evening, which made it more difficult for her to insist I stay at home. Of course, Jake wasn't going to the movies at all. He was off to a political meeting with Marcia to protest the arms embargo on Spain, and neither one of them liked the idea of my tagging along. So for once everything worked to my advantage, and I was only slightly embarrassed when the horn of Pamela's car sounded outside our house. "Wouldn't your friend like to come in and have a cup of coffee while you finish your dinner?" my mother asked. She was keeping us company at the table, looking as if she didn't belong there, for she was already in her evening dress, the small glittering handbag lying beside her long white gloves on the not-too-clean tablecloth Maureen had laid out, as "only the children" were dining.

I shook my head and hurriedly folded my napkin. "We'll miss the newsreels," I explained, kissed my mother's cheek, and rushed out the front door. Richard Gordon's Buick convertible was parked outside in the street, with only its side lights on, and as I stepped through the wire gate, I heard the engine start.

Even in the semidarkness of the car I was startled by the beauty of the familiar face I had half-forgotten, by the smell of her perfume and the sudden nearness of a person who had existed for so long in my mind and then was suddenly there. Her face, framed in the fur collar of her tweed coat, was only dimly visible, and she smiled a little distantly, I thought, and said: "Hello, Carl. Well, aren't you going to kiss me? After all, we haven't seen each other for a long time."

I slid across the leather seat and kissed her cheek while she kept the car from rolling backward, holding it with her foot on the brake pedal. "Let me look at you," she said, touching my face with her gloved hand. "Why, you're altogether a different person, you're so grown up. . . ."

"You've changed, too," I said. The color of her hair seemed darker, although I couldn't be sure.

"Well, I'm getting on," she said with a peculiar little laugh. "Be an old lady soon."

"Why do you say that?"

"Because it's the truth. I'll be thirty the year after next. You'll soon be embarrassed to be seen with me." I started to object, but she laughed and said: "I don't mind, really. I'll be old and wise, and you'll come to me with all of your problems, and I'll be able to tell you just what to do to make all the girls who've fallen in love with you suffer. . . ." We had reached the end of the block. She swung the nose of the big car into Lovers' Lane, reversed, and started back up the street, passing quickly in front of our house again. I was glad to see that it still lay in darkness, that neither my mother nor Jake had come out into the street.

"I'll never fall in love again," I said, and meant it.

She said: "Don't be silly. You'll fall madly in love at least a dozen times before you're twenty-one. But we won't talk about that now. We're going to the movies and then have a bite to eat, because I'm quite hungry already. . . ."

"Haven't you had dinner?"

"No, I sat and kept Karen company . . . but that was hours ago. I'm all turned around, anyway. It's only eleven o'clock in the morning my time, you know."

"We can go get something to eat now," I said.

"But you've had your dinner. . . ."

"That doesn't matter. I'll watch you."

"No, I promised to take you to the movies, and I'm not going back on my word."

"I don't care about the movies," I said.

"You mean, all you really wanted was an excuse to get out of the house? You are clever."

It was almost as if she enjoyed twisting everything I said in order to make me feel like a child. "Well, you decide, then," I said angrily.

"Oh, Carl, you are funny," she said, laughing. "I'd forgotten how serious you are, how earnest. . . . And suppose we go to a restaurant and run into some of your friends, or your mother?"

"What difference would that make?" I asked, although I knew that she was right.

"It might make a great deal of difference if your mother catches you out in a lie," she said. "I'll tell you what we'll do. We'll go to a drive-in, and I'll have a hamburger and you can have an ice-cream sundae, and then we'll decide whether we'll go to the movies. It's what I've missed most, believe it or not, the hamburgers. . . ."

Because I was so on the defensive, her words wounded me, and I couldn't help but think of Edwina's warning that Pamela was not the person she pretended to be. She seemed much more frivolous than I'd remembered her, and I regretted having written so ardently in my letters, and having confessed feelings that were obviously not returned. How she must have laughed while reading them, I thought bitterly to myself.

"Tell me, does that plan suit you?" she asked, glancing over at me. "Or are you thinking about something frightfully important?"

"A drive-in's all right with me."

"But that's not what you were thinking about, was it?"

"No, it isn't," I said.

I looked out at the glistening pavement, at the trees masking the streetlights with their leaves that had not as yet started to fall.

She did not answer at once. She was annoyed. I sensed it in the way she drove. "I don't even think you're glad I'm back," she said finally. "You're so morose and argumentative. . . ."

"D'you want me to get out and walk home?"

She took her foot off the gas, and the car began to slow down in the middle of the street. "Oh, Carl, what's the matter with you?" she said.

"Nothing. Let's go to the drive-in and get you something to eat."

It was not a final remedy, but it helped. The breezy waitresses in their tight red trousers dashed in and out of their brightly lit shelter, carrying trays covered with waxed paper to protect the food against the rain. "Did you want onion on your hamburger, honey?" the blonde assigned to our car asked as she attached the aluminum tray to the steering wheel.

"No, I didn't," Pamela said. "But it doesn't matter. I can remove it." The girl smiled gratefully at having been spared an extra trip through the rain, and holding onto her cap, ran back to the glass-enclosed counter.

"There's nothing like this anywhere in the world," Pamela said. "Life is so simple, even when the weather's bad. Are you sure that you really wanted coffee? You won't be able to sleep tonight."

"I always sleep well," I said boastfully. But at the time was true. She bit into her sandwich. "It's delicious," she said. "Would you like

a bite? You'd better have one, in case I didn't get rid of all the onion."
She offered me a corner of her hamburger. "We don't have to go to the
movies, you know. No, I'm serious. We can drive up to Billy Lovat's
house and say hello to him. We're invited . . . both of us. He called
just as I was leaving. He lives in one of these canyons. I've been there
before. . . ."

But we couldn't find Lovat's house in the darkness. Pamela had been
there only in the daytime, and that was more than a year ago. We
wound our way up several narrow roads, stopped in front of a dozen
bungalows, until finally we found ourselves on the summit of the hills
overlooking the town. It was no longer raining, and the stars were out
overhead, the sky clearer than it looked in the summer. The entire city
lay in front of us, the main thoroughfares marked by more intensely
burning strings of lights. There was the smell of wet sage, mingling with
Pamela's perfume. "I'm sure it's somewhere very nearby," she said
vaguely. "I remember the view from his living room, and it was just like
this."

"We can go down to the drugstore on the boulevard and call," I
suggested.

"No, it doesn't matter. I'll call him tomorrow and tell him we went
to the movies instead." She turned off the engine. "Would you like to
take a walk?"

"Yes. Fine. Anything."

"You're still not yourself, you know."

"I'm sorry."

She shrugged. Then she said: "Come on," as if an energetic command might snap me out of my mood. We turned off the paved road
and followed a stony path along the top of the ridge. There was no
moon, but the glow of the city made it possible to see the path ahead.
"Are you cold?" she asked. I never wore a topcoat in those days, only a
jacket and a sweater. I don't think I owned one.

"No, I'm fine."

"Still a bit grumpy?"

"No, not even that."

"Come closer, I'll keep you warm," she said, putting a corner of her
coat around my shoulders. "Walk in step now. And put your arm around
me. Now, tell me why you're cross."

"I'm not cross."

"What is it, then?"

I said: "I love you, and I know that you don't love me," quite calmly, as if it really didn't matter at all.

She stopped. "Is that all that's wrong?" she asked with the same slightly mocking laugh with which she had greeted me. Then she turned to face me. "Please kiss me," she said. "If you want to, that is."

I brushed her lips with mine, and she pulled her head away and looked curiously at me. "Do you not want to?" she asked. "Or is it really that you don't know how?"

I didn't answer. I could feel her body in the knitted dress she wore, pressing against me.

"Carl?"

"Yes."

"Like this." She pulled my face close to hers, and gently parted my lips with her mouth. I remember that at first the novelty of it was greater than the pleasure, and I also remember her surprised voice as she asked: "Have you never kissed anybody else like that before?"

"No."

"Are you telling me the truth?"

"Yes, of course I am. You have, though, haven't you?"

She moved her head, as if she were trying to avoid the question. "I wish I hadn't," she said in a low voice. I didn't understand. Nor did it matter to me, then. I was concentrating on the purely physical act of kissing, trying to do what was expected of me. She took my hand, and opening the top button of her dress, put it inside her brassiere. "Don't you like to touch me?" she asked, as I removed my hand. I didn't answer, and she laughed softly again. "You prefer kissing, is that it?"

"I like both," I said bravely, and kissed her again. It was less embarrassing than talking; then and forevermore.

"Let's go back to the car."

I nodded obediently. We walked hand in hand along the dirt track. Whatever reluctance or bitterness I had felt was all gone. A car came up the road, and for an instant we were caught in the glare of its headlights. I noticed that Pamela put her head down, as if to hide her face. I didn't say anything. She opened the door of the convertible and got inside.

"It's nicer to kiss sitting down, isn't it?"

"I don't know."

"Well, you'll see," she said, laughing. Then, after a while she straightened and buttoned the top of her dress. "I think we should go home," she told me. I was discovering that her mouth, and the smooth skin I had found inside her dress, were having an effect on me. I felt less nervous than I had in the beginning, but I was still worried by a general feeling of inadequacy. She gave me her handkerchief and told me to wipe the lip rouge off my mouth. "It doesn't look good on you," she said, smiling.

We drove slowly down the twisting road that led us into the darkness of the canyon. Suddenly the figure of a man was visible in the beam of the lights. It was Billy Lovat. He was waving his arms in an exaggerated manner, as if to warn us of a hazard ahead. "I thought it was you patrolling my road," he said. "What were you doing up there all that time, anyway? Did you park and pet?"

"Of course," Pamela said, pinching my leg. "We couldn't find your house, so we didn't want the evening to be a total loss."

"You are clever," Lovat said, grinning. "And you're the luckiest bastard in the world," he added, turning to me. "Come on in and have a beaker, now. Everybody wants to see you, Pam. The whole bloody clan. You're our only courier from home, and we're all panting for news. . . ." He took Pamela's arm and started to lead her down a narrow flight of wooden stairs, with shrubbery on both sides.

"How can you ever expect anyone to find this place?" I heard Pamela ask as I followed her and Lovat, less jealous than I would normally have been, but feeling more out of place than ever. The house was a small bungalow perched on the steep hillside, completely hidden from the road. Lovat had started to sing as he approached the front door. " 'Maxwell-ton's braes are bonny, where early falls the dew . . .' Here she is, chaps. And d'you know what she was doing? Leading this young man astray up on Lookout Mountain Road!"

I blushed, but the room we had entered was so dimly lit that I knew I was safe. The Bennetts were the only people there I had met before. Everyone else was a stranger, which didn't matter for once, even when Pamela disappeared, saying that she "had to go and powder her nose for a minute." It was easier just to accept a Coke and look out at the view and say nothing.

"I heard the car go by," Lovat was saying again, "and I thought it must be you, looking for the house. That's why I went out to have a look." Did I still have lipstick on my face, I wondered, as I stared at the distant lights of the city. I felt that everyone was looking too closely at me, as if I were an oddity merely because I was so much younger than all of them. And then, suddenly, I didn't care. Pamela was all that mattered to me. The rest of the world was unimportant.

four

MANY THINGS were said that I have forgotten, but the scenes have remained clear in my mind, so that it has not been too difficult to supply the missing words. Still, there are phrases I can remember as accurately as if it had all taken place only yesterday, or the day before. Such as the question Pamela had asked while I held her in my arms for the first time, a question that was bound to come sooner or later, I suppose, but that contained the poison that ultimately does harm to all lovers, unless they are so wise and experienced that they know better than to ask it. Under the circumstances it was a perfectly reasonable question, but then, so was my reply reasonable, although it was quite apparent that I had "never kissed anybody else like that before," and equally apparent that she had.

I suppose I was ridiculously innocent for my age, despite the fact that I belonged to a generation that was, as a rule, not that innocent at all. Of course, I pretended to be very well informed about sex, in theory at least, if not in practice, but that attitude was an obvious defense, as I didn't want to appear to be an ass when Jake made allusions to what "really went on between men and women." He had read Pierre Louys, as well as a good many other works of that kind, while I had glanced briefly on various occasions at the illustrated copy of *Fanny Hill* that he had discovered in my father's library, yet I had never thought myself capable of doing the things pictured in that book, not because I was shocked, but because it all looked somehow unreal. The partially clothed men and women wore the costumes of another period, which made what they were doing look outdated as well. In any case, the illustrations failed to incite me, or even interest me sufficiently to make me read the text of *Fanny Hill*, or any of the other valuable source material that was readily available.

As far as *praxis* was concerned, I had never again come as close to the actual experience as I had with Maureen that shaming night, an adventure I already considered a part of my childhood. Since then my "sexual" experiences had been even more innocuous. The most recent one had consisted in joining some of my basketball teammates at a hole in the plaster wall of our locker room, in order to admire the figure of a girl who was getting dressed in the girls' locker room on the other side. I remember to this day that her name was Tracy Hill, and that she had an astonishingly well-shaped body that never looked the same to me again in the navy-blue skirt and white middy blouse that was the required uniform for female high-school students in those days.

Seeing her half-naked at fairly close range had, I recall, aroused no specific sexual desires in me, and although most of my teammates testified vociferously to the contrary, I myself doubted that the graceful form in the "panties and bra" had had all that much effect on them. I had decided that, not unlike most of their other intimate revelations, their reactions had been largely fabricated so that they could impress each other with their manliness. And I found their boasting about their sexual needs just as distasteful as having to listen to their accounts of what had taken place in their parked automobiles on Friday and Saturday nights. I like to think that I was a romantic rather than a prude, which was probably one of the reasons I had fled in such a cowardly manner from Maureen's bed.

Now, suddenly, I was one of them. I had done what they had boasted about doing for years. Yet my experience had been different, or at least so it appeared to me. I had never had any sexual designs on Pamela Gordon. I was in love with her, and had been brave enough to declare my love only because I believed it to be a hopeless cause, a Spain of the heart. When she had taken the initiative, I had at first been surprised and scared. I knew that she wasn't in love with me; certainly nothing she had said or written had indicated that she had ever thought of me as anything more than a tennis friend. What had made her change? I couldn't go to sleep that night, not because of frustrated desire, but because a hundred questions kept filling my brain, unpleasant questions that gnawed away at the generally pleasant feeling that had been brought on by what had happened.

Why had she asked me to kiss her? Was it out of pity, or was she leading me on, in order to make fun of me ultimately? Not that I really believed she was capable of such cruelty; yet I had not altogether forgotten what Edwina had said about her.

I was being an idiot, I decided after a while. I was the one who had behaved strangely. I had been sullen and difficult, and jealous—yes, jealous—as simple as that. Without any reason. Only because she had been away, and because I imagined all kinds of things had happened to her. Yet she had come back and had called me. What more did I want? Furthermore, the only person of whom I should have been jealous was thousands of miles away. Although, strangely enough, I had never felt jealous of Richard Gordon. I was slightly in awe of him because he was famous and because he treated me as if he didn't ever quite know who I was or what the hell I was doing in his house. Still, if I had annoyed him with my too overt admiration of his wife, he had never shown it.

Most of the time he seemed removed, uninterested in what went on while he wasn't there, as if he had complete confidence in his wife. To him Paul certainly didn't present a threat, or Billy Lovat. And I was a child, so there was no reason for him to worry about me. Then I recalled the day when she had pushed his hand away angrily when he had stroked her behind. Yet that was understandable. She had been angry because he had touched her in my presence. Still, I could recall another occasion when he had come home from work and had complained that she had not kissed him. "I'm all hot and sticky from tennis," had been her excuse, to which he had replied that he "didn't care a damn." Still, there was Karen, the undeniable proof that they must have loved each other at some time in the past.

I tried not to think about that. That was a long time ago, I decided, and fell asleep, and had a dream that was so real that I felt certain, even after it was over, that I had been awake: we were riding in a car somewhere near the sea, in Edwina's little Ford, and somehow I had found the courage to ask Pam why she had suddenly wanted me to kiss her. "But why not?" she replied. "Why shouldn't I want you to? It's high time, isn't it? After all of your letters, all that missing me you kept writing me about. We can't go on forever riding around in a car like this." In my dream I had kissed her again while we sat parked above the beach at Castle Rock, with the moon reflected in a smooth sea, hanging low over the water the way the sun did late in the afternoon. Then I realized that it was morning and that I was in my bed. Maureen was knocking on the door, saying: "Get up, night owl. If you're not down in half an hour, you'll not get any breakfast from me."

I got up at once. It was a bright Saturday morning. The rain had washed the world clean, and it was quite warm again. Summer was not dead, and even Hitler didn't exist that day, as far as I was concerned. I finished breakfast and put on my bathing suit. I would go for a walk on the beach, and in that way avoid my mother and the many questions she was sure to ask. But Maureen was not quite so easily avoided. "Will you be home for lunch?" she shouted from the kitchen window as I made my way down the driveway.

"I've just had breakfast," I told her. "And I'm going to play tennis at one o'clock."

"If you were my son, you wouldn't be allowed to just use this house as a hotel," she grumbled. But I paid no attention to her.

My mother was still asleep, and Jake had left over an hour ago. Barefoot, in my faded trunks, with only a towel around my neck, I crossed the state highway. I walked slowly past the lifeguard station to the edge of the sea. The rain had packed down the sand, but it was already getting warm under my feet. The surf was bitingly cold as it came up to swirl around my legs. I saw a couple lying on a blue beach towel farther up the strand. It was Jake and Marcia. They were lying face down, letting the sun beat down on their backs. He was tanned, while her skin was quite pale. My brother had his hand over Marcia's hand. Both of them had their eyes closed. "Lenin says that we need people who are willing to give their lives for the revolution, not just their free evenings," I said.

Jake whirled, grinning as he recognized me. "To hell with you," he said. "And how's my fascist brother?"

Marcia shaded her eyes against the sun with her free hand. "How was the movie, brother Carl?" she asked.

"Not much good," I said, realizing that I didn't even know the title of the film I was supposed to have seen. "You didn't miss anything."

"You should have come with us."

"You didn't want me to."

"Go on," Jake said. "Your plans were already made." He turned over on his back and closed his eyes again.

"How's the water?" Marcia asked. She was making an effort to be friendly.

"Not bad. Why don't you try it?"

"You want to get rid of me? With my lungs I wouldn't last more than a minute at that temperature." I'd forgotten that she had had tuberculosis as a child, although I couldn't help feeling that she rather enjoyed reminding me of it.

I said: "See you later," and started up the beach. When I came back, they had gone. I left my towel on the beach and ran down through the shallow breakers until it was safe to dive. The cold water made me gasp for breath. I took a few strokes, then turned around and swam back toward the shore. It had been a performance for an invisible audience, and as such, rather a foolish one. If you have a cramp now, nobody'll ever know, I said to myself. But even that was a pleasant sensation, the thought of my being mourned. Pamela would be forced to hide her feelings. That was the best part of it. I could already visualize her stoic face under a black veil as she arrived at the funeral. Then my feet touched sand, and I remembered that I had to be back at home at ten for my lesson with Guy Boulard.

He was waiting for me in the garden under the brown leaves of the fig tree. My mother had gone to work at the shop, so I knew that I would have to talk him into driving me to the Gordons' once we had finished. Arriving late was going to make that more difficult, and I cursed myself for having gone for a swim. But Guy said nothing, only glanced at his watch, fondling the golden chain with the Phi Beta Kappa key as he put it back into his waistcoat pocket. We were reading *The Red and the Black*, which I was finding more difficult to concentrate on than *The Charterhouse of Parma*. Lucien Sorel was not as likable a character as Fabrice del Dongo, and the story was different from what I had expected it to be.

"Your mind's not on your work," Guy said after I had asked him the meaning of the same word twice in about ten minutes. It was an accusation that was not easy to deny.

"I was wondering if you'd give me a lift to the Gordons' after we've finished?" I asked.

"I will if you pay attention now."

So I read more slowly, concentrating on every word. Five minutes before the hour had expired, Guy got up, went around to the back of my chair, and put a hand on my shoulder as he stood listening. "We can stop the torture now," he said. "It's absurd to read a great book such as this one if you're not in the mood. We'll go back and reread that chapter again on Monday."

"Who said I wasn't in the mood?"

"Nobody. It wasn't necessary for anyone to say so. Come on, I'll take you to Las Golondrinas."

I wasn't going to argue with him about stopping early. I hurriedly packed my tennis clothes and joined him in the garden. "Lucien Sorel is the most modern character in the whole of French literature," he said as we got into his car. "He exists inside every one of us to an alarming extent." I didn't reply. I hadn't read far enough to understand what he meant. "Did Karen come back from England with her mother?" he asked after a while.

"Yes, but I don't think she's going to start her lessons again until after Christmas. Her father told her she didn't have to do any work after school until he got home."

Guy raised his eyebrows in clownish despair. "That's bad news," he said. "I don't mind if Gordon spoils his child, but not at my expense."

"Pamela says he only promised Karen that because she didn't want to leave without him."

Guy sighed noisily. "The problems of the rich," he said. I noticed he hadn't even asked about Edwina.

He dropped me at the end of Portofino Drive, and I walked the rest of the way, carrying my racket and my tennis bag. I was early, of course, and at Guido's suggestion went down to the court to change. The green concrete playing surface had been washed that morning, and there were large puddles behind the base line at either end. I put on my shorts, recombed my hair, and went out with a broom to disperse the water. After a while I heard footsteps, and Pamela appeared, carrying a new can of tennis balls. She waved as she ran down the concrete steps, her bare legs and arms looking much paler than before. I kissed her cheeks, pleasantly conscious of the familiar scent she wore. Something had changed between us. We had become conspirators, suddenly, without a word having been said.

"Are you all right?" she asked, looking carefully at me, as if she hadn't seen me for a long time.

"Yes. Are you?"

"I'm fine. Did you sleep well?"

"Not really," I admitted.

She laughed. "I'm sorry to have to tell you that I slept like a log," she said. "Amazing, isn't it? I guess I'm just an insensitive lump. I don't know what you see in me." There was the sound of a car door, and approaching voices. She stepped back, as if we had been standing too close to each other. "I wanted to warn you that Edwina has some plan about my driving out to the desert with Billy Lovat and Paul. So if I say that I have a date, don't look surprised and stricken. I just don't want to go, that's all."

I continued my sweeping. We were conspirators, then, although I wasn't sure for what purpose. I could hear Paul Hévesey's voice calling from a distance: "Where is Pam? Where is that most divine creature, the woman of my life?" He came quickly down the stairs and embraced Pamela. "Why, you're more beautiful than ever! God, I've missed you! That lovely pale skin. You must never go out into the sun again. Never. Promise me this minute that you will live the rest of your life in a shadow. Mine!"

"You *are* an ass, Paul," Pamela said. "I'd forgotten."

He turned, and shading his eyes against the glare, stood looking over at me with mock surprise. "Is that huge creature out there really Carl Woolf?" he asked in a loud voice. "Is that truly the adorable boy who once gave me a black eye? I can't believe it. He looks like Dempsey! What's Dempsey doing out there in short trousers sweeping away the water?" He chuckled happily, delighted with his own joke. "Please," he said, coming down the stairs onto the court, "please promise that you'll never raise your hand against me again. No matter what happens, you'll always turn the other cheek. Agreed? Marvelous!" He pulled me to him and hugged me. "I don't know why I should be glad to see you," he said, "because all you do is make me feel old. So stop growing, you hear me. Just stop it. Or we can't go on being friends." He turned to the others. "I really don't think we can play with him, do you?"

For the first time I was glad to see him. Something had changed in our relationship, too, in the year that had passed since our last meeting. He was beginning to treat me like a contemporary. "Not to worry. We'll play on the same side together," I told him.

"No, not even that!" he wailed. "I'll find myself apologizing all the time, and I hate that." He crossed to Edwina. "Send him home," he implored. "Young boys are dangerous . . . hasn't anyone ever told you?"

"Not this one," Edwina said wistfully. "He's not dangerous. I know!"

≫ five ≪

THE SUN had lost its strength, and the air was cool, even though it was still early in the afternoon. Autumn had come at last. But that was not the only change I became aware of as we started our usual game of mixed doubles, for I soon discovered that I was no longer the weakest player on the court. I had spent a good many hours that summer perfecting my serve and learning to volley, and although I was still not as steady a player as Paul, I had sudden flashes of brilliance (inspired perhaps by Pamela's presence) that seemed to justify his warning that "young boys are dangerous."

"You see, you see," he shouted, running up to the net and pointing an accusing finger at me after I had hit one of my best overhead smashes, "he's turned into a monster, just as I thought he would. An untrustworthy Goliath!" He dropped his racket noisily. "I won't play with him," he declared. "Why, in another six months he'll refuse to play with us because it's bad for his game!"

"That's not true," I replied, with the humorlessness of all lovers, thinking I would never *not* want to play with Pamela.

Paul said: "Don't be condescending, you sonofabitch. That makes it worse."

The game continued. Billy Lovat had decided to sit out the first set, and Edwina the second, saying that she found it impossible to concentrate. The Count appeared and took his customary chair in the pavilion. Guido solicitously spread a woolen blanket over the old gentleman's knees, remarking that it was already quite cold in the shade. For his trouble he was sent back up to the house to fetch a coat for Edwina.

It was at this moment that she declared her intention of driving out to the desert after tea to spend the night. Andrea frowned, and asked if she was planning to go alone. The question had an immediate effect on the rally that was taking place at that moment on the court. Paul missed an easy service return and cursed lengthily in Hungarian.

"Billy and Paul are going too," Edwina said calmly. "And Pamela, I hope."

"I'm sorry, but I'm afraid I can't," Pamela called over to her. "I have a date tonight."

"Well, you'll have to cancel it," Edwina said. "I'm sure Carl won't mind. Anyway, the desert air will do you a world of good after the humidity of London."

I didn't know whether to protest or not. But Pamela was better prepared than I was. Without looking over at me, she explained that her date was not with me, but with Karen, therefore uncancelable. She had promised the child that she would take her to the amusement park on the Venice Pier that evening, which was a promise that was impossible to break.

"Don't be absurd—you can take her tomorrow night, or even next week," Edwina said loftily. But Pamela was not to be dissuaded. Sunday night was no good, she explained, because Karen had to go to school the next day, and even if she could persuade her to wait, the weather was apt to change. "It's not much fun riding a roller coaster in the rain, you know," she added, getting ready to receive Billy Lovat's service.

He double-faulted. "Are you going to argue, or shall we finish the set?" he wanted to know.

"There's no point in arguing," Pamela replied. "I'm sorry, Billy. Start the game all over again. . . ."

"But Andrea can take Karen," Edwina insisted. "Guido will drive them."

"I told her I was going to take her." It was the first time I had ever seen Pamela angry. She flushed, her mouth a thin line as she pretended to concentrate on the game. We finished the set in silence. Then, as we returned to the pavilion, the Count suddenly volunteered to go to the desert in Pamela's place. It was obviously not the solution that Edwina had desired, but by that time it was too late to back out. So once they had all showered and had tea, and Guido had loaded the bags into the back of Paul's car, they were ready to set off for Victorville. "Why don't you come along with us?" Edwina said to me as they were leaving the library. "We can ride in the desert after breakfast, and swim and sit in the sun."

"I don't think my mother'd let me," I answered, quite truthfully.

"Nonsense. You've got some other plan for tonight you don't want to give up."

"That's not true."

"Well, then, I'll call your mother and ask her. You'll see that she won't refuse me. . . ."

Paul came to my rescue. "Why don't you stop bullying everybody, Edwina?" he said. "Suppose he did want to come along. . . . Where would he sit? On your knees? Or squeezed in the back between Billy and Andrea? Anyway, if he has a date with a lovely young thing, why should you try to mess it up for him?"

"I have no date," I said, trying to sound very definite.

"Well, you should have," Hévesey said. "At your age I was the terror of the village near where we lived. Fathers would lock their daughters in their rooms on Saturday nights, knowing that I was going to be let out of the castle."

"The castle!" Edwina jeered. "Will you please 'ark at him."

"It was a country house, but the villagers always referred to it as a *Schloss*," Paul Hévesey said.

"And they tipped their hats to you when you rode through the fields, I suppose?"

"That's right. . . ."

"That was in Hungary, luv," Billy Lovat said, grinning. "So there's no way to check up on him."

By that time we had reached the driveway and Hévesey's car. Edwina got in the front seat. "Look, there's lots of room," she said. "We'll stop by Carl's house, and I'll go in with him and ask his mother."

Paul shook his head in despair. "God, you're obstinate," he said. "The boy doesn't want to go, so why insist on trying to make him?"

"Well, at least we can drop him off at his home," Edwina said.

"Guido can do that," Pamela said coolly. "No use your wasting time. It's getting dark."

"If you prefer," Edwina replied. She was looking straight ahead out of the windshield, and as Paul got in beside her, I noticed that she moved with exaggerated haste to the other side of the car, putting as much space between them as possible. "Enjoy yourselves," she added, instead of saying good-bye.

Paul kissed Pamela affectionately and pinched my shoulder. "Aren't you grateful to me for taking Edwina away for a while?" he asked, getting behind the steering wheel of his car. She looked at him with unconcealed hate. The Count had taken his place in the back beside Billy. He nodded to Pamela, raised his hand, and they were gone. We stood in silence for a few seconds, both of us amazed that we had escaped Edwina's machinations.

"She can really be a pain sometimes," Pamela said feelingly. "Get your things, and I'll drive you home."

"Wouldn't it be better if Guido took me?" I asked.

"He has to lay the table. Come on, we'll go in the small car." She meant Edwina's, but couldn't force herself to say so. Karen appeared and wanted to know if she could come along. "I'm just going to take Carl home," her mother told her.

"I want to go too," the child insisted.

"Well, then, run and get a sweater. We'll wait for you."

She had grown, was all legs and arms, I noticed, as she ran toward the house. She returned an instant later, wearing one of her mother's coats. It hung from her thin frame to well below her bony knees, which delighted her for some reason. "I want to sit next to Mummy," she announced, climbing over my legs.

"That coat's just been cleaned, darling. . . ."

"I won't get it dirty. Look, it's not really too long in the sleeves!"

"So I see."

We drove down the familiar road that led to the sea. The crisp evening air whipped through the open sides of the roadster. "We'll have to put on the side curtains if we take this car tonight," Pam said.

"But it's not going to rain, Mummy. . . . And it's much more fun this way!" Karen said. She was sitting on the edge of the seat, her clenched fists braced against the dashboard. The sky was a washed-out red along the far reaches of the horizon, the ocean a cold, glistening gray. "What time are we leaving?" the child wanted to know.

"Right after dinner. So I hope you won't dawdle over your food." We stopped at the intersection of the coast highway. "Shall we ask Carl if he wants to come along?" Pamela asked.

"No. I want to be alone with you." She often spoke in my presence as if I weren't there, and was usually corrected for it. But this time it was Pamela's fault for having asked her a question to which there was only one answer, and obviously not the one Karen wanted to give.

"That's not a very polite thing to say, you know. . . ."

"Well, you asked me," the child said quite logically. "I don't really mind if he comes, but I'd rather it was just you and me."

"If he comes, you'll have someone to ride on the roller coaster with," Pamela said. "Otherwise you'll have to go alone. Because it frightens me." She was making things worse, indulging Karen, trapping her into agreement. I looked over at Pamela, and noticed that she was smiling. So it was a game they had invented between them, a game Pam had invented to make things easier.

"All right. Then he can go," Karen declared.

"I don't know. I have a lot of homework to do," I said, trying to sound doubtful. "And I have to ask my mother, anyway."

"See what a good son he is," Pamela said, laughing. "I hope you'll be as thoughtful when you get to be old enough to go out on your own."

I went along, of course, not quite as satisfied with the arrangement as Karen, but then, I had no special advantages coming to me, such as the roller-coaster ride, which was undoubtedly the high point of the evening as far as she was concerned. In any case, that was what she told me. Like true innocents, we had gotten into the queue without a cent between us, and had even made our way past the ticket seller, so that Pamela was forced to pay our way and hand us our tickets across the wire fence that separated the cowardly from the brave. Then we sat waiting, Karen waving repeatedly to her mother as we were joined in the open car by a couple of sailors and their girls. Still the machine refused to start. Then two young Mexican women arrived. They chose to sit directly in front of us, not knowing that the first seats in the lead car were the most exposed, and nudged each other, and giggled, their fat bodies spilling out over the metal tubing on either side of them as they sat huddled together long before there was any danger.

It hadn't looked particularly frightening from the ground, yet as we clicked slowly up the steep incline of the rickety track, I noticed that Karen had grown tense. "You know, they kill about two or three people a year on this thing," one of the sailors behind us drawled, and Karen looked over at me for confirmation, the first time that evening that she had looked directly at me. I shook my head and tried to appear disdainfully confident, although I had heard the same rumor myself. We could see the crowd below us, hear the distant spiel of the barker's voice on the loudspeaker: "It's a high, free, safe, sensational ride! Three can ride in a seat, if you wish!"

The curved shoreline of the bay was visible to our right, while on the left we could see the pier. The edges of the boardwalk were adorned by hundreds of colored lights that grew smaller and smaller as we climbed. "I hear they're going to condemn this thing soon," the same voice from behind us drawled. "Next summer they're going to take it down and burn all the rotten old timbers. . . ."

We had reached the top of the first steep arch. The clanking of the chain underneath the car stopped abruptly, and an instant later we started down the precipitous incline. Karen grabbed my arm. There was a rush of air and a clatter of wheels. The Mexican women in front of us screamed in unison, while the sailors and their girls behind us were strangely silent. I looked over at Karen. She had closed her eyes. Then, as we were wrenched around the first curve, she opened them, and I noticed that they were filled with tears. I took her hand and held it tightly, forgiving her all of her past antagonism, as curve followed jolting curve. Then we were rocketed to the top of the skeletonlike structure again, the speed of the car decreasing momentarily, until we started down the final descent. Among the dark girders, in the flat stretch of track that warned us that the ride was coming to an end, Karen relaxed her grip on my arm. We were sitting quite normally when we arrived.

"Did you enjoy yourself, darling?" Pamela asked as we walked down the pier, away from the instrument of our brief torture.

"It wasn't as much fun as I thought it'd be," Karen said. She was holding both of our arms, having apparently forgiven me a great many things during her moment of fear.

A girl with bright red hair came lurching out of a place called the Fun House, her powdered face a replica of the huge distorted rubber masks that adorned the façade of the establishment. She was drunk, and as she careened across the pier, two marines in their dress blues appeared, in obvious pursuit of the girl. They caught up with her and kept her from falling, while she wailed out in a rasping voice: "I ain't got my cherry, but I got the box it came in!" I pretended not to have heard, as did Pamela. Other passersby were shaking their heads as they looked after the reeling threesome. Karen seemed not to have heard or noticed anything. She was studying the concessions on both sides of us, trying to decide which of the many attractions to choose for our next adventure.

"Let's go on the Shoot the Chutes," she suggested, her enthusiasm returning now that she knew that she was safe.

"All right. But after that we have to go home," Pamela said.

We walked to the far end of the pier and got into the boat at the bottom of the ramp up which we were ultimately towed by another creaking engine. The young man who took our tickets inside the boat was dressed as a gondolier, with a straw hat and a blue-and-white-striped jersey. There was appropriate music, a Neapolitan love song that the loudspeaker system blared out over the small artificial lagoon. "I want to sit on the outside," Karen announced courageously. Pamela changed places with her, squeezing in between us. In the darkness, as we were slowly hoisted up the long, illuminated ramp, her gloved hand found mine and held it tightly.

"Are you frightened, Mummy?" the child asked.

"Of course I am."

"Then put your arm around me."

"I will. Just a minute." She quickly took off her right glove, and almost with the same movement put her left arm around Karen's shoulders. Her ungloved hand returned to its original place and found my hand again. It was such a different hand from the one I had held only a few minutes earlier, and I couldn't help thinking that my hand and Karen's were more alike. "Someday we'll go to the real Venice, just the three of us," she said. "It's the most wonderful place in the world, you know."

I said nothing. I clung to the naked hand hidden beneath the folds of her coat. "Where are we going after this?" Karen asked, not to be put off by the promise of some future treat.

"Home, I told you. It's late."

"But aren't we going somewhere for hot chocolate?"

"I'll make some when we get back to the house."

"Then Carl won't get any."

"He can come too."

"But how will he get home?"

"I'll take him, don't worry. In any case, you'll be asleep by that time."

"I don't know," the child said playfully. "If I don't feel sleepy, I might come along."

We had reached the top of the ramp. Other men dressed as gondoliers swung the boat into place at the top of the slide, and we went down it at a rather sedate speed, to splash in the water of the lagoon, making the spray shoot up on all sides of us, which delighted Karen. She screamed happily and rose from her seat in order to show Pamela that the sleeve of her coat was wet, as was her hair.

"That settles it. We're going home."

"Please, can't we do it again, Mummy? It was such fun."

"But you're soaked. . . ."

"No, I'm not. I'm dry as can be underneath."

"All right. But this is the last time, and no arguing once it's over . . . and the side curtains go up on the car."

Which Karen agreed to. And so we did not move from our place in the boat, while a new group of passengers joined us. "I don't think the real Venice is any nicer than this," Karen said as we started off again, which made Pamela laugh and hug her child, while I sat waiting for her hand to return to mine in the dark.

ᘒ Six ᘓ

AT TIMES, even now, the light of the moon on a windowpane can take me back without warning to the white-walled house among the eucalyptus trees, and suddenly it is as if I were standing in Pamela's room, looking out across the low stone wall at the end of the lawn to the distant moonlit hills. Then for an instant, as I see that familiar landscape again (although the scenery outside my window might be totally unrelated, a snow-covered mountain, or a black patch of lake, nothing that should be able to stir up memories), it is as if I hadn't aged or changed at all, and I can even remember the strange feeling of my own nakedness as I undressed that night, as well as the violent beating of my heart as I got into the wide bed.

Needless to say, I have lain in other beds since with a pounding heart, but these perhaps equally important occasions do not come back to me as frequently, proof of the strength of the initial impact of love, I suppose. Yet it had all come about so simply and quickly that it is surprising, in retrospect, that it was memorable at all. We had returned home, and as promised, had had hot chocolate and cookies, only vaguely conscious of the insidious moonlight outside. A mist had come in off the sea while we were driving back from Venice, the upper reaches of it straying through the tops of the tallest trees in the garden, so that the moon was only occasionally visible through the fog. We all felt the chill of the moist air after our drive, so that the hot chocolate proved to be more of a necessity than a treat.

Karen had not taken off her coat until she had swallowed her first cup, and even after drinking two more she had protested that she still felt cold. It was a maneuver with which she hoped to avoid being sent to bed, but her mother was not to be taken in so easily, and after glancing at her watch, announced that it was time to say good night. Then Karen asked once more how I was going to get home, and again Pamela told her that she was going to drive me, falling easily into the child's trap. "Then I'll be alone in the house," Karen complained. "I don't like that!"

"Guido is here, and Bessie."

"But suppose I have a bad dream," Karen argued. "They'll never hear me down there where *they* live."

"Very well, then, Carl will take the car and bring it back in the morning."

"But he's not allowed to drive alone at night until he's eighteen. . . ."

"It'll be all right this once."

She appeared to be pacified. "You promise you won't go, Mummy?"

"I promise."

Having won that concession, she finally agreed to go to bed. She insisted on kissing me good night, which was another unheard-of ritual she had suddenly invented; and then, while Pamela went upstairs to hear Karen's prayers, I took a walk in the garden, preferring to face the cold rather than wait by myself in the living room, where I was afraid Guido might find me, having been awakened by the noise we had made in the kitchen.

Very carefully I opened the French doors that led outside. The fog had vanished, driven off by a wind that had come down out of the mountains and was still blowing softly across the terrace. In the light of the moon I walked down to the tennis court and sat in the night shade of the pavilion, where Pamela joined me after a quarter of an hour. "I thought you'd be here," she said, smiling. "The court's still the main attraction, isn't it, the thing that brings you back to us always."

"That's not true!"

She laughed. "I do love to pull your leg. Your entire face changes. . . ."

"How can you tell in the dark?"

"I can tell, don't you worry. The moon's not there for nothing."

I started to take her into my arms, and for a second she resisted me, pretending to be surprised by my boldness. "What's this, now?" she asked. "I mean, really!" But then suddenly she came toward me, into my arms with what seemed almost to be anger, or fierceness. I kissed her, and as I did, I caught a glimpse of the tennis court beyond us in the moonlight.

"You know, there's almost light enough to play," I said.

"You see. . . . Oh, how well I know you." I laughed, and she added quickly: "You're getting pretty fresh . . ." but I wouldn't allow her to finish the sentence. "I guess I'd better take you to bed," she said, withdrawing her mouth briefly from mine. "What have you to say to that?"

I had nothing to say. So she took my hand and led me across the lawn and into the house, up to the room I knew she shared with Gordon, but where I had never been before. Instead of turning on the lights, she opened the curtains, and once she had closed the hallway door, the room was lit entirely by moonlight. I felt nervous, remembering Karen's threat of a nightmare, and while we stood together at the window, I mentioned the possibility of the child suddenly appearing in the room and finding me there.

"Don't worry, she's asleep. She never wakes up at night. All that was merely to keep me from leaving the house."

"But suppose she does come here?"

"She won't. But if it worries you, I'll go in and see her now." She started toward the door. "You get into bed, and I'll be right back," she said.

So I undressed, standing at the window, folding my trousers mechanically, as if I were in my own room, and putting my shirt and pullover down on the same chair. Then, with the curtains still open, I got into bed and lay listening to the sound of my own heart, as well as the muffled noises that the wind was making outside. Finally the slit of light at the bottom of the hallway door became part of the darkness as well, and I knew Pamela had finished her rounds. The door nearest the bed opened, and she appeared in a white dressing gown, with her hair brushed straight back, looking more beautiful than ever before. I looked up at her, watching her in silence as she turned to lock the door behind her. Then she stood over me for a second, her hands holding the dressing gown together as if she were cold.

"Have you warmed up the bed?" she asked in a whisper, and I nodded and put out my hand to her. With a quick movement she took off her dressing gown and let it fall to the floor, stooping to pull back the covers, and with a curiosity I could not control, I found myself staring at her body in the moonlight, surprised to see that she was less ashamed of her nakedness than I was of mine. I also remember feeling surprised at the perfection of her body, and feeling more in awe of her physical beauty than ever, not quite able to believe that she had chosen to make love with me, or that I was there. Then all at once I felt the touch of her cool skin, and with my eyes shut I found her mouth, and kissed her as I had learned to kiss not so long ago.

She pulled away from me for a second. "But you're all dressed," she whispered.

"No, I'm not." I had not taken off my white undershorts, that was all.

"D'you always go to bed in your underwear?"

"No, not always."

"Well, then . . ."

I unbuttoned my shorts and pushed them out of the bed with my feet.

She laughed and said: "That's much better. You're not afraid of me, are you?"

"No. I love you."

She held me close, while I repeated the phrase again and again, trying to put my life and everything I believed in into those three words, attempting, I suppose, to force her into making some reply. None was forthcoming, however, although I could feel her hands on my body, caressing me, holding me tightly.

"I like your skin," she said.

"Is that all?"

"You are demanding, aren't you?"

"No, I'm not. I'll settle for anything." I did not move. I held my burning face pressed against the cool softness of her body.

"Carl . . ."

"Yes?" There was a long pause.

"I don't believe in saying things that aren't true. . . ."

"Neither do I."

"Well, then, I can only say . . . that I love your love for me. Will that do?"

I nodded, and lay very still.

"Would you kiss me now?"

I released her and moved higher in the bed in order to reach her mouth, and she pulled me closer, lifting me up so that she could find her place beneath me.

"You don't know anything about bed, do you, my darling?"

"No, I guess not."

"Well, I'm just as glad you don't, and that I'm the first one. Isn't that silly? And that I can show you. Not that I know all that much."

I felt her hands on the lower part of my body, and gently, very slowly, I began to understand what I was expected to do. The pleasure of the feeling was very strong, yet I was afraid I might hurt her. My body seemed too hard for the softness of hers, and at last she made a noise that sounded like pain, and I stopped moving. "Did I hurt you?" I asked.

"No. Yes. Yes and no. Oh, Carl, Carl . . ." She pulled the covers back, and I could see our two bodies together in the moonlight, locked together. "Are you happy, Carl?" she asked.

"Yes . . . of course I am. I love you."

That was obviously not the only thing she wanted to hear. It even sounded inadequate to me. But I couldn't describe what I felt, was incapable of it. In any case, no matter what I might have said, it was not the answer to her question, as I realized only much later on. Because I was too conscious of everything at that moment, could not forget myself, lose myself entirely, which is what the act of love demands, so that time has no meaning, and the difference between two bodies is lost in all the touching and feeling and possessing.

So that there was no conclusion, no possible ending, and I would have been happy holding her for the rest of the night, half-drunk with the moonlight and the smell of her skin and her hair, and the hopelessness of trying to express with my mouth and my hands and the rest of me how much I loved her. I loved her for her beauty, and for having enough confidence in me to have let it come to this, and for being unattainable, which at that moment I still felt she was, and I felt exasperated by my inability to tell her, to show her, caught up by the tenderness, the novelty of it all, afraid of the violence that is a necessary part of love, a part I still did not know anything about.

Then I knew that it was late, much later than I had ever stayed out before. I looked at the clock on the table beside the bed, and she noticed the movement of my head. "I think you'd better go home now," she said, guessing my thoughts.

"All right."

I would have agreed to whatever she might have said at that moment. I would have stayed for the rest of the night, the rest of my life, if she had commanded it. But instead I got up and dressed without turning on the light, and once I had my pullover on, I returned to her side of the bed and kissed her again. I didn't put on my socks, but stuffed them in my pocket, sensing that such a banal chore might look like a ridiculous thing for a lover to do.

"The keys are in the car," she said. "Drive carefully, won't you?"

"I will. I love you."

I crossed the moonlit room and went out into the dark hallway and down the carpeted stairs, moving as if in a dream. The cold night air brought me back slowly to reality, but it was not until I had turned down the street that I began to worry about where I would leave the Gordons' car. If I left it in front of the gate, my mother was certain to notice it and ask questions.

I decided finally to put it at the far end of the street. But as I passed in front of our gate, a strange car started to move away from the curb in front of our house. Its driver had not as yet turned on the headlights, and I was forced to swerve quickly in order to avoid a collision. The disaster I had narrowly escaped made me break out in a cold sweat. The car had looked familiar. Could it have been Guy's old Chevrolet?

I dismissed the thought and concentrated on parking well out of sight of our house. Then, relieved not to be driving, I walked back up the road and let myself in by the garden gate. For once Prince didn't bark. I saw that there was a light on in Maureen's room, and concluded that she had come home late, and that the car I had almost run into belonged to someone who had just dropped her off. But I was so full of my own thoughts that I forgot about the incident as soon as I was in my bed. I closed my eyes and went to sleep with the smell of Pamela's perfume all around me. It was almost as if she were there, beside me, in the narrow bed.

I woke up early in the morning, took a shower, and went downstairs for breakfast. It was Sunday, and only Maureen was up, moving grumpily around the kitchen. "You certainly were late last night," she said as she served me my fried egg on toast and my glass of milk.

"So were you," I told her.

"Not at all. I didn't even go out."

She stood over me, watching me as I drank the milk. "The poor King," she said. "They're going to make him give up the crown. It was on the news this morning. And all for that American woman."

"Oh, really?" I wasn't at all interested. The King was not one of my heroes, as he'd been photographed too often in Germany.

"Don't you think it's sad?"

"I don't believe in kings," I answered, and she turned away grumbling about Jake's bad influence on me.

I didn't care what she said. I finished my breakfast and hurried out the front door in order not to have to continue the conversation. I found Edwina's roadster where I had left it, and grateful that I had not been discovered breaking the law, I drove very carefully up the coast highway in the morning sun.

I found the garage empty at the end of the asphalted drive, and the front door inside the patio partially open. Pamela was still in her room. She called for me to come up. The curtains were drawn, and I saw that she was sitting in bed with her breakfast tray beside her on a small table. "They're all off to church," she said. "Karen was furious because I wouldn't go."

I sat down beside her and took her hand. "I brought the car back," I said.

"You're a good boy." She was making fun of me, but I didn't mind. "Are you all right?" she asked, smiling.

"I'm fine."

"Not tired?"

"No. Not tired at all."

"That's because you're young and strong," she said, smiling, her hand finding its way up my unbuttoned sleeve. I put my body across hers and kissed her.

"Do I taste of tea and toast?" she asked.

"No. You taste fine."

"How polite you are. Even early in the morning." I wanted her suddenly, wanted her more now that some of the unfamiliarity between us was gone. She was wearing light blue silk pajamas, and I undid the buttons, and she didn't resist. Then I pulled off my clothes, and without a thought of the unlocked door, I took her in my arms, and immediately the violence of love overcame me, overcame us both, and it was as if this were the end of the night, the conclusion that I had been unable to find in the moonlight, and the feeling was greater than I had imagined anything would be.

"Oh, darling," she said. "I'm so glad you came back. I thought maybe you'd be late, and already dressed for tennis. . . ." She kissed me on the cheeks and on the forehead. "This is nicer than tennis, you will admit," she said.

I didn't answer. My brain was clearer than it had ever been in her presence, and it was full of questions I did not quite dare ask. "You'll have to let me get up now," she whispered. "And I think you'd better get dressed. When it's a nice day, the sermon's usually short." She got out of bed, and wrapping her dressing gown around her, left me alone in the room I discovered to be full of framed photographs and small private possessions. Then, as I put on my clothes for the second time that morning, I found my mind rushing on to the weeks and months ahead, the years even, and I couldn't help wondering how it was all going to end, which was something I had never given much thought to before, and suddenly I felt saddened, as if everything had gone wrong. The photographs on the bedside table and the dresser were to blame, I realized, the many pictures of Richard Gordon and Karen that had not been visible in the moonlight and that made me feel like an intruder now that it was day.

After a while Pamela came out of the bathroom, wearing a blue quilted robe. She was brushing her hair with a silver brush, and she, too, seemed subdued and slightly sad. "Let me look at you," she said, turning my face to the light. "Well, I can see that love has not left you unmarked, my darling. So you'd better go wash your face and comb your hair. It won't do, you know, for us both to have bedroom eyes."

PART
V

≈ one ≈

"**I** LOVE YOU. I'll always love you. As long as I live. I'll never love anyone else."

I can still hear myself, repeating the worn phrases over and over again as if they had never been said before, and with the muffled sound of the surf in the distance, I can hear Pamela's voice gently contradicting me: "Don't be silly. Of course you will, darling. You'll meet someone your own age, and before you know it, you'll have forgotten all about me. It's bound to happen. . . ."

It was summer again, with the sun burning down out of a cloudless sky, and the sea a solid, dark blue all the way to the horizon. At that hour of the day the beach around us was too hot to walk on in bare feet, so that the two of us, lying close together on the faded red towel, felt temporarily isolated, the sole inhabitants of a tiny rectangular oasis made of cloth.

"You're wrong," I said. "Age has nothing to do with it. Even if I live to be a hundred, I'll never fall in love again."

"I won't ask you to put that in writing. . . ."

"You can. I'm willing."

"All right. We'll have the document notarized and sealed in a bottle, and then we'll drop it into the sea. . . ."

"If you like."

"Or maybe we'd better have it framed, so that I can hang it on the wall. . . ." She raised her head and lay resting on her elbows, looking out to sea. Fifty or sixty yards beyond our naked legs, I could see the small house Pamela had rented for the season, its board-and-batten walls a tired beige, as if it had been intended not to stand out too sharply against the landscape.

"Do you feel like going in the water again?" she asked.

"Not yet. What about you?"

"I can wait." It was as if nothing had changed—the beach with its smell of salt and dried seaweed, and the brush-covered mountains, in the narrow canyons of which I had gone looking for adventure on my bicycle. And yet everything was different. I had turned a corner in my life, and suddenly found it difficult to enjoy the things I had always enjoyed —the sun, the beach, playing tennis. Only the future seemed to matter, the way it would all turn out, which was why, almost obsessively, I felt I had to try constantly to convince Pamela of the durability of my love, make her believe, as I did, that age and time were obstacles we would easily overcome. "Why do you always make fun of me?" I asked. "Of what I say?"

"I don't. That's not true."

"Yes, you do. Whenever I talk of the future, you make a joke or try to change the subject."

"Because there isn't any point. Oh, Carl, can't we talk about something else? It's such a lovely day."

I turned my head and looked up the beach to where the highway curved along the distant shore. She had been that way for some time. I couldn't understand why. In reply to all of my promises and declarations, she was always skeptical, even appearing distant at times, or worse yet, indifferent. Not that I expected her to share my feelings; I had long ago settled for her merely loving my love for her. Still, I could not understand why she invariably chose to paint such a black picture of the future. In her opinion, all love was doomed. In the end everyone's feelings changed, became habit, and atrophied. Or what was worse, intimacy turned love into hate. When I rejected these arguments, she would always return to the obvious obstacles confronting us, the devastating arithmetic of the differences in our ages. "Things will only get worse with time," she would say. "I'll change as I get older, and so will you. Just think . . . in ten years I'll be thirty-nine, and you'll only be twenty-seven. And when *you're* thirty-nine, I'll be fifty-one, an old lady. Can you imagine how unhappy we'd be?"

As if it were possible to be unhappier than I had been the last six months! For it had been short-lived, our idyll. Edwina had returned from the desert, and ten days later Richard Gordon had come back for the Christmas holidays. What had made matters worse was that he had stayed on, due to a sudden change of plans (a part in a new film that he had decided to accept instead of going back to London), and so I had been relegated once again to the role of the young friend who is asked to play tennis on the weekends and nothing more. For that reason I had seen very little of Pamela that winter, and when I did see her, we were seldom alone. Love had been limited to holding hands in the car when she had had time to drive me home, or to furtive kisses in the tennis pavilion once everyone else had gone in to tea. I had almost started to believe that I had invented our night in the moonlit room, imagined or dreamed it. It had been a strange, disquieting memory for me to take back to school.

Then, in the spring, a marked change in the way of life of the Gordon household had come about that had at least given me hope for the summer. Edwina's first film had come out, and she had been a success overnight, "had attained instant stardom," as the local newspapers wrote. It had not made her any easier to live with, her new fame, coming, as it did, so quickly. There had been unpleasant scenes between her and Pamela (one or two of which I had witnessed on the tennis court), and in the end Gordon had decided that he would rent a house on the beach for the summer in order to minimize the tensions between them. As he had said, "it was bad enough to have crises starting all over the world, without finding one every night at the dinner table," so Pamela had moved into the small cottage a few miles north of Castle Rock as soon as Karen's semester had ended.

The beach house had made things easier for us, and we were together almost every day once the summer started, although there was still Karen to claim her mother's attention, as well as Bessie, the maid who came in the mornings. And of course there was always Gordon, who would return from the sweltering city in the evenings, his coat draped over his shoulders to protect him against the damp, cool air that hung over the edge of the sea. Still, there had been many hours in which we were free to lie in the sun together or walk along the beach that was almost deserted during the week. I suppose that if I had been older I would have known enough to simply enjoy being with Pamela, instead of torturing myself with thoughts of what went on in the small house when I was not there. But I was only sixteen (about to be seventeen that fall), which was why I was incapable of simply enjoying myself and taking what the days had to offer. We learn to accept impermanent arrangements only when we are older and know that we are running out of time.

I remember that my constant daydream during that summer was one of flight to some distant and foreign land in which Pamela and I would be able to live together, and when in my saner moments that dream dissolved, I would visualize countless heroic scenes of farewell instead, dramatic partings that always took place on the eve of my enlisting in the International Brigades and going off to fight for an ideal, as that was the only alternative left to cure my breaking heart. On one occasion I revealed this "romantic" plan to Pamela (perhaps as a threat, or in order to keep her from taking my love for granted), and was astonished to find that she took it quite seriously. "But what would you achieve by doing a mad thing like that?" she asked. "Think of the anguish you would cause your parents . . . and your own life, that you would probably waste!"

"Thousands of others are wasting theirs," I replied. "If nobody is willing to risk his life, then the world is lost."

"It's probably lost anyway . . . that particular world. Your going to fight won't make any difference."

"It might make a difference to me."

She looked intently at me then, taking her eyes off the road for a dangerously long time, and after correcting the course of the car, which was veering toward the sea, she shook her head and said: "Oh, Carl, Carl . . . why do you say things like that? Is it because you want to torture me? Or do you really want me to feel that all I've done is make you miserable?"

This had made me regret my moment of indiscretion, and I had promised that I would never say anything as absurd again, although in reality I had no thought of abandoning my heroic daydream.

I turned over on my side and lay looking at the slender body in the black two-piece bathing suit next to mine. "You're getting very brown," I said.

"I'm not burning, am I?"

"No, I don't think so."

She pulled the shoulder straps down onto her arms and lay with the other side of her face exposed to the sun. "What time will Karen be back?" I asked.

"Not until late," she replied drowsily. "Bessie's taking her to a children's party in town."

So we were to be on our own for the rest of the day. It was strange that she hadn't mentioned it earlier. In the past she had always told me that we were going to be alone the moment I arrived. Perhaps she had decided that it was better for us not to make love anymore. I got up slowly and stood on the edge of the towel. My shadow fell across her legs.

"Where you off to?" she asked.

"I think I'll take a dip."

With her eyes closed she said: "You change your mind every five minutes, don't you?" But once I was in the water, she got up to follow me.

She didn't like the surf, not even the gentle shore break of a quiet day. I watched her as she hesitated at the water's edge, splashing herself before wading out through the small waves. I swam over to join her in the smooth swell just outside the break. I knew she liked to have someone near her whenever she was out of her depth. "Are you hungry?" she asked, keeping her head well out of the water.

"Not really."

"But you *would* eat? Just to be polite?"

"I'd certainly make an effort."

She laughed, and swallowed a little water. "You are a fool, you know," she said, coughing. I put out my hand to steady her, but she was already out of reach. "I'm getting cold. Let's go in."

We washed the sand off our feet with a garden hose that lay coiled up on the edge of the terrace. I started to wash off my body as well. "Why not take a proper shower inside," she suggested. "You'll never get all the salt off you that way."

I followed her into the house, hurrying across the living room so as not to wet the faded green carpet. The place had been furnished in the style of a New England fisherman's cottage, with brown nets hanging from the walls, and a display of seashells on the varnished mantelpiece over the brick fireplace. It was hot and airless inside the low-ceilinged room.

"You go ahead," I said. "I'll wait outside in the sun." I started toward the glass doors that led to the small terrace in the back of the house, but she caught me by the arm.

"We can shower together," she said, laughing. "It'll save water . . . and anyway, it's an old country amusement." I was surprised, not shocked, for although it was the first time I'd heard of that kind of thing, it didn't seem like an unpleasant notion. I followed her upstairs, glad I had decided not to voice my doubts a few minutes earlier.

I remember that the yellow plaster walls of the stall shower were peeling and that the rubberized curtain did not altogether protect the bathroom floor. But none of that mattered. Nothing mattered anymore. Not even the future, which suddenly appeared much less problematical to me. I kissed her, the water splashing over both our faces. "What about your hair?" I asked.

"It doesn't matter. I have to wash it later anyway." I held her close, my eyes shut. "Can you unbutton my bra for me?" she asked.

"I can try."

There were small rivulets of water running down her shoulders onto her breasts as she shed the lower half of her swimsuit. "You're not going to stand there in your trunks, are you? You make me feel positively indecent."

All my doubts and feelings of jealousy were temporarily forgotten as we stood locked together in the warm rain of the shower bath. I was conscious only of her skin against my skin, her mouth against my mouth, and felt grateful to be alive.

"Come with me," she said. The house was silent once she had turned the shower off. We dried ourselves and went into the bedroom that looked out onto the beach and the glistening sea. She had wrapped a towel skillfully around her head, so that it looked like a turban, and with the afternoon breeze that had come up, sweeping in through the open windows, we made love to the music of the mild surf breaking on the sand.

⇘ *two* ⇙

THERE WERE louvered shutters on the windows of the bedroom, which she got up to close after a while to shut out the heat of late afternoon. Then she came back and sat on the edge of the bed and started to brush out her moist hair. I watched the silver brush in her hand as it flicked through the narrow lanes of light that the shutters formed in the semi-darkness, enjoying the graceful movement of her body and the way the hair fell away from the brush, always coming to rest in a thick, blonde mass between her shoulderblades.

"It's full of salt," she complained. "I'll have to wash it."

I put my hand out to touch the white mark the strap of her bathing suit had left on her back, and she turned almost before the tips of my fingers had reached her skin, and noticed that I had covered myself with the sheet while she was gone. "Are you cold?" she asked.

"No, of course not."

"Then you're hiding."

"I'm not."

She smiled. "Well, I do hope you don't mind my lack of modesty," she said. "Because it's so much more comfortable this way."

"I don't mind at all," I said, pulling her down on the bed.

"What about my hair?"

"You said you had to wash it anyway."

"And lunch?"

"Lunch can wait. I love you." Which was truly more important than the touch of her skin, and the shape of her body, and the fact that it was not often that we could be together like this, naked and undisturbed.

"Do you? I wonder sometimes. . . ."

My mouth cut short whatever she was about to say, which I had found out was the best way to silence her sarcasms. Her superiority was easily overcome when we made love, as then there was no difference in our ages. Nor, as I discovered that afternoon, was she always in full control of herself, for the intensity of my passion finally released the inner spring which it seemed had been coiled up inside her, and all at once she responded with equal ardor, losing herself in the act of love, just as I had learned to do the morning after the first night I had been to bed with her. I was amazed that she was capable of such ferocity, and I realized at once that we had passed some strange landmark in our lovemaking, which she confessed was a landmark in her life. "Oh, darling, darling, darling," she said, and clung to me, her body moist with perspiration, as was mine. "That's never happened to me before, you know. Now, please don't ask questions. . . . Just lie very still and hold me in your arms."

I did as I was told. Yet all at once the heat in the room seemed unbearable, and I felt I had to get up. "Shall we go for a swim?" I asked.

"Now?"

"Yes, I'm hot. Aren't you?"

She laughed and said: "What a strange animal you are. All right, if you insist, we'll go for a swim. But then I really must wash my hair. Without interference."

"I won't interfere. I'll help you."

"I've become rather suspicious of your help, you know, but if you promise just to sit and watch, you may." She got up and went into the bathroom. "You haven't got a dry swimsuit," she called out through the partially closed door.

"That doesn't matter."

The light outside on the beach was blinding, but the breeze was warm, so that we did not regret our decision until we had reached the water's edge. I jumped in, diving very flat because of the shallowness of the water, enjoying the shock of the change in temperature that the sea had in store for me. "Oh, how can you dive in like that?" she asked once she had joined me beyond the breakers. "It's freezing."

"It's much worse if you go in slowly."

"Either way is awful. And it was so nice and warm in bed."

"We can go back, if you like." I put my arms around her waist and tried to kiss her, but she pulled away.

"We're not alone on this beach, you know," she said warningly. "I have neighbors."

"I don't see anybody." The beach was deserted at that hour. The other houses along the road had their shutters closed against the sun.

"Everybody's inside having lunch. Which is why I don't think we should put on a show for them."

"I'm sorry." I swam away from her. I resented having to be careful. It reminded me of everything I wanted to forget.

"Aren't you starving?" she called after me. "I'll go fix us a salad . . . so come back soon."

I turned and watched her run across the hot sand until she had disappeared into the house. Then, keeping my head out of the water, I swam parallel to the beach. After a while I went in to rest. I felt weak, but it was an agreeable feeling of weakness. I lay watching the sandpipers feeding at the edge of the water, my mind empty and vague. She had called me an animal, and I felt like one.

When she called, I went around to the patio at the side of the house. She had laid two places for us on the warped wooden table that stood on the uneven brick floor. I noticed that she had put on a Mexican straw hat to protect her face against the sun, which made her look quite different, almost as if she were wearing a disguise. "Were you asleep out there on the beach?" she asked.

"No, just dozing. Can I ask you something?"

"Depends on what it is."

"About love. . . ." She made a face, but I continued: "You said that that had never happened to you before . . . you remember? And I couldn't help wondering why. When you were first married, you were happy, weren't you? I mean, you wanted to be married. . . ."

"Well, it wasn't a marriage of convenience, if that's what you mean. I was very young, of course, and had no idea what it was all about."

"Does that make such a big difference?"

"Of course it does. But why do you ask?"

"Because I want to know everything about you. Is that so amazing?"

"I suppose not," she replied, shrugging, "although it's rather a dreary story. . . ." She pulled the brim of her hat down in order to keep the sun off her face. "On my honeymoon I found love to be rather painful," she said, "which is why, I suppose, I didn't enjoy it much. Then I got pregnant right away. . . . I adore Karen, as you know, but it all happened too quickly, and I felt awful, and then after she was born, I really didn't want to make love anymore. Richard made me go to a doctor, because he thought there was something physically wrong with me, and they operated, did something they thought would make it easier, but of course it didn't. Probably it made things worse, I don't know. Richard thought I was frigid, and we had terrible quarrels. We would argue all night about something you can't really argue about. Perhaps I *was* frigid, although I'm sure I'm not now. People don't really ever change, don't you agree? Anyway, I told him that I thought we should get a divorce, but he wouldn't hear of that. And so we went on, half-married . . . miserable, the both of us, until we got used to living that way, that's all."

"Does it still happen now?" I asked. "Does he still . . ."

She got up from the table. "Don't ask me that," she said. "What does it have to do with you? With everything else in the world going wrong, why do you want to spoil this, too? It's stupid!" She went into the house. I heard the screen door of the living room slam, and I knew that she'd gone out on the beach. I followed her. I felt upset, too, and yet relieved. At least, I thought, she was really happy only with me. And I had broken through to her, had made her talk about her own feelings for once. We were finally on a more equal footing. I caught up with her. She was walking along the edge of the water without looking where she was going. I took her hand, but felt no response to the pressure of my fingers. "I'm sorry," I said. I couldn't think of anything else to say.

"I suppose you have a right to ask these things," she replied. "Although I can't see that it has anything to do with you. It's not at all the same thing, and it happens so rarely . . ."

"But it does happen, doesn't it?"

She hesitated, her head turned away from me. Then she said: "Yes, sometimes," and kicked at a shallow wave that had come up to pull at our ankles. "I told you that you should find someone your own age," she went on, "someone who isn't married and has no children, and no past. That's the sort of person you should fall in love with. Then you can ask all the questions you like."

"But I love *you*. . . ."

A gust of wind carried off her hat, and I ran after it, retrieving it just as another wave came up. I brought it back covered with wet sand.

"Give it to me," she said. "It'll dry. And let's go back. You haven't even finished your lunch."

But I wasn't hungry anymore. I felt a heavy weight inside my stomach. I drank the watery tea in my glass and helped her clear the table. Then we went upstairs, and she started to wash her hair. I sat on the edge of the tub, watching her while she stood leaning over the basin.

Her hair was full of soapsuds, and she lifted her head and looked at herself in the mirror. "That's how I'll look when I'm gray," she said. "I'll cut it short, and wear it like Ethel."

"I won't mind."

She smiled and said, "Oh, you'll be miles and miles away by then." She ran fresh water into the basin to rinse her hair. Then she added soap again and rubbed her scalp with her fingertips. When she asked me to, I got up to help her wash the back of her head. "You're really quite useful to have around," she said. She was trying to keep the soapsuds out of her eyes. "I'd better take another shower. I'll never get all the soap out this way."

"I'll join you. It's an old country amusement."

"Whoever taught you that?" she asked. "Must have been a lecherous old woman."

"Same person who taught me everything else."

She chuckled, pushing her lathered hair back from her face with both of her hands. "There hasn't been much teaching, I'm afraid," she said. "It's rather been a case of the blind leading the blind."

She turned the water on inside the shower, and I helped her rinse off the soapsuds. Her eyes were red when she lifted her face at last and let the stream of water brush her hair into place. "You look as if you'd been crying," I said.

"I haven't, though. My eyes are red from the soap, that's all." I kissed her cheeks and her eyes and her mouth. "It's late, Carl," she warned.

"Not that late. It's only three-thirty." I felt I had to make love to her again, perhaps to make her forget my questions, or perhaps because I wanted to wipe out her answers. I also wanted to prove beyond a doubt that a special, physical bond existed between us, a bond that tied us both with equal strength. Then, too, I had discovered the satisfaction that giving pleasure can give, which was perhaps the most important discovery of all. I kissed her, but she pulled her head away from mine. "I know now why older women prefer young men," she said.

"You do?"

"Yes. Because they're tireless. They can go on forever."

"Haven't you ever made love that much before?"

"You're starting to question me again. Please don't do that. There's no point. The past is dead. Over and done with."

"I'll never ask another question," I promised, knowing even as I said it that it was a promise I would never be able to keep.

The telephone rang. She went into the bedroom to answer it. I tried not to listen, but I could tell by the sound of her voice that it was Gordon calling. I went downstairs into the living room, and unconscious of the heat, stood watching a man and a girl on the beach in front of the cottage. He was trying to pull her into the sea, and the girl was resisting, laughing while they struggled. They obviously didn't care about anyone else. They had nothing to hide.

Pamela called me, and I went back upstairs. She had opened one of the shutters and was sitting naked on one corner of the bed, drying her hair in the sun. "Where did you go?" she asked. "Were you looking for something to eat?"

"No. I was being polite, that's all."

"How refreshing," she said. "Bring me my hairbrush, will you?"

Then, by way of an explanation, she added: "I have to go into town later on. We're having dinner with some people tonight, which is just about the last thing in the world I want to do."

"What about Karen?"

"She's going to stay at Edwina's. I'll call her. She'll be stopping by there for tea." She paused. "I can give you a lift home, if you like. We'll put your bike in the rumble seat."

"I can ride back," I said. "It's not that far."

She looked up at me. "What's the matter?" she asked.

"Nothing's the matter."

"Yes, there is. I can tell. I can't help it that I'm married, you know."

"I know that."

"Then don't look so reproachful."

I went around to the far side of the bed and stretched out in the shade. I heard her pick up the telephone and call Las Golondrinas. She left a message for Karen to wait there until she arrived. Then, once she had hung up, she lay down beside me on the bed. "We still have two hours together," she said, "and after today there's tomorrow. And after tomorrow, there's the next day. So don't be glum. A glum lover is a bore. Are you having dinner at home tonight?"

"No, I'm taking Joan Crawford dancing," I said.

"She's much too old for you."

"Who isn't?"

"Don't make things more difficult than they already are, Carl," she whispered.

I turned toward her, and found that her skin was warm from the sun, and that her mouth tasted faintly of soap, which taste was soon lost in the mutual taste of our kisses. I wanted to tell her again that I loved her, but I had said it so often that day that I thought it was foolish to repeat again the oft-repeated words. So we made love in silence, the heat and the exertion fusing our bodies together as they had never been together before, and then finally, at the end she cried, and her tears running down her cheeks mingled with our kisses.

I didn't really understand why, for I couldn't imagine that her misery was as great as mine, as satisfying a sadness, which was a stronger feeling even than being spent. "Please don't ask me to take another swim," she said later, her head close to mine. "For if I go into the sea now, I'm sure to drown, my darling, and I really don't want to die today of all days."

⇒ *three* ⇐

THE FRONT doorbell rang.

She had finished dressing, was just putting on her earrings in front of the mirror, and thinking that it was a mistake, that the sound was perhaps part of the orchestration of the piano concerto she had put on the record player downstairs; she stood looking at me, still holding the pearl clip in her hand until the bell rang again, and we both knew for certain that it was the brass ship's bell outside the front entrance of the cottage.

She whispered: "Stay here," and pulled the door of the bedroom shut behind her. I could hear her footsteps on the wooden stairs, and then Edwina's voice in a falsely affectionate greeting that was half-lost in a crescendo of the concerto that was continuing as if it were being played as the background music for a dramatic moment in a film. I looked over at the unmade bed, at the twisted sheets and rumpled pillows that might well have served as a shot in the film the music was underscoring. There was nothing I could do. I did not dare make a move to straighten the bed, for I knew that the wooden floor would creak under my feet. If Edwina decided to come upstairs, and found me there, it would be quite apparent to her how we had spent the afternoon.

Yet I felt surprisingly calm. I remember that for a few seconds I even found myself wishing that she would take it into her head to visit the house she had never seen, for there would be an end of hiding then, of lying. We would be forced to face the consequences.

I could almost hear myself defying them all, confessing my love, and doing so with pride. Suddenly I became aware of a familiar sniffing outside the door, followed by a barely audible whine. It was Tim, who had escaped his mistress and was conducting his own investigation of the cottage. I held my breath, as the sniffling at the bottom of the door continued. If I was discovered, there was a good chance that I would be sent away to school in the East, a stern voice within me warned. All Edwina had to do was go to my mother and ask for her help in avoiding a scandal. I felt less brave, less calm.

But Pamela came to the rescue. She called the dog, and sensing the urgency in her voice, Tim obeyed. Then I heard the screen door of the living room open and close, and I knew that the moment of greatest danger had passed. Very slowly I made my way to the window beyond the bed. Through the louvers in the wooden shutters I caught a glimpse of the two women standing on the brick walk that led out to the beach. They were looking at the sunset, admiring the summer-evening sky, oblivious of my existence. Edwina was still in the makeup she wore for her work, which meant she had driven directly to the beach instead of stopping off at home. She was wearing faded blue jeans and a white cardigan, and her hair was wrapped in a piece of grayish gauze in order to protect it against the wind. I saw Pamela lean down and retrieve the dog's leash.

At that moment Edwina turned to look up at the window behind which I was hiding, and startled, I stepped back, reacting before I had time to realize what I was doing. The boards under my feet creaked noisily, and I sat down on the bed, appalled at my own stupidity. Nothing happened, however; the voices droned on, until after a while they moved off. Still I did not move. It was as if my mind had come abruptly out of the fog of an impossible and imagined dream, and now the entire scenery of reality lay before me in an unpleasantly clear light.

I did not like what I saw. I was experiencing my first encounter with guilt, I suppose, which is why I remember the scene so vividly—the room with the untidy bed on which the shutters had not so long ago projected lanes of sunlight across our naked bodies; the closet door that still stood open the way Pamela had left it, so that I could see myself reflected in the floor-length mirror on the inside, sitting there, afraid to move, hiding, like a criminal. It occurred to me briefly that I was after all not the one who was married, but as that line of reasoning merely shifted all of the blame onto the person I loved, I abandoned the idea at once. I was at fault as much as she was. Yet what solution was there for the two of us? If I went to Gordon and confessed, Pamela would be the one who would be made to suffer the most. It would be better never to see her again. But it would be preferable not to live at all than to have to face that. I could foresee what my days would be like without her, and I experienced a moment of true panic. If only I were a little older, then I could at least go to Spain and dedicate my life to the struggle against fascism. I noticed that in my despair I had started using Jake's terminology. Then I began to compare my life with his. Everything was much simpler for him. He had a *Weltanschauung;* he believed in a cause, while I didn't really believe in anything. The struggle against fascism! I hadn't given it a thought for weeks. Jake was right to despise me, to treat me like an idiot.

The bedroom door opened, and Pamela reappeared. She said: "Thank God you're still here," and laughed nervously. "I thought you might have taken it into your head to climb out of the window over the garage just as Edwina was getting ready to drive away."

"You told me to stay here."

"I know, but I wasn't sure you'd wait all this time." She came over to me and took my hand and held it against her chest. "Feel my heart," she said. "It's been beating like that for the past half-hour. God, I was scared. Can you imagine what my dear sister-in-law would have done if she'd found you here? She wanted to see the house, so she said, and breathe a little fresh air. You know, I didn't offer her tea or a drink, or anything." She went over to the mirror. "Look at my hands! They're still shaking. I can't even put on my earrings."

"Tim knew I was up here."

"Yes, that bloody little dog! He nearly did us in."

"Do you think Edwina suspected anything?"

"I don't think so. Why should she, after all? I told her that I had to hurry into town to meet Richard, which is the truth. . . ." She crossed to the bed and started to pull off the sheets in order to remake it with the fresh linen she had taken out of the closet earlier, and which lay folded on a stool near the bed. "Give us a hand, darling," she said. "I do have to hurry now. . . ."

I helped her pull the sheet taut across the bed, and I found myself thinking that Gordon was going to sleep there with her, and make love to her, for all I knew. I said: "Pamela . . ." but she seemed not to have heard me, for she was smiling suddenly, off on some comical fantasy of her own.

"You know, we could always get work as a couple," she said. "If everything fails, that is . . . if Richard throws me out, and your father decides to send you away to school. You're a bit young to be a butler, of course, but I could pretend you were my son, and you could do odd jobs. Although I suppose it would be difficult to explain why we should sleep in the same bed." She looked over at me. "You don't like that idea, do you?"

"I was thinking about something else."

She straightened the blanket on her side, and tucked it in. "Couldn't have been a very pleasant thought."

"It wasn't."

She pointed to the bed cover, and I brought it to her. "You know, while I was waiting for you," I said, "I kept hoping Edwina would come upstairs and find me, just so there'd be an end to all this lying."

"Did you, now? That's interesting."

"I'm serious, Pam. . . ."

"Oh, Carl," she said. "For heaven's sake! You know it's hopeless to think that way. We'd only cause pain and grief to a person who doesn't deserve either one, and we'd be separated forever, you may be sure of that."

Her concern for Gordon irritated me. If it came to a choice between us, there was no doubt in my mind as to which one of us she would choose. I recalled one of Guy's favorite old French sayings, *"L'amant est toujours le plus grand cocu,"* and wondered if he had been trying to warn me, or had merely been displaying his worldliness. I said: "Do you think she noticed my bicycle?"

She straightened, and looked over at me with alarm. "Why?" she asked. "Where did you leave it?"

"In the garage."

"Did you close the door?"

"I don't think so."

She shrugged. "Well, you could have left it there at any time," she said after a moment's hesitation.

"Anyway, that's our story."

She scowled. "I don't enjoy lying any more than you do," she said. "But we have no choice."

"Yes, we have. I can stop coming out here to see you."

"Would you prefer that?"

"No."

"Then why do you suggest it?"

"Because all this makes me feel lousy—your getting dressed to go and meet him, and then coming back here to sleep in the same bed with him, as if nothing were wrong. . . ."

"That's not true. He knows something's wrong, just as well as I do. But he's still my husband."

"You don't love him."

"No, not in the way you mean . . . but I love him in other ways, and we have a child, and a life together. . . . I can't leave him and go off with you. If you can't understand that, or if it makes you too miserable, then perhaps we *should* stop seeing each other, as much as it might hurt for a while. . . ."

It was easy to give up things if you didn't care. "I wonder how much it would hurt," I said in a muffled voice, and left the room. I sensed that I had come close to ending everything, which frightened me. I went into the shower and collected my wet bathing suit, the memory of how happy I had been only an hour earlier making me feel even more miserable. I started down the stairs, my head throbbing.

She called my name, and I stopped and waited for her, thinking that she would take me in her arms once she came face to face with me. But she was more in control of her emotions than I was, and arriving at the bottom of the stairs, she merely held out her hand and said: "I suppose it's good-bye then, Carl." She was much stronger than I was, much more adept at the game, and it was a game, I realized, an unpleasant kind of charade in which one hid one's true feelings and pretended to be someone else. I shook my head, wishing that I had not learned long ago that it was wrong for a man to cry. Although it was that that saved me, that small degree of manliness I had managed to acquire.

"I don't want it to be good-bye for keeps," I said quietly. "I love you, and I always will, even if we have to cheat and lie."

Tears came to her eyes then, and she took me in her arms, or rather we both moved toward each other at the same instant, both of us abandoning our false attitudes.

"I can't kiss you," she said, "because I've just put on my lipstick . . . but I promise I'll make up for it tomorrow, if you let me." I nodded, and held her close, more conscious than ever of the difference between us, aware of her elegance and beauty that contrasted with the way I was dressed, the way I felt.

After she had locked all the doors in the house, we went out to the garage together, and I put my bike into the rumble seat of the car while she started the engine. We both heard another car approaching, but neither one of us paid any attention to it. There was the sharp sound of a horn, and turning, I saw that a large car had stopped on the shoulder of the highway outside the garage. It was Edwina.

My first impulse was to hide, but it was too late for that. She had seen us both, and so I froze instead, and stood staring at her, open-mouthed. For what seemed like an eternity she sat looking at us, an amused smile on her heavily made-up face, until finally she laughed, perhaps because she, too, felt embarrassed. "I took a short drive up the beach," she said, looking past me as if she had expected to find me there, and yet was unwilling to recognize my presence. "You know, I don't blame you a bit for wanting to live down here, Pam. It's never lonely near the sea."

Pamela didn't move. She merely sat looking out through the open back flap of the roadster, her face slightly flushed, but otherwise controlled. "Yes, I love it here," she said in a flat, toneless voice.

"Isn't it rather a long way for you to come on your bike, Carl?" Edwina asked solicitously.

"It's not so bad," I heard myself say. "It takes me a little more than half an hour, that's all."

"And you always get a ride home, I suppose."

Pamela backed the Ford roadster she had inherited from Edwina out of the garage, and pulled up alongside her sister-in-law's car. I closed the garage doors, glad to have something to do that did not require my looking at either one of them, and I heard Edwina ask: "Where was Carl when I stopped by a few minutes ago? I hope he wasn't hiding from me?"

"Of course not. Why should he hide?" Pamela replied, with a genuine note of surprise in her voice. "He was upstairs, changing his clothes."

"Oh, I see," Edwina said, carefully putting the new Buick convertible she had bought that winter in gear, still pretending to be friendly and unconcerned. "Well, I hope I'll see you both on Saturday for tennis," she called out as she drove off.

I got in beside Pamela, and we sat in silence, watching the dark green convertible disappear down the highway. "The bitch!" Pamela said slowly. "Well, you got your wish."

"Will she say anything?"

"Not right away. She's too clever for that. And I'll see Richard before she has a chance to make trouble, and tell him that you were here. There's no reason why you shouldn't come to visit me, you know. And thank God you're still young enough to be above suspicion! But she knows, now. It was just a little too obvious when you didn't appear while she was here the first time."

"You told me to stay upstairs."

"I know. It never occurred to me that she'd come back." Her eyes narrowed. "And it isn't that she gives a damn about Richard. It's just that she can't stand the idea of anyone not falling in love with her instead. She's jealous of everything I have. She always has been." We started off down the highway, the wind whistling through the exposed wheel of my bicycle in the rumble seat.

"And if I weren't 'still young enough to be above suspicion'?" I asked. "If I were older?"

"Well, there'd be trouble then."

"What would you do?"

"You mean if I were really forced to make a choice, or were able to make one freely?" She glanced over at me, and I noticed that her gloved hands tightened on the steering wheel. "Oh, darling, you and your questions," she said, shaking her head. "Of course, in my maddest dreams, I, too, think of our going off together, escaping to some place without husbands and wars and money, so that neither one of us would have any responsibilities, and could lie in the sun and make love whenever we felt like it, violently or sweetly or however you like. . . . But that's only in my moments of purest madness, early in the morning or in the middle of the night when I'm half-asleep. . . ." She pulled off her right glove and took my hand in hers, holding it tightly as she went on: "But when I'm fully awake and sane, and you're far away in your own bed, then I know if

I had to make a choice—and almost every day I feel I must make one—why, then I'd give you up, I'm afraid, make do without you, because I love my daughter and am attached to my husband, love him too, in a different way. And I'd go on, sadly, with my life that I know would seem empty forever after, and incomplete. But that's what I'd have to do. You understand, don't you, my darling? Fortunately, you *are* still above suspicion . . . in Richard's eyes, anyway, if not in Edwina's, and so if you're willing to go on as we are, then we still may have a little time left."

I didn't say anything. She pulled over into the State Beach parking lot. We had passed Castle Rock, which was where she always stopped so that I could ride the rest of the way home. I released her hand and stepped out of the car. "Will I see you tomorrow?" she asked.

"Yes, I suppose so," I said. I lifted my bike out of the rumble seat. It weighed a ton.

"Don't be blue now, angel," she called out to me, her voice faint above the noise of a passing truck. "You know that I hate going."

It sounded like something she might have said to Karen in order to console her because she was leaving her behind. I got on my bike and started pedaling. I thought about how different Edwina had looked the first time I had seen her on the beach with Tim. She was certainly as beautiful now, but her beauty was almost too perfect. I realized that I had changed too, which made it seem even more ridiculous to be riding along the highway on a bicycle. Once again I decided that I must find a job. That was the only way I could stop being an "adolescent."

Although I had made up my mind not to, I found myself thinking of Pamela. She would soon be arriving at the studio, driving her small car past the policeman at the gate, looking tanned and summery in contrast to everyone else, especially Gordon, who would be waiting for her in his dressing room. He would take her in his arms with that professional grace of his, and kiss her cheeks, as I had often seen him do in the past. She's his wife, I repeated over and over again as I pedaled along. Then I tried to make myself think of something else: school, the war, anything that would make me forget her for a few hours—what I would "do with my life," even, which was the last thing in the world I wanted to think about.

But I had no life apart from her anymore, not even a false, heroic one I could escape to for a few hours, for she had taken over my daydreams as well, was always there, constantly in my thoughts, as if she were part of me. "Someday we'll be able to live together without lies," I wrote in my diary, as if putting it down on paper would make it come true.

four

AND IT WAS THAT which disrupted my days most of all that summer, my inability to stop thinking about Pamela while I was separated from her. No matter what I was doing, she would invade my thoughts, so that I found myself leading a tortured, almost schizophrenic existence that was not limited to those first few hours of crisis. For the crisis, I soon discovered, had taken place almost entirely in my mind (and briefly, perhaps, in Pam's mind, while she drove into town that evening), as Edwina had apparently decided to keep to herself whatever suspicions our behavior had aroused in her. In any case, she made no mention of her visit to the beach when I arrived for tennis the following Saturday; she even seemed pleased to see me, offering her cheeks to be kissed, as if nothing had happened.

I had expected her to be hostile, or at least more sarcastic than ever, which was why I had not wanted to go. But Pamela had insisted that "we show the flag," and so I had prepared myself for the worst—a scene, or even a confrontation. But neither one materialized. The Count made some reference to the infrequency of my visits, and Hévesey, when it came time to play, remarked that "we must separate the lovers," which was the kind of thing he had often said before. There were only four of us on the court at that moment, for which I was grateful, as I felt the blood rushing to my face. Edwina laughed, and I changed sides in order to play as her partner, while she agreed quite blandly that "Pam and Carl are much too strong a team."

Richard Gordon did not arrive until late in the afternoon, and there was a lengthy discussion as to where he had been, for he had not had to work that day. Paul suggested that he had had lunch with his new leading lady (one of the dark-haired vamps of the day), but Gordon merely shrugged and said that that would have been a waste of time, as he could have lunch with whomever he liked all week long.

"You are a troublemaker, aren't you, Paul?" Pamela remarked acidly, which attitude I knew was expected of her, but which bothered me just the same. It was all banter, a mock show of jealousy she was expected to put on in order to appear to be a normal wife. Still, it bothered me, for Gordon was far from being "above suspicion" in *my* mind.

"I'm a disgustingly faithful husband," he said, "something quite unheard of in Hungary, I'm sure." He had appeared at the top of the pavilion steps a few minutes earlier, and he seemed quite pleased with the conversation his absence had provoked. Then, with his hand thrust deep into his trouser pockets, he added: "If you really want to know, I've just had my first flying lesson. . . . Not that you're to spread that all over town, Paul, because the studio takes a dim view of anything like that while I'm in the middle of a film."

Pamela turned away from the net, saying: "What on earth did you want to do a thing like that for? It's mad."

"Because I thought it was a good idea," Gordon replied. "I certainly don't want to follow in my dear father's footsteps and join some Highland regiment once the trouble starts." He seemed to be mocking himself by appearing as the caricature of an upper-class Englishman, which was a pose he often adopted, as if he were playing a part which he was in some ways born to play. "I prefer to die a clean death, if you don't mind," he continued, "pampered and well fed. And then, it's really quite fascinating, learning to conquer a new element. Don't forget, darling, the world of the future will see us all flitting around in our own airplanes. Lunch in Paris, and home again in time for tea." He turned to go. "Just have to put on my kit," he called back over his shoulder. "I'll be right with you."

It was an actor's exit, I remember thinking even then. His entire speech sounded as if it might have been carefully planned and rehearsed for that afternoon, so that it would have the maximum effect. But I was too concerned with myself to question his reasons for making such a public display, although I should have guessed what was in his mind, I suppose, when I saw the effect his announcement had on his wife. For Pamela's game deteriorated at once, and Edwina and I came from behind to win the set, much to Paul Hévesey's disgust. He cursed in Hungarian, and forgot to embrace his partner, obviously as aware of the tension as the rest of us. He couldn't fail to notice that something was wrong a moment later, when after telling him that she was sorry that she had let him down, Pamela left the court.

Hévesey raised his hands and made a face. "Trouble in paradise," he said. "Well, the three of us who aren't married will have to play."

Edwina told him not to be such a fool, just as she always did when he started clowning in my presence. She, too, seemed perturbed, and it occurred to me that she had perhaps not been as discreet as I had at first believed, for I noticed that she was strangely silent when Pamela reappeared a few minutes later.

"Don't you want to try and revenge our honor?" Paul asked.

"No, thanks. I think I've had it for the day." She sat down in a deck chair, and staring at her legs, started to bounce the tightly strung racket off the tip of her tennis shoe. "I can't understand him doing a stupid thing like that," she said. "It's just ridiculous. He might at least have told me."

"Well, he hasn't actually enlisted in the Royal Air Force as yet," Paul replied, although Pamela's remarks had not really been addressed to him as much as to Edwina. "Nor is there a war on. You already see him in uniform, taking off to meet the Hun over no-man's-land. He's just decided to learn to fly . . . what's so terrible about that?"

She disregarded him. "Did he say anything to you?" she asked Edwina.

"Not really. . . ."

"What do you mean, 'not really'? Either he mentioned it or he didn't." Her voice was sharp and aggressive, and she looked up angrily at her sister-in-law.

"Oh, he said something about it, but I didn't take him seriously. And, after all, it's a sport like any other."

"You obviously don't know your brother very well," Pamela said caustically. "He does nothing without a purpose. And I certainly don't believe all that nonsense about his suddenly having decided to conquer a new element." She fell silent; she had heard the door of the living room slam in the distance.

Gordon came quickly down the stairs, and went straight out onto the tennis court. "Who's going to warm me up?" he asked cheerfully. "Come on, Pam. Hit a few balls with your old man. . . ."

"I don't think I want to play any more," Pamela said. "It's too hot." She got up and left the court. Gordon pretended to look surprised.

"What's the matter with her?" he asked.

"You haven't exactly made her day with your little surprise," Hévesey told him.

"Nonsense. That has nothing to do with it." He raised his voice and called after her: "You're not leaving us for good, are you, darling?" There was no answer. "Wives don't like secrets," he said, smiling for our benefit. "Their husbands' secrets, that is. Well, she'll get over it." He turned to me. "*You're* not upset, are you, Carl, old man? You approve of my taking flying lessons, don't you? I mean damn it all, us chaps have to stick together."

I knew that he did not expect an answer from me. It was all part of the scene he had devised, which was why he made no effort to hide the sarcasm in his voice. Yet I felt I had to reply. I said hesitantly: "I'd do the same thing, if my parents would let me," at which he laughed, quite naturally, making me feel even more ill at ease.

"You see, I have the approval of youth," he called out to the others. "Tell you what, Carl, I'll take you with me tomorrow. Your mother needn't know a thing about it."

"You'll do nothing of the kind," Edwina said. "Suppose something were to happen?"

"Don't be absurd. There's a sixteen-year-old girl at the field who goes up with her father almost every day. The trouble with you is that you're passé! Why, if Karen were a little older, I'd get her started. What do you say, Carl? Are you game?"

I knew that he was baiting me. He had never shown the slightest interest in anything I had ever said or done, which made it all the more obvious. "I'd like to go," I said.

"All right, then, I'll pick you up at ten tomorrow morning."

We started to rally. Gordon bounded around the court, hitting the ball as hard as he could. "It's even helped my tennis," he called out boisterously. "A man should risk his life at least once each day. Now, where did I read that?"

I noticed that Pamela had changed when we arrived in the library for tea. Her mood had improved somewhat, although she was obviously still upset. She pulled away from Gordon when he tried to put his arm around her waist. I pretended not to have seen their strained byplay, but as I diverted my glance, I caught Edwina's eye. She had been watching me, her face full of suspicion.

"Don't count on Carl for tennis tomorrow," I heard Gordon say. "I'm taking him out to the airfield."

Pamela turned to me, the teapot still in her hand. "You're not going, are you? I won't have it."

"It's nothing to do with you," Gordon told her. "You can't monopolize all the boys. Anyway, Billy Lovat is coming with the Bennetts, so you'll have plenty of players."

She said nothing, obviously preferring not to discuss it until we were alone together. "But why did you agree?" she asked, as she drove me home after tea. "If your mother finds out, she'll be furious."

"He asked me to come along, and it was hard to say no. He would have thought I was chicken."

"But that's absurd! All you had to say was that you'd rather play tennis. He's got some sort of plan in his head. Edwina's undoubtedly said something to him, and this is his little revenge."

"You think he knows about us?"

"Of course not. Oh, he knows you have a crush on me, but he's known that all along. . . ."

"You don't think he suspects anything else?"

"Certainly not!"

She was too adamant, I thought. "Did he make love to you?" I asked. "Is that why you're so sure?"

"Carl, please. . . ."

"I want to know! That's all I think about when I'm away from you. I lie in my bed at night, wondering if he's touching you or taking you in his arms. . . ."

"We've been married for eleven years!"

"What does that prove? He's still in love with you. You said so yourself."

"You promised you wouldn't question me any more."

"I know I did, but it doesn't work," I replied. "It would make it easier if you'd tell me the truth. I'm sure of it. . . ."

"I won't answer you."

"You've got to. I want to know."

"Why—for God's sake, tell me why?"

"Because it's worse if I imagine that it's happening," I said. "I can't help it."

"Oh, Carl . . . I beg you . . ."

"I have a right to know."

She shook her head. She looked miserable. "Yes, you have a right to know," she said. "But why insist on it? Can't you see you're only torturing both of us?"

"Better both of us than me alone," I replied. "Tell me! Did he or didn't he? Is that why you're so sure that he doesn't suspect anything? Because you gave in to him? Is that why he's reassured?"

She didn't answer, and so we drove on.

"Whatever happens between Richard and me doesn't concern you," she said after a while. "Because it's as if it were happening to a different person. It's not *my* body that is forced to give in once in a while. My body belongs to you. My love belongs to you. You should know that, be able to feel it. You have no reason to be jealous, and you never will have. So don't go on with it. I'm faithful to you in a way no one else will ever be."

But the words she said, words I should have understood, meant nothing to me. All that mattered was that I knew that my fears had been justified. I felt the inside of my stomach tightening with a sudden pain that I could not fight against. I shook my head. "I'm glad you told me," I said, which was a lie.

She turned off the coast road and started up the familiar streets leading to my house. Neither one of us spoke until she had stopped the car in front of the narrow wire garden gate. "Good-bye," she said then. "I hope I'll see you tomorrow."

"Good-bye." As it was still daylight, she didn't expect me to kiss her, but she reached out and caught my hand as I started to get out of the car. She squeezed it for a second, before letting me go. I couldn't look in her face. I didn't want to show the extent of my misery. I heard her drive off as I went toward the house.

I went upstairs and stood at the window of my room, watching the sun sink into the sea. It was stupid to look for solace in another person, I decided. We all live and die alone. And for the first time in my life, the idea of my own death seemed quite acceptable to me.

✑ five ✑

RICHARD GORDON appeared early the next morning. I had been hoping
that he wouldn't remember his promise to take me along, as I was not
looking forward to spending most of the day alone with him, but when
the doorbell rang soon after breakfast, I knew that he hadn't forgotten
and that there was no escaping our outing.

"Are you ready?" he asked with the same slightly mocking smile that
had intimidated me even at our first meeting.

I nodded. I was ready. I had told all the necessary lies, had even
packed my tennis things in order to dissimulate the true purpose of our
trip. Yet, as I started out of the house, I realized that there was one thing
I had forgotten. I hadn't said good-bye to my mother, which, as I was
certain that I was going off to risk my life, suddenly appeared to me to
be an important omission. But by that time it was too late to turn back.
Gordon had already stepped through the wire garden gate and was waiting for me on the sidewalk beside his open car.

I got in beside him, and we started off, as amicably as if we were old
friends. "What did you tell them at home?" he asked, without looking
over at me.

"I said I was going to the beach for lunch, and then to play tennis."

"And suppose she calls the house?"

"She won't." His concern made me feel even more that our excursion
was not a completely harmless one. We drove on in silence.

"I trust you have no objection to classical music," Gordon said.
"Toscanini is conducting today." He found the station, but it was still
too early for the Sunday broadcast of the New York Philharmonic.

"It starts at twelve," I said. My mother always listened to the concert
at home.

"Ah . . . you're a fan. I should have known. The good old Austrian heritage has not been forgotten altogether." The news was on, and for a moment the reassuring voice of the President of the United States filled the car. Gordon turned up the volume and said gravely: "Thank God for Roosevelt. He's the only politician in America worth listening to at the moment."

I agreed with him, but felt that it was unnecessary to tell him so. A roundup of news from all over the world followed, and so we sat in silence listening to the grim recital of the day's events, which ended with a statement from a spokesman for the British Labor party who was reported to have declared that war was not inevitable.

Gordon shook his head. "How absurd," he said. "The war has already started. It's just a question of time before we're all involved." He glanced over at me. "What about you, Carl?" he asked. "Aren't you rather concerned about all this? Or do you feel confident that nothing will ever interfere with your tennis and going to the beach?"

It was the kind of question Jake often asked in order to prove his intellectual superiority. Gordon had a different reason. "Of course I'm concerned," I replied. "I'm not an idiot."

"Well, what are you going to do about it?" he asked. "I mean, your life, in general. How old are you now?"

"Seventeen."

He shook his head. "I always forget how young you are," he said, using one of Pamela's favorite phrases. "Still, in a couple of years you'll be military age . . . when do you finish school?"

"Next June. Only I plan to take an exam in German and French, and if I pass I'll be able to graduate in February."

"And then what?"

"I don't know. I was thinking of getting a job so that I can make some money before starting college."

"You *do* plan to go to college, then?"

"Well, my parents want me to . . . and I suppose it's the right thing to do. Of course, if there's a war, there won't be much point."

"I don't think America will get into it for a while," Gordon said loftily. "It'll be like the last time . . . a few years of neutrality, before ultimately they'll be forced to take sides." He smiled, rather sardonically, I thought. "But then, as you're so disgustingly young, you'll probably miss it altogether. I wouldn't count on it, though, because it may turn out to be quite a long, drawn-out affair. That's why I think it's just as well to get prepared."

So he hadn't been joking. He was learning to fly for a specific purpose, exactly as Pamela had said. "You really think it's better to be an aviator than a soldier?" I asked.

"If you're talking about survival, I'm not so sure," he replied. "But while you're alive, flying is preferable. At least, that's my opinion, because I don't fancy living in mud and filth. I'm an actor . . . remember. The role is important to me, the costume, even. Patriotism is all very well, but if I have to be in the damn thing, I want to play a meaningful part . . . not just be offered up as cannon fodder, and die as my father did, taking some hill with a number instead of a name."

My father had spent four years in the Austrian cavalry, assigned, fortunately for him, to the "train," the service of supply. He had never believed in the cause of the Imperial Powers, had felt no trace of patriotism. He had served reluctantly in Serbia and in Poland, ashamed of being an Austrian officer and a representative of the oppressors. And he had survived, which had finally become the most memorable aspect of his military career. Still, in my daydreams I was often an aviator, although I saw to it that I was never shot down in flames. A glorious return was an important part of my future as a soldier. "I suppose you're right," I said hesitantly.

"I know I am," Gordon replied. "For me, that is. But every man has to make his own decision. Plus the fact that *you* have to calculate even more carefully, as you might be able to avoid the whole damn thing . . . stay behind to console the widows and all the lonely women. That's what Billy Lovat plans to do."

"Well, I can't say that I agree with him. Because I feel it's 'our' fight more than anyone else's."

"I suppose it is," Gordon said. "You were certainly the first people Hitler attacked, although if it does come to a war, nobody will be fighting for the Jews, you can be sure of that. So perhaps the best thing for you to do is try to survive. That way, if I get killed, you'll be able to take my place and look after Pam and Karen." He smiled and looked over at me.

I tried not to show that I was embarrassed. The possibility had occurred to me.

"You're shocked, aren't you, Carl?" Gordon said, laughing. "But it is a thought, isn't it?"

"I don't think that's the kind of thing you should joke about," I replied.

"You mean, never paint the devil on the wall. . . . That's an old German proverb, isn't it? Well, you needn't worry. I always keep my fingers crossed. Still, I can't help thinking about what would happen to Pam in case I bought it. I even find myself worrying a bit when I climb into Al Martin's small aircraft. But if a man allows himself to be put off by his imagination, then he winds up never taking a chance on anything. Anyway, you never know . . . you might slip on a piece of soap in your own bathtub and break your neck!"

The news broadcast had ended. Three thousand miles away the violins and the cellos of the New York Philharmonic were being given their final tuning. We had reached the summit of the hills we had been approaching. In front of us lay an immense plain, a partially converted desert that extended all the way to the horizon. The war would never come to this place, I thought to myself, and felt a momentary pang of regret that I had not been born there, so that I could be oblivious of what was happening in the rest of the world. The music had started. They were playing a Beethoven concerto, but I wasn't quite sure which one it was. Gordon moved his right hand in time, conducting an invisible orchestra of his own. "What a ridiculous race we are," he said. "Capable of producing this, and still unable to live in peace among ourselves. It's a trite thought, I know, but it always comes to mind, doesn't it?"

I nodded, although my mind had been elsewhere. I had been watching him, studying his face, trying to understand why Pamela was no longer attracted to him. He was certainly good-looking enough. His hair was attached to his head in just the right way, so that it was barely disturbed by the wind. His features were well formed, his prominent, straight nose contrasting with the gentle curve of his full mouth. And yet there was something about his physical appearance that was unwholesome, perhaps the excessive whiteness of his skin, or the thickness of his hands and wrists. Being with him made me unhappy, and I regretted that I had agreed to come along.

He said: "You don't have to go up in the plane with me, you know . . . if that's what's worrying you. You can watch from the ground."

"No, I'd like to go up," I said, trying to sound casual.

We had arrived at a small airfield. A domed hangar was visible behind a high wire fence, while off to one side of it a rectangular wooden hut stood near the edge of the road. Gordon parked the car. He seemed reluctant to abandon the music, but after a moment's hesitation he turned off the engine. "Enough culture for today," he said. "Let's go."

We followed a dirt path, bordered by weeds, and entered the wooden building through a sagging screen door.

The office in which we found ourselves was empty. A few drawings of airplanes hung from the plywood walls, as well as an aerial map of the southern part of the state. On the desk near the window a dusty telephone rested on a frayed green blotter. Apart from a couple of faded canvas chairs, there was no other furniture in the room. "Hmm, nobody home, I'm afraid," Gordon said. "I suppose we'd better have a look in the hangar."

There were two aircraft parked in front of the building, a Ryan monoplane with two open cockpits, and a small, all-metal machine that Gordon explained was a Lustrom. "That's the one I'm learning to fly in," he added. He touched the wing almost lovingly as we strolled past. I preferred the look of the Ryan, although I didn't say so.

We stepped inside the hangar. A sandy-haired man in a khaki shirt and pale blue trousers was standing on a ladder beside the engine of another small aircraft. On the ground next to him stood a girl of my own age. She had dark hair plaited into two braids, and a small heart-shaped face which she turned toward us as we entered. She was dressed in a faded denim jacket and jeans. On her feet she wore a pair of scuffed brown cowboy boots. "This is Al Martin," Gordon said, not bothering to introduce me by name.

Martin's eyes narrowed against the light coming through the open door behind us. He waved a screwdriver in the direction of the girl. "My daughter, Cynthia," he said with an easy drawl. "I didn't catch your name, son?"

"Carl Woolf."

Martin looked over at Richard Gordon. "Another candidate for the RAF?" he asked.

"No. This is one for your Air Corps. If he decides he likes flying, that is."

"Good. That's even better. Who knows, we may have another Lindbergh here."

"I hardly think that," Gordon said, smiling. He winked at me.

"You never can tell," Martin said, starting slowly down the ladder. The recently accepted German decorations had obviously not discredited the hero's name in Al Martin's eyes. "You ever been up before, son?" he asked.

"No, I haven't."

"Well, we'll damn soon fix that." He rested a friendly hand on my shoulder while we walked out toward the two aircraft. "You can shoot the breeze with Cynthia here," he said, "while Richard is having his lesson."

I liked him, despite his lack of "political orientation," which was what Jake would have called it. He appeared to be a man without pretensions or false attitudes, so very different from Gordon. I looked over at the girl. She seemed to be concerned only with the task at hand. "You think you'll need some help starting up, Dad?" she asked.

"I don't think so, honey. . . ." He looked over at Gordon. "You all set?" he asked.

Gordon nodded and went around the tail of the Lustrom in order to climb in on the right-hand side of the plane, while Al slipped easily through the door nearest us. Cynthia and I stood in silence watching the two men strap themselves into their seats. Al started the engine, and the small aircraft taxied off across the bumpy field. I would have preferred not to have waited, but to have gone up right away. I was afraid that my courage would fail me if I were forced to wait another hour before the moment would finally arrive. But that was only because I had not reckoned with the salutary effect Cynthia's presence would have on me. She looked over at me at that moment, apparently to inspect more closely the charge she had been left with. "You don't want to wait out here in the sun until they get back, do you?" she asked almost gruffly.

"I'll wait wherever you say," I replied.

"Well, let's watch the takeoff and then go on back into the hangar."

I nodded. The noise of the Lustrom's motor grew louder, and an instant later we saw it crossing the dried-out stubble field, trailing a long cloud of dust, from which it seemed ultimately to leap away, severing its final connection with the earth. Its wings wobbled as it rose into the clear sky, the noise of the engine growing fainter with surprising speed.

"I suppose I should go and sit by the telephone," Cynthia said, "but it gets too darned hot in that office."

The hangar seemed preferable to me, too, and so I followed her back into the relative coolness of its interior. The girl crossed to the base of the ladder on which her father had been working and closed the lid of the toolbox with the toe of her cowboy boot. "Is your dad a mechanic as well?" I asked, suddenly conscious of the importance of aircraft maintenance.

"Oh, yeah . . . he does everything. Come on over here and sit in this Rapide. You'll be more comfortable." She opened the door in the fuselage of a twin-engined biplane and swung aboard. "This is a British crate," she said casually. "It belongs to a friend of ours. It's slow, but dead safe."

I inspected the seats and peered out of the small windows at the brittle-looking wings. "Is the Lustrom faster?" I asked.

"About fifteen, twenty miles," she said. "Go on up in the cockpit and have a look." There was a single seat facing a mass of instruments. Cynthia had come up behind me, as if to make certain I would not touch anything I was not supposed to touch. "You really never been up before?" she asked.

"No, this'll be my first time."

"Well, you needn't be scared. Dad's the best there is. He trained with the Air Corps at the end of the war, and then decided to go into business on his own. They begged him to stay in, but he didn't like the army."

I nodded and backed out of the confined space in the nose of the plane. "You sure you don't want to sit behind the controls?" she asked.

"I'll wait until I can go up in the Lustrom," I said, and sat down opposite her in the back of the airplane. She draped one leg over the armrest of the seat and inspected the toe of her left boot. Casually her eyes strayed over to my face, as if it merited the same sort of inspection.

"Is Richard any relation of yours?" she asked.

"No. He's just a friend."

She appeared to be surprised at this. "A friend?" she repeated. "He's twice your age."

"I play tennis at his house."

She nodded, apparently satisfied with that explanation. "I never did try to play tennis," she said. "Although I used to ride horseback quite a bit. But then, when my mom died, and I came to live with Dad, I didn't seem to have time for anything but flying."

"Are you going to be an aviator?" I asked.

"I'd like to be," she said, "although it's hard for a girl. I'd like to be somebody like Amelia Earhart, and fly all over the world. But for that you've got to have money. Dad says he'll back me, if he ever gets a stake. But how's he ever going to make a lot of money at twelve dollars an hour? Half of what he makes goes back into the airplane, and the rest he needs to keep up his insurance policies—and for us to live, of course. But, you never know. Something might happen."

"You like it that much?" I asked.

"I don't like anything else," she said with a quick smile. "That's the only reason I'm still in school, because I want to be able to study navigation and radio. Without that you can only be a bush-leaguer, Dad says. So I guess I'll go to college next year, if I can get in, that is." She sat up suddenly. "They're coming back in," she said.

Her ears had not deceived her. The small silver aircraft was approaching the dirt runway. It touched down briefly, and then took off again. I saw that it bounced rather hard after it touched the ground. "Your friend's practicing landings," Cynthia said, smiling. "Let's go over to the office and sit for a spell."

She had a small waist, I noticed as I followed her across the dry stubble grass in the direction of the office. She turned and waited for me to catch up with her, as if she didn't like being scrutinized. "Why do *you* want to learn to fly?" she asked.

"I'm not sure I do yet," I replied. "Depends if I like it." I felt at ease in her presence. There was no need to pretend about anything with her.

"Oh, you'll like it, all right," she said. "It's expensive, that's the only thing."

I felt like putting my arm around her waist, but I didn't, of course. "I hope to get a job this winter," I said. "Then, if I feel I'm going to be really good at flying, maybe I can go into the Air Corps when the war starts."

"You really think we'll get into another war?" She sounded surprised and concerned.

"I don't see how we'll avoid it."

She shook her head. "I hope you're wrong," she said.

"But if it happens, wouldn't you rather fly than be a soldier?"

"I wouldn't want to do either," she said. "And being a girl has nothing to do with it. I want to be an explorer, and fly around the world, and visit other countries. I don't want people chasing me around up there and trying to kill me. And I wouldn't want to have to shoot down others, or bomb people, or destroy things." She sounded as if she had thought about it all and come to her own conclusions. I admired her for it, more than I'd ever admired anyone my own age.

The sun caught in the metal fuselage of the Lustrom as it came circling back for a landing, and then, as it taxied across the field toward us,

I knew that there was no escaping the test Gordon had prepared for me anymore, the challenge I had so willingly accepted, believing as I did that I had to prove that I was his equal.

⇒ SIX ⇐

"SIT UP STRAIGHT . . . you're not on a bicycle!" Al Martin's nasal voice filled the small cabin, rising above the noise of the engine and the buffeting of the wind. Obediently I shifted the upper part of my body and tried to avoid looking down at the arid fields outside the plexiglass window on my left. The Lustrom was in a tight turn, banking steeply now that we were well away from the ground. "Relax, Carl," Martin shouted. "We're not going to fall!"

He glanced over at me and grinned, but I did not feel reassured. It seemed like folly to trust so blindly in the strength of the tiny propeller, although he had explained it all to me in a brief lecture prior to takeoff —how the vacuum that was created by the curved leading edge of the wing supplied the necessary lift to make us airborne; and how, even if the propeller stopped turning (provided we had gained enough altitude), we would be able to glide safely back to earth. Nevertheless, I found that my hands and feet were bathed in cold sweat and that my stomach was drawn together in a tight knot. I did not like the feeling of being suspended in thin air, found it frightening. Was it cowardice, or merely the initial shock of venturing into a new element? How Gordon would laugh if he could see me, I thought, and tried hard to summon up the remnants of my courage.

"You all right?" Martin asked.

I nodded. I knew that if I had tried to answer him, my voice would have given me away. An instant later the Lustrom leveled out, and I felt slightly less ill at ease.

"Put your hand on the stick," Martin commanded, the expression on his face masked by his dark glasses.

"You want me to fly today?"

"You've got to start sometime."

I knew there was no arguing with him. I put my left hand on the control lever in front of me. "Don't try to bend it," he growled. "Just hold it normally. Now, keep your eyes on that dirt road down there, and slide your feet onto the rudder pedals. O.K. Push down on the left pedal. See how we start to drift? Now, correct with your right foot. That's it. Easy does it! An airplane is a sensitive machine. It's not a car you can wheel around corners. Now, just fly her parallel to that road down there."

I worked the pedals as gently as I could, and yet it seemed impossible to keep the airplane on its course. "I can't do it," I said. "I can't keep her straight."

"That's because you're too tense. Take your feet off the pedals for a minute. You see . . . she flies all by herself." He grinned. "Pull back on the stick now. Not so hard, for God's sake! You'll stall her. You can't ask her to climb that steeply without giving her more gun."

How was I to know about the dangers of stalling? I had never even been up in an airplane before. "You know, this is all new to me," I shouted in his ear.

"O.K. . . . but you want to learn, don't you?"

I remembered our swimming teacher, an overly muscled lifeguard at the beach club we had belonged to, who had pushed me into the deep end of the pool at the age of eight and then had been forced to rescue me when I started to drown; he had been surprised when, instead of thanking him, I had declared my everlasting hate. Was Martin his blood brother of the air? He said: "Let me show you something."

Martin's gloved hand covered the black knob of the throttle. The noise of the engine increased. I felt him pull back on the stick, and the nose of the Lustrom rose abruptly higher. Then he banked the plane steeply, and we went spiraling up into the glare of the sun. I clung to the tubular sides of the seat. "That's a barrel roll," Martin yelled triumphantly. "It's the kind of maneuver you'll have to learn to do if you want to be a pursuit pilot."

I nodded absently. My forehead was moist, and I felt that I was about to throw up. But I didn't complain, for by that time I had guessed that Gordon had put Martin up to this, had told him to frighten me. Well, I would show him, I thought, clenching my teeth, that I could endure whatever tortures were still in store for me. I must have been a pitiful sight, braced pale and perspiring in my seat, for suddenly Martin smiled and reached out to pat me with his gloved hand. "You're a good boy," he drawled. "You'll make them heinies sit up and take notice, if you get the chance."

I didn't contradict him, although I had given up my heroic day-dreams as the first slow roll had immediately made me decide to choose some other branch of the service in which to fight fascism. "Do you think," I shouted in a high voice, "we could just fly straight for a while? My stomach's not in good shape this morning."

He managed to look surprised. "You feel sick?" he asked with pre-tended concern.

"A little nauseous."

"That happens to the best of us," he said, nodding sympathetically. "Anyway, the acrobatics were Richard's idea. Take over the controls now, and you'll feel better."

I was doubtful, but I complied with his instructions. With my toes on the rudder pedals, and my moist hand on the stick, I managed to fly the Lustrom parallel to the road below us. After a while I felt almost normal again. I even managed to execute a turn at Martin's command. He seemed pleased. "Flying a plane is like anything else," he com-mented. "You've got to get used to it. The first time I went up, I got sick as a dog and puked all over the place. They damn near had to take the plane apart to get rid of the smell." He grinned and lit a cigarette. "You're doing good now, boy," he chuckled. "You'll be able to solo in about six hours."

At his command I made another right-angle turn, and we flew back in the direction of the small airport. Soon the hangar came into view, and the brown scar of the landing strip. A thermal bounced us around the empty sky, and yet I kept my hands and feet steady on the controls. Al nodded in silent approval. "You want to take over now?" I asked hopefully.

"Yeah, maybe I will," he replied. Then a strange expression came over his face, a mischievous look that should have served as a warning to me. "You know what I'd like to do?" he shouted. "To even the score, that is. I'd like to buzz our English friend down there, just to scare him a little. You think you're up to it?"

"I guess so."

Martin chuckled and straightened in his seat. "Hang on," he said. He pushed the stick forward, and with his left hand covering the throttle, put the plane into a shallow dive. I grasped the sides of the seat once again and watched the hangar come rushing toward us. Gordon and Cynthia were visible in the distance, standing outside the rectangular building but near the road, and then only seconds later they were clearly in view, two tiny figures frozen in postures of fear and amazement.

I felt certain that we were going to crash, that the prank Martin had decided on would backfire and end in our mutual death, and suddenly I found myself thinking of my mother and Jake, saw them sitting quietly in front of the radio in our living room, and I thought that the disaster that seemed inevitable now was only a fitting punishment for my having lied to them. Then I heard Martin yell, and I knew that the end was near. "Wave!" he shouted. "Wave to them as we go by!"

I raised a feeble hand, managed to pass it once or twice across the window as the plane leveled out, and then, as we rose steeply into the air, I found myself clutching the metal tubing under my seat again, which turned out to be an unnecessary precaution, for I was being pushed into place by the force of gravity. Martin was delighted. He grinned smugly as he banked and turned back in the direction of the field. "Did you see Richard's face?" he shouted to me. "He looked a lot more scared than you."

We came down smoothly over the tufts of dry grass, the wheels touching the packed dirt of the strip so gently that I could hardly notice that we had arrived. Then, with the propeller turning slowly outside the plexiglass in front of us, we taxied back to the hangar. "Don't tell 'em you had any trouble with your stomach," Martin said. "That way the joke'll be on them." Those were his first needless words of advice, as I had already started preparing myself for my reunion with Gordon, composing my face so that it would appear calm and confident.

"Did you enjoy yourself?" he asked as he came striding out toward the plane.

"It was fun," I replied. I glanced over at Cynthia, wanting to make the most of my moment of triumph. She looked concerned.

"Didn't you feel sick at all?" she asked. I could see by the expression on her face that she had had no part in the conspiracy.

"A little queasy after the first roll," I admitted. "But I enjoyed flying the plane."

She was delighted. "Isn't it a wonderful feeling? The world looks so much prettier from up there."

We followed Gordon and her father to the office. "I'm going to get a job and make enough money so that I can come and take lessons," I said, very sure of myself now that I was once again on terra firma.

"You should," she said encouragingly. "I'm sure you have a knack for it."

"Don't worry, I will," I replied, carried away by her enthusiasm and her charm.

Yet, even had I been completely sincere, it turned out to be a promise that was impossible to keep, as a stronger force than my own will interfered cruelly with both of our plans.

Less than two weeks after my first flight, Cynthia's life came to a violent end. She was returning home in the Ryan monoplane with her father, having flown out into the desert on what I remember Martin advertised as one of his "breakfast flights." While they were circling to land, a mysterious "pilot error" had caused them to spin in from five hundred feet, onto the hard, sun-baked earth I had stared out at with such great misgivings.

Gordon brought the news to the tennis court at Las Golondrinas late one afternoon and stood with a pale, washed-out face looking down at us from the pavilion. "Nobody knows what happened," he said, "but it seems Martin pulled up the flaps while they were in a tight turn, or maybe the girl did. . . . Because he was much too experienced a pilot to make such an obvious mistake. Anyway, they're both dead."

I can remember even now how her face had come rushing painfully into my mind at that moment, her freckled nose and forehead, framed by the braided pigtails she had worn that Sunday morning when we had met, and although since then it has become blurred in my memory, I can still recall the instant of pain that accompanied my recollection of her. I wanted to cry out that what he had said wasn't true, but I knew that it was true, could tell by the drained and weary way he stood there facing us.

"My God, how awful," Pamela said. "Just think, it could have been one of you." To which remark neither Gordon nor I had felt like making a reply.

How unfair life is, I thought for the first time. She had been so pure, so thoroughly lovable. I had hoped to make her my friend.

For months following that day I was tortured by a recurring nightmare, in which I found myself spinning through the air in the restricted confines of an airless cabin, falling helplessly toward the earth, which was never there, but that threatened me with a harsh death that was endless in coming. Then, awakening, I would be caught up in a much crueler vision, that of Cynthia's heart-shaped face screaming for help when help wasn't possible anymore.

That was the first real wounding I received. By the next day the weather had changed. A storm arrived in the middle of the night, and I opened my eyes in the morning and found the rain, like tears, streaming down the windowpanes of my room.

PART
VI

➳ one ᴥ

CYNTHIA'S DEATH cast a shadow across my life. It was as if I had lost someone very close to me, and I found, in the days that followed, that I could not shake off the feeling of depression that had come over me. There was no way of explaining my reaction to anyone else, as I had fabricated a relationship with her in my own mind, a relationship that her death magnified and extended into the romantic realm of the unrealized. Then, too, I couldn't stop thinking that I might well have been the unlucky passenger in the plane with Martin, a selfish retrospective fear that accentuated my distress. I even began to imagine that Cynthia's fate was perhaps a punishment for my own wrongdoing, a retribution that only I knew I had earned. I had never had a formal religion of any kind, yet I still believed in an all-powerful, all-seeing God, which was no doubt the early influence of a Catholic nurse making itself felt, whose explanation of why Christ had died on the cross was the only religious teaching that had left its mark on me. Even if the doctrine of original sin had always seemed unacceptable to me (as I had never really understood the exact nature of Adam and Eve's transgression), I nevertheless believed in a system of Divine Book-keeping that exacted payment for wrongdoing from all of mankind.

I remember that Jake had come down from Berkeley for the Thanksgiving weekend, and although I had a fairly good idea of what his opinions might be, I decided to discuss my problem with him. I was probably looking for comfort more than anything else, but that was something I would never have admitted to myself. He must have sensed that I was seriously troubled, because for once he didn't laugh at me. Instead he began to pace the floor of my room, puffing thoughtfully on an Egyptian cigarette, the brand he favored at that period in his life. "You mean to say, Carl, that you still believe in God?" he asked incredulously.

"I don't believe in an old man with gray hair who sits in heaven and passes judgment on mankind," I told him, "but I do believe that a God exists somewhere. . . ."

"And you think He punishes sinners, and rewards those who live by His law?"

"Yeah, I guess so."

"But then, how do you explain the condition the world is in?" he asked exasperatedly. "How can there be a God if Hitler is allowed to exist? Not to mention what's going on in Spain and China. And where was He during the World War? I mean, if you believe in Him, then quite logically it follows that he must have consented to the slaughter, just as He puts up with everything else that's going on. And what about the past, the centuries of suffering mankind has had to endure? The Hundred Years' War and the Inquisition, and the Crusades, even. . . . You mean to say that was all a part of His Divine Will?" He shook his head as he paced up and down in front of me. "I can't accept that," he went on, sounding very much like a professor. "It's all a myth, don't you see? Man invented religion because he couldn't explain why we're here on this earth, and because he had to have some answer to the question of what happens to us when we die. The invention was useful in the beginning, beneficial even, because it helped people to distinguish between right and wrong, and comforted them when their lives were miserable and without hope. But it's one of man's inventions, just the same."

"Then you don't believe Christ ever lived?"

"I didn't say that. I believe he lived, but I don't believe that he was the son of God. He was a genius, a great man trying to teach people to love each other . . . and because he was a man of his time, he reinforced his teaching with mysticism . . . or rather, the mysticism was invented after he was crucified. But I don't believe in the resurrection, that Christ went up to join God the Father in heaven. Why should I? Only because I can't accept the idea that there's nothing after death?" He shook his head. "I believe in mankind," he said, "and in the continuing struggle of the inhabitants of this planet who are trying to improve life as it exists in their time. That's enough for me. . . . And I want to contribute to whatever progress they are trying to make. Isn't that nobler than just hoping to corner a little private place for myself in eternity? Isn't that better than the egotistical notion that my eternal soul will never die?"

I didn't answer him. I admired him for his courage, and I suspected that he was right, just as he had been right about the mechanics of procreation, and that Lancelot had had an affair with the Queen. Yet I wasn't prepared to accept that once I was dead everything was over and done with, that Cynthia was gone forever merely because of some harsh quirk of fate. There must be more to it than that, I thought. I couldn't believe that we had been born merely to die. And how could the world be as beautiful as it was if no one had created it?

"You don't believe me, do you?" Jake asked.

"Mother believes in God," I said.

"Mother is a product of another time," Jake replied impatiently. "She was educated differently than we were. Anyway, what brought all this on?"

I swore him to secrecy and told him what had happened. He was impressed, I could tell, because I noticed that he looked at me with new interest, as if he for the first time realized that I was more than just his tennis-playing kid brother. "You mean, you wanted to learn to fly in order to go and fight in Spain?" he asked.

"Well, not exactly. I sort of got roped into it."

"Boy, would Mother be upset if she knew," he said after I told him a carefully doctored version of the story.

"You promised that you wouldn't say anything," I reminded him.

"I won't," he assured me. "But still . . . I would like to convince you that direct action isn't the answer. If you want to take part in the struggle against fascism, you should join an organized political party . . . otherwise your actions will be meaningless. Because there's not going to be a war. The ruling classes of England and France are in league with Hitler. Only the revolution of the proletariat will finally destroy fascism."

He was off again. It seemed to me that he was brilliantly intelligent up to a certain point, and then became blinded by his own beliefs. I told him so, and surprisingly enough he did not get angry, but merely shrugged, more interested in my problems for once. "This girl who was killed . . ." he asked. "She was just an acquaintance, wasn't she? I mean, you weren't in love with her?"

"No, I wasn't in love with her."

"I didn't think so. You're involved with someone else, aren't you?"

"I'm not involved with anyone," I lied.

He lit a fresh cigarette and said: "Well, that's not what Mother thinks."

His remark caught me off guard. "Why? What did she say?" I asked too quickly.

"Nothing. I don't know. What difference does it make, anyway? It's your life, not hers."

"I'd like to know."

"She didn't say anything specific. She just intimated that you're involved with someone a lot older than you are, and that's why you're unhappy."

"I'm not unhappy. . . ."

"All right, then, let's forget it. If you're not unhappy, then everything's O.K." He smiled his old, slightly superior smile, which I found just as irritating as I had in the past. "You're seventeen years old," he went on. "Not that that makes you a man, but still, the time has almost come when you've got to make up your own mind about those things. Anyway, you know what Mother's like. She'd never interfere with your love life. Of course, taking flying lessons is something else again."

"I only went up once, that's all."

"Well, I don't think you should do it again," he said. "Mother's got enough worries of her own, without your contributing a few more. If you've decided to be another Eddie Rickenbacker, you'd better wait until you're twenty-one." He hadn't changed, I realized, even though he had given up trying to convert me. He still looked upon me as an immature younger brother who needed to be lectured to, but who really couldn't be taken too seriously.

I didn't really care. What worried me much more was what he had said about my mother. It made me realize how completely oblivious I had been of her problems. I had suspected for some time that she was lonely, but I had no idea that there was any more serious reason for her loneliness than my father's absence. I had always taken at face value the explanation that it was his work that was keeping him abroad. But in referring to "her troubles," Jake had insinuated that there was more to it than just that.

"What kind of problems does Mother have?" I asked guardedly.

Jake shrugged. "Every kind," he replied. "It's not easy for her, living by herself like this. . . ."

"I'm here."

"You sleep here, but that's about all," he said. "Not that I blame you. Everybody has his own life to live."

"Do you think Father will be coming back for Christmas, and then she won't be so lonely," I said hopefully.

"I doubt that," he said.

"Did she write you that he wasn't?"

"No, but she prepared the ground, if you know what I mean. She said that he might be going to Vienna, while it's still possible to go. He wants to see Tante Liesel . . . and Grandfather's not getting any younger, you know."

"Is Tante Liesel still in Vienna . . . ?"

"Of course she is. They all are. Where do you expect them to be? It takes money to emigrate. And Grandfather's an old man, who's set in his ways. He could sell the factory, but only at a great loss. And then where would Uncle Leo find a job?"

How remote and unreal it all seemed. I could remember Uncle Leo only vaguely as a balding man with an enormous stomach, who had given me pony rides on his well-padded knees in Vienna a long time ago. I couldn't even recall his last name, knew only that he had married my father's sister and had gone to work in the modest furniture factory my grandfather owned. "They should get out," I said.

"Sure they should. And Mother's family should get out of Poland, too. But it's not that easy. Where can they go? You have to have a visa in order to get into the United States, and some sort of a guarantee of a job. So you can see that Mother has enough worries without your adding a few unnecessary ones."

"I only thought it would be a good idea to be prepared in case there's a war."

"There won't be a war," Jake said with finality. "Halifax and Chamberlain will see to that. They're the undertakers of Europe. They'll sell out Spain, just as they sold out Ethiopia, because they prefer fascism to any left-wing government. And that includes Blum, too, the traitor." It almost seemed as if he wanted the worst to happen, as if he enjoyed being the prophet of doom.

He continued, "That's why all private gestures such as your 'preparing' yourself by learning to fly are utterly useless," he said with finality.

I didn't agree. To me it was obviously better to prepare for the battles that were coming, just as Richard Gordon was doing. But he was his own master, and I was not. I was still an "adolescent," which word infuriated me, but nevertheless described my status. I had not as yet graduated from high school, had never earned a cent, and was still dependent on my mother for pocket money every week. The only "adult" part of my life was the clandestine love affair I was carrying on with the wife of a man I supposedly admired. That was undoubtedly why my chance meeting with Cynthia, and her accidental death, had taken on such an exaggerated importance in my mind. Wasn't it about time to start scrutinizing myself a little more realistically? Jake was undoubtedly right when he said that there was no God. I was just too cowardly to accept the facts, was precisely what he had accused me of being before returning to his beloved Berkeley, "a timorous agnostic." I was merely massaging my ego when I talked of joining the Americans fighting with the Abraham Lincoln Brigade and my own personal heroes, Hemingway and Malraux and Saint-Exupéry.

I would change, I decided resolutely, would learn to control my natural cowardice. There was no reason to believe that I couldn't learn to fly a plane. It was merely a question of willpower. I would also make an effort to straighten out my "private life," I decided, for despite my many doubts, I could not quite abandon the belief that the virtuous were more apt to receive protection from whatever Divine Power might exist than the immoral. I resolved to work hard and finish high school. And in order to make up for my past neglect, I would spend more time at home with my mother and less time with Pamela. It was a childish plan, a slightly less romantic daydream than any of the others, but I acted upon it.

My mother became aware of the change in me, and was baffled by my strange behavior. "What's the matter, Carl?" she asked. "Has something gone wrong? You seem so unhappy. You haven't played tennis for two weeks, and you've stayed home every Friday and Saturday night since Jake left. . . ."

"It only stopped raining yesterday," I replied. "The courts are still wet."

She smiled sadly. "You don't have to confide in me if you don't want to," she said. "I don't mean to pry into your affairs. I want to help, that's all. If I can, that is, and if you'll let me."

"There's nothing wrong, Mother," I said. "Please don't worry. . . ."

"I can't help worrying. . . . Because I love you." She smiled sadly. "You don't mind, do you?"

"Of course I don't," I said, feeling embarrassed. "But everything's all right. I promise you."

And so I sat with her in silence, listening to the news broadcasts before dinner, and did my homework in the living room, while she played records until it was time to go to bed. When I kissed her good night she held me briefly in her arms.

"I'm sorry that I worry so much," she said. "But I'm frightened. I know the war is coming, and I feel so helpless about you and Jake." I couldn't admit to her that I prayed every night that it might come soon. There was no use upsetting her needlessly.

The next day the weather was gray and cold, and then finally it cleared and was warm again, almost as if the spring had decided to appear four months early. Pamela called late in the afternoon. She sounded cheerful, although there was a slight overtone of reproach in her voice. "I haven't see you for ages," she said. "Have you been ill?"

"No, I'm all right."

"It's a lovely afternoon. We could play a set of singles if you like, and maybe go to the movies later."

"I've got a lot of work this term," I said. "I want to try to graduate in February."

"But is that a good idea?" she asked.

"I think so. I can take an exam in French and German, and get six years' credit if I pass."

"That sounds very ambitious," she said. "But why not work hard this afternoon, so you'll be free tonight. I could pick you up after dinner. . . ." Gordon was obviously going to play bridge, or working late at the studio.

"What time?"

"Around eight?"

I agreed, for in spite of all my resolutions, I was longing to see her.

≈ *two* ≈

THE HORN sounded twice outside the gate. I got up from the table, and my mother smiled and said: "Have a good time." I waited for her to tell me not to be late, that at my age it was still important to get a lot of sleep, but she controlled herself at once. "Have you got a key?" she asked.

"I don't need one. I can get in the back door."

"Well, don't wake Maureen," she said, holding on to me for an extra second. "And be happy. You have more than enough time to be sad." I straightened. "Give my best to the young lady," she added.

It was the first time she had given any indication that she knew where I was going, although she had obviously known for a long time. "I'll see you tomorrow afternoon," I said, and went out through the living room, where the silver coffee service was already waiting for us on the low wooden table in front of the fire. I felt badly about leaving, but there was no point in both of us being lonely together.

The night was very clear, with the stars far away and the smell of wet earth on the cold air, rather than the smell of the sea. I opened the door of the car, and it was like coming back after a long separation. In two weeks I had almost forgotten how beautiful she was and what it was like to desire her, knowing that she felt the same way. "I hardly recognize you," Pamela said. "It's like being kissed by a total stranger." She put the car in gear. "What do you want to do?" she asked. "Have you decided which movie you want to see?"

"I want to make love to you," I said. "The movies can wait."

She squeezed my hand. "You're very forward this evening. I approve." She turned left at the end of the street, heading for the coast highway instead of the town. "I brought the key to the beach house just on the off chance that you might have something like that in mind," she said. She was making fun of me, but I didn't mind. We drove to the cottage in silence, sitting close together like high-school students on a date.

"Are you sure it's all right to go to the beach house?" I asked.

"I'm sure. You're not frightened, are you?"

"No. Not at all."

"Then don't ask silly questions."

It was cold and damp inside the cottage. Pam kept her fur coat on until she had lit a fire in the bedroom fireplace and had turned on the electric heater in the bathroom. There were no sheets on the bed, but it didn't matter, as it was warmer lying between the woolen blankets while I was waiting for her. Then finally she appeared, and I could see that she had put her coat on over her naked body, and when she took it off and got into bed, it was almost a painful feeling holding her again. The flickering light from the fire lit her face, and her long blonde hair fell like a soft curtain over me, touching my shoulders and neck. "It's very cold in this room," she said. "I'm afraid I'm not very good at building fires. I was never in the Girl Guides, you see. . . ."

"It doesn't matter."

"It does to me."

But I wouldn't let her go. I held her, while she struggled halfheartedly to get free, my face pressed against her, wishing that I had five mouths to kiss her with. I pretended to myself that this was the last time we were going to make love, which I knew wasn't true. Yet I wanted to please her more than I ever had before, make certain that she was as dependent on me as I was on her. Then, once it was over, and we lay joined by the warmth of our bodies, with the familiar slapping of the shorebreak outside the windows, I knew that I had been deluding myself and that I would never be able to leave her of my own not-so-free will.

She put her hand on my chest. "Your heart pounds so," she said. "It frightens me. It sounds as if it might burst. Although I'm certain mine will give up long before yours."

"No, it won't," I said. I could see the future clearly in the calm of our released tensions, and I knew that there would never be anyone that I would love in the same way, that there would never be another body I would respond to as completely, and I put my hand out and touched her face, my fingers tracing the curve of her mouth and her nose and her cheeks, until she kissed my hand and pulled away from me.

When she came back from the bathroom and got into bed, she shivered, and I held her close, covering her with my body to make her warm. "That's the only good thing about not making love every day," she said. "When you do, it's better than it ever was before."

"The voice of experience."

"Don't be such a clot. Anyway, it was your fault that we didn't see each other last week. You didn't call."

"I wasn't sure you wanted me to."

"Don't be ridiculous. *You* didn't want to. Richard said that you were too upset to call . . . because of the girl who died in the crash."

It was part of the reason, but I hated him for having mentioned it. "Sure, I was depressed," I said. "It was a terrible thing to happen."

"Were you attracted to her? Be honest. There's nothing wrong if you were. It's absolutely normal."

I shook my head in the darkness. "She was a child," I said.

"Your age. . . ."

"Not really." I turned away and lay on my back, looking up at her familiar ceiling that was visible now because of the light from the bathroom. "I felt awful about it because she was so young . . . and a decent person. Much better than me."

"And you thought that if you could fall in love with her everything would be simpler. Isn't that true?"

"Not really."

"My poor darling," she said.

"I love *you*," I said. "And I always will."

"You don't have to say that."

"I know I don't."

She sat up, and turning, rested her body on mine, looking down at me with a strange expression on her face that I had never seen before, almost as if she were angry. "Well, true or not, it doesn't change anything, not about the way I feel, anyway. You're part of me, I've discovered, and I felt terrible when you didn't call, as if you'd deserted me, and I realized that if you *did* leave, it would hurt me more than it would hurt you, because I love you, Carl. It's the worst thing that could happen to me, I know, but there you are. Now, take me somewhere where I can get something to eat, because I can't live on love alone, no matter what they say."

We dressed in the semidarkness, for which I was grateful, for I didn't want her to see my face, knowing that she would read my thoughts and see that I was pleased in a way that she probably wouldn't like, as if I had won a victory, for her first confession of love was something I had wanted from the beginning, although I had always denied it.

She said that she knew a place where we could go and not have to worry about being seen. Then, while we drove back down the coast highway, she talked about Edwina and everything that had happened at the house, as if she wanted only to talk about things that had nothing to do with us, and not be reminded of what she had said in the darkness of the bedroom back at the cottage. I listened in silence while she went on to tell me that Andrea, despite his age, had decided to go back to Italy, and that Gordon was trying to dissuade him. "Richard thinks it's mad, because the war might well start in six months or a year, and then Andrea would be caught there. Of course, the old boy is frightened that if the war does begin he'll never see Italy again, and that he'll die out here, and be buried in one of those awful cemeteries, far away from his country and his relatives. He talks about nothing else now . . . except how he wants his flesh and bones to become a part of the Italian earth. Poor Andrea. It's terribly depressing for the rest of us."

"But doesn't he worry that he might not be able to come back here if there's a war? The Italians have signed a pact with the Nazis."

"He doesn't believe it. He says it's all propaganda that the newspapers have invented, and that in the end Italy will be on the side of the Allies, just as they were the last time. There's no use arguing with him. It's really rather pathetic," she said, and sighed. "Oh, how I hope that I'll never get to be that old. *Courte et bonne.* That's what life should be." She turned quickly off the highway, into a narrow street that wound its way into the hills above Castle Rock.

"Let's not end it all tonight, though," I said.

"All right. If you'd rather not." She smiled and slowed down a little. After a while we came to an old Spanish house that faced out onto the sea. There was a small electric sign over the gate, but that was the only thing that made it look like a restaurant.

"Have you ever been here before?" I asked.

"Yes, once . . . last summer. But you needn't worry . . . at this time of the year there isn't anyone." We stepped through a heavily curtained doorway, and were met by an elderly Mexican headwaiter in a frayed dinner jacket. "For two?" he asked.

Pamela nodded, and the man bowed slightly and indicated that we should follow him. We went down a narrow passageway, on the left of which were a number of small alcoves protected by red velvet drapes, so that it was possible to catch only a glimpse of the tables behind them. In the third alcove there was a dark-haired girl in a white dress, and seated across the table from her was Richard Gordon.

⚞ *three* ⚟

HE LOOKED UP as Pamela went by, and released the hand of the girl with him, which he had been holding. I could see the startled expression on his face, which changed almost at once into a smile as he recognized me. He started to say something, but obviously thought better of it, and I followed Pamela to the alcove beyond the one where Gordon was seated.

I noticed that she had taken her compact out of her handbag and was looking at herself in the mirror. "Well, that's a bit of a surprise," she said. She looked flushed, although she was very controlled in her movements. "If he asks, we've been to the beach house in order to see that everything was all right," she told me in a low voice.

A moment later Gordon had appeared at our table. "You're dining rather late, darling," he said. "And you've picked a strange restaurant to take this young man to."

Pamela's eyes met his gaze. "I might say the same thing to you," she replied. "Who's your friend?"

He laughed, seemingly not at all embarrassed. "An actress," he said. "I don't think you know her. She's in the film with me."

"Were you rehearsing your parts?"

"No, we've already done that."

"Well, then, have a good time."

"Are you sure that you don't want to join us?"

"I don't think we will," Pamela said. "But thank you for asking us."

"As you like." He bowed slightly, mocking himself as much as her, and disappeared. Neither one of us spoke. I was thinking only of the room in the cottage, wondering what it would look like to Gordon if he took it into his mind to go there once he had finished dinner. Suddenly Pamela got up from the table. "I don't want to stay here," she said.

I followed her out of the restaurant, making an effort not to glance to my right as I passed Gordon's table. The Mexican headwaiter looked confused, retreating in front of her as she approached. "Is something wrong, madame?" he asked. Pamela didn't reply.

"We'll be back," I said to console him, and hurried after her. But I had taken only a few steps when I heard Gordon's voice calling my name. I stopped, and he caught up with me.

"Do you mind," he said, resting his hand lightly on my shoulder, "but I think I'd better have a word with Pam." He didn't appear to be at all upset, was actually smiling, as if our encounter were a comic incident that he enjoyed. I watched him as he approached the car in which Pamela had taken refuge. She had just gotten in behind the wheel, and for a moment they seemed to be struggling with the door, as if she were trying to prevent his getting in beside her. Then she, too, must have realized the ridiculousness of the situation, for she released the door handle and made room for him on the front seat.

I stood there in the middle of the road, not knowing what to do, feeling like an idiot, a child who has been told to go upstairs so that the grown-ups can argue in peace, and trying to look as dignified as possible, I started up the road that ran past the restaurant. I walked very slowly, until I got to a place where the cliffs fell steeply away on the left-hand side of the macadam. There was a narrow cement curb that had been built high enough so that it would serve as a guard rail, and although the abrupt drop in front of me was disturbing, I sat down on the cold concrete and pretended to look out at the view. There was very little traffic on the coast highway, and the ocean beyond it was smooth, the red neon lights of a distant hamburger stand coloring the surface of the water.

I tried not to think about the scene that was taking place in the car at the bottom of the hill, as I knew there was nothing I could do about it. I tried to whistle, forgetting that whistling had never been one of my greatest accomplishments. I heard a car starting up the hill, and a few moments later Pamela stopped directly behind me. She rolled down her window as if nothing had happened and asked: "What are you doing there?"

"Waiting for you," I said. "What does it look like?" I went around the front of the car and got in beside her.

"Don't tell me *you're* in a bad mood?"

"Why? Is that not allowed?"

"Well, hardly tonight."

She was right, and yet I found that I was ill-tempered, as if what she had said to me earlier had meant nothing. Because that was what she was referring to, her confession, and the making love that had prompted it. I noticed that there were tears in her eyes and that she drove rather too quickly up the narrow road. "What happened?" I asked.

"It's none of your business."

"The hell it isn't."

We had reached the end of the paved road, and she stopped to see if there was enough room to turn the car around on the small dirt plateau on top of the ridge line. "It isn't," she said quite calmly, although she had obviously noticed that I had spoken to her in a way I had never spoken to her before. "What happened in the restaurant concerns only Richard and myself." She shifted from reverse into first gear, and stalled the engine. I leaned forward and turned off the ignition.

"Do you mean that?" I asked, feeling my empty stomach tightening inside me.

"I do."

We sat rigidly in the darkness, not hearing the noise of the crickets around us, not looking out at the string of lights that lay along the distant shore beyond the hood of the car. "You were jealous when you saw him with the girl in the restaurant," I said toughly.

"Don't be ridiculous."

"I could tell by the look on your face. That's why you didn't want to stay. . . ."

Her hand reached out for the ignition key, but I pulled it quickly out of the lock. "You were jealous. I know you were," I said, almost hating her. She was so calm and controlled. She turned away from me as if to get out of the car, but I grabbed her arm and pulled her back.

"Let go of me," she said, breaking free of my grasp. She was angry suddenly, uncontrollably angry.

I struck out at her with my open hand, not knowing why I wanted to strike her, acting out of frustration, as I had done so often with Jake. I felt the back of my hand come into contact with her nose, and appalled at what I had done, I tried at once to take her in my arms, tried to kiss her. She wrenched her head away. "Nobody can do that to me," she said, her anger making her voice sound strange and choked as she struggled against my embrace. "Let me go, you swine. . . ."

I relaxed my grip, and we sat next to each other, both of us short of breath, as if we had just finished making love, only there was a bitter taste in my mouth. "Pam, for God's sake . . . I don't know what made me do that. I'm sorry. I really am," I said, my apology sounding feeble and absurd.

"Give me the car keys," she said coldly.

"Pam . . . please. Forget what happened."

"If you don't give me the keys, I'll walk," she said, and got out of the car. I opened the door on my side and ran after her.

"Pam. Please. Listen to me. . . ." I took her by the arm. "Can't you put yourself in my place? I'm jealous of anybody who comes near you, and tonight, when for the first time I thought that you loved me in return, you suddenly turned to ice because you saw him sitting there with this girl. . . ."

"Because I said I loved you, you thought you had the right to hit me, is that it?"

"I didn't feel I had the right to do anything," I said. "You were excluding me, making me feel that I was an outsider, a kid who has to wait in the road until you'd finished with your grown-up conversation. And then when I asked you what had happened, you told me that it was none of my business!"

"You said that I was jealous."

"Because I wanted you to deny it; I don't know what you felt."

"Then you're just a bloody idiot," she said harshly. "I had to pretend something was wrong, didn't I? I couldn't just sit there with you and have dinner, with Richard in the next booth."

"Why not? Why couldn't you?"

"Because I'm married to him, and we don't have that kind of arrangement," she said. She stopped. "Look, give me the keys, and let's go home and not see each other for a while. Isn't that the best thing to do?"

"No. I want to settle this now. I want you to understand what made me do it."

"I understand," she said. "Hitting a person is the easiest way to deal with things you don't like. Well, I won't put up with it."

"It'll never happen again," I said. "I promise that it'll never happen again."

She seemed to hesitate, her eyes studying my face in the darkness. "All right. But I'd like to go home now."

"Kiss me."

"I don't feel like it," she said, touching her nose. "You hurt me."

"I didn't mean to. I don't know why, but when I get angry I seem to lose all control. When I was a kid and I fought with Jake, he always said I'd wind up in the penitentiary. . . ."

"He may be right."

"Don't say that . . . please."

"I don't like being hit."

"But it was an accident. I didn't mean to do it. Can't you try to forget it happened?"

"I don't know if I can," she said. "You hit Paul, too, I seem to remember."

"That was different. Please, Pam." I held her tightly in my arms, until finally she let me kiss her. But she didn't respond.

"Everything gets spoiled," she said. "I suppose it's my fault. I always forget that you're still a child." I released her, and she shivered suddenly. "I'm going to have a huge mark on my face," she said. "That'll look fine in the morning, won't it?"

We walked back to the car, and she turned on the interior light to study her face in the rear-view mirror. "Is it bad?" I asked.

"Bad enough. Nobody has ever hit me before."

"It'll never happen again."

"I hope not." She didn't sound convinced.

"Did he say anything about me?" I asked, as if I'd already been forgiven.

"No. . . ."

"What did you talk about?"

"Nothing to do with you, as I've already told you. He merely said that it was my fault that it had come to this, and that I had no right to complain."

"And what did you say?"

She shrugged. "I agreed with him."

"Then why were you gone for such a long time?"

"Because I didn't know where to find you, and I was upset, and so I just sat by myself for a while, thinking you'd come back. Then, when you didn't appear, I realized that you'd probably gone for a walk up the hill, and I came after you. That was my biggest mistake."

I could feel the blood rushing to my face, but I controlled my anger. "Then you can't forgive me for what I did?" I asked.

"I don't know . . . but I think we should go now."

"You're not hungry?"

"Not anymore."

I wanted to stay with her and talk and try to win her back, but she said that it was late and that it was no use talking any more. I sat beside her, feeling helpless and defeated, while she drove me home with both of her hands tightly clutching the wheel.

➤ *four* ➤

I COULDN'T SLEEP, thinking about what had happened, found myself remembering every detail of my unforgivable behavior, as if my brain, quite independent of my will, was continuing to search for a valid excuse for my actions. Only a madman or a bully was capable of striking a woman. In order to escape my thoughts, I got up and dressed. The first fog of winter had arrived in the early hours of the morning, providing me with a suitable background for my mood. I went down to the beach. The sand was wet, as if it had been raining. I took off my shoes and let a small wave wash up over my feet.

I felt depressed. Everything had gone wrong. Thinking about the past, I realized that I hadn't made an entry in my diary for a long time. Well, I had something to write now. "Last night I struck Pamela across the face!" That was an item that would make interesting reading in the years to come. Still, it was better to be honest and put it down on paper, as a safeguard against any convenient lapses of memory. And to make certain that it would never happen again. Yet I suspected that it might. That was what frightened me most of all.

Then it occurred to me that it would perhaps be better to write what had happened in the form of a short story, using the confessional "I," a more mundane version of Sherwood Anderson's "I'm a Fool." That would be a wiser course to follow, I thought, especially as I had lost the key to my diary. I could imagine the effect an account of my actions would have on Jake or Maureen, or my mother. If I wrote it as a short story I could easily pretend that it was all an invention, something I had written for my English class. And if it turned out well, I could show it to Pam, as an additional explanation of what had made me behave in such an abominable manner.

I hurried home, eager to get my story down on paper. Guy Boulard was standing in the living room. "Your mother invited me to lunch," he said. "You don't mind, I hope?"

"Not really."

I noticed that he had shaved off his moustache. I thought to myself: "He looks much improved, more like an American." We shook hands.

"*Comment tu vas?*" he asked.

"*Ça va,*" I replied curtly. "How about yourself?"

He smiled, somewhat smugly, I noted in my dark mood. "*Pour moi, ça va très bien,*" he told me. "Probably because I've given up the profession that was a source of so much of my misery. I am no longer a tutor of the progeny of the rich, you'll be glad to hear."

"What are you doing? Selling apples?"

He pursed his recently liberated mouth and looked more like a Frenchman again. "You know, the wisecrack has never been my favorite manifestation of the American spirit," he said. "Especially when it comes out of the mouths of the young. However, I'll answer your question. I am not selling apples. Far from it. I am working as a part-time 'personal' assistant to a famous movie producer. I act as his confidant and his secretary. During office hours I perform the latter function, while during meals, and on weekends, I merely keep him company and speak to him in French. . . ."

"You mean you're his tutor!"

He managed to grin. "I thought Jake was my enemy and that you were my friend," he said.

"I still am. I don't see anything wrong with being a tutor. It's better than being a secretary or a male companion."

"Well . . . if you say so."

"What about the French army? Have they called your class yet?"

He sighed, and lit a cigarette, and looked sad, although I sensed it was an artificial sadness. "They may have. . . . In any event, it no longer is of any concern to me. I've taken out my American citizenship."

"No kidding?" I was amazed. He had finally won a victory over his mother. Or perhaps she had seen the light. "That calls for a drink," I said. "What did Madame Boulard have to say?"

"She cast the deciding vote."

"Don't tell me she's decided to become a citizen too."

"No . . . she feels too old, she says, to change her allegiance. But she's glad I've taken the step." He ran his forefinger around the edge of his collar. "They were really after me," he said, grinning. "I could smell the hot breath of the gendarmes on my neck. I just couldn't face it," he added. "I couldn't face eighteen months of life in a barracks somewhere in Alsace-Lorraine, with only the war to look forward to. So if I have to fight, I'll fight for this country." He paused. "By the way, you know who I ran into this morning . . . Richard Gordon. It seems he goes to the same tailor as my boss. He was actually very friendly. Asked me to come by for tea tomorrow afternoon. And he said to be sure to bring you along."

My mother appeared at that moment, giving me time to consider my reply, for I was puzzled by Gordon's message. I hadn't required an invitation for tea on Sunday at Las Golondrinas for years. Why was he trying to make certain that I'd be there? Did he know more than he pretended to? My mother's voice interrupted my thoughts. "It would be nice if my son said good morning to me," she said good-naturedly. "He used to have such nice manners. I wonder what happened to them?"

"I used to click my heels and bow. Hitler put an end to that."

"America," Guy said.

"*Ne dis pas du mal de ton pays,*" I told him.

He grinned sheepishly. "Insolent, but grammatically correct. So I won't punish you."

"He's too old for that, anyway," my mother remarked. "Go and see if Maureen is ready for lunch, will you, darling?" She seemed in a better mood than I had seen her in for a long time. She looked better too, I thought, noticing that she was wearing a new blouse and skirt that suited her slender figure. That she had put it on in order to lunch with Guy astonished me. Was it possible that she found him attractive? That was something that had never occurred to me. Suddenly the memory of the car I had seen more than a year ago outside our gate in the middle of the night came back to me, but I dismissed the suspicion that had passed through my mind with an uncomfortable feeling of shame. Although, why shouldn't my mother have a love affair? She was a normal woman, and it would be unnatural if she lived completely cut off from men. "What she does is none of your goddamn business," I said to myself.

Yet I watched her more closely while we ate lunch, and found my suspicions dispelled almost at once. She seemed genuinely surprised when Guy told her that he had given up his French citizenship, which was a matter she would certainly have heard before if they were on more intimate terms. "Will you ever be able to go back to France?" my mother wanted to know from Guy.

"I think so," Boulard said, his naked upper lip clamping down hard on the lower half of his mouth. "I've notified the consulate of my decision, so I hardly think I'll be considered a deserter."

"Will Father be coming home for Christmas?" I heard myself asking. Was it the word "deserter" that had prompted my question? I wondered.

But my mother did not appear to be at all disconcerted. "No, I don't think so," she replied unhesitatingly. "I believe he's going to Vienna to see your grandfather and Tante Liesel. He'll be coming home in the spring, though. . . ."

Jake had been right. I felt momentarily resentful that he should be better informed, but then, I hadn't exactly shown a great interest in my own family of late.

"It's better to go to Europe now, while one still can," Guy said darkly.

We finished lunch and moved into the living room for coffee.

"Are you going to play tennis, or shall we all take a walk?" Guy asked. "I see the fog's lifted."

I told him that I didn't feel like tennis, nor like taking a walk. He suggested a drive up the beach, to which I agreed. My mother declined the invitation, saying that she had an important letter to write, which sounded vaguely ominous to me. But I put all of my suspicions out of my mind, and we set off, and we were once again professor and pupil.

"Forward, Candide and Panglos," Guy said, reading my mind. "It's not the best of all possible worlds, but it's the only one we've got."

And while we drove along the edge of the ocean, with the gray sky hanging low above us, he told me of his new job, giving me to understand that the rich, well-dressed, polo-playing producer who was his pupil now was an important man in "the industry," all of which was certain to work toward Guy's ultimate advantage. "If all goes well, I might even make a career in the movie business," he said, grinning.

"As an actor?"

"Oh, come on . . . although it would be funny if I were called upon to play a French lover opposite Edwina."

"Maybe you'd better start growing your moustache again."

He laughed good-naturedly. "You know, I find that the little respect you once had for me has been dissipated during my absence," he said. "Not that you had all that much while you were my charge." I was watching him, considering how I could best describe him if I were to write a story about him. "Are you listening to me, or are you off on one of your daydreams?" he asked.

"I'm listening to you."

"Well, I hope you'll watch your step at the Gordons' tomorrow. My new boss might be there. . . ."

"I'll be careful," I promised, "although I'm not sure I'll go." It would be better to stay home and work. There were so many stories I could write. It was probably easier to start with one that was not quite as painfully personal as the one I had attempted. Then I couldn't help thinking: "Perhaps Pamela will call while I'm gone! If the license plate of the next vehicle we pass ends in an even number, she's sure to call." I leaned forward in my seat, straining my eyes. It was an eight, but the car turned off into a service station as we pulled up alongside of it, making it a dubious signal from the powers above who controlled my destiny.

SHE HADN'T TELEPHONED by the time we got back. As it was Saturday night, Guy suggested that we go to the movies together, but I declined his invitation. There was always the chance that Pamela might still call, which was why I didn't want to make a date that would be difficult to get out of. I told Guy that I had to finish a term paper that was due on Monday, which prompted him to remark that I hadn't changed, that I still left everything to the last.

But nothing anyone might have said to me at that moment would have mattered. I felt physically ill, the unavoidable truth I hadn't wanted to face suddenly very clear. Pamela would never forgive me for what I had done. I had violated the unmentioned boundary of respect that had always existed between us. That was what had hurt her most of all. I had behaved like a child that exceeds the limits of a game with its elders in order to test their patience, I realized. Only I had been testing her love, for love, I thought, gave one the right to exceed all boundaries occasionally, as it presumes forgiveness for any mistake blindly made. That is, if it exists as a mutually recognized condition between two people.

But our relationship had turned out to be as one-sided as it had always been, despite the fact that she had confessed her feelings a few hours earlier, deciding to do so in order to finally answer all of my insistent declarations. Because she felt that it was high time. Or perhaps because she had truly felt a greater degree of affection for me at that moment. Which was why later she had found the need to go on quickly to other things, make conversation, and thus avoid the possibility of my questioning her. And sensing this, I had become more demanding in my attitude toward her life with Gordon, assuming there was nothing she should keep from me now that she had declared herself. That was the missing explanation I had been searching for, the hidden reason for my sudden violence, for when she had pulled away from me in the car, I had sensed that her actions were a denial of what she had said, almost as if she had regretted having gone that far, realizing too late that I was still a jealous adolescent, and that she was jeopardizing her marriage with a love affair that was hopeless and would never be anything else. It was obvious that she didn't love me, or why would she willingly prolong the torture of our enforced separation at this moment, as during all that day she could certainly have found an excuse to go to the telephone. Just to have called would have been enough. Just to have said, hello, how are you, are you coming over tomorrow? But she hadn't done so, which was proof she didn't really care.

I ate my dinner alone in the breakfast room, as Maureen didn't believe in using the dining room whenever my mother was invited out. It made me feel like a child again, a humiliation she might have spared me. But of course she didn't know what I was going through, or she wouldn't have insisted on serving me in the small, brightly lit room where Jake and I had always dined whenever there were guests. It was easier for her, a few steps less to carry the dishes, and she could chat with me through the open kitchen door. She was in a hurry to finish up, as she was going to a dance the Celtic Club she belonged to was giving that

Saturday night. Probably with the poultry man, who I suspected was her lover, as his car was parked outside our gate now. I had finally realized that it was his car I had seen early that morning when I had driven back from Las Golondrinas, and not Guy's. "Is Paddy taking you to the dance?" I asked.

"What business is it of yours?" she replied from the kitchen.

"I was just wondering."

"Do I ask to know who you're off with at night?" She appeared in the open doorway, a dish towel in her hand. "Of course, you can come along with us, if you want to," she said. "There's often a lot of young people your age at the dance."

"I'm going to work," I told her.

Which was my intention at that moment. But once I was seated at my table with the desk lamp casting a lonely circle of light around the typewriter I had borrowed from my mother's room, I knew that the deserted house would soon prove to be unbearable, and so I went downstairs again, to find Paddy in a tightly buttoned blue suit waiting in the kitchen. "Have you decided to come along?" he asked, his thick gray hair standing up steeply above his flushed face.

"No, I don't feel like going to a dance. But maybe you could drop me off in town at the movies."

"The Society's at Venice Pier tonight, at the Rose Ball Room," he said.

"I can go to the movies there," I told him.

"And how'll you get home? Walk?"

"I can take the bus. They run until midnight."

But I hadn't reckoned with the memories the pier would bring back, and that night the film was a Shirley Temple picture, which was the last thing in the world I wanted to see at that moment. So I walked up the broad esplanade, among the drunken sailors and their girls, past the Fun House, and the Hall of Mirrors, to the "Shoot the Chutes," and stood mournfully beside the glistening water of the tank, thinking about past happiness, watching the boats with their swarthy Mexican gondoliers and their cargoes of shrieking girls and sailors come sliding down into the circular basin. Painfully I recalled the feeling of Pamela's cool, naked hand in mine, and Karen begging to be allowed to go up again in order to experience the pleasant terror of the slide down the ramp. And when it had all become unbearably sad, I started back, avoiding the crowds by walking along the far side of the pier, behind the concessions, where all I could hear was the dark, murky sea washing up under the pilings.

I passed the carrousel, and crossing the boardwalk, started up into the town. There were groups of elderly people huddled together on the benches overlooking Muscle Beach, and a gray-haired woman with a shawl asked me what time it was in Yiddish. I told her that it was a quarter to ten, but she didn't seem to understand until I had repeated the word in German, which made her look at me with unconcealed curiosity. "You're a Deutscher?" she asked.

"No, I'm not," I told her, anxious to be on my way.

"But a Yid, no?"

I nodded, and went on, unwilling to be asked further questions, not because I was ashamed of sharing her destiny as a refugee, but because I was not in the mood for anything but my own sorrow. The small frame houses standing close together along the dried-up Grand Canal looked squalid and sad, and I almost regretted not having gone with Maureen and Paddy, to dance at the Celtic Ball with some wet-palmed creature I would never have to see again. At least I wouldn't have been forced to think so much about the past, the untortured, it seemed at that moment, past, which was all I felt I had left.

In the empty bus I decided I would go with Guy to the Gordons' the next day. That way I would be able to see Pam, and maybe in the pantry, or on the tennis court, I could ask once more for the forgiveness I so desired. She wouldn't be able to avoid me all afternoon. And even if she told me that forgiveness was impossible, it was better to hear it from her directly. If only the sun would come out, I could go earlier, pretending that I had come to play a set of singles before the other guests arrived. Please, God, make tomorrow a nice day, I heard myself praying as I made my way home from the station, pushing aside all the doubts about an all-powerful Being Jake had planted in my mind.

For once I found that my prayers were answered, although the appearance of the sun was of no immediate help, as I still had to wait for Guy to arrive. He arrived later than he had promised he would, so that there were already quite a few cars parked in the driveway of Las Golondrinas. The tennis court was occupied by Paul Hévesey and Edwina, who urged me to go and snare Pam for a game of mixed doubles. Guy stayed behind with them in the pavilion, while I made my way into the house through the kitchen entrance. A strange man in a white serving jacket glowered at me from the sink, but I paid no attention to him, and went out through the pantry into the dining room, where I found the table covered with bottles and glasses, and enough hors d'oeuvres to feed a hungry army. From the living room came the babble of voices, and I caught a glimpse of Guido and another servant in a white jacket moving among a dense crowd of guests. I wanted to turn around and flee to the safety of the tennis court, but Gordon had noticed my arrival. Above the general din I heard him say: *"Chérie, ton amant est là,"* as if the family joke still hadn't turned sour, despite everything that had happened.

Pam got up from the couch in front of the fireplace, where she had been hidden from view. I noticed that she was wearing a black dress with a deep décolleté, which aroused my immediate jealousy, as it seemed pointedly provocative. "If you've come to play tennis, you're much too late," she said, giving me her hand instead of offering me her cheeks to be kissed, as she would normally have done.

"I'm sorry, but I had to wait for Guy," I mumbled.

"It doesn't matter. Edwina's on the court with Paul, and I'm sure Billy would like to make a fourth."

I found myself staring at her face, noticing the slight swelling along the bridge of her nose, and I experienced the same feeling of shame that had come over me a second after I had committed my outrageous act. "I don't care if I don't play," I replied, but Lovat was already on his way across the room toward us, waving the half-eaten potato chip he held in his right hand.

"Come along," he said, taking me by the arm. "A bit of fresh air will do both of us a world of good. . . . And anyway, you're much too young for this sort of a do."

"I only wish *I* were," I heard Pamela say, which comforted me slightly. I changed together with Billy in the dressing room of the pavilion, where only recently, or so it seemed, I had put on the shirt Gordon had lent me that first afternoon. "We'll make old Paul work," Billy was saying. "He doesn't like to lose against you. I think he still remembers the black eye you gave him when you were a kid."

At least one person had noticed that I was no longer a child, I remarked to myself, but that wasn't enough to steady my nerves, and we lost handily despite putting on a wild display of power and speed. Paul and Billy occupied the shower first, and when I had finished dressing, there was not even Guy around to help me make my return appearance among the guests. I would wait there, I decided. Perhaps Pamela would notice my absence and come looking for me.

She did finally, although it was almost dark by the time she appeared. "What in God's name are you doing here?" she asked, as she came slowly down the steps, so as to make sure that she didn't fall.

"Waiting for you," I told her. The truth was obvious, so why try to lie.

"But aren't you frozen?" she asked, shivering.

"I'm all right." I had noticed that she had made no move toward me, although we were alone in the place where we had so often furtively kissed. "I can see that I haven't been forgiven," I said, not intending to express the self-pity I felt, but blundering into it despite all of my resolution.

"Please, let's not start that again."

"I want to know. . . ."

She looked exasperated, understandably so, I realize now. "I just don't want any more scenes," she said.

"There won't be any more, I promise."

"All right. Then come in and act like a normal person."

"I'll try."

She smiled, making me realize that my sad face in the darkness appeared more comic than tragic. "And try not to expose your broken heart for all the world to see, darling," she said, touching my cheek. "My God, you are frozen. How silly you are, Carl, sitting out here by yourself for hours. Go in through the kitchen now, or everyone will notice that we've both been missing at the same time."

I caught her wrist and pulled her to me, the scent she wore and her cool cheeks a painful reminder of everything I was about to lose. "Isn't there anything I can do to make you forget what happened?"

"I'll forget in time," she said. "I can't kiss you, because I'll smear my lipstick."

"You don't want to kiss me. . . ."

"Of course, I do. Please, Carl, let me go."

"You've changed. You don't love me anymore."

"You mustn't say that."

"Because you never really did; is that why?"

"No, because you mustn't ever say that to anyone. It's demeaning."

"I don't care what it is," I said. "It's what I feel. I can't play games, or pretend. You can, perhaps. . . ."

"You promised there wouldn't be any more scenes."

"I know I did. . . ."

"Then behave normally. . . ."

"What do you consider normal? Not really caring about anything?"

"Carl, please. You frighten me when you're like this. You're so violent, and aggressive. I'm almost afraid you're going to hit me again. . . ."

I released her. "I'll kill myself first before I do that," I said.

"Don't say things like that."

"Don't you tell me what to say!"

We stood facing each other, more estranged than ever. From inside the house came the distant sound of a record someone had put on the Capehart. "I have to go," she whispered. "Don't hate me, Carl. Please. I can see the hatred in your eyes." She turned and went up the steps, leaving me behind in the pavilion. I heard her stop on the top landing. "You're coming, aren't you?" she asked.

"Of course. I wouldn't want to spoil your party," I said testily, and with my hands cold and wet, I followed her into the house. In the dining-room mirror I could see that my face was pale and drawn. I took a glass of champagne from the table and drank it all. Then, with the warmth returning to my face and hands, I went in to mingle with the guests. The Wilsons were there, and the Bennetts, all of them eager to tell me that I'd grown so much since our last meeting that they could hardly recognize me. I moved on in order to avoid their compliments, and stood near the fireplace, where there was no one I knew. A slim woman with short, very blonde hair joined me. "I'm Terry Sangster," she said, offering me an equally cold, damp hand. "I've heard a lot about you. You're the wife-fixer, aren't you?"

She had obviously had too much to drink. "I'm afraid I don't understand," I said rather stiffly.

"Oh, you don't have to pretend with me," she replied, laughing. "And don't, for God's sake, put on an act of injured innocence. I want to be friends." She sipped her highball, her eyes on my face. "See that man over there," she said, pointing with her little finger. "That's my husband. He's a writer. Very famous, very successful. Avoid him like the plague. He's a terrible bore. Much older than you and me." She swung her body around to face me. "It's a shame I don't play tennis," she said, "but I do other things. I ride and I swim . . . and I used to do a lot of ice-skating, believe it or not."

"I used to skate too," I said, glad to find myself on safer ground.

"Well, then, I'll call you, and we can go together. What's your number?"

I told her rather reluctantly, and she wrote it down on a paper napkin with her lipstick. "I still go to school," I added, as a warning.

"You do? So do I. Phil's idea. He thinks I haven't got enough culture for a writer's wife. You see what I mean? But then, he shouldn't have married a showgirl, should he? He should have married some dark, hairy thing if he wanted brilliant conversation." She chuckled happily. "I shock you, don't I? That's because I'm just a little bit high. I'm not always like this." She sipped more of her drink, as if it were perhaps an antidote. "Now, why are those two coming over here to bother us?" she asked. "The young one looks like a drip, and I know the other one is a dirty old man."

"That's my former tutor," I explained, "and his new boss. I think he wants me to meet him."

"I'd better go, then," she said. But she turned to face me again before Guy had arrived. "You had a tutor?" she asked with mock pity. "You poor boy. We'll have to make up for that somehow." She winked broadly and fled.

Guy was smiling self-consciously as he introduced me to Mr. Levin. "*Mon ancien élève*, Carl Woolf," he said.

Levin had a deceptively firm handshake, the result of playing golf, no doubt, for he was a small man, given to fat. He wore a pale pink shirt with a blue polka-dot tie which looked admirably neat inside his double-breasted blazer. "I'm pleased to meet you," he said in a deep, well-modulated voice. His eyes were elsewhere, however, as if he were searching for an old friend in the crowd behind me. "Guy said he might bring you to the studio someday, when you've finished school."

It was the first I'd heard of the plan, but I managed to say that I'd be most pleased to come. Mr. Levin was already moving on to another part of the room before I finished the phrase. Guy patted me reassuringly on the shoulder and followed his new boss through the crowd. An instant later Mrs. Sangster reappeared, pretending to skate the last few steps. "My, how that little man's hair shines," she said. "A girl would need dark glasses if she had to talk to him any length of time."

I observed that her skin was smoothly tanned and that she appeared to be much prettier than on our first encounter. Her even teeth shone invitingly inside her delicately painted mouth. "Have you met him before?" I asked.

She nodded. "Lots of times," she said. "Phil, my husband, that is, worked for him last year, and we were invited to endless dinners where I had to dance with the little bastard." She giggled. "You'll have to get used to my language," she added. "The chorus, as Phil says, has left its mark on me."

"It doesn't bother *me*," I said. She was friendlier than anyone there, especially Mr. Levin, who was standing next to Pam a short distance away, looking down the front of her dress. Pam's glance met mine for an instant, and she raised her eyebrows slightly, making a silent comment on Mrs. Sangster. I looked away and smiled pointedly at the well-formed face in front of me, hoping that I could make Pam jealous, which I realized was not even vaguely possible anymore.

"I wish I was in New York," Mrs. Sangster said. "Right now. This very minute."

"I guess I'm not very good company," I mumbled.

"Oh, not because of you, ducky," she said, and I was grateful that she grasped my arm. "I wish we were both in New York, instead of this lousy town. You've never been, have you? Well, I could show you a thing or two. But I guess we'll have to go skating instead." She finished her drink, and insisted on taking me with her to the dining room, where she said she felt sure there was another drink waiting for her.

SIX

HER FACE, at times, was capable of an expression of such gaiety (although Pamela always said she had a vacuous look) that it is difficult for me to believe, even now, that she would wind up taking her own life. That was later, after I had lost touch with her, after the war, which changed so many things. I remember reading about her death in a Paris newspaper, and experiencing a feeling of disbelief that she could have been driven to such despair, making it impossible for her to laugh at whatever misfortune it was that had come her way. I felt sad, and wished, as everyone does on those occasions, that I had behaved differently with her. I saw her face again, as it had looked the first time when we went skating together, her tanned skin slightly flushed as she moved gracefully backward along the edge of the artificial rink; and her sad end, alone in a car in the garage of her house, seemed like a false invention someone had tacked onto her life, a pretentious screenwriter, perhaps, like her husband.

"You know how I learned to skate?" she asked, catching the curved wooden barrier that separated the ice from the stands of the old Palladium. "I was out of work for a change, and I heard somewhere they were looking for girls for a Sonja Henie musical, and because they were paying ninety dollars a week, I told the casting director I was an expert skater. . . . I had to, otherwise I wouldn't have gotten the job." She giggled nostalgically. "Luckily it turned out that I wasn't the only one who'd lied . . . only about six kids out of the forty who reported for work had ever had skates on their feet. So they taught us, because there wasn't anything else they could do. Come on, put your arm around my waist, dummy, and keep in step."

We circled the rink, while "The Blue Danube Waltz" poured out of the public-address system. "I'm not very good at keeping the time," I said apologetically.

"You don't say? And I thought all Austrians knew how to waltz."

"I'm not an Austrian."

"You're not? Then I want my money back!"

It didn't rankle when she made fun of me, and I was glad that she had telephoned, as she had promised she would. "My father says that the false notion of Austrian charm, and everything that goes with it, is one of the things he's hated most all of his life."

"And what do you say?"

She surprised me by her irreverence, which I later learned spared nothing she encountered. I tripped over the tip of my left skate, and regained my balance. "I agree with him," I said.

"Why? Because he's your dad? I never agreed much with mine, the old bastard!"

I said: "No, that's not why. But let's not go into it."

"You mean because of Hitler? Well, as I always say, Hitler, Schmitler . . . *sei gesund*." She grinned, blinking her eyes. "Not bad for a *schickse*, eh? Come on, I'll buy you a Coke, because you've been a good boy."

"What are you going to have?"

"None of your damn business."

But she had a Coke too, making a face to express her disgust as she tasted the first swallow. "What do you say we get rid of these things on our feet," she said suddenly, "and go to the movies."

"It's too late."

"O.K., then let's go home and neck." She laughed impishly. "Don't look so petrified, sweetie," she said. "I was only foolin'. We'll take a walk in the hills . . . that is, if you'll carry me."

I answered: "Sure, why not," but Pamela's face was suddenly there, even as I said it. Walking in the hills was somehow connected with her, as was everything to do with enjoying nature. "You'd better get over that," I warned myself. I hadn't heard from her since the Sunday evening, and it was now Friday.

"But first I'm going to the ladies' room," Terry said, camping outrageously, "and then I'll meet you in the foyer."

I watched her go, swinging her hips as she crossed the splintered wooden floor of the bar, walking on the full blades of her skates, clowning for my benefit. It didn't go well with her lovely face and her slight figure, but I didn't say anything. I didn't know her well enough at the time.

We drove up one of the canyons and stopped in a vacant lot under a sycamore tree. The night was clear and cold. Terry shivered inside her camel-hair coat. "Good God, it's freezing," she said. "We should have brought our skates." She took a firm hold on my arm, and we started up the deserted road. "Now, tell me about yourself, young man," she said facetiously. "When did you first decide to go into show business?"

"You're never serious, are you, Ter?"

"Sure I am, but then I'm a bore. Anyway, don't call me 'Ter.' If you don't like 'Terry,' call me 'Teresa,' and if you don't like that, call me 'honey,' or 'lamb,' or 'sweetie-pie,' or anything else that comes into your tiny head." We walked on, following the winding road, leaving the sycamore trees and the dark hills behind us. "How far do I have to go before you make up your mind to kiss me?" she asked.

"I don't know. A little farther." I discovered that I felt less unhappy than I had for quite a while. "You know, when we first met, you said something that bothered me. Remember what it was?"

She laughed, tightening her hold on my arm. "You mean that crack I made about your being a wife-fixer? I don't know why I said that . . . maybe because I'd heard some gossip about you and Lady Pamela, or just because I was a little tipsy and had to say something. But don't worry. . . . Now that I know you, I'm sure none of that's true. Because you're the most innocent character I've ever met. How old are you, anyway, honey, eighteen?"

"Not quite."

"Well, I wish I'd been as pure and starry-eyed when *I* was eighteen. I was working in some crummy club on the East Side by that time, dodging all the cheap mobsters that used to hang out around the joint. I got married the first time when I was sixteen. How about that? But it didn't take. My fella turned out to be a fag. That was bad luck, wasn't it? I tried again when I was twenty . . . because I admired Mr. Sangster's superior mentality. Boy, what a drag." She breathed deeply. "Well, there you have my life story. You'd *better* kiss me now!"

Her mouth was different from the mouth I was used to, as was her scent. "Do you want to turn back?" I asked.

"You mean go back to my place? Why, sure."

"I didn't mean that."

"You didn't? Aw, gee. . . ." She was making fun of herself as well as me. "You don't have to worry, you know," she said quickly. "There's nobody home. He's in Palm Springs with his boss, or that's what he told me, anyway. Come and have a drink. I won't bite you. Not hard, anyway," she aded, laughing.

Her house was in the next canyon, a rambling one-story structure built in the style that was known as "modern" at the time. She led me through the living room, which I found to be large and overheated, into a small study that she said was hers. There was a half-decorated Christmas tree on a small table, and a record player, which stood precariously on the arm of a couch that was littered with records. "He doesn't believe in Christmas, so this is the only place I'm allowed to have a tree," she explained. "Are you going to have another Coke, or d'you want something else?" she asked.

"A Coke's fine."

She left, and I wandered nervously among her private possessions—a huge rag doll that was propped up in an armchair, and a leather-bound book of clippings she had saved during her brief career. I was looking through it when she returned carrying a wooden Mexican tray with our two drinks, her Scotch and soda, and my Coke. "I wasn't bad, was I?" she said, looking over my shoulder. "I made quite a hit in that costume. A French count wanted to marry me, or so he told me one night when he was oiled. But he was forty, can you imagine? Forty! I'd as soon have married my uncle Oscar. So I said, *non mercee*." She closed the book on my hand. "Enough of that, honey." She raised her glass. "Here's to us." She continued, "Two livin' dolls." She took a sip of her Scotch and soda. "He wasn't really a count . . . and he was nothing as nice as you," she said, putting her arms around my neck, and I kissed her dutifully. "Don't spill Coke on the rug, baby," she warned. "It stains."

I found a place for my glass on the table near the exiled Christmas tree. "I like you, Terry," I said, sounding stiff and insincere.

"You do? Honest Injun?" She giggled happily. "Then it's not just physical?"

"Of course not."

"My, you're polite. You're the politest fella I ever met. And just for that I'm going to take you to bed with me." She took my hand. "You can bring your Coke if you're still thirsty." She led me through a bathroom and on into an adjoining bedroom where there was a double bed covered with a beige fur blanket. "Wait here," she told me, and disappeared. After a few minutes there was a muffled sound of a jazz quintet that I discovered came from a small speaker near the bed. I made an effort to listen, and tried to keep my mind blank. I wanted to say something that might win me a little time, but when she came back into the room, she crossed the floor too quickly for protest, the white negligee she had put on for my benefit revealing a frilled pair of underpants and a lace bra. We kissed with desperation. I sensed a mutual fear, which, although it was never to be confessed, helped make me feel braver.

"You're very beautiful, you know," I said. The skin on her stomach was smooth and tanned.

"No, I'm not. I'm flat on top, I warn you, and I'm not in as good shape as you are. But girls are supposed to be soft, aren't they?"

I pulled off my shirt and trousers and took her in my arms. "I can feel your heart beating," I told her, realizing that I was unfaithful even in my words.

"That's good," she said, and laughed softly. "Please take off my panties for me. I can't reach them. And don't tear them. They're expensive." I felt ill at ease helping her undress. Yet, once she had wound her legs around me, my heart seemed to slow up inside me. She unbuttoned my shorts and pressed the lower part of her body against mine. "You'll wait for me, won't you?" she whispered. "Because sometimes I'm a little slow off the mark."

I nodded, embarrassed. I was used to most things being left unsaid. When I opened my eyes in order to push the picture of Pamela's face out of my mind, I discovered that Terry was indeed very "flat on top," just as she had said, but her skin was soft, and her girlish body well formed. Yet I felt less desire than I did with Pamela, so that the act of love was prolonged, and finally fierce, which seemed to excite her more. She pulled her mouth away from mine for an instant. "Fuck me," she whispered. "Don't stop. . . ." The words sounded raw, and disturbed, I turned my head in order to look at her. Her eyes were tightly closed, and I noticed that she had been crying. "What's the matter?" I asked.

"Nothing, darling. Nothing. I'm happy, that's all."

But she didn't look happy. I had no idea whether I had satisfied her or not, but I found that it didn't matter to me. She touched my forehead with her cool hand and kissed my cheeks. "It's hot in here," I said, my voice sounding strange to me above the music that was still playing.

"I don't find it hot. It's nice."

I felt a strong desire to get up and take a shower.

"Maybe we should open a window," I suggested.

"All right . . . if you like." She got up out of bed and crossed the thick carpet on her toes. "Don't go away," she said. "I'll be back." I lay on my stomach on the fur rug. After a while she reappeared, wearing her negligee. She sat down on the edge of the bed. "You want to go, don't you? You're restless. I can tell."

"Maybe I'd better get dressed."

"There's no hurry, for God's sake. . . ."

But I got up and put on my shorts. Then I sat down beside her on the bed. "You all right?" I asked, not knowing what else to say. I felt empty.

"I'm fine. Why shouldn't I be?"

"I thought you were upset a little while back."

"I wasn't. Don't be silly."

"But you cried."

"What's wrong with that? Haven't you ever made anyone cry before?"

"No, I guess not."

"Well, you've been going around with the wrong kind of people, dummy." She caught hold of my hand and kissed it. "Come on. You want to be off. I know it," she said. "There's a clean blue towel on the edge of the tub, so take a shower, or do whatever you want to do, and I'll buy you something to eat."

We went to a drive-in on the boulevard at the mouth of the canyon where she lived and ate deviled-egg sandwiches and drank lime Cokes through cardboard straws. Then we drove back to the beach and stopped near the public park above the palisades. "I'll walk home from here," I told her.

"All right. If you think that's better."

I kissed her on both cheeks, avoiding her painted mouth. "I'll call you tomorrow," I promised.

"I can call you, if that's easier." She held on to my arm as I started to get out of the car. "You won't talk, will you, baby?" she said. "I mean, to your pals. Because that wouldn't be such a good idea."

"What do you think I am?"

"I'm sorry I asked." She leaned forward and kissed me on the cheek, without clowning for once. "Sleep well, sweetheart," she said, and drove off. I felt relieved to be alone.

The lights were on in the living room, I noticed as I let myself in through the gate. I went down the driveway and into the house through the back door. On the kitchen table there was a message from Maureen, saying that Mrs. Gordon had called after I had gone out. I reread it twice. Why couldn't she have called earlier, I thought angrily. At that moment Jake appeared from the breakfast room. "Well, this is a fine time for a red-blooded American boy to be coming home," he said, grinning.

"When did *you* arrive?" I asked, disconcerted.

"About half an hour ago. I drove down with some friends, and their car didn't quite make it. We had to hitchhike from San Luis Obispo. Come in and meet them." He took two bottles of beer out of the icebox, and I followed him into the living room. Marcia was seated on the floor next to the radio, and standing beside her was a young man with unruly dark hair, dressed in a heavy black leather jacket. "This is Bart Hecklin," Jake said. "My brother, Carl, the aristocrat."

Hecklin smiled, and we shook hands. He had thick, work-hardened fingers and a strong grip. Marcia waved from the floor. "Been to the movies?" she asked. "What did you see?" She was trying to be friendly, although she made sure that the effort was thinly concealed.

"I left early," I said. It would have been impossible to admit that I had been ice-skating. "It was a soap opera, starring Shirley Temple. . . . What happened to your car?"

"Just about everything," Hecklin replied. "T.B., high blood pressure, pleurisy. All the diseases of poverty and old age. They're going to try to fix it," he added, "and I'm going to try to raise the money to pay them."

"Why not sell it to Japan as scrap iron?" Jake suggested.

"That's not a bad idea," Hecklin said. "They need all the hard metal they can get."

Marcia made a motion with her hand, asking them to be quiet. The commentator's voice was being partially drowned out by static. I stood listening for an instant. He was discussing the international implications of the Panay Incident, which had occupied the front pages of all the newspapers for the last few days. "What's the loss of a gunboat between friends?" Hecklin said. "Believe me, nothing'll come of it." He took one of the bottles Jake was holding, and drank from it. "We're not going to fight anybody that might someday help us in a war against the Soviet Union."

They were all so sure of the infallibility of their own point of view. I excused myself and went upstairs. For once my own problems seemed more insoluble than those of the outside world. How could I face Pamela after what had happened? I examined my face in the bathroom mirror, and except for a trace of lipstick on my mouth, discovered that no great change had taken place.

But I had changed; I was so sure of it. I turned out the lights and got into bed, unable to suppress a feeling of disgust with myself. What we had done had nothing to do with love. Or desire, even. The word Terry had used had been the correct one, which was probably why it had disturbed me so at the time. It had been too accurately descriptive, too honest. "You think you're a lot better than you really are," I told myself. I longed for sleep, knowing that it was the only antidote, and fortunately, sleep came quickly that night.

⇒ *seven* ⇐

BUT MY DISGUST with myself didn't last. Instead I awoke the next morning remembering brief glimpses of Terry's body, with an undeniable longing that I couldn't explain to myself. I would have liked her to be there with me in my bed, in the cool of the early morning, to make up for whatever failings I had shown as a lover, and I was disappointed, surprisingly enough, when Maureen announced outside my door that "Mrs. Gordon wants to speek to you on the telephone." It was not pleasant to realize that my infidelity had gone that far, but I knew that talking to Terry would not involve recriminations of any kind, or even hurt feelings, which was certainly not true of any conversation I was about to have with Pamela.

My misgivings were justified an instant later. The familiar voice was more pointedly distant than ever. "Are you still in bed?" she asked.

"No, I'm up," I replied cheerfully.

"Of course you're up now," she said testily, "but you weren't when I called. You must have had a late night."

"Not really." I silently cursed Maureen for her lack of discretion, and wondered if some instinctive malice had not prompted it. There was a long pause, which was ultimately broken by Pamela.

"We must talk," she said, too calm. "We're going away to the mountains over Christmas, but when we come back I'd like to see you."

"I'll be here," I replied, secretly relieved that our meeting was thus postponed at her own request. "When are you off?"

"Oh, in a few days. Probably not before the end of the week. But I have all the Christmas shopping to do, and I'm sure you're busy too."

I had never been too busy to meet her whenever she wanted me to. I sensed that the game had gone too far, and that I was losing her. I felt helpless. I was standing in the breakfast room, with Maureen probably listening in the kitchen, and Jake about to appear at any moment. "I'm not busy," I managed to say. "There's no school next week."

"There isn't? Well, you *are* fortunate. Karen doesn't get out until Thursday." That was all. She had gained the upper hand again, and was conscious of it. I could tell by her voice. "I'll try to call you before we leave," she said.

"All right."

"You sound rather strange. You're not alone, I take it."

"No, I'm not."

"Well, then perhaps you'd better try to call me later sometime," she said, her voice almost friendly. "I'm usually home early in the afternoon."

"Yes, I remember," I said with mild sarcasm. I felt that I had to see her at least one more time. She was going away to a place I didn't know, and at once I visualized her in a romantic setting, a snow-covered mountain lodge full of elegant, wealthy people, where I was sure she was going to meet someone new. Despite everything that had happened, the small vengeance I had taken (which I knew was all that my making love to Terry had been), she had aroused all of my old feelings of jealousy and possessiveness merely by being distant, and although I knew that it was all probably pretense, I still couldn't control myself and play the game she was so expert at, and answer her with some vague, disinterested remark. "I'll call you later today," was all I managed to say.

"Not today. Today's Sunday," she said. "Call me tomorrow. Or Tuesday."

"All right, Tuesday," I replied, and hung up. It drove me crazy that I was unable to win even a skirmish in the struggle between us. For it was a struggle, I had realized by that time, a struggle, not a game. I wanted it to stop, and go back to the way it had been at the start. If only I could see her, I thought, and shout at her, or make love to her, or plead with her, then perhaps I could repair the breach between us. But that wasn't possible now, would probably never be possible again, and so, out of weakness, or desperation, I did the thing that was easiest for me to do— arranged to meet Terry when she called an hour or two later, ostensibly to go to the movies, although of course that was not where we wound up.

It was a gray, wintry afternoon, bleak and almost cold, threatening rain, and Terry closed the front door on it, locked out everything she didn't want to see, the "Sunday people," who, she said, always made her feel sad, "and the God-awful weather." Then, without much help from me, she lit a fire in the small study which was her domain, and we sat on the floor together, with the record player behind us on the couch, starting to make its way through the large collection of melancholy music she had collected over the years. After a long silence, during which we sat listening to the mechanical noises the machine made as it changed records, she suddenly altered the position of her body, pivoting neatly on the bottom of her black silk pajamas, put her head in my lap, and looked up at me with fluttering eyelids, which I knew by then was one of her favorite comic expressions. "You don't want to go to bed with me again, do you?" she asked, her face frozen in a wide-eyed look of expectancy. "I'm not your type, I guess, or it wasn't any good the first time."

"Sure, I want to."

She shook her head. "No, you don't," she insisted. "And I know why. You're carrying a torch big enough to light up the whole town. It's that English broad. She's giving you a rough time. I got the message the first day I met you." She grinned. "Well, that's what you get for going around with married women."

"I guess I'd better leave."

"Don't do that," she said, holding on to my legs. "Anyway, I'm different. I don't make anybody suffer. Maybe that's what's wrong with me? Also, I don't really work at being married, so you're O.K. on that score."

"What about that warning of yours last night, not to talk to any of my pals?"

"That was only for the sake of my reputation," she said, laughing. "I don't want to be known as a tart or an easy lay at Warren G. Harding High School. Funny thing is that I'm *not*, as a rule. It's you that has this bad effect on me. Because you're so damned reluctant. All you want to do is skate, or walk in the hills, or go to the movies, and that kind of attitude is enough to start me off. Kiss me, you idiot, will you please?" She held tightly on to the back of my neck, then suddenly let me go, as if something important had just occurred to her. "Anyway, it's never any good the first time," she said. "You, as a junior Casanova, ought to know that! Or was it wonderful right away with Lady Gordon?" She put her hand over my mouth. "No, don't tell me. I don't want to know."

"I wasn't going to say anything."

"You weren't. Good. Come here. Lie next to me, please."

"Don't you want to go into the bedroom?"

"No, I want to stay right here by the fire." She got up on her knees. "Don't go away now," she said, and hurried into the next room. She came back an instant later, bringing the fur blanket with her. "Why are you so nervous?" she asked. "Are you afraid somebody's going to ring the doorbell? Because you needn't be. I talked to Palm Springs ten minutes before you arrived, and all is well. It's sunny in the desert, and he's staying an extra day."

"I wasn't worried about that."

"You weren't? Well, I was. I'd hate to get caught *in flagrante*." She made the Latin word sound as American as possible, and I found myself laughing with her, despite the unpleasant picture her words had brought to my mind. And so we made love on the floor, partially dressed, and she didn't say anything to shock me, or cry, and when it was over, I felt a little less like getting up and going away. "Wasn't I right?" she asked, stroking my face. "You *were* happier this time, weren't you?"

"Yes."

"My God, a girl really has to work to get a kind word out of you. I didn't ask you to tell me that you loved me, or *liked* me even."

"I do like you, you know that."

"Thanks so much," she said, laughing. "For nothing. Although I had that coming to me. Now, listen . . . I'm not going to be able to see you for a few days, so while you're on your own, pal, I'd wish you'd try to cure your bleeding heart. Will you really try? Is that a promise? All right, then, I'll make you a melted-cheese sandwich. It's a specialty of the house."

We did finally go to the movies then, after she had fed me. She wanted to see *Camille*, and I agreed, provided we didn't have to stand in line. It was early in the evening, and so we got into the theater quite easily. Terry was looking forward to seeing Garbo, who was the only actress she admired, and she was impatient with the cartoons and the newsreels that preceded the feature. "We could have stood in bed another half-hour," she whispered in my ear while a Japanese destroyer slid across the screen, looking like some evil and rapacious fish.

"It doesn't hurt to know what's going on in the world," I told her.

She shrugged impatiently. "What's the use?" she said. "You can't do anything about it. So why bother?"

But the appearance of her idol soon calmed her, and she took my hand in the darkness, saying: "If I ever decide to cheat on you, it'll be with her. If I get the chance, that is." I withdrew my hand, and turned to look at her with surprise, which made her giggle happily. "I thought that'd shock you," she said. "Now, be a good boy and hush." She settled herself still lower in her chair. "Isn't she divine?" she asked in an awed whisper. It was not an opinion I could agree with at once, as I was still thinking about what she had said. I knew that it had been a joke, and yet I couldn't help wondering if, despite her ingenuous manner and all of her protestations to the contrary, she wasn't after something more exciting than making love with me on a Sunday afternoon.

However, I didn't pursue my doubts, for I was soon caught up in the atmosphere of the film. Its heavy romanticism brought me back at once to my own problems, as well as making me realize that the pretty girl sitting there beside me in the darkness was no more than a friend. Pamela was truly the only person I cared about. She was what she had always been, from the first moment on, my Madame de Renal, my Anna Karenina, my Catherine Barkley, for I had superimposed her face over that of every heroine I had read about after meeting her, and now in the hushed movie theater I found her face crowding Garbo's tragic features off the screen, disrupting my attention, so that I was soon confusing the complications of the film with the events of my own story, which egotism was ridiculous, I realized, but impossible to cure. As much as I wanted to, I couldn't dismiss Pam from my mind, and when Terry withdrew her hand in order to take a handkerchief out of her handbag so that she could wipe the tears from her eyes, I found myself sitting beside her remote and estranged, and far from tears, which, of course, was a condition she couldn't understand.

"Don't you even feel like crying one little bit?" she asked.

I shook my head regretfully, and reached out for her hand again, the comfort of which she seemed to require. Armand was a fool to let his father influence his opinion of Camille, I had decided by that time, just as I was being an idiot to let pride interfere with my relations with Pam. I would wind up losing her, that was all, and then be miserable for the rest of my life. I made up my mind that that wouldn't happen, that I would force her to see me. I would wait for her on the road to her house and make her take me along in her car, and if she failed to stop, then I would follow her home, even if that meant behaving like a character in an old-fashioned novel, the kind of thing Guy Boulard enjoyed reading. And once I had decided on my own plan of action, I felt better about everything, less distracted, quite happy to allow myself to be carried away by the sad ending of the movie.

The house lights came on, and Terry wiped her eyes and blew her nose noiselessly. "My God, that was sad," she said. "I could easily sit here and see it all over again."

"I couldn't," I confessed.

"But didn't you fall in love with her? Be honest. How can you bear to look at any other woman's face after that?"

"I have no choice," I answered glibly.

"Oh, you're a doll," she said sarcastically. "D'you want to come home and have a drink? I'll try to remember to cough once in a while, if that'll help."

"It's late, I'd better get back."

"Not that late, for Pete's sake. It's not even ten o'clock, and tomorrow's Sunday."

But I insisted, remembering that Pamela often went to buy flowers for the house on Sunday morning. "I've got to get up early," I explained. "I'm working on a term paper."

And so the next morning I set out on my bike, as I didn't dare wake my mother to ask permission to take the car. There was a heavy fog hanging over the crumbling cliffs above Castle Rock, and I felt doubtful about how long I would be able to stand waiting in the moist air. There was very little traffic, even though it was Sunday, and I had just decided to ride a little farther up the beach when I saw the familiar outline of the Ford convertible coming down the road.

But it was Edwina who was at the wheel of the car, and she waved to me and stopped on the verge of the road. I went over to her, trying desperately to think of an excuse for my being there, but my mind was blank. "Well, fancy meeting you here," she said. She was bundled up in a tweed overcoat, with a pale blue scarf around her head, the color obviously carefully selected to match her eyes. "You're still riding a bike, I see."

"Just getting a little exercise," I told her unconvincingly.

"Well, why not come along with me, then," she suggested. "I'm going to the Jonathan Club for a swim in the pool. It's much too cold to do anything out of doors."

"I haven't got a bathing suit, and there's no place to leave my bike."

She smiled acidly. *"Plus ça change, plus c'est la même chose,"* she said, sounding very pleased with herself. "I see you're still waiting for the better offer. Well, she'll be along in a while."

"I'll go with you tomorrow," I said, but she shook her head and put the car in gear.

"Who knows what I'll be doing tomorrow?" she said.

Laughing at me, then, she drove off, leaving me at the side of the road not knowing what to do. Now that Edwina had seen me, it was perhaps better to return home and forget about my plan. I got on my bike and started down the highway, cursing my luck. I was just riding past the lifeguard tower at State Beach when Pamela drew up alongside of me in Gordon's car.

➳ eight ➴

I FELT SHY in her presence, more so than I had for a long time. And it wasn't only because I had been unfaithful to her that I felt ill at ease. It was suddenly being confronted by her familiar face, the beauty of which caught me off guard, just as it always had in the past whenever I hadn't seen her for a while. Only this time the idea of losing her (the moment I saw her I always seemed to become aware of the possibility) was even more painful than before, so I abandoned my resolutions to tell her everything that had happened, admitting only that I had gone down to the beach that morning to meet her, as I knew that she often went to buy flowers on Sunday.

"That's exactly where I'm going, as a matter of fact," she said. "You can come with me if you like. Leave your bike here."

"Edwina came by in the Ford while I was waiting near Castle Rock," I told her, getting into the car.

She shrugged. "That doesn't matter," she said. "She's done all the harm she can." She put out her gloved hand, and we turned inland, through the sedate residential district that lay behind the palm-lined park on the palisades. The big houses on the left of the road, with their well-kept lawns, looked remote and uninhabited. "You've been rather busy, I take it," she said. "At least, you're never in when I call."

"I didn't expect you to, or else I'd have been home," I replied.

She made a face that suggested her disbelief. "I got the distinct impression that you didn't want to see me again," she said.

"That's what I thought about you."

"Really? Why?"

"The way you acted at the cocktail party. I was certain that you hadn't forgiven me."

"Is that why you flirted with Mrs. Sangster?"

"I didn't flirt with her."

"You mean she flirted with you?"

"She was kidding."

"Was she? Are you sure?"

We were starting to play the game again, the ridiculous game I despised, because it always ended in a quarrel. "You were pretty busy flirting on your own," I said.

"I never flirt," she replied. "I don't like it. It's a boring social habit, a complete waste of time."

"I agree with you."

We were approaching the Veterans' Hospital, with its flat green graveyards that bordered on the road, the endless rows of white crosses blurred now by the movement of the car. Pam turned left at the traffic light beyond the cemetery, and we drove along the edge of a huge field of poinsettias inside a high wire fence. She parked near the gate of the nursery, in front of the main greenhouse. "We'll have to find my little Japanese friend," she said. "I get on better with him than with his wife."

I followed her, thinking that she got on better with him because he liked to flirt with her, but I didn't say so. "I want to know if you've forgiven me?" I said, walking behind her. We were moving down a narrow lane, the scarlet fields of poinsettias on both sides of us, the noise of the distant traffic growing more distant with every step.

"I suppose I have," she said. "I didn't like your talking to Mrs. Sangster, though."

"I didn't like your talking to Mr. Levin," I replied childishly.

"Mr. Levin! You're joking, I hope. I was only trying to be civil, because he was my guest. Anyway, let's not bicker like husband and wife. It's a bore."

"All right. But you could have called earlier. You knew that it was difficult for me to call you. That's why I thought you weren't particularly anxious to see me again."

She turned to face me. "How childish you are sometimes," she said. "I wanted *you* to call. You could have invented any excuse, tennis or going to the movies. . . ."

"It was raining. How could I call you about tennis?"

"You're not very ingenious. You could have called me and asked me to play in case the rain stopped."

"I guess I'm not ingenious," I admitted. She had turned to face me, as she had come to the end of the lane, and wanted to start back.

"I wanted to see you, because I had something important to tell you," she said, "and then when you didn't call, I thought maybe it was better not to say anything."

"What was it?" I asked, but at that moment someone whistled, and we both saw the owner of the nursery, the Japanese gardener she "got on so well with," approaching in the distance. She waved to him as if he were an old friend.

"Later," she said in a low voice. "I'll tell you later," and hurried off to meet him.

And so I waited around while she bought a large bouquet of poinsettias with which the smiling Japanese filled the back of the car, the scarlet leaves protruding from inside their paper wrappings, looking even more scarlet against the black leather; I waited some more while she bought two plants for the house, and her admirer gave her three yellow roses as a present, which made his plump, disheveled wife scowl slightly, waited, as I had done for years in all the markets and flower shops, feeling certain that every man who served her was secretly in love with her. Then, when we were finally alone again, driving back in the direction of the beach, I asked her what it was she had wanted to tell me, thinking that it was all still part of the game.

"Do you really want me to?" she asked. "Because I'm not sure there's any point. . . ."

"You said it was important."

"It is," she said.

"Well, then, I think you should tell me without torturing me."

"You think that's what I'm doing? Oh, Carl, what a ridiculous thing to say."

"I'm sorry."

She shook her head, and suddenly I noticed that there were tears in her eyes. "I've never wanted to torture you, never in all the years I've known you, and especially not now," she said, without looking over at me.

"What is it, then? What's wrong?" I asked.

"Nothing that you can do anything about, I'm afraid," she said. "You see, I've been worried for weeks now, and yesterday I went to the doctor again, and he told me that what I feared was true. I'm pregnant, Carl. There's no doubt about it anymore. The worst of it was that I had to pretend that I was pleased, or at least not as dismayed as I felt, because it seemed quite natural to him that I should want another child."

I sat staring out at the road, with the heavy smell of the roses in my nostrils, and I felt like a traitor, for all I could remember was the room in which I had made love to Terry, with the rag doll propped up in the armchair, and it suddenly seemed worse than a betrayal. It had been a final breach of trust. "What are you going to do?" I asked, as if she were alone in her despair.

"I don't know," she said. "I hate the idea of doing anything unnatural, or getting rid of it, but I hate the idea even more of doing what most women would do . . . going back to their husbands, because that's the easiest way."

"I don't want you to do that."

"Nor do I, because that's betraying everyone at the same time, and it's distasteful and false, a lie you have to live with forever." She shook her head. "What an idiot I was," she said, "thinking everything would be all right, trusting in that stupid little gadget, when I should have known all that lovemaking wouldn't be for nothing."

"The night we went to the restaurant at the beach . . . did you know then?" I asked.

"I didn't know for sure, but I suspected the worst. That's why everything seemed so unbearably awful when we had that fight. Oh, Carl, Carl . . . what a terrible burden all this must be for you."

"Don't be silly. That has nothing to do with it."

"Yes, it does. Because it's all so much more complicated a thing than you're prepared for at your age. That night I wanted to tell you, but we ran into Richard and that absurd girl, and when I saw them together I realized that that one way out was impossible, that everything had gone too far, because he wasn't embarrassed, quite rightly so, or didn't try to hide. He'd made an adjustment to having a frigid wife, the only adjustment a normal man can make, and he told me so in the car outside the restaurant. But you were jealous, and I couldn't explain everything at once. It just wasn't possible." We had come to a stop light, and she turned to look at me with a sad smile. "What a mess it all is," she said.

"Do you have to go away over Christmas?" I asked. We needed time, I felt, time to talk, and make love even, so that I could prove to her that my feelings hadn't changed.

"Yes, of course I do," she said. "Richard's going back to England right after the New Year, and he feels a brief family holiday is the least we can do for Karen, and I think he's right. Then, when I come back I'll have to face it all by myself." The light was green, but neither one of us had seen it. A car behind us blew its horn.

"But you're not all by yourself," I said.

"Well, I am almost, my darling," she replied. "I know that you'll try to help me, but there isn't much you can do. Oh, if you were only ten years older, Carl," she added with a desperate little laugh. "Oh, how I'd trap you then. But you're not, my angel, so there's no alternative but to do the thing I despise most." We were approaching the sea. The fog was blowing in toward us like billowing smoke. "I suppose we have to pay for being happy in this miserable world," she said. "Yet in the end we only wind up adding our own misery to that of everyone else." She took my hand without looking over at me. "The worst of it is that I would have so loved having your child," she said.

PART
VII

≈ one ≈

MY DIARY contains a number of
blank pages for the days that followed (as I have never been eager to
record my own unhappiness), and my memory is somewhat hazy when I
try to recollect the exact continuity of events with which the old year
ended and the new one began. I can clearly recall, however, that that was
the first Christmas holiday I failed to enjoy, which is not surprising
under the circumstances, although there were other, equally important
factors contributing to the general lack of "yuletide cheer."

For there was an atmosphere of fear and apprehension hanging over
the end of the year 1937 that affected almost everyone. The news was
bad from every corner of the world, so consistently bad that it was becoming more and more obvious that the Second World War was unavoidable and that it would be only a question of time before it would
begin. We were not as conditioned to disaster as we have become since,
nor had the feeling of helplessness in the face of history as yet become
a habit of our lives. Thus it seemed inconceivable in the bright sunshine
of a southern California winter that men everywhere would soon start
killing each other again.

There were those who scoffed at the much-publicized threat of a
general conflict. Hitler was too smart a man to take on the whole world,
and wanted only to rectify the "injustices" of the Treaty of Versailles.
And when it came to the Far East, many of the same people felt that

this was the natural process by which the Orientals adjusted their ever-increasing birth rate. Anyway, a war against Japan was "an affair we would begin on any Thursday, and tell you how we won it on the following Monday."

The newspapers painted a grimmer picture. Japanese troops had already taken Nanking, and on Christmas Eve Hangchow was captured. In Spain the loyalists had launched an offensive near Teruel, but their victory was short-lived, and in ten days the besiegers were in turn besieged. At the same time, the British and the French governments, as well as the American, were still abiding by the Arms Embargo, thus maintaining a false neutrality in the face of flagrant German and Italian violations of the agreement they had signed.

For a variety of reasons, the victors of the First World War were behaving as if they were the vanquished, and the advantages of the peace that had been won only twenty years earlier had already been dissipated. Twenty years appeared to me to be a much greater span of time than it does now, and yet I remember that we all continued to believe in the potential strength of France and Britain, certain that the former allies had only to take a firm stand in order to bring the fascist dictators to heel. But the governments of Chautemps and Chamberlain seemed disinclined to assert the potential power of their respective nations, and continued to yield to the demands of the Axis.

Only the politicians of the left were not amazed by this unreasonable behavior, and Jake, as their representative in our household, continued to express their point of view. "Can't you understand, they don't want to stop Hitler," he insisted. "They've made up their minds that a strong and aggressive Germany is the best possible bulwark against Bolshevism. So they feed the wolves, hoping that they'll someday devour the red dragon. Anyway, how can you expect them to behave normally? They never have in the past. Are you listening to me?"

"Sure, I'm listening," I replied. "But you've said all of it before." I was thinking of my own problems of morality. I hadn't heard from Terry for more than a week, had been hoping that she wouldn't call, although that morning Maureen had reported that a strange lady had asked for me on the telephone, and had hung up when she was told that I wasn't in. "Do you think the Soviet Union behaves in a moral manner?" I asked.

"I don't know. There's no reliable information available about what's going on inside Russia. But when it comes to their foreign policy, they're the only ones who behave halfway decently. They support the republican government of Spain. Of course, they behave suspiciously when dealing with us, but what do you expect? Less than twenty years ago we sent an expeditionary force to help put down their revolution. So why should they trust us?"

"Why should we trust them? They want to see our form of government overthrown, and they admit it. They send agents and money to try to undermine our institutions. . . .'"

"They don't send all that much money," Jake interrupted, "because they don't have much to send. You mustn't believe what you read in the papers. The Red Menace is a bogeyman, used by every crooked politician, every demagogue from Hitler to Father Coughlin. Moscow Gold is not going to contaminate our fair land, don't worry."

"You don't have to talk down to me. I'm not an idiot."

"I didn't say you were. I just think you're a little too gullible, that's all." He paused and glanced over at me. "Why are you smiling?" he asked. We were seated on the terrace, both of us facing the garden and the midday sun.

"I was just thinking about how many times we've argued about all this," I said.

"What does that prove? Except that nobody listens. I may not be able to convince you, but someday perhaps, when the forces of the left are victorious, you'll remember what I said."

"And suppose they're defeated?"

He shrugged. "That won't make any difference to me," he said. "I'll never change my opinions. I'm a socialist. I believe that socialism is the only solution for the world, the only possible way out. Because there'll never be peace until economic injustice has been stamped out, until the workers of all nations own the means of production. No other system man has devised can solve man's basic problems—hunger and inequality. And once that's been accomplished, there'll be no more race hatred, no more war, and people will live in peace with each other everywhere!"

"It sounds great, but I doubt that it'll happen."

"Well, you'll see that it will. And sooner than you think. It's that, or the extinction of the human race."

It seemed a bleak prospect to me. I could visualize endless athletic fields with people of different nationalities doing mass calisthenics, which was the picture world socialism always brought to my mind. But I didn't dare voice such a frivolous thought, for I knew that Jake's desire to convince me was prompted by true brotherly affection. And perhaps he was right.

Yet the doctrinaire discipline of his new religion bothered me. No matter what the ultimate ends were, the dictatorship of the proletariat in Russia had turned out to be just another dictatorship, an authoritarian government that deprived the people—for whose benefit it had supposedly been created—of all their liberties.

"They'll ultimately get them back," was Jake's answer. But when? How? Was it worth living for years under a dictatorship for this promise of a better life? I longed to be better informed so that I could answer him, and perhaps persuade him that he was wrong, for I felt that he was jeopardizing his future by his dogmatic belief in a political system that would make him an outcast in the country in which he lived. He was my brother, and I couldn't help worrying about him.

"The United States will never be a socialist country," I said. "Not in our lifetime, anyway."

He smiled calmly. "I've tried to tell you so often that you and I are really not that important," he said. "Which is where I seem to lose you. You want to be rich and successful and 'happy' in the current meaning of the word, while I believe that none of us can be really happy while the greater part of the world lives in misery. 'While there is one man in chains, I cannot feel free.' I don't know who said that, but that's the way I feel, too."

Maureen appeared, looking as if she were one of the millions who were waiting to be liberated by Jake's dream. She scowled and said: "There's a lady on the telephone for you, Carl. And lunch is ready, so don't be too long."

I felt relieved that our conversation had been interrupted. It was like arguing about the existence of God with Jake. He was thoroughly convincing, yet giving in to his logic could only result in a rather cheerless capitulation. There was no solace in letting oneself be persuaded that God was a myth, just as there was no consolation in his argument that England and France were governed by a group of conspirators and weaklings who would finally sell out all of Europe. It was better to believe that someday soon things would change.

Terry's voice brought me back to my own, more immediate problems. She wished me a belated Merry Christmas and asked what I was doing. "I've got the evening off," she added cheerfully, "so I thought I'd call."

"I'm not doing anything in particular," I said, the tone of my voice presaging the unpleasant decision I had arrived at.

"Hmm . . . you sound grim," she said. "Hasn't Santa Claus been good to you?"

"I was in the middle of an argument with my brother," I told her.

"Is he bigger than you are?"

"Not really."

"Then relax, honey. Where'll I find you?"

I suggested a drive-in I could reach by bus, and she said she would meet me there. Then I joined Jake for lunch. Although it was Saturday, we ate alone, as it was a busy time for my mother at the shop. People were returning their Christmas presents and exchanging them for something they really wanted.

"Have you made up your mind where you want to go to college?" he asked while we ate our sandwiches and salad.

"I'm not sure. Maybe in the East somewhere," I replied.

"And what are you going to major in?"

"English and history."

"With what end in view?"

"I don't know. Maybe I'll try to become a writer," I said. It was the first time I had confessed my secret ambition to anyone.

He made a face, to express his surprise and doubt. "A writer? What made you decide that?"

"I haven't decided. I've been thinking about it, that's all."

"It's a very difficult vocation. D'you think you've got talent for writing?"

"I don't know."

He grinned. "Well, at least you're not overconfident," he said. "But have you ever written anything? I mean, apart from the annual birthday poem for Mother?"

"Yes, a few things," I replied, purposely vague.

"I'd like to read them."

"I don't think you'd be interested."

"You never can tell. Are they about tennis?"

"No, they're not. Anyway, I'm not ready to show them. What are *you* going to do when you finish college?"

He shrugged mysteriously and said: "I don't know. Maybe study some more. It depends on what's happening in the world by then. I really haven't made up my mind."

Was he planning to be an active revolutionary, an American Trotsky? "You thinking of going into politics?" I asked.

"Not in the way you mean," he said, laughing. "I'm not an activist. Maybe I'll try being a teacher. Who knows? Anyway, I've still got plenty of time."

"And Marcia? What's she going to do?"

"You'll have to ask her. She was thinking of becoming a labor organizer. . . . In any case, she's not going back into the garment industry, that's for sure." He got up from the table. "How can anybody really decide what they want to do?" he said. "Everything's in such a mess. All you can hope to do is something positive, serve whatever cause you believe in."

"You have to make a living," I said, conscious that I sounded a little like Andy Hardy. "I mean, you have to earn enough money to be able to stand on your own feet."

"I don't intend to starve," Jake said, "or live off Mother. Nor do I plan to make a million dollars and become President of the United States." He stretched lazily. "In any event, you don't have to worry about me. I'll keep out of jail."

He returned to the terrace, having retrieved from the downstairs toilet the book he was reading. I remember suddenly being conscious of the stillness of the afternoon, of the clear blue sky. I felt as if we were both suspended momentarily in time, and I felt a genuine regret that I couldn't halt the progress of the sun, in order to put off for a minute or two the end of the day.

"How about a walk on the beach?" I suggested, and to my surprise, he agreed to come along.

"Go get Prince," he said. "He needs the exercise even more than I do. . . ."

⤜ *two* ⤛

THERE WERE NO TEARS, no remonstrances, even though I confessed everything. Terry sat slouched against the door on her side of the car, sipping an ice-cream soda through a straw. I noticed that she had eaten only half of her sandwich. She asked: "Have you been to bed with her since you and I . . ."

"No, I haven't."

"Well, don't snap my head off. It's a fair question."

"I haven't seen her, except for that once."

"But that was enough for you to discover that your feelings hadn't changed? Am I right, dear boy?"

"Don't be sarcastic."

"Sarcastic! Me? Teresa Slane Sangster. You must be off your stick. Sad, yes, but not sarky. That's not my style. Anyway, it's all my fault. I was the one who led you astray. You had very little to do with it, as I remember."

"And don't make me sound like a jerk."

"I'm sorry," she said. "I can't seem to do anything right today. But you see, I *did* have an idea that you were stuck on the lady in question the day we met. I just thought I could make you forget all about her," she added, smiling. "Turns out it's me you want to forget." She began to sing softly, mocking herself. *"I thought I'd found the man of my dreams. So it seemed. This is how the story ends. He's going to turn me down and say: 'Can't we be friends?' "*

"Can you be serious for a moment, Terry?"

"But I am serious," she said. "More than that. I'm sad. I loved our little life of sin. I'm going to miss it. Unless I can get you to change your mind, that is. . . ."

"That wouldn't be very fair, would it?" I said, sounding pompous even to myself, so that I wasn't surprised by her answer.

"Fair?" she asked. "To whom, for God's sake? You sound like the village parson. All's fair in love and war. Hasn't anyone ever told you?" She straightened and took my hand, her mood changing. "I didn't mean that, darling," she said more gently. "You do what you think is right, that's all. I feel sorry for Pam. And for you too, as a matter of fact. But there really isn't much I can do about it. If you decide that we shouldn't see each other anymore . . . well, that's it. Flash the lights, and we'll pay and be off."

"There's no hurry."

"No? All right, then. Let's relax. What'll we do tonight? Skate or screw?"

"Terry. Sometimes you really . . ."

"Shock you? That's good. Because you're too serious for your age. You should have two girls, three girls . . . any number. And if one of them gets knocked up, well, that's baseball, darling."

"The more the merrier. Has that been your motto?"

"Mine? Oh, no, honey," she said, "that wouldn't work for me. I don't get that many evenings off!"

She was suddenly in good spirits again, contagiously so. I laughed, in spite of myself. "I wish I could follow your advice," I said, "but I can't. . . ."

"Well, at least try. You only live once. Anyway, I've heard that in hell all the girls you could have laid and didn't will come to haunt you."

"I'll have to take that chance."

"I don't like your attitude," she said, and giggled. "No, that's not true. I really approve of you. Honest, I do. I guess that's why I decided you were for me. Because you're such a nice, clean-cut kid. And so did Lady Pamela, I'll bet, poor thing." The waitress came for the tray, swinging her hips and smiling. I paid and backed the car away from the counter. Once we were out on the boulevard, Terry slid across the seat to sit close to me. "Have you read any good books lately?" she asked in her comic, seductive voice.

"I haven't had time."

She giggled. "That's better," she said. "I don't like you when you're too serious. Shall we go and see Greta Garbo again? That's about all we have left."

I didn't want to go to the movies, and I didn't really want to go home. "Isn't there anything else playing?" I asked.

"Everything else is a waste of time." She slapped my knee hard, so that it stung. "Listen to me, friend," she said gruffly. "I haven't had a very nice Christmas, and it looks as if it isn't going to be much of a New Year, so you'd better think of something to do on this, my one night out."

"Let's take a long drive up the beach, and on the way back you can drop me home."

"Oh, that sounds exciting."

"Would you like it if while you were pregnant your boyfriend was fooling around with somebody else?"

"I don't intend you to fool around," she said.

"I asked you a question."

She moved abruptly over to her side of the car. "I wouldn't like it even if I weren't pregnant," she said. "But that still doesn't mean that what you're doing makes any sense. She's too old for you. She has a kid, and a husband she'll never leave. So you'll always be odd man out. If you're lucky, that is. And you'll never be able to relax and enjoy being young, even, always thinking, where is she, what is she doing?"

"While if I fall in love with you . . . ?"

"With me? Ha!" She laughed gruffly. "First of all, you never will, dumbhead, and should you, by some wild stretch of the imagination, get a slight, a very slight crush on me . . . why then I'd give Sangster the heave-ho, and go back to the chorus, and boy would you be in trouble then, lover! Why, you'd be as good as married and hog-tied all at once." She shook her head. "As a matter of fact, I've changed my mind. You're better off the way you are, tied to Lady Pam's apron strings, or to whatever you're tied. Go on. Don't stop. Keep driving. You wanted to ride along the beach for a spell, and that's what we're going to do. And then we're going to stop and have a drink, and I'm going to tell you some more things you don't want to hear." She opened her handbag and took out a cigarette, which she lit. "No, I take it all back," she said. "I'm going to be sweet and affectionate, so that's the way you'll remember me. Isn't that a better idea?"

"A little better."

We stopped at a place called the Hula Hut and sat at the bar, with the glistening ocean available behind us whenever we wanted to turn our heads away from the neon-lit rock garden in front of which the barman plied his trade. "How old are you, anyway, son?" the bartender asked as he served us our drinks, Terry a highball, and a lime Coke for me.

"How old is he!" Terry repeated, outraged. "You can't be serious. You think I'm out with my kid brother tonight?"

"Could be, lady."

But he was intimidated enough by her question so as not to pursue the matter. "Can't you learn to order something a little stronger than a Coke?" she asked testily once the man had gone. "He wouldn't have given you a second look if you'd ordered a Scotch." She shook her head. "It's just as well that you're on your way," she said gloomily. "I'll wind up getting pinched for corrupting the morals of a minor in the end, and wouldn't that be just great for all concerned? You off with your pregnant duchess, and me out in the street with a police record and not a dime to my name." She shook her head. "Don't laugh. It's not funny." She swiveled around on her barstool and stared moodily out at the Pacific. "If I weren't so chicken, I'd do a Freddy March. Right out to sea. Like in *A Star Is Born*. Only it's not worth it, is it, baby?"

"Nothing is," I said, without much insight into her character.

"Oh, I don't know. You mean to say you wouldn't be tempted if Lady Pam bowed out of your life? Not even for a second?"

"I don't think so."

"Well, I'm glad to hear that." She tapped the bar with the bottom of her glass. "One more for Ma," she said, "and then we'll hit the road."

We drove back an hour later, passing scores of other couples, sitting close together in their cars. "You know why they drive around like that on Saturday night?" Terry asked rhetorically. "Because they've got no place to go. Not like us." I was almost regretting my newly found morality, but I held on to my resolve. We stopped in front of our house, I kissed her gently on both cheeks, and got out of the car. "You're a stupe," she said. "You know that, don't you? As well as a goddamn fool."

"I know."

"Well, ring me tomorrow if you're on your own." She sighed and slid across the seat in order to take the wheel. Then, with a clownish grin she drove off, crashing the gears as she disappeared into the night.

I let myself in by the front door. The lights had been left on in the living room, undoubtedly for my benefit. I turned them off and went upstairs. As I was getting undressed, I heard the telephone ring. It was almost one o'clock. I hurried out into the hallway, but it had stopped ringing before I was halfway down the stairs. I picked up the receiver in the breakfast room, certain that it was Terry calling from a telephone booth or a gasoline station. Then I heard my mother's voice saying: "It's for you, Carl," as calmly as if the call had come in the middle of the afternoon.

"I'm sorry."

"It doesn't matter. I was reading," she said, which I knew wasn't true. She hung up, and then I heard Pamela's voice very faintly on the other end, as if she were a thousand miles away. "Carl? Oh, darling, I'm so sorry that I woke your mother, but I couldn't help it. I just had to talk to you."

"I can barely hear you."

"It's this damn telephone. Is that better?" Her voice sounded strained, frantic, but before I could ask what was wrong, she said hurriedly: "I've had a terrible row with Richard, and I've told him everything. I couldn't help it. I was so tired of all the lying . . . of pretending that I was a neurotic female. He asked me point-blank if I was having an affair with you, and I told him yes, I was. . . . I didn't think he'd take it as badly as he did. We haven't lived together for almost two years, but tonight for some reason . . ." She broke off, and I knew that she was crying. "I'm an idiot, I guess," she said, pulling herself together. "It would have made things so much simpler, but I can't bear for him to touch me, even. . . ."

"Where are you, Pam?" I asked, although I knew that I couldn't go to her. Yet I felt I had to make the offer.

"Oh, miles away, darling . . . in the mountains near Lake Arrowhead. You can't possibly come here now. Anyway, I'm all right really. I only wish I were with you. Oh, darling, everything's in such an awful mess. He took the car and went off in a rage. . . . That's why I had to call you. He said he was going to see you, and he was full of all sorts of stupid threats."

"Is he on his way here now?" I asked, surprised at the calm tone of my own voice.

"No, he's probably gone to see his girl friend. But he might call tomorrow or the next day. You'll have to be careful, that's all."

"What do you mean, be careful?"

"Don't see him, if you can avoid it. Because it'll only make matters worse. . . . Just have whoever answers the telephone say you're not in."

"But I can't do that," I said, thinking of the questions Maureen would ask, or Jake, or my mother. "What kind of threats did he make?"

"Oh, the usual ones, saying that he's going to give you a good hiding. I told him that if he was going to beat anyone it had better be me. Because I was the one who was responsible for everything."

"That's not quite true."

"Oh, yes, it is true. You were a child when all this started. Anyway, let's not argue about that now. I know how irritated you get when I say anything at all about your age. The important thing is for you to keep out of his way. He'll come to his senses before long. He has this girl . . . he's admitted it to me, so why should he care what I do? It's his vanity, that's all. . . ."

"When will you be back?"

"In four or five days. It's Karen's vacation, and she's having such a lovely time, I don't want to cut it short, although I suppose a day or two won't matter. Promise you won't see him if you can help it."

"I'll try," I said, "but it may not be possible. I'm not going to run away from him."

"Oh, don't be ridiculous, Carl!"

"Suppose he comes here, to the house. I can't crawl over the back fence and hide."

"He won't do that."

"All right. Then there's nothing to worry about. Will you call me when you get back?"

"Of course I will. Don't forget to make my apologies to your mother."

"I won't forget. Take care of yourself. I love you."

"I love you, too."

It still sounded a little like a confession made under duress. But I didn't say anything. I replaced the receiver and started slowly up the stairs. I felt relieved. At the same time, I felt frightened. And it wasn't really the possibility of physical violence that disturbed me at the first moment. It was being totally in the wrong. What excuse could I present for my behavior? I had fallen in love. That was all I could say in my own defense. I could imagine how Gordon would scoff at that statement. Well, that's too bad, he would say, because the lady happens to be my wife. I visualized the scene, played it again and again. Inevitably, it sounded like something out of a movie with George Brent and Ronald Colman.

As I reached the landing, I saw that my mother was waiting for me in the doorway of her room. She asked: "Is something the matter with Pamela? She sounded so upset. She's not ill, is she?"

"She's all right," I said curtly. I didn't want to talk about it.

"You weren't with her tonight, were you?"

"No, I wasn't."

My mother hesitated an instant. "You know, it's very easy to hurt someone who's in love with you," she said. "And most of the time it's not necessary."

"I know. I'll see you tomorrow, Mother."

She nodded. "I'll try to come back early," she said. "Although I doubt I'll find anybody home."

"I'll be here," I told her.

She closed the door of her room. I knew that I had offended her. I had been unnecessarily abrupt. Yet at that moment there was nothing more I could say. I certainly couldn't explain what was wrong. I'll make it up to her someday, I told myself, which was another one of the many promises I was never to keep.

➳ three ➳

THE TELEPHONE CALL I had been warned to avoid never came. Instead, two days after my conversation with Pamela, a letter arrived in the mail for me. It was written by hand, in a rather elongated scrawl that was easy enough to decipher. It read:

> *Dear Carl Woolf* [the use of my full name made my heart beat faster],
>
> *I would like to see you about a personal matter that has caused me considerable anguish, and that concerns you. As I do not want to involve the other members of my family, I suggest we meet at eleven o'clock this coming Saturday morning at the beach cottage*

*you know so well. If for some reason you are unable to make it,
would you please call my house and leave a message to that effect.*

*Sincerely yours,
Richard Gordon*

The tone of the note was controlled—there was no doubt about that
—and still I found myself more than a little uneasy after I had read it.
Why had he chosen a place as deserted as the beach cottage in mid-
winter? ("the cottage you know so well"—I didn't like the sound of that
either.) Was he really planning to give me a beating, and if so, why was
he suggesting such a simple way for me to escape? It seemed as if he
anticipated my refusal. I could only guess that he wanted me to beg off
so that he could demonstrate that I was a coward, a child who could not
be taken seriously.

Perhaps if Pamela hadn't called I would have tried to avoid meeting
him, but as she had warned me, it would seem like even greater cowardice to take her advice. For hours I debated with myself about what I
should do. If I didn't go, I would have to hide from Gordon forever, as I
could certainly never face him after having shown that I was afraid. That
was probably his intention, I reasoned, to frighten me away, so that I
had no choice but to accept his invitation.

Yet there was always the possibility, I couldn't help thinking, that he
intended to do more than just beat me up. Almost every day there was a
story in the newspapers about a jealous husband shooting his wife's
lover, and although I doubted that Gordon had any such extreme measures in his mind, I couldn't altogether dismiss the idea. It would be
ironic, I thought, if after all of my worries about getting killed in a war, I
ended up being shot by Richard Gordon. I could visualize the headlines:
ACTOR SLAYS WIFE'S BOYFRIEND . . . SCREENLAND MURDER IN BEACH
COTTAGE. My photograph would appear on the front page and bring
shame and embarrassment to the entire family.

But my imagination did not stop there. All day long I found myself
visualizing the various aspects of the entire drama, and I played out
every scene, from my meeting with Gordon at the beach (it was almost
like a duel in my daydreams, only I didn't have a gun) to the funeral
(mine, of course), which would be attended by members of my family,
as well as some of my school friends, and perhaps even one or two of my
tennis partners. Hévesey would certainly come, and so would Guy.

Everybody would be suitably solemn, even if they were not deeply moved by my early demise.

My mother would undoubtedly be heartbroken, blaming herself for not having intervened while there was still time. And Pamela . . . her tragic grief made for an endless reverie that I allowed, with considerable pleasure, to pass through my mind. She would certainly never forgive Gordon; I was convinced of that. She would take Karen back to Europe and live with her somewhere on the Italian Riviera, having renounced love forever. Men would still pursue her, I reasoned with all my worldly knowledge, but she would never go to bed with any of them. She would devote the rest of her life to her daughter's welfare, which would keep her busy for as long as she was still attractive. She would probably remain married to Gordon, as it would be difficult for her to ask for a divorce while he was in the penitentiary.

Strangely enough, I remember that I didn't like the idea of Gordon going to jail. I preferred that he should run away, drive across the border to Mexico, and then continue on to England, where he would enlist in the army. If he were killed fighting the Germans, it would all somehow end with greater poetic justice. The fact that I would be ignorant of the outcome of this romantic story disturbed me considerably. It would be preferable, I couldn't help thinking, if I were only wounded. The dramatic possibilities were almost as good, with the added advantage that I would be there to witness it all. Only Terry's part in the proceedings would be seriously curtailed if I were to survive, while if I were killed, she would have the chance to appear at the funeral, a mysterious mourner, her blonde hair partially hidden by a black veil.

But the luxury of all this daydreaming soon came to an end, for our family was invited to a dinner party at the Pojawlskis' that evening, a yearly event that was unavoidable, as they were old friends as well as my mother's employers. I remember that I was even less communicative than usual during the long meal, and almost failed to enjoy the stuffed cabbage and kasha Mrs. Pojawlski had prepared for us. The dinner-table conversation was mainly concerned with a discussion of the fates of various acquaintances who were still trapped in Germany and Austria, which led me to think of my father, whom I hadn't included, I suddenly realized, in the various scenes of mourning I had conjured up during the preceding afternoon.

I knew that he would be sad. But he would be terribly disappointed as well, I concluded. That was what he had hated about the war, the waste of young human life, and that was undoubtedly what he would resent most about my possible demise. Although he would understand better than anyone how I had come to such a premature end. I had followed the "voices of my heart" more than was wise. I smiled grimly at my own morbid joke, realizing that my *Galgenhumor* was another trait of character I had inherited from him. Suddenly I found myself missing him more than I had ever missed him before. He was the one person I might have been able to confide in, I thought, mainly because he was prone to the same romantic weaknesses.

When we arrived home, I went straight to my room and made an entry in my neglected diary that I hoped would explain (should it turn out that way) the circumstances of my premature death. "Am meeting R.G. tomorrow," I wrote. "At his request. Don't really want to go, but feel that I must. There are things that are unavoidable in life, that one must face. I hope my father and mother will understand." With pen in hand I was a better moralist than in action, even then.

≫ *four* ≪

IT WAS AS IF there had never been such a morning. The sea was smooth all the way to the horizon, and the hills guarding the gently curving bay stood out sharply against the cloudless sky. There was no traffic, as, with the sun at my back, I drove along the familiar road, watching the gulls stunt lazily in the mild breeze. Everything appeared benign—the milkman hurrying from house to house with his tray of bottles; the motorcycle patrolmen parked side by side behind the filling station; the solitary fisherman with his trousers rolled up to the knees, wading in the spent surf. Even the live-bait boats lying at anchor beyond the kelp beds looked like innocuous toys that intended no harm to any of God's creatures. Only I alone, it seemed, was on a desperate mission that day, while all the rest of the world was happy and secure.

If only I had had the strength of character, while there had still been time, to stick to one of the many resolutions I had made. . . . Or if I had listened to Pam, right in the beginning, and had fallen in love with someone my own age! But that was an absurd idea, I realized, brought on by the panic of the moment. And even if I had been miraculously prophetic, it wouldn't have made any difference. For I had certainly never thought it possible that I would end up as Pamela's lover, had never dreamed that she would pay any attention to me. I had been truly guiltless, at least in the beginning. "Tell it to the judge," I said aloud, my own moral traffic cop for one brief, self-mocking moment.

Then I thought: "Cynthia might have saved me." But even that episode, I realized, had been nothing more than another one of my daydreams. Had she lived, it was most improbable that she would have fallen in love with a coward. For I was a coward. I had learned that much about myself. And Terry had come along too late. No, that wasn't true. I could never have fallen in love with "Mrs. Sangster." In any case, the same dangers existed there, no matter how little interest she said she had in her husband. "Stop regretting what you've done," I told myself. "It's a useless pastime."

The truth was that I had been damn lucky. Everything had happened the way I had wanted it to, including this final confrontation I had been seeking all along.

And despite the nervous tension of the moment, I found myself recalling the past with unashamed longing, saw the moonlit room again at Las Golondrinas, a single, unforgettable photograph that would never fade, and Pamela sitting naked on the bed in the sun, brushing her hair, or lying on the beach beside me, trying to burn out the mark the strap of her bathing suit had left high on her back. If only I had let things go their own way, I thought, instead of spoiling so much of our time together by my idiotic questions. For in the end nothing had mattered except the knowledge that my feelings had ultimately been returned, that I had been, or was, loved by the one person I had considered worth loving. Whatever might happen at the cottage toward which I was traveling, with such great trepidations, it had been worth it, was truly worth it.

The straight stretch of highway lay before me now with the small beach house on the left, and I saw that Gordon's car was parked in front of the garage, the new Chrysler phaeton he had bought in November, standing like an ominous reminder of his presence in the diminishing distance. Without taking my foot off the accelerator, I continued on, and once I was safely around the next curve in the road, I turned my mother's car off onto the summerway so that I could wipe my perspiring palms dry on the legs of my corduroy trousers. I looked at my pale face in the rear-view mirror, a last check to see if my cowardice was actually visible. It was. I toyed with the idea of calling from a gasoline station farther along to say that I had been detained.

The engine was idling patiently. I said to myself: "Perhaps he's gotten tired of waiting, and left." "You have no *Zivilcourage*," I added aloud, using the German word my father had used so often in the past. The die was cast. The decision that I thought I had made days ago was unavoidable now.

The highway behind me was deserted, and without putting out my hand, I made a U turn and drove slowly back down the road. The cottage came into view again, as did Gordon's car, and with a surprising feeling of calm, I pulled up behind it, switching off the engine before I had stopped rolling, in order to save gas. The gate leading to the house was open, and with a fleeting sense of admiration for my own temerity, I went through it and knocked firmly on the weathered front door. There was no sound from inside the house. I knocked again, a little louder, in chorus with my pounding heart.

Gordon's voice coming from inside startled me, which was ridiculous and comical. Who else did I expect would answer? "Come in," he said gruffly. "The door's unlocked." I noticed that the curtains were still drawn in the living room, while the door leading out to the beach stood open. "I'll be down in a minute," he called from upstairs.

He was inspecting the scene of the crime, I thought to myself, which did little to reassure me. I wandered out across the brickwork to the edge of the beach, remembering how not too long ago I had hidden in the bedroom upstairs and had watched Edwina on her unannounced visit. Was *he* watching me now? Or was he merely making me wait so as to increase my nervousness?

I heard his footsteps on the bricks behind me, and turning, saw that he had followed me out onto the terrace. He didn't appear menacing or dangerous. He looked tired, rather, like a man burdened down with problems that he had not prepared himself for. "Well, Carl," he said. "Here we are. We meet like characters in a trite play. . . ."

"I'm sorry I was late," I mumbled.

"That," he replied wearily, "is the least thing you should feel sorry about." He glanced around the empty terrace, as if looking for a place where we could sit. "Let's go inside the house," he said. "The sun's too bright for my eyes today."

There was dust on the furniture and on the faded rug, a fine dust that rose through the shafts of sunlight that angled in through the drawn curtains. He lit a cigarette, while I sat watching him, feeling like a schoolboy who has been called up in front of the principal for a breach of discipline. Neither one of us spoke for a long time. He seemed to be searching for the right words with which to begin, pacing up and down in front of the painted stones of the small fireplace. "I'm sure Pamela called you," he said after a while, "although I asked her not to. It doesn't really matter if she did . . . I suppose in a way it's better. At least you know what I want to talk to you about."

"I'm not sure that I do. . . ."

"Don't act the part of the perfect little gentleman," he said gruffly, "because you certainly haven't behaved like one up to now." He raised his hand warningly. "No, don't interrupt, please. I'd rather you heard me out. You owe me at least that small courtesy."

He had apparently decided against violence; at least, he was not going to shoot me, because he probably would have done so without lecturing me beforehand. I felt relieved, although I tried my best not to show it as I sat waiting, feigning humble attentiveness. Because I was obviously in the wrong, I owed him that much, just as he had said. He stopped in front of the window nearest him, pulled open the curtains, and stood for an instant squinting out at the sea.

"You first came to my house as a boy," he began, his eyes still narrow, although he was no longer staring into the sun, "which is why you can't wholly be blamed for what has happened. You became attached to my wife, for which I can't really blame you either. I don't know who took the first step to change that relationship into a love affair, nor do I think it really matters. Pam says it was all her fault. All right, let's accept that. After all, she's a fully grown woman, and you're still not a man. However, I still can't absolve you from all of the blame. You're not an idiot . . or even a fool. Granted that love, or sexual attraction, provides its own rules, or is a strong enough stimulant to make people willing to disregard what's decent. Yet, you must have known that you were violating my confidence." He lit a fresh cigarette and inhaled deeply. "No matter what the circumstances might be, Carl," he said slowly, "adultery is a nasty betrayal of the rules of human conduct. You'll discover that one day, if you haven't already."

I wanted to ask him if his behavior had always been above reproach, but I didn't dare. I didn't have to, as it turned out, for he added: "I'm speaking from experience, if that's what you're thinking. However, in my case, adultery was rather forced on me. Or at least there were mitigating circumstances. I suppose Pamela could make a similar plea. But that still doesn't excuse your behavior." He shook his head. "Let me finish," he said, as if I was about to interrupt him, although I wasn't, for I was listening to him, not entirely untouched by his words.

"I've never spent all that much time with you," he went on, "but I know that you have a strong sense of what's right and wrong when it comes to politics. You wouldn't be normal if you didn't, considering your background and your race." I felt myself flushing, partly out of embarrassment, partly out of anger. But he anticipated my objection. "Not that I think your race makes you behave in any special way," he said with a knowing smile. "I am not an anti-Semite, as you well know. But being a Jew has influenced your *Weltanschauung*, has it not? It's made you distinguish right from wrong quite clearly. That was why I was even more surprised by your actions, your lack of morality. For in all of your other attitudes and opinions you appeared to be a decent young man." He must have become aware of the sullen look on my face, for he smiled suddenly, an almost friendly smile, intended, no doubt, to be disarming. "Very few people are any different," he added. "We all love to preach a moral sermon for mankind, while pursuing our own private immoralities. You'll agree to that, won't you?"

I nodded and said: "Yes, I agree." What else could I say?

He made a face, a rather contemptuous one. "Congratulations," he said. "At least you're being fairly honest. And I suppose, since you're intelligent as well, it must also have occurred to you that there might well be unpleasant circumstances attached to this schism in your morality. Or did you think you would never be found out? Because if that was your hope, you were being a little naïve. . . ."

"I wanted Pam to leave a long time ago," I said aggressively.

"You did, eh? I suppose that's commendable? And what else did you want her to do? Abandon Karen and come to live with you at your mother's place?"

"I finish school in two months," I said, trying to keep my voice low, without sounding reticent. "I plan to get a job. Pamela could work, too. We've never discussed it, but . . ."

"Obviously not," he interrupted with heavy sarcasm. "That would hardly have been the manly thing to do. You wanted her to make the break all on her own. But after that, what did you think would happen? Did you see her getting a job as a salesgirl in a department store, or did you expect her to work nights as a carhop?" He threw his cigarette into the fireplace and clasped his arms in front of his chest as if he wanted to make certain that he wouldn't use them to strangle me. "Or did you think at all?

"She's never had to earn a dime in her life," he continued, "and neither have you. And what did you think she was going to do about your child? I suppose you expected her to get an abortion? Or did you see yourself as a father at the age of nineteen?" He ran his hand nervously through his hair and started to pace again. "You're both immature idiots, that's all you are. Only Pam's case is a little more serious than yours. She needs psychiatric care. . . ."

"That's not true!"

"Don't raise your voice," Gordon said menacingly, turning to face me. "Oh, how I have been so blind as not to see all of this happening!" His despair was as great as my own, I realized, and for an instant I felt sorry for him. But then he gained control of himself again, and his voice changed, reverting to a tone of anger. "Now, listen to me carefully," he said. "Two things are certain. Pam is not going off with you on some half-baked plan that can only lead to disaster, and she's not going to have an abortion. Because I'm not going to allow it, you understand? It's just not on. The risks are too great, and besides that, it's not the sort of thing I want any part of—her going to some quack doctor and having her insides messed about with. I won't have it. And I *am* her husband, remember . . . I can go to court and have you put away in a school for juvenile delinquents. The only reason I've decided not to do that is because of the scandal that would result." He stood in front of my chair, his hands thrust deep in his coat pockets. "You're going to stop seeing each other, that's step number one. Then, in a month or so, she'll join me in England, where she'll have the child. It'll just have to be an unpleasant reminder of our stay in this ridiculous place, that's all. You can do what you like with *your* life, but you're not going to muck up our entire existence. Is that clear?"

I got to my feet with my fists clenched. My knees were shaking, as was the rest of my body. "Where are you going?" he asked.

"Home," I said, the misery of my whole existence exploding in that one pathetic word. Pam had been right. It was ridiculous to have agreed to meet him. I had proved nothing, except my own inferiority. For what he had said was true. It was all hopeless, everything I had planned.

"Well, as long as we understand each other," he said coldly. "If you make an attempt to see my wife again, if you even call her on the telephone, I shall take the necessary steps to have you put in a reform school, no matter what the consequences might be. Is that clear?"

I didn't reply. I started toward the door. Then I felt his hand on my arm, was spun around roughly, so that I almost lost my balance and fell. "You don't really know me, Carl," I heard him say. "I can get quite rough, if necessary. Rougher than you can imagine." I stared up at him. His face was very close to mine, and I could see the beads of perspiration on his forehead, covering his pale skin. "You've gotten away with a great deal, but I advise you now . . . don't push your luck!"

I pulled free of his grasp. I didn't feel frightened. I wanted to get away from him, that was all. I hurried out of the house and through the wooden gate at the side of the garage. He caught up with me as I was getting into my mother's car, and he said: "I'm not bluffing. I hope you realize that. And I've told Pam the same thing. I'm tired of playing the fool."

If I had only known where to find her. But I had no idea of where to call her, even. Without looking at him, I stepped on the starter, trying to concentrate on what I was doing so that I wouldn't stall the engine and be made to appear more ridiculous, while he stood there beside the open window, watching me with a cold look of outraged authority. "I'm going to talk to her," I said defiantly, and put the car into first gear.

"I advise you not to," was all he had time to say before I drove off.

≫ *five* ≪

I<small>T WAS NOT</small> a defeat. A defeat implies that a battle has been lost or that a struggle has unsuccessfully ended. But neither the one nor the other had taken place. There hadn't even been an argument. I had sat there listening to him like a recalcitrant child, a juvenile delinquent without any rights or convictions. But why . . . why? There were so many things I could have said now that it was too late. At the time I hadn't heard the French expression *l'esprit de l'escalier*, which so aptly describes the brilliant things that occur to you as you go running down the stairs, else I might at least have been able to laugh at myself.

Instead I drove back through the bright sunshine of that winter day, planning a dozen different actions, each one more desperate than the last. I couldn't believe at first that there was nothing I could do, although with time even that realization became apparent to me. I had no money, which was finally the decisive argument against anything I might decide to undertake. Gordon was right. I had pinned all of my hopes on a childishly conceived plan for a dream future that was unrealizable. That he was also right about my lack of morality disturbed me more. Not only had I taken part in an underhand betrayal of his confidence (which I still found a great many excuses for), but I had contemplated getting rid of my child with Pamela without any particular feelings of horror or distaste. For her to have it, even though she wanted it, or had said so, had seemed utterly impossible to me from the first moment on.

Of course, I hadn't known that there was a real risk involved. I wasn't a monster; I was merely selfish, as well as naïve. Looking back now, I cannot believe that I was as uninformed at the age of eighteen as I obviously must have been. I had heard of illegal operations, and of women dying as a result of an infection, but I had always imagined that these circumstances existed only among people too poor to get first-class medical attention. I had been much more concerned with the moral aspect of her having an abortion, had worried about what it would do to her, because she had said she hated the idea of it. I had never imagined (nor had she even mentioned the possibility) that she was risking her life. "Almost everybody I know has had a *curetage*," she had said (using the French word, which somehow made it sound less sordid), "so I suppose I'll survive, too." Which had made me come to accept the idea. But it was Gordon's description that stuck in my mind. If it was true that she would have to go to some "quack doctor" and have her "insides messed about with," then almost any other alternative was preferable.

Yet the idea that she would go to England and have the child seemed impossible too. I would never see her again, I was certain of that. Nor could I imagine going through life knowing that a human being I had caused to be brought into the world was forever out of my reach. "It'll just have to be an unpleasant reminder of our stay in this ridiculous place," Gordon had said, which was a sufficient indication of what the child's fate would be. It was like something out of *The Forsyte Saga*, a *fin de siècle* punishment so cruel and old-fashioned that I could not conceive of it happening to us. But he was capable of forcing both of us to submit to it; I was convinced of that. In order to avoid a scandal; he would prefer to accept the child. And he would appear righteous and forgiving in doing so.

The only other thing to do was to defy him, to go off on our own and somehow make enough money to live until the baby was born. Gordon was right in thinking that I didn't look forward to being a father at the age of nineteen. I would have to give up going to college. But even if I got a job, how would we manage to make ends meet? I would hardly make enough to keep myself, much less a small family. I would certainly have very little time to write. And what would I write about? The war I had planned to go to, either as a soldier or a foreign correspondent, would be out of the question. William Bolitho, another one of my heroes, had written that "adventure starts by running away from home," but that was hardly true if one ran away to a home of one's own making. And would our love endure under such circumstances?

Suddenly I found all of Pam's many previous warnings ringing in my ears, of how I would get tired of her and fall in love with a girl younger than myself and want to leave her—all of the arguments I had scoffed at and dismissed so many times. They seemed most menacing now, the handwriting on the wall. Perhaps she had been right all along. I found myself thinking, perhaps love did die as a result of familiarity and habit. And if that should happen, then what would I do?

But still I couldn't accept his ultimatum, couldn't let her go away with him to England, to live under his self-righteous rule, like the tragic heroine in a nineteenth-century novel, and lose her forever, as well! For the first time in my life I understood how one could be driven to suicide, a way out that I had never believed as being remotely possible up to that moment. What a relief it would be just to stop thinking! But I knew that I was incapable of doing away with myself. I was too much of an egoist. The thought of an eternal void was still worse than any of the other alternatives. There was always the chance that things might change, that somehow a solution would suddenly present itself: an accident in which Gordon died a quick and painless death, or the discovery that the doctor had made a mistake, that Pam wasn't pregnant after all. No, it was better to go on living, I decided, no matter how miserably. And so I returned to the seemingly dreary routine of school, and sat listlessly in class among my friends, even more of an outsider than I had been before, unable to join them in their interest in the success of the basketball team, or the senior prom, or even the College Board exams that were a part of my immediate future.

Nor was I particularly interested in the news of the world anymore, the battles that were going on in Spain and China. I accepted the fact that things were going badly, that the poison of fascism was spreading. It was almost as if I had lost my partisanship in the cause I always believed in. Gordon's face with its neatly trimmed moustache appeared constantly before me, reminding me that I had no right to pass moral judgments, as I was not above reproach myself. I couldn't shake off his presence. At the same time, I felt lonely, even lonelier than I had been in the days before I had met Pam. I felt the need to talk to someone, to unburden myself. I couldn't go to my mother, because I knew that she had her own worries that any belated confession of mine would only add to, and so I refrained from going to her, not realizing, as I did later on, that she would probably have been able to comfort me more than anyone else.

In the end I called Terry, thinking that she would not hesitate to give me advice, although I suspected that it might be tainted by a certain bitterness. At least she was acquainted with all of the facts, which would spare me having to make a long explanation. But Terry was not available, as it turned out, or at least that was what the maid who answered the telephone told me. "Mrs. Sangster is out of town for a few days," she informed me in an apathetic voice. I concluded that she had gone to the desert to join her husband, which I couldn't help thinking was a good thing, and so I hung up without leaving my name.

There was always Guy Boulard, although he had never inspired confidence, his tutorial manner making him appear cold and removed. He was a friend, but not one on an equal level. But there was nobody else, and so toward the end of the week I went to see him in his new apartment, which was where his mother had suggested I call him. Rather than confess everything at once, I had made up my mind to ask his advice about getting a job.

He looked slightly astonished at my request, his thin mouth turning down at the corners, causing the saliva to gather around the stem of his pipe. "You mean a temporary job," he said. "Something you could do this summer."

"I'm graduating in February, thanks to you," I told him. "I'd like to start then."

He smiled, Professor Panglos again for one brief moment. "Ah, congratulations. You see . . . all our hours of toil were not entirely wasted. At least you wound up with a few French credits, not to mention the benefits to your personal life."

I disregarded his remark, although it was the opening I required. He had changed since going to work for Mr. Levin, had taken on an air of smugness that was irritating. "Both the French and German exams I took helped," I said. "I got three years' additional credits for each."

"And now you want to make some money before you start college, is that the plan?"

"If I go at all."

"What makes you say that?" He glanced over at me suspiciously, taken aback.

"Well, I'll never be able to finish," I said. "The war's sure to begin in a couple of years, if not before. . . ."

He assumed his most professorial manner. "Although I know a tempest will soon destroy this house, I must continue building it," he said. "I'm misquoting Schopenhauer, I believe, but you get the point. . . ."

"Not really. Anyway, I have other reasons."

"Have you discussed this with your mother?"

"No, and I hope you won't either."

He made a face, and got up to shuffle around the room in his slippers, stopping to clean his pipe over the wastebasket. "Why are you in such a hurry?" he asked. "Making money is not a virtue in itself, you know."

"It is when it's a necessity."

He shrugged. "Well, you can do both—work and continue your education, just as I did." He started once again to tell me the long story of his travail, the years he had spent teaching French while studying for his degree. But he noticed that I wasn't really listening, and so he stopped. "What do you plan to do with yourself, anyway?" he asked. "Are you still thinking of becoming a writer?"

"I'm not sure. All I know is that right now I want to make a living."

"I see." He paused thoughtfully. "And what makes you think I can help you?"

"Well, I thought that as you're working for a man who runs a big company, you might be able to put in a word for me."

"With Mr. Levin?"

"Sure. Why not?"

"Well, I could, I suppose," he said, sounding as if I had asked him to divide a personal treasure with me. "But what do you know how to do? Mr. Levin is not going to give you a job just because you're a friend of mine. The studio is overrun with friends and relatives as it is. Then, there are the unions. They don't make it any easier. He might offer you a job as a messenger boy, but that isn't really what you want, is it?"

"I don't care what kind of a job it is," I said.

He nodded absently. "You must be in trouble," he said. "I know you pretty well, Carl, and although you've grown up a lot, I'm pretty certain you wouldn't give up a summer of tennis and the beach without a damn good reason." He smiled, apparently pleased with his insight and his brilliant deductions.

I disliked him for both. Still, there was no use procrastinating any longer. He would never do anything unless he realized that I was serious about my request. Also, that was why I had gone to him, although his manner hardly invited confidence. "I need to make enough money to support myself," I said. "There are various reasons for this. . . ."

"Such as?"

"I'm trying to tell you. . . ."

"Go ahead. I'm sorry."

It was more difficult than I had thought it would be. "A long time ago you were kind enough to take me along to the house of one of your pupils," I began rather pompously.

"And you fell in love with her mother. Is that what you're going to say? Because I know all about that. I'm not as insensitive as you must think I am. I knew you'd fallen in love with the lady almost the minute it happened. . . . And that you've been in love with her ever since. Still, I don't see how getting a job will help. It'll only make it more difficult for you to see her, that's all. She's married, and she has a life of her own, apart from you. Your giving up college won't solve anything."

"It's gone beyond just being in love with her," I said.

"You mean you're having an affair with her. Well, I guessed that had happened some time ago, too." He looked searchingly at me, as if something quite incredible had suddenly occurred to him. "You're not going to tell me that you're planning to live with her, are you . . . to get married? Because that would be madness. She's at least ten years older than you are. . . ."

"Twelve."

"All right, twelve. That only makes matters a little worse."

"She's expecting a child."

He stood facing me, openmouthed, clutching his empty pipe in his left hand, his right hand raised to his forehead in a gesture of both horror and amazement. "Good God," he said slowly. "How long ago did this happen?" As if an automobile accident had occurred, something that could be pinpointed in time. "Not that it makes any difference," he added, "but for God's sake, how long have you known? I mean, why didn't you come to me sooner?"

"What could you have done?" I asked, irritated by his manner. "The reason I came to see you is because I need your help now."

"Of course. I realize that. And I'll do everything I can. But still, I don't want you to rush into something you'll regret for the rest of your life. And what about Mrs. Gordon? Have you discussed this with her? I presume you have, but still, I can't believe that she approves of your giving up college."

"I haven't seen her for almost a month."

"But does she know what you have in mind? Is she willing to give up her marriage in order to go and live with you?"

"I don't know."

"But, Carl, for God's sake, you're acting as if it were a *fait accompli*, her leaving Gordon and the child. What about him? He might have a thing or two to say about it."

"I've spoken to him," I said quite calmly. "He threatened to have me put in a reform school if I didn't stop seeing Pam. Of course, that's absurd. . . ."

"I'm not so sure it is," Guy interrupted. "I remember reading about a case not long ago. Alienation of affection was the charge. And I think they did send the boy off to some sort of truant's farm. Anyway, think of the scandal if this comes out. Your poor mother . . ."

"I don't think she'd be all that upset."

"You don't!" He was standing over me openmouthed with surprise.

"She wouldn't panic, I know that," I said, "not because there was about to be a scandal. Anyway, that's beside the point. Gordon's not going to do anything, because he doesn't want a scandal either."

"Then what is the point?"

"Are you going to help me, or not?"

"Of course I am, if I can. But I don't want you to count on it. Anyway, I want you to think a little more before you decide. And you *must* talk to Pamela. She stands to lose much more than you do, you know." He shook his head. "What a mess," he said, kicking off his slippers and going off into the adjoining room. "Couldn't you have fallen in love with someone your own age?"

"It's a little late for that suggestion," I called after him. I heard him muttering to himself, and got up to follow him. I caught a glimpse of him standing in front of the mirror in his bedroom, adjusting his necktie. He had put on a pair of shoes and a raincoat.

"I have a date tonight," he said, "else we would talk about this some more." He put on a ridiculous little hat that made him look like a mannequin in the window of a cheap clothing store. "I'll drop you off at home, if you like," he said, apparently satisfied that he was well turned out for his "date."

"I'll walk. It's not far."

"When'll I see you again?" he asked, following me to the door.

"Whenever you like. Call me, especially if you have some news from Mr. Levin." We went down the stairs together, and out into the street.

"I hope you won't do anything until we have a chance to discuss this again," he said.

"I won't." We shook hands beside his car. I noticed that he had bought a new one, but I didn't feel like commenting on it. I watched him drive off, his absurd silhouette, complete with hat, visible through the rear window.

I turned and started off in the opposite direction. The town I had always enjoyed walking through at night suddenly looked sad to me. The streets were empty, although it was only seven-thirty. In the alley behind Fourth Street the last traces of Christmas were still in evidence, a few pieces of crumpled tinsel in the gutter, and one or two dried Christmas trees sticking out of the garbage cans that were assembled there. I crossed into the public park on the palisades, thinking how often I had walked there at night hoping to meet someone I could fall in love with. The wind was moving through the trees, blowing in from the sea. There was only school to look forward to the next day, a few more classes that would require no effort on my part. Everything was coming to an end; I was experiencing an empty sadness, as if I had been trapped in a world of permanent melancholy. I had done everything wrong. (Oh, how often I was to feel the same way in the years that followed, although never again did things seem as hopeless as they did that evening.) Before I was halfway through the park it started to rain, the cold rain of winter that penetrated everything. But I walked on at the same pace, without seeking the shelter of the pines that grew among the palm trees.

≈ SIX ≈

I HAD WALKED down the same halls so often, climbed the same stairs, taken the same paths to all the familiar places, the gym, the auditorium, the chemistry laboratory, the registrar's office, only now I was seeing it all through different eyes, with regret and farewell. Why had I been in such a hurry to leave? It would have been far better to wait and graduate in June with the others, and that way have the whole summer in which to decide what to do. And it would have helped, not being free until then. Yet how could I have foreseen everything that had happened?

The messenger who had come for me (he was a B-team letterman in basketball) walked sternly beside me, conscious of his official function. "Did they say what it was about?" I asked him. It was unusual to be called out of class in the middle of the day.

"Nope. They just told me to bring you to Stanton's office."

Stanton was the vice-principal. He was also in charge of sending our transcripts to the various colleges to which we had wanted to apply. That was probably the reason for this urgent summons. "You a sophomore?" I asked my taciturn guide as we made our way down the empty main hallway.

"That's right." He acted as if he were a policeman who had been sent to bring in a suspect.

"Going out for the varsity next year?"

"I guess so. My old man don't want me to play football." We had arrived at the main entrance of the building. "In there," my guide said imperiously, indicating the glass door I had known so much longer than he had.

"Thanks for telling me." My sarcasm was lost on my companion, who returned to his post and the open book he had left behind when called to duty. I went into the vice-principal's office. Miss Dunlap, the school secretary, looked up from behind her desk, her pince-nez astride the bulbous nose that was the outstanding feature of her face. In all the years I had known her, she seemed not to have changed at all. Nor had she smiled, as far as I could remember. She greeted me by name, and went to the door on her left to announce my arrival. Then, nodding to me, she ushered me into Mr. Stanton's office.

I found him standing at the window that looked out on the campus, which was his usual place of vigilance, from which he could control the work of the gardeners, or the unauthorized movement of students while classes were in session. The blue-and-gold state flag and the Stars and Stripes flanked his unoccupied desk, to which he stepped now.

He was a huge man with a powerful body, famous for his effective intervention in the fights that the school had been noted for in the first years of my attendance. Looking up, he smiled, so that I knew I had not been called in for a breach of discipline. In contrast to the principal, Mr. Cavanaugh, a pale stick of a man who scowled always, Stanton was as well liked as any member of the faculty, despite his position of official disciplinarian. "There was a telephone call for you a quarter of an hour ago," he said. "It sounded as if it were urgent. The lady said she'd call back in a little while."

His relaxed manner had not prepared me for a message of this kind, and I stared at him, alarmed. "Was it my mother?" I asked.

He shook his head. "I don't think so." He glanced at his watch. "She should be calling again any minute now. No use getting all upset until you know what it is all about," he added.

I noticed that he had moved back to the window and was gazing out at the campus again. "You graduate in a few weeks, don't you?" he asked. He seemed to be making conversation.

"Yes. At the end of the term."

"Well, you can come back and get your diploma with the others," he told me. "You'd probably enjoy that, wouldn't you? In any case, you won't be starting college until the fall."

"If I get in, sir."

"You won't have much trouble. I seem to remember that you've applied to a couple of schools in the East." That had been the idea of mine during one of my periods of strong resolution, when I had thought it better to go away somewhere out of reach of all my involvements. "They like to favor applicants from other parts of the country," Stanton said. The fingers of his right hand were drumming on the top of his desk. "It'll be a change for you. I went to school in the East, too, you know, and I enjoyed it."

"I suppose I could still get into the state university?" I asked hesitantly.

"I think so. You've got the grades, I seem to remember. But why do you ask? Have you changed your mind about going east?"

"I don't know if my parents can afford it."

He nodded and said: "Well, that's quite another matter. It *is* expensive."

Miss Dunlap appeared in the doorway. "The call for Carl Woolf is on the line," she announced.

"Put it in here," Stanton said. Then he left the room, closing the door firmly behind him. The telephone on his desk rang, and I picked it up, feeling like a trespasser in the empty office, with the pictures of Roosevelt and Lincoln on the wall behind me as my only companions. Then I heard Pamela's voice over a meaningfully discreet click; Miss Dunlap had hung up, and immediately I forgot my surroundings.

"Carl, is that you?" she asked hesitantly. "Oh, darling, I hated so to call you, but I didn't know what else to do. I'm not well, and I need your help. . . ."

"Where are you?"

"I'm here in a restaurant, in town. I'll give you the address. . . . Because I can't make it home by myself, I'm afraid, and there's nobody else I could call. Can you take a cab and come for me?"

"I'll have to ask," I said.

"Do ask, will you, darling? I'll wait on the line."

I put down the receiver and went quickly to the door. Mr. Stanton was standing in the outer office beside Miss Dunlap, a sheaf of papers in his hands. He looked up, squinting at me over his glasses. "It's a friend of the family's," I said. "She's not well, and she needs me to drive her home. Do you think I could be excused for an hour or two?"

Miss Dunlap frowned, but Stanton merely nodded, as if he had been expecting such a request. "I presume it's an emergency?" he said calmly.

"Yes. There isn't anyone else who can help."

"Well, then, I think that'll be all right." He glanced at his watch. "Lunch recess is in half an hour. If you could be back by two-thirty . . ."

"I can make it."

He said: "I'll write out a pass for you," and smiled. "I wouldn't want you to be picked up by the truant officer this late in the game. . . ."

I thanked him and hurried back to the telephone to get the address of the place where Pam was waiting. There was a taxi stand a few blocks from the school, and I decided that it was better to go there directly rather than ask Miss Dunlap to call one for me. I didn't want to wait in her office, confronted by her disapproving presence.

I found a cab and told the driver where I wanted to go. Then I sat tensely in the back as we made our way through the traffic, which appeared to be worse than ever that day. Still, it was only half-past twelve when I walked into the restaurant. I remember that it was a small place on one of the main boulevards, and that the interior was decorated in an imitation of an English pub, with a bar facing the main door, and a row of wooden booths behind it. Pamela was seated at a table in the back, and she waved to me as I entered. I noticed that she looked very pale as I sat down beside her.

"I'm so sorry about this, darling," she said, putting her hand over mine, "but I really couldn't help it." Her fingers felt cold, but she managed to smile as I kissed her cheek. "Will you have a drink, angel?"

"It'll have to be something nonalcoholic," the white-jacketed barman said. He had followed me to the booth without my noticing it.

"I'll have a lime Coke," I told the man, hating him. He nodded, and I felt relieved when he went away.

"When in heaven's name will you be twenty-one?" Pam asked, laughing. "I know . . . please don't tell me. It's still quite a few years off." She took a sip of her drink, a brownish liquid with froth on the top. "Oh, I feel so much better now that you're here," she said.

"What's wrong?" I asked, leaning across the table. "You must tell me."

"I will, angel. But not now. Anyway, it's all over, my private horror, so there's no use talking about it and bringing it back."

The barman brought my Coke, with a piece of lime perched on the edge of the glass. "Would you care to order lunch now, madam?" he asked.

"I'm afraid we won't be having lunch today," Pam told him. "But we'll be back next week, I promise."

"Be glad to look after you anytime, madam," the barman said, and slipped the bill under the bowl of imitation flowers. I took a sip of the Coke. It tasted like medicine.

"Didn't he make it right?" Pam asked, putting her hand on mine.

"I'm not thirsty." I could tell by her face that she was ill. Her lipstick looked very bright against her skin, and I could see by her eyes that she had been crying. "I was afraid to call the house," I said. "I thought it would only make more trouble for you."

She nodded. "I know. Richard told me everything. And I couldn't call you, because he was always there."

"What are we going to do?" I asked.

She patted my hand. "Nothing. But don't worry," she said. "Everything will be all right. Just have to get through today and tomorrow, that's all. You can drive me home, can't you?"

"Sure. Only I have to be back by two-thirty."

She glanced at her watch. "Then we'd better get going, hadn't we? We can talk in the car."

She took the red leather billfold I knew so well out of her bag, and paid. The barman held open the door for us, and we went out into the street. Pam put her arm through mine, and tightened her grip on my hand. "You don't mind if I hang on you, do you? I'm not very strong. That's why I telephoned the school . . . because I really thought I might not make it all the way home." She indicated the parking lot with a movement of her head, and we went down a steep cement drive to where she had left her car. "Have you got fifty cents, darling?"

"I think so." I gave the attendant who had come over to us all the coins I had left in my pocket. He counted them in his palm without taking the cigarette out of his mouth.

"Thanks, buddy," he said. He looked to be about my age, and was wearing cords with the name of his high school printed in ink across the knees.

Pam slid across the leather seat, and I got behind the wheel. I drove up the steep drive and turned left on the boulevard. Pam shivered and held on to my arm, pressing her side against mine. "Have you just come back from the mountains?" I asked.

She nodded. "I got back this morning," she said, "and went straight to the doctor . . . some terrible woman Billy Lovat recommended. I should have known better, I suppose. She could hardly wait for me to get dressed before she pushed me out into the street. I guess she was frightened I'd pass out there. It was all so awful, darling, so cold-blooded and brutal. I couldn't believe that it was the result of loving you. It was as if I were being punished." She started to cry, clinging to my arm as if she were afraid of falling. "I bled and bled," she said through her tears. "I just wouldn't stop bleeding. And that made the old bitch even more impatient with me, as if it were my fault. She stood over me like a butcher, and I felt I was going to die, and never see you again."

"But why didn't you wait until we'd at least had a chance to talk?" I asked, although secretly I felt relieved that she had made the decision by herself.

"Because there was no point in waiting. Every day only made matters worse. Richard was threatening to take me with him to England at the end of next week, and so I decided to get it over with, even if it meant another bad row. . . . I knew I couldn't do what he wanted me to, go off with him and have your child, and then have him hate us both for the rest of our lives." She shook her head. "Anything's better than that, don't you agree?"

"What do you think he'll do when he finds out?"

"I don't know. I'm going to tell him I had a miscarriage, and if he doesn't believe me, well, then he doesn't, that's all. I don't care anymore. I just want to go home and lie in my bed until I feel strong again. I'm not going to die . . . I made up my mind to that when that beastly woman was standing over me, telling me to get up."

We had left the main part of the town and were passing through a residential section again. There was a row of old-fashioned mansions on our right, with the hills rising steeply behind them, the same hills where we had parked the night we had gone to Billy Lovat's party. I stopped for a traffic light in front of a supermarket. A newsboy was hawking the early edition of the evening paper. In the market a loudspeaker system was playing *"The Skater's Waltz."* It made me think of Terry for a moment, and I felt worse than ever about everything. I put my hand on Pam's knee. "Are you all right?" I asked her.

"I'm better," she said bravely. "I don't feel quite as weak as I did. I have a blinding headache, that's all."

"Will you call the doctor when you get home?"

"I hope I won't have to," she said.

The light changed, and I said: "It's all my fault," not meaning for it to sound as dramatic as it did.

Pam laughed. "Well, not all your fault," she said. "I had something to do with it too, you know. But let's not talk about it, please. Did they make a fuss at your school when I called you?"

"No. I told them that you were a friend of the family's, and they didn't say anything."

"That was very civilized of them," she said. "You'll thank your teachers for me, won't you?" She sounded more like herself again. "Tell them I'll see to it that you make up for lost time."

"Will there be anyone at the house to take care of you?" I asked.

"I hope not," she said. "Of course, Andrea'll be there, and probably Edwina, if our run of bad luck holds true. Oh, wouldn't it be lovely if we had some place of our own to go to, so that you could stay with me until I felt better?" She sighed. "Never mind. Someday we'll be free to do what we want. I only hope it won't be too late. Kiss me, darling, will you, please? I'll watch the road."

It was as if nothing had changed. We were together in a car with no place to go, about to be separated without knowing when we would be able to see each other again, only now things were worse than ever before. "Are you sorry that Guy brought you to the house that day a hundred years ago?" she asked.

"No. Are you?"

"Not really," she said, smiling, and closed her eyes, and I knew that she was in pain.

ᗌᗌ *seven* ᗌᗌ

BUT OUR RUN of bad luck *didn't* hold true, for Andrea was at home alone when we arrived. He was walking in the rose garden near the gate, and he waved to us with his cane as we passed. I remember thinking that he suddenly looked very old, his face caved in and gray, his shoulders sagging under the weight of his tweed topcoat. He turned to watch us as we stopped in front of the main patio, a frail, solitary figure among the rosebushes. "Poor old boy," Pamela said. "He seems so sad these days . . . and detached." I held the wrought-iron gate open for her, and followed her across the smooth tiles, ready to take her arm if she should falter. I had noticed that the garage at the far end of the garden was empty, which was why I felt that it was safe to go with her into the house.

We stopped for an instant in the library so that she could catch her breath. She stood leaning on the oval table around which we had so often had tea, her pale face reflected by the polished surface, her features blurred and distorted in the imperfect mirror of the high polished wood. "I must call a cab for you," she said. "They take awhile to get here, you know, and you mustn't be late. Not after they've been so helpful. Have you got enough money for the fare?" I had to admit that I didn't, and watched, ill at ease, while she emptied her purse and then insisted that I take a five-dollar bill because she had nothing smaller. "Don't be silly. I won't need it now that I'm home," she said.

I took the money and followed her slowly up the carpeted stairs. Tim, Edwina's dog, stood wagging its tail in the hallway above us, watching us with happy expectation, as if our hesitant progress were part of a game. Before we had reached the top, Pamela had to pause again. She felt dizzy, and I put my arm around her waist and half-carried her into the bedroom. Then, while she waited on the upholstered stool in front of her dressing table, I pulled the cover off the double bed, trying not to think that Gordon would be sleeping there that night. "Shall I help you undress?" I asked, folding the heavy material as best I could.

"No, not today," she said with a faint smile. "I'll just lie down for a minute the way I am. Will you close the curtains, darling?"

I crossed to the windows, and stood there thinking that I had looked at the moonlit hills from that very same place long ago when suddenly I caught sight of Andrea crossing the flagstone walk that led from the tennis court to the pool. He was staring up at the house, his face set in an expression of doubt and disapproval, which made me feel that I should leave at once. But Pamela said: "Come sit here with me for a second until I feel strong enough to telephone," and I went to her and took her hand, which was even colder than mine.

"Do you want me to call?" I asked.

"Perhaps you'd better. The number of the people we always use is in my little black book."

Then, once the taxi was on its way, I felt less nervous about being there, and sat in silence beside her on the edge of the bed as if we were together in our own house. She asked me to get a glass of water for her out of the bathroom, and she drank half of it before putting it down on the bedside table with a trembling hand. She said: "Don't look so frightened, Carl. Everything's going to be all right. I know it will. The worst is over now."

"But what'll happen when Richard comes home?" I asked. "He's bound to guess the truth."

"He won't do anything," she said calmly. "He's not a monster, you know, and he's bound to realize that I was right."

"Will you still have to go to England with him?"

"I shouldn't think so," she said. "There'd be no point in Karen and my going now. He knows that we're better off here. He's always said so himself . . . especially with the world the way it is. But I don't want to think about all that now, darling. Is it very warm in here, or is it me?"

I told her that I didn't find it particularly warm, and helped her off with her coat. Exhausted by the effort, she lay back on the crumpled pillows, her eyes closed, still holding my hand. "Don't you think you'd better call Dr. Dostal?" I asked, remembering the name of the physician I had often met at their house in the past.

"I don't think so," she said. "Not unless I start bleeding again. Anyway, he's better for children than adults, and then, what's wrong with me is a rather special thing." She opened her eyes and caught me staring at her face. "Don't look at me like that, angel," she said. "I'm not going to die. You don't have to worry."

"I wasn't worrying about that," I said, lying. "I was just thinking you'd be more comfortable if you got undressed and into bed. I don't mind helping you."

"But I mind," she said. "I hate for you to see me like this."

"Don't be silly." I slid my left arm under her shoulders, and pulling her up into a sitting position, unbuttoned the front of her sweater.

"You know, you're a very forward young man," she said, laughing. She slipped out of her cardigan, and shuddered slightly. "It's cold now," she complained. I helped her pull back the covers, and she got into the bed, crossing her arms over her bare chest. The pearl necklace she wore was visible above the top sheet, which she had pulled up over her. "How often have I told you that a lady's jewelry has to come off first?" she said. "We all look like tarts, naked in our pearls. . . ." She raised her hands to her throat and unclipped the single strand of pearls. "Perhaps that should be the title of my autobiography. *Naked in My Pearls.* Do you like that?"

"I like you," I said, joining in the forced game. "Anyway, you're not naked. You've got your bra and your skirt on."

"So I have," she said, almost gaily. "Still, that's as naked as you're going to see me today. Now, will you please go and wait for your taxi out in the road? Bessie'll help me with the rest of this. Then she can make me some soup, and I'll feel all well again."

"Are you sure you want me to leave?"

"Very sure."

I didn't argue with her. She was right. There was nothing I could do except hold her hand and look worried, which only made things worse. But I couldn't help feeling frightened. Seeing Andrea in the garden, looking like a scarecrow among the clipped rosebushes, had made me think of death when we had first arrived, and although I had tried to suppress my fears, they were still there in the back of my head. It was as if death had suddenly become a mystical presence lurking outside the house, and although I realized that it was ridiculous to think that way, I couldn't shake off the feeling of death waiting there in the gray light of afternoon, like the character in a German legend. I knelt beside the bed and kissed her on the neck and cheeks as I had always done after we had made love. "All right, I'll go," I said. "But please call me as soon as you can. You don't know what it's like to have to wait without knowing what's happening."

"I promise I'll call you tomorrow," she replied, turning her head to look at me. "Around four. That's a good time, isn't it? That is, if you'll promise not to worry. Not about my having to go away, or dying, or any of the other silly ideas you like to plague yourself with." She touched my face gently with her hand, stroking my cheek with a spent kind of tenderness. "The things we're most afraid of rarely happen, you know," she said gravely.

"All right, I won't think or worry at all. How's that? I love you. You know that, don't you?"

She smiled and said: "I'm glad you do. Because that's all I have now."

And as if we were starting all over again at the beginning, I found that her answer was not quite what I wanted to hear, that I would have preferred it if she had replied with a declaration of her own, which I realized at once was an absurd thing to expect at that moment, for I knew that what she had been through must have come close to curing her of love altogether. And yet I would have felt better about going if she had repeated the words I had used too often in the past, so that they had become a greeting almost, a way of saying good-bye.

"Do you think you'll ever want to go to bed with me again?" I asked shamelessly, and she shook her head, tears coming into her eyes for a second.

"Of course I will, you silly idiot," she said. "What makes you say a thing like that?"

"Because I am an idiot, I guess," I told her. She didn't reply, but merely looked away as if there were something on her mind she didn't want to tell me. After a while I got up to go, knowing that I had to, but feeling as if I were abandoning her just the same. What if she should die, I couldn't help thinking. I would never forgive myself for having left.

"Leave the door open, please," she called after me. "That way Bessie won't have to struggle with it when she brings the tray." When I looked back she raised her hand and waved to me, managing to smile a smile of encouragement, as if I were the one in jeopardy. I stepped out into the hallway, where Tim was still waiting for his mistress. He wagged his tail as a sign of recognition, looking up at me like an old friend who expects to be neglected. I went quickly down the stairs and out of the house. In the patio I ran into Andrea. He didn't put out his hand, but stared at me with hostile, watery eyes. "Are you leaving?" he asked.

"I have to get back to school," I replied, too embarrassed to be anything but truthful.

"But you have no car," he remarked suspiciously.

"It doesn't matter," I said, and hurried past him through the wrought-iron gate. At that moment the taxi appeared, proving me to be a liar as well as a troublemaker. I gave the driver the address of the school, which he acknowledged with an irritated grunt. Andrea had stepped through the gate in order to get a better view of my departure, and our eyes met for an instant as the taxi started to pull out of the drive. There was not enough time for me to transmit even a last apologetic glance; nevertheless I will always remember the expression on his face, the hurt, bewildered look that seemed to be asking why it was that everybody lied to him now about everything.

I never saw him again. He had a stroke and died late that same afternoon, hopefully ending all loneliness for him forever. The end came while he was climbing up the back stairs on his way to his room, and it was there that Bessie found him, lying face down on the wooden steps, his topcoat still buttoned tightly around his neck. Seeing the purple face, the terrified woman thought that he had fallen and been choked to death by his own collar, which awful assumption the doctor dismissed as soon as he had examined the body: "Count Tucci has died of natural causes," he stated categorically, thus dispelling any possible accusations of neglect that might have been brought up once the first shock of the old man's death had been absorbed.

Yet, even while Pamela was describing the events of the previous day on the telephone, I couldn't help thinking that I might have been able to help the old man, at least have made it possible for him to die in bed instead of alone, on the back stairs, like an aging servant in a Russian novel, for I recalled how aware I had been of the presence of death that afternoon, had recognized its threat in the pasty color of Andrea's skin, as well as in his labored movements. But I had been solely concerned with Pam's welfare, had not registered any other dangers. Only her life had mattered, only her survival, and so I had transposed my observations and had reverted to a childish mysticism that I was ashamed to admit to her now. "I thought Andrea didn't look well when I saw him in the garden," was all I could find to say.

"There was nothing any of us could have done," she replied, guessing what was going through my mind. "Poor old boy. His heart just gave out on him." Then she told me that she would call me again as soon as she possibly could, that she felt much better, was well enough to go to the funeral with Gordon and Edwina, which made it seem that she had been completely reinstated in the family. "He left a letter, asking that he be cremated, and that his ashes be returned to Italy, so he obviously knew that he didn't have much time left."

"And will that be done?" I asked. "I mean, is Richard going to do it?"

"Yes, I think so," she said. "It's not all that difficult, you know."

"Then he's still leaving for England? He hasn't changed his plans. . . ."

"No, of course not," she replied. "He has a film to do there." She sounded almost distant, I thought, or at least as controlled as she had always sounded on the telephone, which disturbed me.

"And will you have to go?"

"No, I'm staying here, just as I told you. But there's no use going into all that now. You promised not to worry, remember? Not about us, anyway. There's no reason to. I'm perfectly all right again. I must go," she added, as I didn't reply at once. "Good-bye, my darling. Work hard."

"I will," I said. "I love you." I was being relegated to my old role again. "*L'amant est toujours le plus grand cocu*," I thought grimly. "You won't forget to call," I said, as she hadn't left the line.

"Don't be silly. Of course I won't. Try not to be so pessimistic."

"You mean because the things we're most afraid of rarely happen?"

"That's right." She laughed and said, "Good-bye, darling," as if someone had come into the room, forcing her to end the conversation.

⇜ *eight* ⇝

BUT IT WASN'T altogether true, I discovered soon enough, her private counsel of comfort, or at least it didn't apply to the events of that winter, for the evening papers that arrived a few days later brought the first news that Schuschnigg, the Austrian chancellor, had been called to Berchtesgaden and had been handed an ultimatum that presaged the end of Austria as an independent state. The late-news roundup confirmed the beginnings of a new crisis in central Europe, supplied all the frightening rumors that soon turned out to be true. The Nazi party was to be reinstated in Austria, where it had been illegal, and all the assassins and their helpers were to be set free. Seyss-Inquart was to be appointed Minister of the Interior, and another Nazi was to be made Minister of War.

We sat in front of the radio, my mother and I, after a hastily eaten dinner, and it became apparent that our worst fears were about to be realized. Vienna, the city where my father's family still lived, was no longer safe. The brown-shirted bullies of the SA were about to make their reappearance in the wide, elegant streets I so dimly remembered, commandeering the red streetcars, as if the revolution they had been waiting for had come at last. It was difficult to believe that it was going to happen in Vienna, too, the attacks on Jewish shops, the arrests of hundreds of people. My aunt was there, and my uncle. And their children.

"I have to cable them," my mother said, as the broadcast had ended. "They have to get out. In a few days they won't be able to. If only Uncle Ludwig doesn't persist with his idiotically optimistic view of everything. He's always been so sure that the Nazis will never take over Austria. . . ."

"Father isn't in Vienna, is he?"

"No, he's in London. But I must cable him too, so that he doesn't go there in order to persuade the others to leave." She was pale. Her hand shook as she took a pencil and a piece of paper and started to draft the first of the messages she intended sending.

"I don't think there'll be a war," I said to reassure her, hoping that the opposite would turn out to be true.

"No, there won't be a war," she replied. "Not over Austria. But for those who stay behind it'll be much worse than war." She sighed wearily. "I only thank God that you and Jake are here, in this country," she said.

Now, more than thirty years later, it is difficult to recall the feeling of gloom that hung over those days early in February, 1938, although we had an idea of the greater disasters that were to follow. We could sense that the trap was slowly closing, that every day counted now, every hour. "Maybe it won't happen," I said, influenced by Pam's counsel of optimism in the face of disaster. "Maybe the other nations of Europe will come to Austria's aid. . . ."

My mother shook her head. "Nobody will help," she replied. "Because nobody really cares."

She was right, of course, although a month was to pass before her prophecy was to be proven true. The government of Austria struggled like a small fish on a steel hook, and the world watched apathetically. The end came with surprising speed. Schuschnigg announced that he was going to hold a plebiscite on March 13, to determine how many Austrians favored *Anschluss*. That last desperate act of defiance on the part of the Austrian chancellor provoked Hitler into setting the wheels of the Wehrmacht's tanks and trucks in motion, and on the morning of the thirteenth of March, the German army started to cross the Austrian border.

I remember that life changed, too, in that month of crisis. I graduated from high school, and Guy transmitted to me Mr. Levin's offer of a job as a filing clerk with the motion-picture company he controlled. I accepted at once. That was the first money I had ever earned, the blue Thursday paychecks, relieving me of the last of my childish fears: I would not die in the trenches without having proved myself capable of earning a living, even if it was a slender one. My other boyish concern, that I would be offered up as cannon fodder while still a virgin, had obviously been dispelled a long time ago.

A week after I reported to work for the first time, Gordon departed for England, taking Edwina with him, ostensibly to accompany her stepfather's ashes to the small Mediterranean town where he was born. Las Golondrinas was rented to an English writer and his wife, with the proviso that they would give it up should Gordon return. Pamela and Karen, with Bessie to look after them, moved to the cottage on the beach. In the interests of economy, Gordon had apparently chosen to ignore all unpleasant associations that the place might have had for him.

The winter rains started by the middle of February, the skies closing in on the mountains permanently, so it seemed, for the ceaseless downpour did not let up until the middle of March. The main boulevards were flooded, the brown water spilling out over the banks of the shallow riverbeds, nature thus providing an atmosphere of disaster that was once again in concert with the disasters that were taking place thousands of miles away. The wilting letters that the postman delivered almost daily to our house brought only news of fear and despair. My aunt had been beaten and forced to wash the floor of the local police station on her hands and knees, while the Nazi stormtroopers, who had seized power before the arrival of the German troops, stood over her with their whips, jeering at her ineptness. Just as my mother had feared, Uncle Ludwig had reacted too slowly to my parents' warnings, and it was only by signing over his factory to a Nazi foreman that both he and my aunt were able to escape to England. My father's best friend and comrade during the Serbian campaign in the World War was less fortunate, for he was beaten to death in the same police station a week later, ostensibly because he insisted on wearing his uniform when he was called for by the Brown Shirts to take his turn at being degraded.

One of the letters the rain-soaked postman delivered was for me. I recognized Gordon's handwriting on the envelope. He had apparently written it on the eve of his departure. It was a little less austere in tone than his first note, although equally unpleasant in content. He addressed it to "Dear Carl" (not Carl Woolf, as he had the last time), "I don't suppose you will pay any more attention to my wishes now than you have in the past, but I want, nevertheless, to say that I hope that in my absence you will conduct yourself in a more honorable manner toward me. I don't think I have to elaborate on the meaning of these words, as I am certain that you understand what I am referring to. I do not blame you alone for everything that has happened, if that is any comfort to you, nor do I think that you alone will decide on what your future behavior will be. However, I do want to remind you that a man is responsible to his own conscience for the things he does in life, which fact I hope will influence your actions."

The edge of the sea was brown as I started up the coast highway that first Saturday morning after Gordon's departure, the beach strewn with rubble left by the storm that had subsided at last, and as I rode along on my bike, I found myself wondering if in reality my conscience wasn't a lost cause, that was doomed to defeat. Because I realized that I was more concerned about whether Pamela was waiting alone for me at the cottage than anything else, for I wanted to make love to her again, thus making certain that she hadn't changed toward me, been cured of love, which selfish fears I seemed unable to control. And as the cottage came into view, I said a small doubting prayer, that should there be a war, it might at least be delayed until the fall, so that we would have the benefit of another long summer's grace.

PART
VIII

≫ One ≪

Looking back now (from the vantage point of a sometimes unwelcome maturity), I find the past obscured by an almost constant nostalgic mist, which tends to make everything appear innocuous and old-fashioned, like a family album collected by a kindly *papparazzo*. And although I get impatient with my part in the story, there seems inescapably to be, by comparison with today's standards, a quality of guilelessness about it all that gives off an aura of unreality. In self-defense, let me say that it is not by intent.

Then, too, mine was anything but a typical youth, although I can't recall that any of my friends lived a much more tortured existence. Some of them were poorer, and perhaps more adventurous, yet none of them were led to serious crimes or excesses of a vicious nature. Their most rebellious acts conformed with the then current notion of youth. They made love in parked cars, and cut school in order to go to the beach on hot days, and a few, I remember, smoked "loco weed," but those were the fastest of the "fast," as that was then considered to be a rather wild thing to do.

Violence was not as big a part of our daily lives as it is today, although the world was certainly an equally violent place. But America didn't seem to have been as infected by the germs of savagery as the rest of the world, at least not that part of the country. There were political demonstrations, of course, even in the land of the lotus-eaters (which was how my father always referred to California in his letters), as it was an intensely political time. But even these confrontations were fairly self-controlled, not nearly so violent as today's counterparts.

I remember going to one with Jake during the early days of the Czech crisis. We went to heckle and protest, for it was a meeting of the German-American Bund, held in a house in the eastern part of the town. A couple of swastika flags had been lowered out of the second-story windows of the place, and the booing crowd, which Jake and I joined, grew quickly into an angry mob. There were all kinds of people on our side, members of the Young Socialists League, Jewish War Veterans, a few men and women from the anti-Nazi organizations, as well as a group from one of the local unions belonging to the garment industry. When the Germans inside the house began singing the "Horst Wessel Lied," we did our best to drown them out with a rendition of "America, the Beautiful," and it was at that moment, I recall, that the police arrived, led by a man who was known to most of the demonstrators as Red Hines, the head of the vice squad. He and his men were there to protect the "meeting," and they faced the protesters with clubs in hand, which stirred up the more militant elements in the crowd.

A couple of hefty young men in T-shirts, whom Jake seemed to know, produced a crate of half-rotten persimmons, and we helped ourselves to the fruit and began to throw it at the curtained windows behind which the enemy was gathered. When someone added a rock for good measure, the police replied with tear gas in rather limited amounts, enough, however, to disperse the crowd, and I remember standing shoulder to shoulder with Jake and his comrades, our eyes stinging, as we threw with our well-trained baseball arms until there were no more persimmons left. Then we retreated as rapidly as we could, for the police had started using their clubs just as indiscriminately as they do today. My last view of the battlefield was most satisfying, and it is still vivid in my mind—the cream-colored plaster walls of the Nazi bastion covered with the red polka dots our missiles had inscribed on it. Marcia, who had appeared in time to join us in our hurried withdrawal, was shouting hoarsely for us to hold our ground, but neither Jake nor I paid any attention to her as we ran up a narrow alley at the end of which we had parked my mother's car.

The police followed in halfhearted pursuit, but there were few arrests, as once the crowd had dispersed, it was difficult for them to locate the worst offenders. Long hair in those days was worn only by artists and intellectuals (though always, on the stage, by young revolutionaries), so that once we had left the scene of the riot, they were unable to proceed against us with any degree of certainty. And although we were stopped by a patrol car after a few blocks, we escaped arrest by telling the harassed officers that we were on our way to a nearby movie. Our appearance hadn't given us away, partly because the police didn't take the time to examine our clothing (which was covered with persimmon stains), and also because we looked no different from any of the other kids who were out on that Friday night. We hadn't really accomplished our mission (which was to break up the meeting of the local Bund), but I remember that we drove back to the beach full of the exhilarating feeling that direct action always seems to bring with it, especially when motivated by political solidarity. My eyes were still smarting from the tear gas the next day, and my right arm was sore, which minor discomforts I felt as proud of as if I had received an honest wound.

However, I never took part in a political demonstration again. Jake urged me to on various occasions, but I felt that the causes were not mine; the real enemy was out of reach. I believed dogmatically that any action that didn't combat Germany directly was a juvenile waste of time. And so I stayed away. I realize now that my point of view was motivated by a romantic snobbism that made going off to defend Madrid seem admirable, while demonstrating in front of the British embassy against the embargo seemed a way of emphasizing the fact that one did not really have the courage to go. Anyway, submitting to the discipline of the various organizers bothered me. I didn't want to be ordered around like a soldier without being one.

Then, too, I was busy with my new job, which demanded my being at the office at a quarter to nine in order to "punch in," which only true proletarian moment of the day brought with it its own feeling of satisfaction, as it started the pay clock on its way. I didn't enjoy the eight or nine hours that followed. As a filing clerk in the story department of Mr. Levin's private production company, I saw very little of the amusing side of studio life, especially during the first couple of months, when I was confined to a room full of metal cabinets, with the mission to bring order into the voluminous story files of the department. I rarely saw anyone but my direct superior's secretary, a rather forbidding spinster who made it her business to see that I was busy most of the day.

Every story that had ever been submitted had been synopsized and buried in one of these cabinets. The left-hand corner of the synopsis was marked with a colored clip, the purpose of which was to catalog it as a possible vehicle for one of the company's stars. Red clips meant that it was a suitable vehicle for Carole Lombard, with whom Levin had a promised commitment. Blue was for Ann Harding, green for George Brent. And so on. My predecessor, an elderly lady, a friend of Miss Grossman, the secretary, had spent a considerable number of hours designing this complex filing system, which, as the contractual obligations of the various stars had changed, had become obsolete. My job, or at least my first assignment, was to rectify the system and bring it up to date, using a new list of players that the great man himself had issued. And so while the Sudeten Germans clamored for their alleged rights, I spent hours pulling colored clips off the sheets of onion paper on which they had been carefully attached.

Every few days Guy would come to visit me in my cell, to see "how I was getting on," as he announced with relentless monotony. It occurred to me that his calls had an ulterior motive, that he intended to emphasize what was already quite apparent to me, that a job was in itself not the answer to my problems, that the dreary routine of filing was worse than any school or college, and that I was probably condemning myself to years of just this kind of drudgery by giving up my education. "There are people who have to do this kind of work all of their lives," he always began, in reply to my as yet unuttered complaints, because it gave him a lead into his favorite sermon of self-improvement, which he had obviously come to preach.

He needn't have bothered. I had already realized that the job I had wanted so much was not the solution. Aside from the boredom of the work, I was finding it difficult to be with Pamela. Gordon had exacted a promise from her to behave "honorably" as well, which she interpreted to mean that we shouldn't be seen together in public, nor that I should be around while she was with Karen. Therefore we were limited to the hours when Karen was at school. But as I was busy with my filing most of the day, we were reduced to furtive lunches in the small restaurants near the studio, and long walks on the beach at night when Karen had gone to bed. It was as if Gordon had cleverly devised a way by which he could leave, and still make certain of his wife's fidelity, and it seemed almost comical at times, the invisible chastity belt he had imposed.

Even Bessie, the cook, appeared to be part of the conspiracy against us, as she refused to be left alone in the house with Karen. She was afraid of the sea, so she said. She had been born and raised in Kansas, which was why she hadn't minded the solitude of Las Golondrinas. It was different at the beach, she maintained. The constant sound of the waves frightened her, made her think a huge fish would crawl out of "all that restlessness" and attack her, so that Pamela was forced to stay within earshot of the cottage at all times.

I decided that if we were ever to make love again, I would have to find a place away from home. Then Pam and I at least would have a place to go whenever she was free. But I couldn't leave my mother to live alone in the house with Maureen. Once again everything seemed to be rigged against us. "Be patient," Pamela would say; "things will change. It won't always be like this." But I didn't believe her. I was certain that the weeks and months would pass and that Gordon would return, and we would be separated by the same obligations that had always separated us in the past.

Sometimes in desperation I felt that we had already come to the end of our love affair, and that she had realized this long ago, the night we had quarreled and I had struck her, but that she hadn't had the courage to tell me and had been looking for a slow, relatively painless way out, a separation due to the unalterable circumstances of both of our lives. I confronted her with my suspicions, accused her of wanting us to grow apart, which she denied, of course, exasperated by my lack of faith in her, in myself. "Why do you always say things like that?" she asked in a voice that she was forced to control, as we were seated in the Blue Diner, a small restaurant frequented by the less-well-paid white-collar workers at the studio. "If you don't want to see me anymore, if it's all too difficult, you don't have to call, you know. But don't invent elaborate theories to serve as an excuse for what you yourself want to do."

"I'm not inventing anything," I said, glancing at my watch to see how much of my lunch hour there was still left. "I just feel that it's going wrong, that we only quarrel now when we're together."

"You like to quarrel," she said. "I noticed that a long time ago."

"No, I don't. I hate it."

She shrugged doubtfully. "All right. Then I'll tell you what we'll do. We'll make a pact, a very simple one. If you ever want it to end, not to see me again, just send me a note, or leave a message for me, saying you're at the Blue Diner. I'll understand what that means, and I'll do the same thing if that's how I feel. . . ."

"That's a ridiculous idea," I said, glancing at my watch again.

"No, it isn't. I think it's a fine plan. Maybe neither one of us ever will, but if we want to, we can. You have to get back, don't you?" she asked. "I'll stay here and finish my coffee, if you don't mind. . . ."

"No, come with me, I hate to leave you sitting here by yourself. It makes it more difficult for me to go."

"But why? I'd enjoy being quiet for a minute or two. I'll see you tomorrow, anyway. Unless you decide to send our coded message," she said, laughing.

"I don't think it's much of a joke," I said, rising.

"Oh, come on, let's not quarrel about that, too."

But we did, all the way back to her car, and parted without really making up again, which had rarely happened to us before, but was happening more and more frequently now. There was no release for the tensions between us, except to meet again at night and walk endlessly up and down the beach in front of the cottage, like sentinels on guard, never going more than a hundred yards away, because we were afraid that Karen or Bessie might wake up and find that Pamela had gone. Karen did once, and ventured out onto the terrace in her nightgown, so that Pamela had to run back and reassure the child that she had only gone out for a breath of fresh air. I waited for a long time in the darkness, hoping that she would be able to come back, cursing Karen, with the still wintry sea as my only witness, which was fortunate, as Pamela would never have forgiven me had she heard.

Once, to please me, she brought a blanket out of the house, and we made love on the beach, which, despite the discomfort, helped heal the wounds of my frustration, although I could tell it hadn't been of much satisfaction to her. "You didn't really like it, did you?" I asked as she lay beside me on the moist sand.

"Of course I did," she replied. "Why do you say that?"

"Because I can tell."

"Well, it wasn't as nice as being in bed together, but that doesn't matter. I love being close to you again, and having you touch me. It's better than nothing, just as you said."

"That isn't enough. I don't want you to do it just for me. I don't want you to 'sacrifice' yourself. You've had to do that for too many years. . . ."

"But it's different with you," she said. "Oh, Carl, how can you even think a thing like that, much less say it?" She got up, and smoothing her skirt down around her legs, started back in the direction of the house. I picked up the blanket and followed her.

"I want it to be the way it was before. I don't want you to make love with me just to please me."

"I didn't," she said. "You're mad. It's all in your head. You think that because I became pregnant, I don't want you anymore, and that isn't true." I caught up with her and took her in my arms. "Why do you always say things that hurt me?" she asked.

"I'm sorry. Would you rather I stopped coming to see you?"

"No, of course not." We were standing directly in front of the bricked-in terrace of the house, her disheveled hair catching the light. "Let me go, Carl," she said. "Please. I'll call you tomorrow." She took the blanket and turned away from me.

"Will you come and have lunch?"

"I don't know. I'll call you."

I watched her cross to the front door. She hesitated a moment before going inside, in order to shake the sand off the blanket, and I waved to her, but she didn't wave back. I remember walking on past the house and crossing the beach to the highway, where I had left the car, thinking that it was all over and that she would send me a note the next day, or a telegram with the coded message she had invented for just such an eventuality. But she didn't. She called instead to say that lunch was impossible, but that she was free in the evening, as Karen was going to a birthday party, and that Bessie was taking her, all of which she had arranged so that we could be alone together. And so we made love undisturbed once again, and the breach was healed, and the crisis passed.

Toward the end of May of that year the world looked better for one fleeting moment. Beneš, the slight, professorial-looking president of Czechoslovakia, suddenly mobilized his country's armed forces, and for a while it appeared as if the Germans were going to be held in check. It was the first time anyone had defied the Nazis, and there were rumors of a military revolt inside Germany, the old, optimistic rumors nobody had paid any attention to for a long time. Hitler declared that he had no aggressive intentions against the Czechs, and the whole world breathed a little easier. But it didn't last long, the spring *détente*. Chamberlain and Halifax and Henderson saw to that, the three "undertakers of Europe," who were making their arrangements for the sellout of Czechoslovakia even then.

But we lived in ignorance of their secret meetings and private retreats, at least during the early months of the summer, when it still seemed possible that a war might be avoided altogether. The European tourist season had begun, with some Americans venturing inside Germany to "find out for themselves about the Nazis." Gordon wrote Pam that London was "its old normal, gay self" again, and urged her to return. She declined his offer without any hesitation.

"Nowhere in the world is as pleasant a place as the beach outside my own house," she told me, "especially on the days when I can be there with you."

Those days were becoming more numerous, as Karen often went to play with the neighbors' children. And as the weeks passed and the warm weather set in, Pam became less punctilious about keeping her promise to Gordon. After all, he was having a good time. At least, that was what her friends in London reported to her, trying perhaps to make her change her mind and come home. "It's such an old-fashioned tactic," she said, folding one of the many letters that had arrived for her at the cottage. "I'm glad he's enjoying himself. I don't want him to grieve and become a monk just because we don't live together anymore."

"But don't you sometimes feel that you'd like to go back? You used to talk about it a lot."

She sat up in her deck chair and looked out across the tranquil water, her eyes squinting against the afternoon sun. "I don't know why, but I don't miss it anymore. Quite apart from you. . . . It's being out here on my own, in this little house. I suddenly feel as if I never want to leave." She laughed uneasily. "I'll probably change my mind someday. Or maybe I'll become even more of a recluse, and move off to some island in the Pacific. That's after you've left me, of course. Then at least I'll be able to console myself with some gorgeous beachboy who will have become my slave. He'll probably seduce Karen and turn me out of the grass hut . . . that's how those stories usually end. But all that's still a long way off. For the moment I feel quite happy here."

⇛ *two* ⇚

I FELT A DEGREE of contentment, too. But I couldn't dispel the conviction that it wouldn't last, that we would soon have to pay for "our long summer's grace." For despite the rumors of peace and agreement, I felt certain that the war was finally coming and that there would be no way to avoid it this time. The total apathy of most of the people I encountered in my new job only helped strengthen my conviction that we would all be called to account for having escaped the turmoil of the rest of the world for so long. Even "the Greeks without brains," who were returning to their favorite playgrounds again, would ultimately be affected. I was convinced of it. It gave the summer a strange atmosphere of desperate seeking after pleasure, as if we were all at a party at which death would soon appear.

While I swam in the ocean with Pam, the unrest in the Sudetenland was increasing. While we lay on the hot sand, Lord Runciman was visiting Prague and proving himself to be just another partner in the firm of funeral directors headed by Neville Chamberlain. While I worked half-heartedly in my hot cubicle, the Germans were mobilizing their army. The newspapers and newsreels were once again full of pictures of goose-stepping troops stamping across the cobblestone squares of German towns. On the day General Franco's troops reached the Mediterranean, I bought my first car, and recorded both events in my diary, as if to expiate my guilt at being happy on the day that Madrid was isolated.

Madrid! What a ring of defiance the name had that summer. But would its defenders be able to hold out until the war against Germany had started? Or were they doomed to defeat, the Spanish republicans? The International Brigades were being withdrawn. The last crusade was ending. There were well-verified stories now of bitter strife inside the loyalist camp. The Communists were intriguing against the men of the

POUM, trying to gain control of the government. Was it still a cause worth dying for? A man's death was so quickly forgotten.

I had made friends with my boss, an unsuccessful writer, who had given up the struggle of literature in order to become the story editor for Mr. Levin's company. His name was Benson, and although he had been educated at Virginia Military Institute, he had been too young to serve in the First World War. He was a big, nervous man who had accepted all of the personal defeats of his creative life with a wary sense of humor, had learned to control his ambitions and take the money that the movies paid him, in order to raise his family and enjoy himself. He had a sailboat, a small sloop that required an extra hand, and so he frequently invited me.

I was a willing apprentice, anxious to learn the art of sailing, which he enjoyed trying to teach me. As we sailed slowly up the coast, he liked to reminisce about his school days at VMI, which had marked him for life with a slight stammer and an uncontrollable habit of using the word "sir" too frequently. "I should have gone to West Point," he often told me. "I'd be a major now, and a lieutenant colonel ten minutes after the outbreak of any war. Instead I'm an overly subservient sergeant in Mr. Levin's command. Pull in the jib, a little, will you, Carl? It's fluttering."

He was not altogether serious about his regrets, because part of him despised the military life, as he knew what his early encounter with it had done to him. Still, he was anxious to give me good advice, knowing what my problems were. "If I were you I'd join the army," he said to me one day while we were returning to port in a slack breeze, with a following sea. "You did your ROTC in high school, didn't you?"

"No, I was excused because I was an Austrian."

He frowned. "Well, then, join the army now as a buck private. The war's coming, and the sooner you get prepared for it, the better. If you go in now, you'll be commissioned in a year or two. Then, by the time this country goes to war, you'll have company grade; and just remember that the higher you rise, the better chance you'll have to survive. It's going to be a century for soldiers, for American soldiers, too. And if you still want to write, you'll have something to write about. War and sex . . . those are literature's favorite subjects, and you'll know plenty about both before you're twenty-five."

"But suppose America stays neutral?" I asked. "I'd look pretty silly in my soldier's suit."

"America's not going to stay neutral for long," Benson said. "No matter what Mr. Roosevelt says. He's just being careful. Oh, you can be sure we won't fight for the Czechs, and probably not for the French. But we'll fight for the British; you can bet your arse on that . . . because we're tied to them by blood. Also they know how to lure us in on their battles, our British cousins."

"It's everybody's fight," I said in a controlled voice.

"I know, I know. But even if it wasn't, they'd see to it that we'd be there in time to pull their chestnuts out of the fire."

For a man who appeared to have few prejudices, Benson was surprisingly anti-British, which bothered me, as it usually went hand in hand with a tendency to be pro-German. When I asked him why he hated the English so much (he had an English name), he shrugged and smiled his easygoing smile. "I'm not half-Irish for nothing," he said. "And my mother was French, so what the hell, I've got a right to hate their guts. But I admire them, too. Nobody can hold a position as well as the British infantry. But that's all they can do. Dig in and defend. They have to get their backs against the wall. Otherwise they won't fight. It'll be the same old story again this time. Wait and see."

I told him that I didn't agree with him, which didn't disturb him in the least, as he was obviously not too impressed with any of my opinions. He tolerated them, because he realized that as my boss it would be unfair to contradict me too emphatically. I ultimately told him that I had thought about joining the Royal Flying Corps, even recounted my one attempt to learn how to fly.

He grinned happily, delighted with my confession. At the same time, he considered the idea with greater seriousness than I had expected him to. "The Royal Air Force, eh? Well, it's very glamorous, of course, and the uniform's smarter than most. But from what you tell me, you're not really suited to be a flier. You've got too much imagination, and that's no good for an aviator. Especially if you want to survive."

"The infantry's not exactly safe, is it?"

"I didn't say the infantry. I said the army. There are a lot of jobs besides being a rifleman, you know. And you speak the language of the enemy . . . that should be a help. And French, too. Well, there won't be too many fellows around who can do all that."

It was too practical an approach, and it didn't fit in with my plans. I couldn't see myself joining the army as a peacetime soldier, signing up for a three-year hitch. I preferred to wait until the war started. In the meantime, there were other, more pressing decisions to be made. What would I do in the autumn, which was fast approaching? I had applied to several colleges, and had been accepted by two of them, both in the East. That meant leaving Pam, and to go away to another part of the country while she remained behind was unthinkable, especially while she was living alone.

I decided to discuss the problem with her, thinking that she would agree with my decision not to go East to school. But as always, she was too reasonable, too undemanding. She seemed incapable of possessiveness or jealousy. I didn't want to leave *her* because I was afraid that she would find somebody else, which thought never seemed to cross her mind. Or if the thought did occur to her, she was too proud to mention it, too much in control of her emotions to let it bother her. She was always too self-controlled, it seemed to me; only when we made love was she capable of suddenly abandoning her restrained manner, and only then did I sense that she did occasionally feel as I felt nearly all of the time. But when we were seated in a car or in a restaurant, she was somehow remote, level-headed to a painful degree, just as she was on this occasion. "You must do what's best for you," she said. "If you have to go East to college, well, then, you must go. I'll still be here when you get back."

"Do you *want* me to leave?" I asked.

"Of course I don't. But neither do I think it's right for you to change all of your plans just because of me."

"I don't care about anything else."

"Oh, Carl, don't be so silly. There are other considerations that are far more important. Someday you'll regret you didn't go."

"I can just as well go to the university here."

"But you said it was too late to apply."

"I can go to the extension division for the first term. Then, in the winter I can transfer and become an undergraduate. The credits will count just the same."

"Don't you think it would be good for you to go away?"

"Why should it be?"

"Because you'll meet new people, experience new things. You shouldn't tie yourself down to this place just because I'm here. You're too young."

"I'm not that young. I'll be eighteen in a couple of months."

"I know, my darling. You're ancient. A tired old man." She squeezed my hand. "Watch the road," she added, as I tried to kiss her. "An automobile accident is all we need."

Why was it that everything always threatened to part us? She seemed to accept this, take it for granted.

"Going East to school is too expensive, anyway," I said, knowing that that was an argument she could not contradict. "I don't want to become a burden to my family."

"But haven't you been able to save some money this summer?"

"I spent it on the car."

"That wasn't very prudent, was it?"

"If I didn't have a car, I'd never be able to come and see you," I said, not quite truthfully.

"There you are. It's all my fault again. . . ." She laughed cheerfully. She was right, I realized. It was ridiculous to let future problems spoil what little time we had together. And although I did not succeed as well as she did in enjoying "our evening out," I made no further reference to college or the war, or the possibility of Gordon coming back from England.

Karen was spending the night with Bessie somewhere on the other side of the town, an outing she always enjoyed, as she was pampered and spoiled, and allowed to eat and drink whatever she wanted to. "Richard would probably disapprove," Pamela said as an afterthought, "but I think it's good for her to get away from 'Mummy' once in a while."

"And good for Mummy."

"That, too," Pamela replied pensively.

We went to the movies and saw Hitchcock's *The Lady Vanishes*, which reminded us both of what was happening in Europe, and so we drove back in silence to the beach, aware more than ever that we were living on borrowed time.

It was a warm night, and after we got back to the cottage we sat for a long time on the terrace, facing the ocean, content to hold hands and listen to the steady splashing of the surf. After a while Pam got up, and shivering slightly, announced that it was "time to go to bed," as if we were already married.

It was a luxurious feeling not to have to worry about what time it was, and to be alone together without being concerned about somebody coming to the door, or the telephone ringing. The night seemed to stretch endlessly ahead of us as we got undressed in the small room that was pleasantly familiar to both of us. We had never spent the night together, and when I was awakened by the first light that came in through the window, the room, and her presence there beside me, had about it a sense of fulfillment that I couldn't express. I pulled on my clothes in the semidarkness, trying not to wake her, but when I started toward the door, she turned and slowly opened her arms, and I went to her and took her in my arms and kissed her good-bye, and even though I knew that I would see her again in a few hours, I felt like a soldier leaving his wife to go off to war. "Take care," she said. "Don't fall asleep on the road."

She didn't realize that sleep was out of the question. I felt more alive than ever before in all of my almost eighteen years of living, aware of every detail of the deserted road I knew so well, of the color of the sea and the summer sky, wanting not to forget any of it, ever. When I got home I made a long entry in my neglected diary, hoping that the description of that early-morning drive would make it possible for me to recall the details of the preceding night that I did not dare write down. The page began with "Spent the night with P," which inadequate code anyone could have deciphered.

A few days later I told my mother that I had decided not to go to college in the East and that I wanted to enroll in the extension division of the local university. She accepted my decision calmly. "I'm glad you're not going away to college," she said after I had explained to her the reason for my change in plans. "I'd have missed you. And you're right, the financial burden *would* have been difficult for me."

I experienced a distinct feeling of relief. I knew that had she argued with me, I might well have been swayed, as I was not at all certain that I was doing the right thing. I said: "It's better this way. The colleges out here are just as good as anywhere."

She hesitated an instant, and I sensed that she, too, wanted to unburden herself of something that was on her mind. "I really didn't know how I was going to manage," she said. "That's why I had decided to take in a boarder . . . a young man who works at the shop. That probably won't be necessary now."

"It's still not a bad idea," I replied. With another person living in the house it would be easier for me to propose that I rent a room somewhere, using the excuse that I needed a place of my own in order to concentrate on my studies. "What's his name?" I asked, still preoccupied with my plan of deception.

"Riesener," she said, as if that would mean something to me. "Edmund Riesener." Then she added almost defensively: "He's a friend of Father's."

≫ *three* ≪

I HAD NO IDEA at the time who the Rieseners were, or what they represented, so I was not impressed by the fact that he was one of them. Still, I realized the moment he walked into our living room that he was, or at least considered himself to be, a very special person. He was certainly unlike anyone I had ever met. It was a hot afternoon early in September, and despite the heat, he was dressed in a well-cut gray flannel suit, complete with shirt and tie, which, as he was only a few years older than Jake and myself, made both of us take notice. We exchanged conspiratorial glances (which we hadn't done since Guy Boulard had come on the scene), prompted, no doubt, by the strong suspicion that we were facing a similar emergency.

Just as Guy had done, Edmund Riesener kissed my mother's hand, but he did it in a completely different way, almost carelessly, not as if he were conscious of his good manners, which overtone had been apparent in Guy's case. Nor did he pay any further attention to either one of us. He merely returned our curious stares with a rather superior smile, making it obvious that the relaxed way we were dressed had made him think some uncomplimentary thoughts about the lack of civilization we had acquired during our stay in America. "I know your father," was all he said after we had both shaken hands with him, and again the same slightly superior smile passed over his round face, which was framed by an abundant head of hair. I noticed that his eyebrows grew together above his prominent, pointed nose, which made him look a little like the illustration of the Neanderthal man in my edition of *The Book of Knowledge*. Except for the uninterrupted line of his eyebrows and the too-straight part in his hair, he was really not that bad-looking, I decided after a second glance, although his skin was surprisingly pale, and his handshake a little soft for a young man of his age.

He had come to see the room he was to occupy, and as tea was not ready, my mother decided to show it to him at once. Jake and I stayed behind, as there was no point in our going to visit father's study, where a bed had been installed in order to accommodate "our boarder." "He's rich," Jake said disdainfully as soon as Riesener and my mother were out of earshot. "Did you see how he was dressed?"

"He can't be all that rich," I replied, "or else why would he rent a room here?"

"His family is," Jake said knowingly. "They're the ones who always manage to get out. I think his father was a publisher in Berlin. In any case, we're stuck with him, or you are, that is. I go back to Berkeley next week."

"Maybe he won't like the room," I said hopefully.

"He'll like it," Jake said. "Why shouldn't he? It's well furnished, and it's near the beach. The food's good, and there are lots of books to read. It's the perfect bourgeois setup."

He never failed to irritate me on occasions such as these, first of all by his pessimism, and then by his habit of disassociating himself from the family, as if his political persuasion gave him the right to stand aside and observe our troubles. "He may turn out to be a very nice guy," I said. "Remember how sure we were that Guy was a fairy? Anyway, Mother won't be so lonely if he comes to live here."

He looked at me quizzically over the tops of his steel-rimmed glasses, which were a recent acquisition of his, probably in imitation of his idol, Trotsky. "He's a little young for Mother," he said, "even if the European ideal is for a young man to fall in love with an older woman."

I was shocked. It had never occurred to me that my mother's notion to have the young man as a boarder had been motivated by anything more than household economics. "But you don't really think . . ." I started to ask, and then changed my mind as the sound of footsteps became audible on the stairs behind us.

Riesener reappeared, followed by my mother, and Jake and I rose with a display of manners that was usually reserved for older guests. "It's a very nice room," he said, "and it will certainly be a relief to get away from the boardinghouse atmosphere of the place I live now."

The issue had been decided, I realized, although I suspected, because of what Jake had said, that it had never been in doubt. Tea was served by Maureen in a freshly laundered apron, and I noticed that she, too, looked over our new boarder with great interest. She nodded politely when my mother introduced her, which was nothing out of the ordinary. She was too important a member of the household to be left out, which was why she was always presented to the guests who mattered. "When will Mr. Riesener be moving in?" she asked, standing by the table for a minute or two.

He seemed surprised by the question, or rather the source of it, and turning to my mother said: "In a few days . . . if that's convenient, of course." He spoke English fluently, although with a marked German accent that was made more noticeable by the occasionally British pronunciation of a word. Yet his grammar was perfect; probably better than mine, I thought enviously.

My mother said: "You can come whenever you like," which for some reason Maureen took as a signal for her exit.

Riesener smiled as he watched her go. "She's been with you for a long time," he answered, insinuating that servants were more discreet in the households to which he was accustomed.

"She's part of the family," my mother replied.

"Yes, that's pretty obvious." He grinned, and took a piece of the chocolate cake Jake offered him, without realizing that my brother's *politesse* was motivated only by his eagerness to have a piece himself. The conversation turned automatically to the subject of the day, the Czech crisis. It was impossible to talk about anything else, especially as Hitler was due to speak the next evening at the Nürnberg party rally, which promised to be the culminating moment of the tensions that had been building up for more than a week. Would his speech include an ultimatum, my mother wondered? And if it did, then what would the reactions of England and France be?

Riesener seemed to assume that he was being asked to express a definitive opinion, for he started to lecture us with all the assurance of a foreign commentator who felt obligated to share his knowledge with his listeners. What was even more irritating was that he spoke condescendingly, with an overtone of amused cynicism, as if he were lecturing children. Nobody in Europe wanted war, he said, not even the Germans, and so there wouldn't be one. It was as simple as that. He, himself, had been in London and Paris only a few months ago, and he was certain that the atmosphere hadn't changed much since then. Hitler would have his way again, because nobody was willing to fight.

To my amazement, Jake contradicted him, for I knew that he shared the same pessimistic view of the future. But Edmund Riesener's manner had irritated him so much that he had temporarily abandoned his dialectic, and was arguing as I might have done, had I dared. "This atmosphere you've observed might change," he said. "People's opinions are not static, you know . . . especially when they're conditioned by their instinct for self-preservation."

Riesener nodded and said: "Exactly," then smiled disarmingly. "It's their instinct for self-preservation that makes any course of action that will avoid war seem preferable. Only the Germans are somewhat different, because even if they're not entirely pro war, they'll go in the end. They like soldiering. That's why they're so good at it."

"You seem to take pride in that characteristic. . . ."

"No, not at all. It has nothing to do with me."

"They lose every war," Jake said sourly.

"Only the last one," Riesener corrected him. "They won in eighteen-seventy. Perhaps it's their turn again."

He was baiting Jake, and yet I suspected that there was a degree of sincerity behind his opinions. He was a pessimist because his experience had made him one. I had noticed the same tendency to expect the worst in other refugees, most of them much older than Riesener.

Jake said: "I don't believe it's a question of taking turns." He was using the same condescending tone of voice he always adopted when speaking to me. "History doesn't pay much attention to the rules of sportsmanship. And when you say the Germans are better soldiers, I'm not sure you're right. Convictions make people fight. . . . Look how badly the Russians fought under the czar, and how well they defended their country under Trotsky."

"The Germans have convictions, too," Riesener told him. "You forget that, because you disagree with them."

"We'll see how long they last under fire."

"I doubt that we will . . . because the English and the French won't support them. And alone, the Czechs can only fight bravely and lose."

"Poor Beneš," my mother said, trying to bring us all back to a common ground. "It's tragic to think that he will have to give in to the murderers."

"It would be even more tragic for him to involve his people in a war they can't win," Riesener insisted. "I think Daladier and Chamberlain know that their countries aren't prepared, and will do everything they can to avoid a conflict."

My mother sighed. "I hope you're right," she said. "I just don't see how anyone can contemplate another war."

I said: "I hope you're wrong."

My words fell squarely into the silence that had followed her remark. Jake scowled, and Riesener turned to face me. "Are you willing to go if it starts?" he asked. "Because you might have to."

"Of course," I replied. "Aren't you?"

He shrugged, and a vague smile appeared on his round face. "I'm not looking forward to it," he said. "But then, I'm not the heroic type."

We had arrived at an impasse in our discussion, and my mother suggested we go for a swim. The idea seemed to appeal to Riesener, although he hadn't brought his bathing suit and was obviously too thick-waisted to wear one of Jake's or mine. In the end he borrowed a pair of trunks my father had left behind, and the three of us walked down to the beach together, Riesener keeping a towel draped over his round white shoulders, presumably as protection against the weak rays of the setting sun.

I can still remember with what superior glances Jake and I had sized up his plump white body, but he was not at all self-conscious about his shape, and made his way steadily across the beach and into the water, starting to swim almost at once, with his head above the surface, like a young walrus. Jake, standing waist-high in the water, warned him of the undertow, but he merely smiled and assured us both that he was a good swimmer and that we needn't worry.

Not that either one of us was particularly concerned. We rode the waves, while Riesener swam into the sunset with his steady breast stroke, which it turned out he was able to keep up for a long time, as he was soon out of sight.

"He's a strange guy," I said to Jake while we treaded water, waiting for the next big breaker that would take us in to the shore.

"He's typical of his class," Jake replied. "They still love the *Vaterland*, even though the heinies kicked them out."

"Maybe he was just trying to get your goat?"

"I don't think so. You know, there were actually Jews in Germany who marched through the streets with signs on their backs that said: *Wir sind gegen Uns.* And even if he isn't as bad as that, deep down inside he's still a German patriot."

I didn't agree completely with Jake, but I realized there was something to what he said. Along with the pleasure Riesener obviously derived from telling people what they didn't want to hear, there was undoubtedly a remnant of pro-patria within him. He was also a cynic, as I discovered before very long, shrewd and independent, as well as irreverent of all current thought and opinion.

Years later, when I woke him on "that fateful Sunday morning" and told him that the Japanese had bombed Pearl Harbor, I remember that he grinned sleepily and said: "Well, now, that should make things more interesting . . . at last two unbeaten teams." I was used to him by that time, had come to like him as well as respect his judgment, so that I could forgive him his cynicism. Also, the world looked a little better to me that December morning, believe it or not, for I felt certain that with the United States in the war, the defeat of Nazi Germany would be only a matter of time.

I was less optimistic on the afternoon we first met. It seemed then that Hitler would never be defeated, that his self-proclaimed one-thousand-year Reich might last long enough to destroy mankind, instead of only a part of it, as it finally did. The Nazis had supporters everywhere. There was talk of an influential group of people in both England and France who were not at all opposed to the plans of the Nazis, who preferred a German domination of Europe to an alliance with Soviet Russia. It was a theory Jake had drummed into my head, and it seemed now that he might even be right. And as I walked along the beach with him that evening, I was curious to find out what had made him change his tune.

"I haven't," he said dryly. "I just couldn't stand listening to him," he added, jerking his thumb in the direction of the orange-colored ocean from which Riesener had not as yet appeared. "That's why I argued as I did. Although I really think he's right. Beneš and Co. are doomed . . . they're going to get sold down the river by the Cliveden Set, who are in league with Monsieur Bonnet and his French fascist friends. . . ."

"The news wasn't so bad today," I interrupted somewhat hesitantly, as he always turned out to be much better informed than I was. "There are rumors that the British fleet has been mobilized, and is steaming back to Portsmouth."

"Well, I might be wrong. I hope I am. Look, here comes Edmund, the baby whale."

Riesener was walking down the beach toward us, his long dripping hair hanging down on both sides of his face. "Why didn't you come for a swim?" he asked. "It's quite safe out there beyond the waves."

Jake explained that we preferred to body-surf, which Riesener didn't seem to believe. "You get a lot more exercise swimming," he said. "By the way, does either one of you have a comb?"

We didn't. We wore our hair cut short in the American style. He said it wasn't important, and combed his hair into place with his fingers. Then he dried himself carefully, without neglecting any part of his heavy body, quite unconcerned that people were watching him. "It's a nuisance that there are no cabins where one can change," he complained.

"Your trunks'll dry quick enough," I told him. We started back, the asphalt of the road still warm under our bare feet, for it had been a hot day. Jake went on ahead, leaving me to walk with our guest. He interrogated me about my work, as if he were truly interested, which made me feel that he was trying to make up for not sharing my opinions about the war.

"Your mother tells me that you're going to give up your job and go back to school," he said.

"To college," I corrected him.

"I think that's wise," he said. "You don't want to work as a clerk any longer than you have to. The university will prepare you for a better position."

"That's what they tell me."

He took me seriously. "It's true," he said. "You'll limit yourself if you don't get a degree. What do you want to do, or have you decided as yet?" I told him that I hadn't, which answer he accepted. "You still have time," he told me patronizingly.

A Good Humor was parked at the end of Lovers' Lane, and Riesener offered to buy me an ice cream. Then, remembering that he had no money on him, he apologized that the treat wouldn't be possible after all. We continued up the street in silence, as we really had nothing more to say to each other. I helped him wash the sand off his feet with the garden hose, and he gasped as I splashed the cold water on his legs. Then, glad to have discharged my duties as a host, I directed him to the downstairs shower.

Maureen called me to the telephone, and I was surprised to hear Pam's voice on the other end. She said that she was coming into town after dinner, and if I was free, she would pick me up. She sounded perturbed, but when I asked her if there was anything the matter, she told me that it was nothing that couldn't wait.

Yet the moment I got into her car, I knew something serious was wrong.

"I've had a cable from Richard," she said. "He's joined the Royal Air Force."

I sat stunned for an instant, while she drove slowly up the street, the radio playing some idiotic song that was popular that summer. "But he's in the middle of a picture," I said.

"They're almost finished. Anyway, he probably won't have to report for duty for a few weeks. He wants us to come back to England."

"Even if there's a war?"

She nodded. "He wants to see Karen again. I can't refuse him that."

"But isn't it better for her to be here? If the Germans bomb London . . ."

"I've written him all that," she said, indicating a sealed letter beside her on the leather seat. "But I know what he'll say . . . that we're English, and that we belong in England at a time like this."

"When will you have to leave?" I asked.

"I don't know," she replied. "It all depends on his answer to my letter."

four

She seemed completely resigned to going. At first I didn't argue with her, because I was amazed by the calm way in which she accepted the whole thing, as if Gordon's decisions were irrevocable as far as she was concerned. What puzzled me most was that she had quite easily asserted her own will while he was still present and could press his demands. Now that he was thousands of miles away, he seemed to have acquired a much greater power over her, for he had merely sent a cable, and that had been enough to persuade her to risk her own life, as well as that of her daughter.

She ridiculed that particular argument of mine, accused me of being melodramatic. "There are millions and millions of people living in London," she said. "You think the Germans are going to kill them all?" We were driving to the studio together on the morning after my first meeting with Edmund. She had agreed to accompany me, as I was going to stay there only long enough to say good-bye and collect my belongings, for I had already given up my job.

"Well, if the Germans start bombing in earnest, they'll kill a lot of people," I replied.

"But they won't," she said very positively, "simply because they know we'll retaliate and bomb Berlin."

"They have superior air power . . . at least that's what Mr. Lindbergh says."

"They won't have for long. Anyway, I've written Richard and told him that it was madness for us to come over now. There's a good chance the war will be avoided, and if he's training, or whatever he's going to be doing, he won't be able to see very much of his daughter anyway."

"Suppose he insists?"

"I already told you, I'll have to go. . . ."

"I'll never see you again," I said grimly.

"Oh, don't be silly . . . I'll go for a few months, and then I'll be back."

"You really think it'll be that easy?"

"Of course. Otherwise I wouldn't go. I don't want to be stuck there forever."

"You might well be," I said. "Wars have a funny way of changing people's lives."

"Do they really? Has that been your experience, Mr. Woolf? Tell me about it, won't you?"

I controlled my irritation. "You think the war will start, and nothing will change?" I asked. "Well, it won't work out that way. There'll be travel restrictions, and submarine warfare, and the ships will be reserved for troop movements. . . ."

"Only if America gets involved, and then you'll have to go, if you haven't already volunteered. So actually, if I'm in England I'll have a better chance to see you than if I stay here. Because you won't be coming back to California on leave. Not unless they make you a general straight away." She was right. I was just as unrealistic about the future as she was. It was ridiculous to try to make plans. "If there's a war, why, then, we'll meet in London," she was saying, "and you'll be in uniform and won't know where to go, and I'll show you the town. It'll be my patriotic duty to look after you . . . take care of one of the boys." She laughed, quite cheerful once again, and I couldn't help thinking that she didn't really mind going.

I felt miserable. Yet that had been one of my favorite daydreams, the possibility she was describing. How often I had seen myself in uniform on the platform of a foreign railroad station, holding her in my arms in a romantic picture of farewell. Or I had seen myself coming back to find her in a small town behind the lines, where she was waiting for me in a cottage with snow on the roof, all of these scenes borrowed from Hemingway, and rewritten, with slight changes incorporated, such as her not being pregnant, and I not wounded.

"Don't you think it would be better to wait and see what happens?" I asked. "Most people think there won't be a war this time, that the British and French will make a deal with Hitler."

"That's exactly what I wrote Richard," she said. "But I'm afraid that won't make much difference to him if he's already enlisted. Once he's in, they'll never let him out. . . ."

"If there's no war, they will," I said hopefully. Which alternative I had dreaded for weeks, only now it seemed less of a catastrophe, a further postponement of the final battle against fascism. I decided that I really didn't know what I wanted anymore.

I left her sitting in her car and hurried off to see Benson, hoping that he wouldn't keep me waiting too long, as time seemed suddenly more precious than ever before. Fortunately, I was ushered into his office at once, as even his secretary seemed in a generous mood that day.

He was in his shirtsleeves, seated in the upholstered swivel chair behind his desk, with the venetian blinds casting their shadows on the worn carpet. "What a day to be stuck in this goddamned place," he said. "There's a nice south wind blowing, and the water temperature's just right for sea bass. . . ."

"I've come to say good-bye," I said, breaking in on his end-of-summer reverie.

"That's right. You're off today, aren't you? Back to the academic life, complete with co-eds, and the beginning of football season."

"That is, if Herr Hitler doesn't interfere."

"He won't, don't worry," Benson said, rubbing the bowl of his pipe along the greasy side of his nose. "It's not in the cards, as yet. Everybody's still making too much money. Next year, maybe . . . or the year after that. That way you'll be able to get a commission once the fun does start."

"Anyway, I've enrolled," I said. "Classes start on Thursday."

He got up and shook my hand and wished me well, "especially in your extracurricular activities," a remark that apparently stirred up old memories. "Did I ever tell you what a cop said to me in Central Park years ago?" he asked. "I was out with a co-ed, sitting on the grass, just reading a little poetry, mind you, and this big dumb Irishman ambles up and says: 'Sorry, buddy, but the rules are the same as last year. No fucking in the park!'" He roared with laughter at his own joke. "That's about the only bit of advice I can give you at this time, boy," he added. "Of course, the job's yours next summer if you want it." He took me to the door, after warning me again to have as good a time as I possibly could, and I hurried down the hall to see Guy, knowing that as my sponsor he would think me ungrateful if I left without thanking him for everything he had done.

I found him in a more serious mood than Benson. A radio stood on a small table beside his desk, crackling with static. He went back to it as soon as he had greeted me, and began fiddling with the dials. "They've only installed this thing a few hours ago," he said. "The reception is no good at all." He glanced at his watch, and went on to explain that Hitler's speech to the Nürnberg party rally was to be broadcast directly in less than a quarter of an hour.

"It'll be rebroadcast tonight," I told him. "I can wait until then."

"It might mean the beginning of the war," he said. "You don't want to hang around and translate for me, do you? Mr. Levin would appreciate it."

"I'm off the payroll," I told him.

He grinned halfheartedly at my joke. "We might all be off the payroll in a few hours," he replied apprehensively.

But he left the radio, and walked with me to my cubicle, where I collected all of my belongings. I asked him to thank Mr. Levin for me, which he agreed to do. "I understand you might be back with us next summer," he said. "Benson seems to like you."

"I'm a good deck hand."

"Well, there are all kinds of ways to make a career," he replied, and went back to his office.

I said a not-too-fond farewell to the filing cabinets that had been my charges throughout the summer, collected my books and papers, and returned to the car, where Pamela was waiting for me. "That didn't take long," she said. "Were they all sad to see you go?"

"They managed to control their tears. Benson said the job was mine if I still want it next summer."

"You're a success, then. In a few years you'll be the head of the studio."

"I doubt that."

We drove down one of the main boulevards leading to the sea, the sun slanting in through the windshield out of a clear sky. I turned on the car radio to see if I could locate the broadcast of the speech. Pam looked over at me questioningly when I found the station and the noise of the crowd in Nürnberg filled the car. The cheering stopped, and we could hear the opening bars of the "Horst Wessel Lied."

"Do we have to have that?" she asked.

"It might decide a lot of things."

"I can wait for tonight's résumé," she replied. "Why spoil a nice day?"

I turned off the radio. "I've made up my mind," I said. "If you leave, I'm going too."

"Where? What are you talking about now?"

"To Canada. I'll join the army there. I don't want to go on living here without you."

"But, darling, that's absurd," she said with a greater prophetic sense than mine; "you're going to have to live most of your life without me, no matter what. So it makes no sense rushing off and doing something you're sure to regret."

"I've made up my mind."

"Oh, Carl . . . don't be so silly. You can't decide things like that on your own. And you mustn't threaten me in that way. It's not fair."

"All right, let's not talk about it. You said you didn't want to spoil the day."

"I don't, it's true. But it's almost spoiled now." She turned the radio on again. "I know I'll have to go," she said. "I have no choice, if he insists. So you mustn't make things more difficult by telling me that you're going to enlist if I leave. It's ridiculous . . . and old-fashioned. Like something out of one of the novels of Baroness Orczy."

"I apologize." The frenzied shouts of the crowd at Nürnberg were brought into the confines of the car on waves of pulsating static. Then the hysterical voice we had all come to loathe resumed its diatribe.

"What's he saying?" Pam asked.

"Insulting Beneš, asking for justice for the Sudetendeutsche . . . it's incredible nobody's tried to shoot him."

"They love him, the Germans. . . ."

"I can't believe it. They must realize that he's a maniac."

But the speech was less maniacal than everyone had feared. It contained no declaration of war, no ultimatum, even.

I lay sprawled in the sun on the beach in front of the cottage, worn out by my own feelings of hate and frustration. Pam joined me after a while. She had prepared our lunch, as Bessie had not come back from her weekend off, which, as a surprise for me, Pam had extended to include most of Monday.

She lay down beside me on the sun-bleached blanket, quite cheerful again. "You see, it's not as bad as you thought it would be. There's not going to be a war, and I'll come back after Christmas to find you more erudite and more passionate than ever before."

We swam in the warm sea, and made love before lunch, going naked from the shower to the bed, as we had done long ago, it seemed, in another lifetime. "What a simple remedy it is for everything," she said, lying beside me on the sunlit bed. "Now we're as happy as we always were."

"Or as miserable, you mean."

She laughed and said: "You're very brooding and German today. Like your new friend Edmund whatever-his-last-name-is. Maybe it's because you're hungry."

"That's probably the reason."

"Well, then, let's eat. Eat and be merry, for tomorrow we may die!"

"Did you make that up?"

"Uh-huh. I did. Do you love me because I'm sexy or clever?"

"I'm not sure. I'll have to think about it."

"You'll let me know, won't you?"

"Yeah . . . I'll write you a letter." She made a face, but didn't reply. "I love you for a hundred reasons," I said. "Is that what you want to hear?"

"It'll do," she said.

Hitler's speech was rebroadcast in the evening, and I had to listen to the ogre's rantings all over again, as I was the only one who had heard it earlier. Riesener was there for dinner, undoubtedly to sample Maureen's cooking, or at least that was what Jake and I assumed. Despite the inaccurate translations of the American commentator, who broke in continually on Hitler's frenzied shouting, it was interesting to hear it all a second time, and I was forced to agree with Edmund's analysis that there was a considerable amount of willingness to compromise hidden in all the raving.

"He doesn't want war," Edmund said. "Or, even if he does, he knows the German people won't follow him with much enthusiasm."

"They'll go, if they're ordered to," Jake said. "Just as they shout whenever it's expected of them. Because they've been conditioned to do just that."

"It's dangerous to make generalizations about an entire nation," Riesener replied coolly.

"But your generalizations are acceptable, I suppose," Jake said acidly.

"I was commenting on a mood of the moment, which is quite a different matter. I wouldn't contradict you if you had said that the French don't want war, for example, because you would be referring to a temporary state of mind, not an inborn attitude."

Jake grinned facetiously. "I don't mind your contradicting me. I'm not a German."

I excused myself and went upstairs. I wanted to get away from their useless arguments, which I knew were based more on Jake's dislike of Riesener than anything else.

The next morning the news was worse again. The moment of hope had been short-lived. As a result of Hitler's speech, riots had broken out in the Sudetenland. There were heavy casualties on both sides, among the supporters of Henlein as well as among the men of the Czech police who had managed to put down the disturbances. Still, I went to the university and signed up for the classes I had to take that fall. Because I was in the extension division, and not an undergraduate, nearly all of the lectures I would have to attend would be in the afternoon. There was only one exception, a geology lab period that was scheduled for eleven o'clock every Friday morning.

It was not the best way to go to college. I would be an outsider, I realized, and yet I would also have time to start writing in earnest, and nothing else I could do would make it possible for me to avoid being a nonentity all of my life. I would write a novel, I decided. I would work on it every morning, just as if it were a paid job. And I wouldn't write about myself. That's where I had gone wrong before. I would invent a character, a young man who grows up during a time without war or persecution. I would make him an American with no ties to the Old World, and I would invent a love affair for him with a girl his own age. The only recognizable part of my own life I would use was the countryside in which I had lived during the last years, the beach and the hills beyond them, which I had explored on my bicycle before I had met the Gordons.

For more than an hour I wandered aimlessly among the still-deserted red-brick buildings of the campus, lost in the nostalgic mood of the novel I planned to write. I would have to work hard, I warned myself, because there wasn't much time. Not if I wanted to finish the book before the war would start. I had wasted most of my life already, only because I had lacked discipline. I looked up during my wandering, and discovered that one of the campus gardeners had been following me. "You lost?" he asked suspiciously.

I grinned, because of the ridiculousness of his question, for I had never felt as little lost as at that moment. "Just getting to know the campus," I replied, and made my way back slowly to where I had parked my car. Then I drove home, dreaming happily about the effect my having written a book would have on everybody I knew. And as I sat waiting for a light to change at an intersection in the middle of town, I saw the headline of the evening paper, announcing Chamberlain's trip to Berchtesgaden, where he was going to see Hitler "in the interests of peace."

⇒ *five* ⇐

THE HOT WEATHER continued. The Santa Ana blew steadily across the open reaches of the bay, raising whitecaps on the grayish-blue water. Yet, despite the south wind, and the climate of summer it brought, I remained faithful to the resolution I had made my first day on the campus. Every morning, with my books and looseleaf folder on the seat beside me, I drove to the cottage on the beach, as if I were reporting to a job. Then, while Pam helped Bessie clean the house, I would sit in a corner of the living room and work on my novel.

It went well in the beginning, the words coming more easily than they have ever come since, for I found it enjoyable to invent an existence that was so unlike my own, and yet transpose into my hero's mind many of the secret thoughts I had had as a boy, such as my brief conviction that I was Christ reborn, which I had never been brave enough to admit before. It was enjoyable as well to describe the countryside, and to improve on it, make it more rural, and in that way create an ideal setting for the story I wanted to tell.

Pam took my writing seriously, or at least she pretended to so artfully that I was convinced that she believed in the successful outcome of the venture as much as I did. Looking back, I find her faith in my talent astonishing, for she must obviously have been aware that many young men my age (or at least that was the case then) set out to write novels that they never finished, much less published. If she had any doubts about my work, she kept them to herself. More than that, she did everything she could to facilitate my efforts, such as not allowing Bessie to use the vacuum cleaner until I had come to the end of my daily session, as well as protecting me from all outside disturbances (the ones she could control), thus playing the part of the perfect writer's wife.

When I had finished for the day, we would go for a long walk on the deserted beach and let the waves swirl around our knees and thighs before venturing into the cold water. "Where do you tell your mother you're off to every day?" she asked me one day during the first week of my new routine.

"I don't tell her anything. She thinks I go to the university every morning."

"And how do you explain that you're not losing your tan?"

"I don't."

She smiled and said: "You know, you're very fortunate. I don't think I'd be as lenient if I had a son." She looked disturbed after she had made the remark, and I knew she was thinking of the child she had denied herself.

"What about Bessie?" I asked quickly. "Does she mind my coming here?"

"She hasn't said anything . . . although I'm sure she suspects the worst, as there's no tennis court."

"There's the ocean."

"That's what I told her you're here for."

"Then she did say something."

"Only once. 'He sure must be crazy about swimming,' she muttered the other day, and I told her that indeed you were."

She had arranged for Bessie to take over the daily chores of going to the market and picking Karen up after school, so that we could at least have a few hours alone in the early afternoon. It was, she said, a farewell present for both of us, a last fortnight of summer by the sea. "I'd never realized how spoiled I've become," she said, "living here and taking all this for granted."

"When do you think you'll have to leave?"

"I don't know . . . in two or three weeks."

"Have you heard from Richard?"

She nodded, and I felt my stomach tightening. "I got a cable this morning. He's been rejected for pilot's training. He's too old."

I felt relieved. He was doing no more than I was, except, of course, that he was there. "Will you have to go soon?" I asked. "Even if there's no war?"

"It's bound to start someday," she said, "and Richard would rather we leave now, before conditions become more difficult. I suppose it's expensive, too, having to run two different establishments."

"You once said you'd get a job if you had to," I reminded her. She was looking off at the hills behind the house that were lost in a haze of heat and salt air, her eyes narrowed against the glare.

"I suppose I wasn't being very realistic, was I? If I went to work in a shop or an office, who'd look after Karen? Bessie would never stay here alone all day, and I'd hardly be making enough money to pay a governess."

"But it's absurd that money should decide things. . . ."

"It usually does, darling."

"You said you were only going for a little while. That isn't true anymore, is it?"

"Oh, Carl . . . how can you expect me to know for sure? The world's in such a mess that it's foolish to make promises. I *want* to come back, because I don't want to lose you. But if there's a war, I don't know what will happen, and neither do you. You said so yourself."

"Have you known for a long time that you'd have to go back?" I asked.

"Yes. But I tried not to think about it," she said. "I don't even want to think about it now. Because it's not very nice what I'm doing, taking his money and living here with you."

"We're not living together."

"You know what I mean."

I lay there in silence, thinking about what she had said. Then, because I felt ill at ease, I looked at my watch. It was nearly two-thirty. "I have to go," I said. I got up and started into the house. She ran after me and took me in her arms.

"Don't be sad yet, Carl," she said. "We still have a few weeks left. I've decided to take a freighter through the Canal, so that it'll take a long time to get there, and maybe everything will have changed when I finally do, and I'll be able to come back right away."

"Sometimes you're as unrealistic as I am."

"Am I? Am I, darling? I don't mean to be."

I didn't hear a single word of the lecture I attended that afternoon. I might as well not have gone, I thought, sitting in the suffocatingly hot hall, except that I knew that I had had to go, because Karen was coming back to the house with Bessie, and that was the only part of Pam's agreement with Gordon she had never broken. After the lecture I went home and sat in silence throughout dinner with my mother and Riesener, unable to contradict his pessimistic forecasts for the immediate future. He was probably right anyway, I felt; we were all doomed to a lifetime of defeat, of having to live in a world partly dominated by Hitler and his brown-shirted butcher boys. The destruction of Nazism was nothing more than another one of my wish-dreams.

Jake had left for Berkeley, so there was no one to contradict Riesener, and he rambled on about the hopelessness of Europe, saying that the French and the British had been bled white in 1917 and 1918, that they had no national pride left, and that the Americans should have taken over the leadership of the world, but didn't because of their provincialism and selfishness.

I didn't contradict him, although his condescending attitude enraged me. But I knew I didn't have the knowledge to argue with him, and so we moved into the living room after dinner and sat listening to the voices that were coming from all over Europe to confirm us in our gloom. The Poles and the Hungarians were pressing their territorial claims against Czechoslovakia, so that now the Czech people were threatened by enemies from three sides. Yet, despite their desperate situation, they had rejected the Franco-British plan for more concessions to Germany, and were getting ready to fight. "Americans, I tell you our powder is dry!" the strained voice of Jan Masaryk said from London, which phrase brought tears to my eyes. I had other reasons to be emotional that evening, but suddenly they seemed less important than they had a few hours before.

Riesener shook his head and said: "What good are heroic slogans at a time like this? The German army will be in Prague in five days once the fighting starts."

"What do you want him to say?" I asked, unable to control myself any longer. "We're outnumbered? We surrender?"

"No, of course not. I want him to be factual, and cold-blooded, and to tell the world that they've been abandoned by their allies, betrayed."

"And what good would that do?"

"More good than pretending that they're going to resist, which they can't possibly do."

"Perhaps they will. A number of commentators have suggested that they might, and that then the force of public opinion will bring down the Chamberlain government, and Churchill will come to power."

"*Dein Wort in Gottes Ohr,*" Edmund said with a superior smile. "Your word in God's ear."

"I understand German."

"But obviously not British politics. Or else you would see that Chamberlain's policy is a reflection of the will of the British people, who want peace at any price, and who, incidentally, have always preferred the Germans to the French."

My mother intervened. "Carl may have a point," she said hesitantly. "I can't believe that the world will stand by and watch Czechoslovakia be devoured."

Riesener shrugged. "Well, there's no use in our fighting among ourselves," he said smoothly. "We're all on the same side."

"Sometimes I wonder. . . ."

"Don't be rude, Carl," my mother rebuked me.

"That's quite all right," Edmund replied, laughing. "In a political argument we all say things we don't really mean. I'm often guilty of it myself." He was being magnanimous, which didn't make me like him any better.

I said: "I have some work to do," and got up to say good night.

"We're not enemies, are we?" Edmund asked, extending his hand. I took it without enthusiasm.

"No, I guess not."

"You don't sound very convincing." He appeared to be amused by my truculence.

"I'm sorry."

"You needn't be." He patted me on the back, as if I were a little boy being sent up to bed. "I hope that we can be friends in spite of our differences. . . ."

"I hope so," I said without enthusiasm. Still, I managed to smile as I left the room.

My mother knocked on my door as I was starting to get undressed. I could see that she was upset when she came in, and was making an effort not to show it. "Why are you so antagonistic toward Edmund?" she asked very calmly. "Both you and Jake are impossible when you argue with him."

"Because he enjoys saying that everything's going wrong. He seems delighted that the Germans are winning."

"That's ridiculous. He's suffered more than either one of you from the Nazis."

"Well, it's made him a defeatist, a middle-European Cassandra. . . ."

"He has a right to his opinions," she said. "Furthermore, he's a very intelligent young man."

"I'm not impressed."

"You don't have to be. You have to be polite, that's all."

"I was polite."

"No, you weren't. And don't act like an American lout."

"I apologize."

She hesitated, her eyes filling with tears. She said: "You have no reason to behave like this. Either with me, or with Edmund," and turning her back on me, left the room.

I stood for a long time facing the door she had closed so firmly behind her. Why did she defend him so? I asked myself angrily. Was she really involved with him? He was such a pompous bore, and he was half her age. Then I realized the ridiculousness of my objection. "It's none of your goddamn business," I said angrily to the empty room, which fleeting moment of honesty only slightly tempered my rage, for as I started to get undressed, I found myself cursing everything and everyone, Edmund, Richard Gordon, Hitler, the way my life was changing, and the fact that I was helpless to do anything about it.

❧ *Six* ☙

ONLY IN THE MORNINGS, I soon discovered, was I able to escape the feeling of frustration that hung over me during the rest of the day. For seated at my typewriter, in the small living room of the beach house, I found that I could temporarily forget the Czechoslovak crisis, and even the fact that Pamela would soon be leaving me. While I worked I felt at peace, too absorbed by the problems of the young man I had invented to worry about my own. Even the news that Chamberlain had decided to return to Germany for a second visit failed to distract me for very long, although the meaning of his decision was fairly obvious. There would be plenty of time later in the day for despair, I realized, with a provisional wisdom I had seldom managed to attain.

Pamela was nearby, either upstairs trying to decide what to take, and what to leave behind, or out on the terrace "making the most of her last few days of sunshine." In either case, her proximity reassured me, and I felt instinctively that it was not possible to achieve greater happiness, even though it was all too brief. She was still adamant about coming back in the winter, which promise I never doubted early in the day, probably because I was too preoccupied. But to watch her pack would have been torture, which made work an even greater necessity, a way of shutting out all thought of the void I knew was surely to follow her departure.

Around noon Bessie would start off on her daily round of chores, the noisy engine of her car warning me that it was time to relax my efforts. I would go to the terrace door for a breath of sea air, or Pam would come downstairs, her naked legs visible through the railing of the banister before she would appear beside me in her bathing suit. "Has Bessie gone?" she would inevitably ask. "Is it that late already? Lord, how the time seems to fly."

It was true. The days were passing with greater speed than ever before, the month coming to an end, and the October sailing date of the freighter on which she had reserved passage approaching relentlessly. It seemed like madness to me that she was actually going, as all of Europe was preparing itself for the war that appeared to be more unavoidable with every passing hour. But there was nothing I could do, no way I could persuade her that fulfilling her obligation to Gordon was an act almost of sacrifice. She appeared to be so certain that no matter what happened, she and Karen would escape unharmed, that I gave up trying to dissuade her, as any discussion of the dangers inherent in her decision led inevitably to a quarrel. And I didn't want to quarrel with her, not during the last few days of our final summer together, for it was still summer on the beach.

Then it was Monday again, Monday the twenty-sixth of September, my diary tells me, and Hitler was scheduled to speak, this time at the Sportpalast in Berlin. "An ultimatum is expected," I wrote. "I wonder what it will be this time?" There follows a lengthy account of the quarrel I had with Pamela that day, "the worst ever," and as it turned out the final one, which, of course I didn't realize at the time.

Bessie had departed, and Pam had appeared beside me, not in her bathing suit, but in the dressing gown she often wore when she was undecided what to do. She rested her hand on my shoulder and glanced at the half-completed page in my typewriter. "Did it go well, today?" she asked. "Was your muse kind to you?"

"Kind enough."

"Then if you're finished, I think we'll do without our daily swim, if you don't mind. The wind is too strong, and I've just washed my hair."

"I don't mind," I said, reaching up under her robe to touch the smooth skin of her body. How the quality of love changes when it is influenced by the threat of a long separation, and made more intense by longing yet to come. The brain knows what is going to happen, and so, it seems, does the skin.

We lay together in the warm wind that made its way into the sunlit room, satisfied and still full of vague wanting. She said: "I wish I could put you in one of my suitcases and take you with me wherever I go. That would be the most practical thing to do. Keep you in a closet nearby and let you out whenever I was alone."

"All of me, or only the parts you like best?"

"All of you. I'm greedy."

She turned over to lie on her stomach, and ran her fingers gently along the edge of my mouth. "The hero of your book . . . does he have a girl?" she asked.

"Yes. I told you that he did."

"Is she older than he is?"

"No. The same age."

"I like that better. And apparently so do you. What happens to her in the end?"

"She's learning to be a trick rider for the rodeo circuit, which is where her father works in the summer. In the end she's killed, when her pony falls on the beach."

"That seems very drastic. Are you sure that's a good idea?"

"Fairly sure."

"Not too melodramatic?"

"It's a novel, and it has to end dramatically."

"Well, you know best. But in life things don't usually end that way."

I thought of Cynthia, but didn't say anything. "I haven't come to the end," I said. "Maybe I'll change my mind when I do."

"And is he faithful to his girl, your hero? While she's still alive, that is?"

"Yes, of course."

"Just as faithful as you've been to me?" I flushed involuntarily, and she said: "I shouldn't have asked that, should I? I made up my mind a long time ago that I never would, and now look at me."

"Why shouldn't you ask that?"

"Because I wouldn't want you to lie to me."

"I wouldn't lie."

"You're about to."

"No, I'm not."

"Skip it, darling." She got up and went into the bathroom, to return a moment later in her robe. Then she sat down on the edge of the bed and began brushing her hair. I was conscious of my own evasiveness, and the silence out of which I couldn't seem to find my way. "Are you hungry?" she asked. "Because when you're silent or grumpy, that's what's usually wrong."

"No. Not really hungry."

"What are you thinking about? Terry Sangster?"

I said: "What makes you ask about her? I didn't even think you knew her."

"You met her at my house."

"But why should I be thinking about her?"

"Because I asked you a ridiculous question you refused to answer."

"I didn't refuse."

"You avoided it! Don't misunderstand me. I approve. I would like you a lot less if you attempted to lie."

"There's nothing to lie about."

"You didn't have an affair with her?"

"Why do you ask me that?" I said, trying to sound exasperated and perplexed at the same time. "I hardly know her."

"But I know her . . . and well enough to know that she doesn't believe in wasting her time in useless flirtations."

"What does that prove?"

"You went to the movies with her . . . to see a Garbo film, I believe it was, and you had the look of a rather well-established couple."

"Who told you that?"

"What difference does that make?"

"I want to know!"

"Billy Lovat."

"What a bastard!"

"Just as big a bastard as you are for sleeping with her while I was away!"

There was no use denying it. The expression on my face had betrayed me long ago. And it seemed somehow cheap to lie at that moment, offensive. Also I undoubtedly had realized that I would feel relieved, and cleansed, even, if I told her the truth. The only thing I didn't foresee was the pain that I would be inflicting on her, especially by going into detail, by telling her the whole story, as if she were a priest, or my mother. Of course I was idiotically proud, too, that another woman had found me attractive enough to take me to bed, and wanted to let Pam know, without meaning to be cruel. After all, she had guessed it, and seemingly had forgiven me.

"And you liked her . . . that awful, flat-chested chorus girl!" she asked.

"I didn't *like* her. I was lonely, and . . ."

"I'm afraid that you'll be lonely like that very often again," she said mockingly. "Oh, Carl . . . how could you have slept with her? It's so stupid and so sad, the whole thing, especially finding out now."

"But you asked me. And you sounded as if you knew."

"I was guessing, using the same ridiculous, jealous trick every woman uses. But I didn't have to guess long. I read your faithlessness in your eyes the minute I asked you the first question. Oh, Carl, Carl . . . isn't it absurd that it should hurt so? It's all vanity, too, vanity and the feeling of having misplaced one's confidence, trusted someone who wasn't worth trusting really."

"You were unfaithful to me, too."

"When? Tell me when?" She got up from the bed on which she had been lying as if in pain, her face outraged now, when before it had only been sad. "I was never unfaithful to you."

"You were. You admitted it tacitly, if not in so many words. You slept with Gordon . . . once or several times, I don't know. . . ."

"But he was my husband. Is and was, and probably always will be. . . ."

"Do you mean that?"

"Yes, I mean it." Her voice was loud, filling the small room, and then ceding its place to the wind that was hooting at both of us.

I picked up my things and started to get dressed. "I'm leaving," I said, still fairly certain that she would feel bereaved by my departure.

"Good-bye. Have a lovely life in your fine, untouched, unspoiled country," she said violently.

"I'll try to."

"And keep the hero of your book pure. Just for contrast with the author."

"I'll do that." I pushed my shirttails into my trousers, and picking up my shoes, started down the stairs. I might have run out of the house if it hadn't been for my manuscript, which I remembered I had to collect. Suddenly I felt ill, as if some very potent pill full of poison had just blossomed out inside my stomach. I sat down at the table on which my typewriter still stood, the sweat starting to break out of the pores all over my body. Then I heard her footsteps on the stairs, and her voice, hoarse from all the shouting, call my name. "Carl? Could you leave like that? Could you really go, without at least saying good-bye."

"No, of course not," I said.

She came over to the chair where I was seated, and put her arms around me, my head against her stomach under the smooth silk of her dressing gown. "I feel awful," she said. "Oh, Christ, don't ever do that again, don't ever tell me about who you've gone to bed with, as if it were something fascinating that happened to you, an interesting story I shouldn't miss . . . because that's where your cruelty lies. Not in what you've done. That was bound to happen. But in having to tell me, not just admit it, but tell me in detail. No matter what happens, promise me that you'll never do that again."

"I promise," I said, releasing her slowly.

"Do you have to go? Right now, I mean."

"Karen's coming back, isn't she?"

"No, not for a while. Not until four anyway. Bessie's taking her to buy a pair of shoes she very much fancies."

"Then I'll stay," I said. "I only ever go because I have to." We went upstairs together. The early-afternoon heat filled the room, despite the open windows. "Do you want to go for a swim?" I asked her, without thinking what I was saying.

"I knew you'd suggest something like that," she said, laughing weakly. "No, I don't want to go for a swim. I'll take a shower with you, but that's as much water as I can take right now."

We stood in the shower together, and she put her head against my shoulder, with her eyes tightly closed. "What a wonderful thing a cold shower is," she said. "Really much nicer than the sea. And not nearly so salty."

We returned to the bedroom, and she put her bath towel across the open bed so that we could lie down and let the sun dry us. I kissed her, noticing that her eyes were tightly closed. "You've made a remarkable recovery," she said.

"It's the cold water."

She pushed my head away from hers, and held me at arm's length, and looked at my face for a long time, and then, shaking her head, held me to her again. Then we made love, fiercely, in silence, with only the act counting, only the moment, no thought of any tomorrow that might be coming, together or apart, and then we lay exhausted and entangled with each other, worn out by the physical strain of completion, which blurred all thought and feeling.

ᘈ *seven* ᘇ

THE END OF EVERYTHING came quickly, without a change in the weather or an improvement in the news. The final conference in Munich was no more than an obscene last act tagged on to a dishonorable and cowardly play. There was no surprise at the outcome of the plot, only the feeling of nausea for the spectator who had followed all the twists in the story. Yet it seemed to be what everyone wanted to see. The final curtain was applauded by all but a small group of dissenters, a minority nobody paid any attention to, and even my own feelings of outrage and disgust were mitigated by the knowledge that Pamela would not be setting out across war-torn seas.

"Peace in our time," the chief undertaker had declared. Well, at least it would last until her ship had reached the other shore. The papers were still full of photographs of the cheering crowds that welcomed Daladier and Chamberlain upon their arrivals in Paris and London, and already it was time for Pamela to make her final arrangements, buy a farewell present for Bessie, go over the inventory of the cottage with the real-estate agent, and sell her car. Then the last day was suddenly upon us, bright and hot, with only the slightly colder temperature of the ocean to make us realize that summer was leaving, too.

We spent the morning together walking on the deserted beach, the final minutes racing by with the speed of the breaking waves that rose to meet us. Then Billy Lovat arrived with two bottles of champagne in a bucket of ice that he had brought all the way from town. I had promised Pam that I would make no mention of his betrayal, which was a difficult promise to keep, as his cheerful manner aggravated me, as did his insipid jokes about the peace that he so blithely assumed was going to be permanent. "I may even be able to go back to England myself," he said, "now that there's no danger of being called up anymore."

Pam laughed and said: "What a patriot you are, Billy. Thank God they're not all like you."

"I have but one life to give," he replied. "Which is why I'm going to be damn careful who I give it to."

Half an hour later Hévesey appeared with a red-headed girl whom he introduced as his personal assistant. As we shook hands, it seemed to me that I hadn't seen him for years. His accent was unchanged, although he looked slightly more elegant than before, a natural result of his recent success as a movie director. "Carl, my old friend," he said, putting his arms around me. "You look as sad as I feel."

To which statement there was no possible reply, and fortunately he didn't seem to expect one. He turned at once to Pamela, and insisted on kissing her again, "as soon there will be no more time for this sort of thing." I didn't feel jealous, which was some small proof of maturity. "Carl and I will load the car," he said ostentatiously, "but I warn you that we'll expect our full share of champagne when we're finished."

There was a mountain of luggage, and in the end Billy was forced to give us a hand, which he did willingly enough. He made a show of his efforts, however, gasping for breath each time he lifted one of the heavier suitcases, puffing out his round stomach, which protruded like a watermelon above the line of his belt. "I don't think anyone in my family has done this much manual labor in three hundred years," he said.

"Don't boast," Hévesey told him. "Three hundred years ago your relations were still squatting around a fire in a cave."

Once the car had been loaded, we returned to the terrace for a last glass of champagne. Hévesey toasted Pamela's safe return, which prompted her to ask: "Return where? Here or England?"

"Here, of course."

Karen clapped her hands and said: "I agree. I want Mummy to come back soon."

"But you're going with me, you noodle," Pam reminded her.

"I know that. That's why I don't want you to stay in England too long. Because I want to come back too."

Everyone laughed, and Karen grinned happily, very proud of her joke. She had perched herself on the knees of Hévesey's girl friend, whose name turned out to be Arleen, and who appeared to be more at home in the company of the child than anyone else.

"Well, you won't be gone all that long," Billy Lovat said. "You'll be back next summer, the both of you."

Pam excused herself and went into the house. She reappeared a few minutes later with Bessie, and Lovat poured out what was left in the last bottle, so that she could share in the farewell toast. "Just a swallow is all I want," she said. "'Cause I'm going to have to stay here and clean up. . . ."

"You can come back tomorrow," Pam told her, but Bessie shook her head.

"No, sir . . . once you all have gone, I don't want ever to have to look at this place," she said.

Which was how I felt, only she had put it into words. Not the beach, nor the ocean, nor the brown hills behind the house. I didn't want to see any of it ever again, I thought. If only I could have arranged my life so that I would be leaving too. It was somehow worse being left behind.

"We must go," Pam said, rising. "It's Saturday, and there's bound to be a lot of traffic. Incidentally, does anyone know the way?"

Nobody did, as the harbor was on the other side of the city. "I have a map in my car," Paul announced. "A Hungarian in a foreign country is always prepared."

"Well, I suggest you study it while I take a last turn around the house," Pam said. She crossed the patio, looking very elegant and citified in her high-heeled black shoes, and I felt what I had so often felt before, the certain knowledge that I would never find anyone as beautiful and desirable in a hundred years. I went to the edge of the terrace and looked out at the sea in order not to have to talk to any of the others while she was gone, but she called me from the upstairs window, and I ran up the stairs to join her, thinking that she had forgotten to take one of her bags down to the car.

But she hadn't, of course, was merely waiting for me in the empty bedroom, and she opened her arms, and we held on to each other for a long time in silence. "We won't have another chance to say good-bye properly, you know," she whispered. "Anyway, not without an audience."

"I love you," I said. "And I always will. Please don't forget that."

"Don't you."

"There's no chance."

"Well, we'll see. But write me, anyway." She took a folded piece of paper out of her handbag and slid it into my shirt pocket. "This is the address I want you to use," she said. "It's my brother's house in the country. I've written him and told him to keep all of my mail until I arrive. So I hope that there'll be a small stack of letters waiting for me."

"There will be. I'll write every day."

"No, only when you feel like it," she said. "And don't be sad, and don't be too gay."

"I'll do my best."

"Oh Carl, Carl . . . I'm going to miss you." She shook her head, as if to clear her eyes of her tears. "The French say, *partir c'est mourir un peu*, which I've always thought a terrible cliché. Now it turns out that it isn't. Although it's probably easier to die. Who knows. Well, good-bye, my darling. Take care." There was the sound of Hévesey blowing the horn of his car from the road. Pam touched my cheek with her gloved hand. Then she kissed me gently on the mouth, letting her lips linger against mine. "Wipe the lip rouge off before you appear," she warned me, and hurried out of the room.

The drive was a final torture, devised no doubt by the righteous God I had always secretly believed existed, for there were still so many things I wanted to say and to ask, but I couldn't because Paul was there beside me at the wheel, chattering away to Pam, who had chosen to ride in the back. I turned sideways and let my left hand hang over the seat, and she took it, establishing a last surreptitious contact, which brought no satisfaction with it at all.

The traffic was heavy through the ugly outskirts of the town, the late-afternoon sun slanting in through the windows. There were endless rows of low buildings and hamburger stands and used-car lots, and then, as we approached the port, the oil wells began, a black man-made forest that gave off an evil odor with no sign anywhere of the mad magician who had caused it to grow. Then at last the smell of the sea invaded the car, although there was no sea in view. We made our way along a series of low warehouses and turned onto a concrete quai where the freighter Pam was to take lay tied up, its red-and-white smokestack standing out against the rapidly graying sky.

Billy Lovat, who had followed us in his car with Karen and Paul's red-headed girl friend, pulled up behind us, and we all went up the covered gangway of the ship and crowded into the small cabin a blue-shirted sailor had led us to. It was like an oven inside, and as soon as the porter appeared with the luggage, we all filed out again onto the covered deck, like the characters in an old-fashioned comedy film. "That's about as long as I'd want to stay in that place," Billy Lovat mumbled to me.

Hévesey overheard him. "It'll cool down once the ship puts out to sea," he said. "They've been moored here for days."

Pam had been directing the stowing of her luggage, and she reappeared at that moment, fanning herself with the envelope that contained her tickets. "My God," she said, "I hope it isn't going to be like that all the way. I'll need a bottle of champagne every hour."

"Well, we have plenty on board, madam," a cheerful British voice said from behind us. He was apparently one of the ship's officers, for his navy-blue uniform was well cut, and his white shirt starched and fresh-looking despite the heat. He had come down a steep ladder from the bridge, and seeing Pam, had stopped to investigate. "Welcome on board, Mrs. Gordon," he added with a pleased smile that he made no effort to conceal.

"Thank you very much," Pam said.

"If I can be of any assistance, I'd be only too delighted," he continued smoothly. "My name's Jenkins. I'm the first officer." He was handsome in a very English way, with blond hair and a sunburned fair skin, and he saluted elegantly before continuing on down the deck.

"That one should make for an interesting trip," Billy said, laughing. "Did you see his face when he discovered that you were one of the passengers? He probably assumed that Mrs. Gordon would be a fat Scottish lady with varicose veins. . . ."

I felt my stomach tightening with hate and jealousy, hate for Billy and his stupid jokes, and jealousy for Mr. Jenkins, who had looked like a cat approaching a pitcher of cream someone had left on the breakfast table. He would be after her for three long weeks, night and day, and I felt a numb misery descending on me. Why had I insisted on coming to see her off, I asked myself. It would have been better to say good-bye to her alone on the beach, or in the bedroom of the cottage where she had suggested we part on the previous day. I turned to lean on the wooden railing of the deck, and stared out at the bare hills beyond the port. Then I saw Karen's hands appear next to mine on the varnished wood, heard her shoes banging against the metal deck scuppers as she pulled herself up in order to share the view. "Will you be coming to England someday to visit us?" she asked.

"I hope so," I said.

"I don't think you'll like it."

"Why not?"

"Because I don't think I'll like it much either."

"Of course he's coming," Pam said, putting her arm through mine. "Anyway, we'll be back in California soon."

"With Mr. Jenkins?" I asked.

"Don't be an ass."

But Mr. Jenkins had already returned, accompanied by the chief steward, who wanted to take our order for a last drink before the ship sailed.

There was an endless wait on the covered deck, too much time to say anything, except all the banal things. Then the warning blast of the ship's whistle told those of us who were being left behind to go ashore. Pam came to me after she had kissed all the others. She put her arms around me slowly and held me to her despite the audience she had so worried about before. "You've asked me so often," I said in a low voice, "but it's only now, for the first time, that I wish we'd never met."

"Don't say that! And don't think it, please."

"I love you."

"I love you, too." She kissed me on both cheeks, and with tears in my eyes I let her go, and started toward the gangway aft.

"You've forgotten to kiss me, Carl," Karen said shrilly.

"I'm sorry."

Her thin arms wound themselves tightly around my neck. "Good-bye," she said with childish finality.

"Good-bye, Karen."

I followed the others down the gangway onto the pier, and we stood endlessly again, waiting for the thick hawsers to be lifted and thrown into the water and the tugs to begin their brief work, and we waved and waved, starting too soon and going on for too long, while the *Duchy of*

Lancaster slowly moved out into the calm water of the passage. The sky was a blue-gray curtain, distinguishable only from the color of the sea by the red streaks the sun had left on the far edge of clouds, and the ship's horn blew a final few blasts as the tugs released her, and she was on her way.

Now there would be nothing, I thought, no more kisses, no more swimming in the surf after we had made love, no more holding hands in movie theaters, or eating in drive-ins, or going to the market even, no more soft skin to touch with my mouth, or lips held tightly against my lips, or wanting her, or having her, feeling the almost painful pleasure of being one. There would be only empty days now, days of waiting for the mail, days of writing letters that would take weeks to arrive, and not be answered until what I had said was well forgotten. How slowly the silhouette of the vessel moved away from the land, gliding across the orange sea. Was that the final twist of the knife? Or was there an infinity of tortures yet to come?

"Well, at least it's sure to be a safe voyage," Paul Hévesey said. "Thank God for that."

"Isn't it silly of me," his girl friend replied. "I always cry when I see a ship leaving port, no matter who's on board."

PART
IX

❧ one ✍

Despite the thousands of miles that soon separated us, I did not lose contact with her, for I wrote every day, as I had promised I would. It quickly became a habit, although at the expense of my diary, as I found that my letters were invariably a summing up of my daily activities. Unfortunately, her replies arrived much too late for any true exchange of opinions or feelings, but these last were constant anyway, unaltered by the slow passage of time. I always wrote to her as soon as I had finished my day's work, for I had not abandoned my novel, as I had been tempted to do immediately after her departure. It, too, was a remnant of our life together, and I felt that I owed it to her to finish it. While I worked, it seemed as if she were still there, and I was again conscious of her unspoken encouragement, although I realized that I was behaving like one of Dr. Pavlov's dogs, responding to a conditioned reflex.

Her letters, when they finally began to arrive, were what I most looked forward to every day, and nothing gave me greater pleasure than to read and reread them, until I could quote certain passages by heart. She seemed to know instinctively what it was that I wanted to hear, and I was seldom disappointed. She wrote me long descriptions of her daily activities, giving me to understand that she was being faithful, which, foolishly enough, concerned me as much as ever. Gordon, she said, was being distant but friendly, trying hard to create a civilized way of life for both of them, despite what had happened.

He was making a film in London, which was where they lived now, in the cold, foggy city that she had to learn her way around anew after her many years of absence. Karen was attending a school not far from the house they had rented, complaining about the weather, and asking every day when they would be going back to the cottage on the beach. "She's amazingly tactful for a child, for she never mentions your name in front of her father, although she often asks me about you when we're alone," she wrote. "She gives me the feeling that I'll soon be able to talk to her as a friend, which makes me happy."

All that anyone else talked about was the war, she added, the war that would soon be coming, despite Munich and the absurd agreement that was signed there. "Peace in our time" was a phrase that was quickly being forgotten, or at best was being used only as a sure way of getting a laugh by the comedians in the music halls. "I don't know what I feel about it myself anymore. Of course, one is more frightened living here, but I think when 'doomsday' finally does come, I'm sure I'll feel relieved, as it's awful living under the threat of it all the time. Then, stupidly enough, I sometimes think that once the war does start, it will mean the end of our separation . . . although, Lord knows, I don't want you to have to go—you, or Richard, or anyone else. Still, I can't help but feel that there has to be an end to this awful tension that divides the world, and once it's over and done with (quickly, I hope), we'll all be able to go on with our lives."

I clung to the same unrealistic dream, the only difference being that mine was a more romanticized version, in which I still saw myself playing a heroic role, that being one of the last vestiges of immaturity I could not seem to shed. And so I clung stubbornly to my favorite daydream of our meeting in London, or somewhere in France, confidently believing that our separation was a temporary state of affairs, a long, difficult period to be survived until fate would graciously provide a happy ending.

⇌ *two* ⇌

TOWARD THE END of October my father returned from Europe. I had
expected to find a change in him, and still I was deeply shocked when I
saw how much he had aged. He was not quite fifty, and already his hair
was completely white, his face lined and marked by tension. He had
always been a nervous man, but now he was excessively so, given to sudden rages that I discovered later were partly attributed to his diabetes.
Contrary to his doctor's orders, he smoked incessantly, his hands trembling more than ever when he lit a cigarette.

Now that I have reached the same age myself, I can better understand how he must have felt at that critical period of his life. Everything
had gone wrong for him. He had been deprived of his nationality, which,
although he said it didn't matter to him, had left him without a passport
and therefore the freedom to go where he wanted to go in order to earn
a living. Worse than that, the ideology he despised with his heart and
soul was spreading across central Europe like a cancer, victimizing his
friends and his family, so that even if they managed to escape with their
lives, their economic survival was still a constant problem for him. Nor,
as I had discovered soon after his return, did he believe that there was
any chance for an improvement in the world situation, for he saw in the
war that he was convinced was soon coming a general period of destruction and upheaval that would bring with it no positive results. Millions
and millions of people were going to be killed, he felt, and yet once the
holocaust was over, the world would be worse off than before.

He was obviously unhappy for other reasons as well. I had never
forgotten the conversation we had had years ago, on the eve of his departure, and I suspected now that if "the voice of his heart" was responsible
for having taken him away, it was probably not an unimportant factor in
having brought him home. That was undoubtedly why he was so restless.
He wished that he hadn't come back, which he did his best to hide, as he

didn't want to offend his family, who had shown how delighted they were to see him again. I could tell that he was pretending to appear equally pleased, but it was difficult for him, as he was incapable of hypocrisy.

The atmosphere of the "happy family reunion" was soon subjected to even greater tension, for on the seventh of November, a young Jew named Grynszpan shot and killed the third secretary of the German embassy in Paris, and the anti-Semitic pogrom that followed inside the Third Reich cast a pall over all of our lives.

My father was more devastated by the news from abroad than the rest of us. He had left there less than a month ago, so that the stories and photographs in the newspapers had an even greater reality for him. He was unable to sleep, and spent the nights listening to the radio in the living room or pacing up and down in front of it once the late news broadcasts had ended. Early in the morning he would still be there, seated in front of the burned-out fire, listening to the first reports of the day, which were inevitably a résumé of everything he had already heard. The uncertainty of what was happening to so many of his friends made it impossible to think of anything else, and he was unable to work or keep any of the business appointments he had made when he had first returned. Everything irritated and upset him, even the time difference that complicated contact with Europe. "If only I had stayed in London," he said repeatedly, not bothering to hide his feelings any longer.

"There is nothing more you could do from there," my mother told him, which was not the sort of logic he wanted to hear.

"Well, at least I wouldn't feel cut off from everything," he replied testily. "As if I were living on another planet."

"That's because you've made up your mind to feel that way. It's not my fault."

"Did I say it was? Have I ever blamed you for my mistakes?"

"Perhaps not overtly, but the inference has often been there."

"Now we're talking about something that exists only in your mind," he said, and left the dining room, where, as usual, their brief altercation had taken place.

There were obviously other factors responsible for the tension that existed between them. Riesener had moved out of the house a week before my father's arrival, but he still came to dinner occasionally, which didn't help matters. He was quite a different person in my father's presence, however, reticent to speak, and surprisingly guarded in his opinions whenever he did become involved in a discussion. But that was not due solely to the complex personal situation he found himself in. It was not a time for cynicism or prophecy. He, too, had relatives and friends in Berlin, and was as devastated by the news as everyone else.

Nevertheless, his visits did little to improve the tense atmosphere. This became so apparent that my father was ultimately compelled to comment on the fact that Riesener annoyed him, although it had been his introduction that had brought the young man into all of our lives. Jake was already safely back at Berkeley by that time (a refuge that I was beginning to envy him), so that it was quite natural for my father to confide in me. He chose to do so on one of our evening walks in the park on the palisades, which were still his favorite diversion.

"I really have nothing against Edmund," he said, stopping to rest at the base of his favorite palm tree. "He's an intelligent and cultured young man. Only he's too well fed . . . too sure of his opinions, like all the sons of the rich German bourgeoisie. To see him here, in this dehydrated *Schlaraffenland*, irritates me. I know it's unreasonable, but I can't help it. What does he expect to accomplish here? Why does he stay?"

The question, even though it was rhetorical, made me feel uneasy. The relationship between my parents was not anything I wanted to speculate or comment on. "Where else should he go?" I replied. "New York? San Francisco? I'd stay here, too, if I had to make a choice."

"That's different. This is where you were brought up. It's your country, your language. But Edmund is a European. He must feel as I do, that this place is an artificial oasis in which he'll stagnate with time."

"But then, why *did* you come back?" I asked boldly.

"Because I wanted to see Jake and you, and Mother, of course. For no matter what has happened between us, she's still an important part of my life. And she always will be," he added pointedly. "Then, also, I'm not infallible in my judgments," he continued with a wry smile. "I make mistakes. I thought my family might need me, which was most probably only vanity on my part."

I started to object, but he shook his head. "Forgive a bad joke," he said. "We all need each other, more than ever these days. No matter how stubbornly each one of us pursues his own private despair." He started across the worn lawn, the evening breeze disheveling his hair. He put his hand on my shoulder affectionately, as if just touching me was all the support he required. "It looks as if it might rain," he remarked, glancing up at the darkening sky. "A few of God's tears, falling on the wrong place."

"Why the wrong place?" I asked. "We need rain."

"I didn't mean it literally. It seems the wrong place to me, simply because I'm stranded here."

"Can't you go back to London?"

"Not without a job or a passport. That was another reason I had to return. The least pleasant one."

"But once you get a passport, you'll be able to, won't you?"

"Yes. In five years. By then it'll be too late. Oh, perhaps with influence I could arrange to travel as a 'stateless person.' It's nothing I could count on, however. That's why I decided to cut all my ties. It's unfair to ask a person to wait—especially a woman. Nobody can divide himself in two, Carl, live on two continents at the same time. Yet mine is a very minor tragedy, compared to the lives of most of my friends."

Was he trying to warn, or console me? I wasn't sure. Nor could I quite follow his reasoning. I still believed, quite unrealistically, that anything was possible, that nothing could stand in the way of love. "Will you stay in this country, then?" I asked.

"I have to," he replied. "I have to work and make money. I can't allow your mother to carry all of the burden of sending you to college and paying off the mortgage on the house."

"Don't worry about me," I said.

"I don't, really. I know you'll be all right. And so will Jake. If only America doesn't become infected by the sicknesses of Europe, and can keep from becoming involved."

I was of a different opinion. But I didn't argue with him, for there was still a gulf between us at that moment, a gulf that his nervousness had imposed, and his long absence. We walked home together in silence, each one of us far away in his thoughts, yet strangely united, intent on a part of the world that was out of reach, but never out of mind.

⮞ *three* ⮜

THE AUTUMN ENDED, and the winter began. Pamela wrote regularly to say that she was well, that she missed me, and was being faithful. Her life was settling down into a routine, which she said suited her, as doing the same things every day made the weeks pass more quickly. The weather was the only thing she found hard to bear, the fog and the endless rain. "California now seems like a lovely dream," she wrote, "or the memory of a holiday by the sea that can never be repeated again. How fortunate we all were living there, although we didn't realize it at the time. Or did we?"

The melancholy tone of her letters made me feel that I was losing her, for in them she seemed to be saying good-bye over and over again, as if the distance between us was increasing, the contact becoming more remote. As a result, my daily declarations of love and loyalty became more desperate, which in turn made her assume that I was unhappier than I really was. So I was forced to write denials, or contradict what I had written before. I began to suspect that my father had been right when he had said that it was impossible to live on two continents at the same time, that the distance and the difference in time were insurmountable obstacles for any relationship.

Pam was becoming a part of my imagination, was joining the unreal images that floated through my daydreams. I found myself going back constantly to my diary, reading the passages that were concerned with her, and cursing the code I had invented because I had been afraid that the leather-bound volume would fall into someone else's hands. The code deprived my descriptions of flesh and blood, and I began even to feel unsure of my memory. Her physical image was becoming blurred as well, and so I asked her to send me a photograph. It arrived a few weeks before Christmas, slightly mauled by the mail, and I trimmed away the tattered edges and pasted it in the back of the looseleaf notebook I used at the university.

She had gone to a portrait photographer, as she said she had no decent snapshot of herself, and the result was a rather lifeless study of her in a tweed jacket, which was not at all as I remembered her. Her hair looked darker, which she explained was due to not ever being out in the sun, and she had cut it short, I noticed, which made her look older. "But I *am* getting older," she wrote in reply to my complaints; "there's nothing I can do about it. Every day I find a few new gray hairs, and even though I pull them out, they come back in greater numbers."

That again. How often we had argued about the difference in our ages, only now it was impossible to end the argument by making love to her, so that I could say: "Do you really think this will change, the way we feel when we're together like this?" Instead, all I could do was write words that were beginning to sound more inadequate to me with each passing day, crippled, repetitive phrases that didn't really express the longing I felt. Although it was not so much making love to her that I missed, as proving to her that we belonged together, which had always been the end result of going to bed together. How could I hope to hold her with written promises that my feelings would never change? A Mr. Jenkins would surely appear one day at a cocktail party or a luncheon, and would flatter and pursue her, with more time than an ocean crossing in which to persuade her that it was ridiculous to wait forever for the much-too-young man she had left behind.

I knew from my own experience that this was possible, remembering how I had met Cynthia at the flying school and had been drawn to her. Now there were other Cynthias who came daily into my life. I saw them in the lecture halls, or crossing the campus, girls of my own age who reminded me again that there was a simple way to end all the waiting and longing. As yet I had only observed them from a distance, had taken no active step in their direction, but their existence made me realize that what might eventually happen to me could certainly happen to Pam. Only Gordon's presence would make things more difficult for her, and for the first time I was glad that he was there, living beside her as a permanent guardian. Of course, there was always the chance that she might go back to him, which thought tortured me as well. They were probably sharing a room, if not the same bed, so that it was reasonable to suppose she might ultimately weaken and go back to the old way of life that she had put up with for so long. All I had to go on was her promise to be faithful, and to wait, both of which she reiterated constantly in her letters. But then, what else could she do? She would never be able to write me and tell me that she had changed her mind.

A few days after Christmas I ran into Terry Sangster. She was coming out of a market to which I had been sent to do some last-minute shopping, and we almost collided in the side entrance of the building. "My God, are you still alive?" she said, smiling happily. "I thought you'd vanished from the face of the earth." She was loaded down with parcels, and so I helped her carry them to her car. "And how's the boy lover?" she asked as we crossed the parking lot together, just as I had done so often with Pam.

"All right," I replied uncomfortably.

"Your lady friend's left you, hasn't she? Gone back across the big water."

"She had to. . . ."

"I know all about it, honey. Daddy wanted her back. That's why you have that awful unfucked look." She put her hand over her mouth in mock embarrassment. "I shouldn't talk like that, should I?" she giggled. "I seem to remember, you don't like it. But you do have that slightly horny air about you, angel, I can't help it. . . . Or even if I could, I won't," she added. "Because I don't enjoy being dropped any more than you do."

"I tried to call you a couple of times," I said, "but you were never home."

"You did? I'm sorry. I should have called back, but I guess I couldn't find a nickel that day. . . ."

"It doesn't matter."

"You forgive me? That's good. And how long do you think you'll have to wait for Lady Pam this time?"

"I don't know. . . ."

"Poor old Carl. Never fall in love . . . if you can help it. It's bad for the heart." She got in behind the wheel of her car. "Call me again if you get really desperate," she said with a sly smile. "I don't want you throwing yourself out of a window or taking an overdose of sleeping pills."

"I won't, don't worry."

Many years later I was to recall that last remark of hers again, and realize that that particular solution was probably always present in the back of her mind. At the time I paid no attention to it, assuming it was just another one of her wisecracks. I watched her drive off and wondered if I had done the right thing, for her attitude had not been all that unforgiving. Still, I knew that it would have been pointless to get involved with her again, pointless and immoral. I went home and wrote Pam a long letter in which I made no mention of running into Terry Sangster.

It was a lie of omission, but a permissible one, I thought as I sealed the envelope, because I had nothing to hide. I had been unfaithful to her only in my thoughts, and for a very brief instant. Yet, it would have been pleasant to return once more to Terry's room, where the rag doll and the record player were undoubtedly still waiting, but I had resisted the temptation by remembering the ultimate feeling of self-disgust that would be as unavoidable as the telephone calls that would have to be made and answered later. It was better to abstain for at least a while longer, and remain loyal, if not virtuous.

As a reward, or so it seemed at that first moment, a letter arrived from Pamela the next morning which contained a ray of hope. Gordon had befriended someone high up in the RAF, who had promised to help him surmount the age barrier that stood between him and his ambitions. Pam was vague about how it would all work, but the plan now was for Richard to get a commission as a ground officer, and then ultimately transfer to pilot's training later. It would all take a while to arrange, but it could be done, the unnamed wing commander had assured them. "He sounded just like the headmaster of one of those schools that it's ever-so-difficult to get into," she wrote, "and I felt like telling him that I wasn't all that anxious for Richard to become a pilot, that I'd prefer to have him in uniform and safe on the ground in Canada. But that would have meant a really gigantic row, so I said nothing, and smiled, and behaved like the perfect British wife, which I'm not, as you well know. . . ."

The important part of the story, the reason she had written me about the incident in such detail, was that it might mean their having to go to Canada in the near future, for that was where most of the RAF training would be done, "once the hostilities start." "At least then there won't be an ocean between us, but only good dry land, and who knows, we might be able to come back to California for a month's leave. . . ." She sounded as if she were quite resigned to being Gordon's wife, which, strangely enough, didn't matter so much to me either anymore. I was more concerned with putting an end to our being separated, would have gladly settled for the old arrangement, which appeared almost idyllic in retrospect.

And hurriedly reading through her letter (I knew I would be rereading it at least a dozen times later on), I felt encouraged. Everything was not hopeless. The day would come when I would see her again. I could visualize it. She would be waiting on the beach in front of the cottage, and I would run across the sand and take her in my arms. Like a character in a nineteenth-century French novel, I could feel my heart beating more rapidly at the thought. But once the momentary surge of optimism had subsided, and the letter had been studied more carefully, I realized that nothing had changed, that our being reunited still depended solely on the war, the beginning of which lay ahead in the remote future, like some bright if murderous Judgment Day.

Looking back, I am amazed at my childish faith in my being able to control my own destiny in the midst of what I must have known would be a fairly turbulent and disorienting event. But at the time I didn't think of the beginning of the Second World War in such realistic terms. My imagination was influenced by what I knew of the past, and so I assumed that it would be a day of flags and marching men, of charged emotions and a general unity of purpose, the beginning of a crusade against fascism, which no matter what the cost might be, would make for a better world. And somehow bring me closer to Pam.

≫ *four* ≪

BUT IT WASN'T like that. When the day finally came, there were no flags in view, no soldiers on parade, no great surge of emotion, until George VI spoke to ask for the support of the empire for his cause, and even then, his words had a ring of resignation and somber purpose that was noble, perhaps, but not inspiring. Right up to the last few hours it had seemed questionable whether England would live up to its treaty obligations with Poland (in Paris the cabinet was still in "secret session," although by that time it was almost certain that France would be forced to follow its ally's lead), so that the general mood was one of relief that an honorable decision had finally been arrived at, but nothing more.

We all sat in silence in front of the radio in the living room, while a band five thousand miles away played "God Save the King," and we were moved in spite of ourselves by the familiar melody, for the music transmitted more of a feeling of finality than anything else. England had declared war at last! Maureen's eyes filled with tears, and she sighed heavily as the song ended, and blew her nose before going back to the kitchen from which she had appeared for the historic moment. My father crossed to the radio and turned it off, as he was in no mood to listen to the local commentator's explanation of the day's events.

I got up and went out into the garden. The sun was shining, I remember, and I could see a section of blue ocean beyond the branches of the fig tree. Prince was asleep against the back fence, enjoying the shade that the neighbor's Japanese pavilion cast on our small patch of lawn. For the first time in many months I felt that life was truly worth living, was not, as advertised, only a vale of tears. I heard the screen door on the terrace behind me open and close, and saw my father coming slowly toward me, his hands clasped behind his back. He said: "After all the orators, it's a pleasure to listen to a man who has to struggle with a stammer."

I knew what he was trying to tell me. He had grown up in a country whose principal illnesses had all stemmed from an ineffectual monarchy, so that he had come to detest the mentality that accepted as normal the rule of a king. His remark, I realized, was the first step toward a mutual reconciliation, as the political events of the preceding week had caused a rift between us that appears ridiculous now, but was anything but ridiculous at the time.

The "pact" was the reason for it, the nonaggression pact that the Soviet Union had signed with Nazi Germany. My father and Jake had tried to justify Russia's actions by insisting that England and France had forced Stalin's hand, and the bitterness of our arguments had alienated us to such a degree that we had given up discussing anything to do with politics and the war.

I nodded, although I was far removed from kings and dictators in my thoughts, on another continent. It was late afternoon in London, I was thinking, and the evening of the first night of the war was only a few hours away. In all probability Göring's bombers would soon be appearing over the city.

On the sea the Germans had already struck the first blow by sinking the passenger liner *Athenia*, so they could be expected to strike momentarily from the air as well. Where was Pamela, I wondered. Had she already moved out into the country with Karen, as she had planned to do? I knew that Gordon was still a civilian, but it was unlikely now that he would remain one for long. The commission he had been promised was "in the works," Pamela had written. More than ever before, I found myself envying him. He was there, where I most wanted to be, with her. Soon he would be actively engaged in fighting the battle I felt was more mine than his.

"Do you think that it'll go on for a long time, now that it's started?" I asked my father.

He glanced over at me, his dark, intense eyes meeting mine. "Why? Are you afraid that it might be over before you get there?"

"No. I just wanted to know what you think."

"I think it'll go on for years and years," he replied gravely. "Longer than last time. And even more innocent people will die."

"But how can the Germans fight on two fronts?" I asked. "They haven't got the resources. . . ." That was what the military experts were saying, that the enemy would be unable to fight a long war.

"They'll manage," my father said. "They always do. They obey, and die, because that's easier than to think and live. And the others will imitate them, proud that they, too, have learned a contempt for life."

"They started this war," I said, irritated by his lack of partisanship. "And if we're not prepared to defend our ideology, and die if necessary, they'll take over the entire world."

He nodded and said: "I know, I know all of that. But it's easier for you to say . . . because you don't have a son. I have two, and so I hesitate." He smiled and drew deeply on his cigarette. "Also, I've always hated the slogans almost more than the wars." He snapped his fingers, and Prince, who had been awakened by the sound of our voices, came to him to have his ears scratched.

The discussion was over, the first one, that is, for there were countless others that followed, a series of passionate debates in which my father tried to make me see that it was foolish to rush off to the war as if it were a holy crusade, which, despite the passage of time and the lack of betterment in the state of the world, I still think it was.

That Sunday morning I left him with the subject hardly touched. The most advanced elements of our points of view had clashed briefly and then withdrawn to reorganize. The military simile came to my mind as I hurried off to the beach, and I remembered it later, and included it proudly in my diary, an adolescent literary flourish that has an absurd ring today. I also noted, for future reference, that I felt my father was guilty of a pessimism that was an integral part of his background, the traditional "European view" of things. He had no confidence in the strength of America, its youth, its industry, which in the end, I felt certain, would resolve the conflict and impose the just peace that it had been swindled out of the last time by the corrupt politicians of Europe, who always insisted on planting the seeds for future wars while they made peace. . . . And more in the same vein, a long discourse that I wrote that evening after returning home.

The beach was crowded on that final summer holiday weekend, as if nothing unusual had happened. The volleyball game in progress near the lifeguard tower was as hotly contested as on any other Sunday, and the tanned lovers lying against the stone wall at the farthest reach of the sand were as unconcerned with anyone but themselves as they had always been. They seemed not to have heard the news, or if they had, they were intent on disregarding it, apparently unconscious that the tides of history would soon reach out for them, demanding their involvement and sacrifice.

The surf was up, the water cold and refreshing, giving new life to the citizens of Muscle Beach whenever they felt themselves becoming lax and stale in the heat of the afternoon sun. I walked along the moist edge of the sea to the jetty where the waves were the best for body-surfing, and dived into the foam of a small breaker and swam out to join the other enthusiasts of the sport. But unlike most of them, I was conscious of the pleasure of every passing moment, every onrushing wave, for I sensed that this was by way of being a farewell performance, a final last day of childish pleasure in the company of the as yet uncommitted, and keeping to myself the secret of what I knew lay ahead for us all, I joined in the game I knew I had already played for too long, and put off my total commitment to "the cause" for half a day more.

≈ five ≈

MY UNCLE DAVID, my mother's youngest brother, was the only member of the family who, like myself, loved sports. I had hazy childhood memories of him on a tennis court, a tall man with reddish hair and freckles who hit the ball so hard that the spectators would step back out of the way when his turn came to serve. He had played soccer for Poland, and according to my mother's stories, had been capable, when they were children, of galloping across the fields like a cossack, with each foot on the back of a pony. I hadn't seen him since I was five years old, and couldn't really recollect what he looked like, but I could recall that he had been considered something of a problem, because he was unwilling to settle down to a permanent job and a disciplined life.

He had had a love affair with one of the Polish maids in my grandparents' house, and after she had borne him a child, had married her, much against my grandfather's wishes. It was this *mésalliance* that was ultimately to cost him his life, for he returned to Poland after the Nazi takeover of Austria because his wife and child were there, and because she had friends who had volunteered to help him. When the invasion began, he joined the Polish army under an assumed name, although he was well over military age, and was captured during the third week of the German blitzkrieg on the outskirts of the small town where he had grown up. Someone in the village denounced him as being a Jew and an Austrian, so the Germans charged him with being a traitor, forced him to dig his own grave, and shot him.

The tragic news reached us early in October. It was all I needed to make up my mind, a final, indisputable argument for direct action, and despite my father's protests, I refused to register for college and announced that I was going to Canada to enlist. I was nineteen, and therefore needed my parents' consent, which, despite many heated discussions, was not forthcoming. My father said he wouldn't try to stop me, but neither would he sign a paper that would imply that he approved of what I was doing. I considered that fair, as thus neither one of us was being forced to abandon his convictions.

Years later, long after the war was over and my father gone forever, I was told by an old friend of the family that immediately after my departure my father had had a change of heart and had written the authorities in British Columbia asking them to send me back, which small treachery I could readily understand by that time, and would gladly have forgiven him had he still been alive. But as I started off in my car that warm October morning, I had no idea that anything might go wrong with my plan, and even today I still think it unlikely that my father's letter had anything to do with its ultimate failure.

I had finished the final draft of my novel and had mailed it to a publisher in New York, so that I felt fully liberated from all obligations. There had been a number of farewells, one or two of them tearful, but most of the others anything but sad. Benson, my first boss, surrounded by his wife and noisy family, admitted that he envied me, although he said he didn't relish the idea of fighting in a British unit. "It's better than joining up with the French, anyway," was his final judgment. Billy Lovat and Paul Hévesey were both full of honest admiration. "You're sure to be sent to London, and there you'll see Pam and Richard," Paul told me, as if that was not something I had figured out for myself long ago. "I'll be there too, someday," Billy said with a sigh. "There's no avoiding it now, I'm afraid."

My friends at school were more doubtful about the wisdom of my decision. They thought that it might have been better to finish another year of college before going off to war, although they were forced to admit that Canada and the RAF might be equally rewarding. For literary reasons, as well as sentimental ones, I called Terry, as saying good-bye to an ex-girl friend seemed to me to be a required part of the story, but I couldn't find her. She had gone east, the maid who answered the telephone told me, without specifying how far east she had gone, the Mojave Desert, or New York.

Edmund Riesener was the least enthusiastic of anyone outside my immediate family. "You're doing something nobody's asking you to do," he said, "and although I know what your motivations are, it seems foolish to me."

"I didn't think you'd approve," I said.

He raised his eyebrows questioningly. "Approve, no. Of course not. But I admire your courage. . . ."

"You don't have to say that."

"I know I don't. However, it's the truth. I only hope you won't be disappointed." He smiled thoughtfully. "Both you and Jake are so different from myself. You feel the necessity to do something for the future of the world. I only want to survive as comfortably as possible. I hope you don't despise me for that."

"I don't." I didn't at that moment.

"Well, then, good luck," he said, putting out his hand. "I hope you'll be back soon."

Leaving my mother was the most difficult part of it all. The death of her brother had upset her terribly, and the fresh flood of tears brought on by my stubborn refusal to take my father's advice and wait for the war to come to me almost made me change my mind several times. But no matter how much my going might upset her, I couldn't postpone my trip. It was too late by that time to register at the university, and I had already written Pam. I also knew that no matter when I decided to go, my mother would react in the same way to my actual departure. So I managed to console her somewhat by telling her that the period of training would be long and arduous, giving her the hope to cling to that it would all be over before I was sent off to active duty. She had probably already made up her mind to write the authorities in Canada on her own, if my father was unwilling to do so, for in the end she was suddenly quite reconciled to my going, insisting only that I take along enough long underwear as a precaution against the Canadian winter, which she was worried I might have trouble getting used to after so many years of living in a mild climate.

But all that was behind me now, I told myself as I drove through the broad valleys of the eastern High Sierras. The sky was an unblemished blue curtain beyond the distant peaks. The golden stubble fields of the high mesas reflected the late-afternoon sun as if they were immune to night. I saw a group of cowboys riding along the barbed-wire fence next to the road, which made me return for an instant to my childhood and all the abandoned dreams of the West that my reading of Karl May and Fenimore Cooper had inspired. Was I running after another illusion, another romantic world that no longer existed? I didn't pursue my doubts for too long. It was great to be alive, I felt, which commonplace sentiment brought to mind my father's varied arguments against what I was doing.

Wars were historic events that made all individual destinies of little or no consequence, he had warned me. Furthermore, it was not a war that was being fought for the benefit of the Jews, so that the compulsion I felt was an erroneous one. "You think of this thing as a duel between yourself and the monster that shrieks at you from across the sea," he had told me. "He says Jews are weak, and you want to prove to him that he's wrong." Then again, he had warned me that no individual sacrifice had ever changed the course of history, not in modern times, in any case. "Jesus was the last martyr who left his mark on the human race, and even his death didn't help all that much, one is apt to feel today, in the time of the Austrian antichrist."

I had no intention of giving up my life for the benefit of mankind. I wanted to fight the good fight, and survive to tell the tale. All of which became increasingly clear to me as I neared my goal. By the time I had crossed the Canadian border, I was secretly willing to enlist as a member of the ground crew of the Air Force rather than insist on being accepted as a flying cadet. For I felt estranged, suddenly less certain of what I was doing. The monotonous scenery of the wheat country depressed me, the narrow towns with their somber-looking grain elevators and their staid red-brick houses huddled together in a futile defense against space.

My journey, I remember, ended in Edmonton, Alberta, a gray city that appeared to have been constructed for no reason. I went to the best hotel, which was too expensive for my limited budget, but less depressing than the smaller ones. The first meal I ate was as tasteless as my mother had warned me it would be. I forced myself to finish it, however, determined to harden my spirit in face of the coming ordeal. Then I went for a brief walk through the badly lit town. It was a windy night, with sudden flurries of cold rain. There was almost no one else in the streets. The small number of uniformed men I encountered looked bored and unhappy, even those in RAF blue. It was nothing like I had imagined it would be, this life I had condemned myself to so recklessly.

Early the next morning I presented myself at the RCAF recruiting station, where, in the company of a seedy-looking group of young men, I filled out the required forms that appeared to be the first, most difficult step toward serving his Majesty the King. Then I was told to take off all of my clothes and pass into the adjoining room, where a gaunt Air Force doctor with halitosis examined my body. My right eye had always been weak, but it seemed weaker than ever when I tried to read the letters on the chart. The light seemed inadequate, and I found that I was sweating nervously, as if my life depended on deciphering the distant symbols. I guessed wildly at the last two, then dropped the card I was holding over my left eye, and realized that I had guessed wrong. The gaunt doctor said nothing, made some notes on my form, and nodded to himself, as if he had suspected my eye was weak right from the beginning.

Across the room I caught a glimpse of a naked body that looked startlingly different from all the others around me. The torso had only one sound leg. The other one ended in a short stump, cradled in a primitive device that might well have served for a model of an illustration of Long John Silver. The man was enlisting as a cook, the doctor explained curtly in answer to my question, having "lost his leg as a trooper in the Black Watch during the nineteen-fourteen war." It was not a vision calculated to make the idealistic recruit's heart beat faster, the gross body, with the sweat-stained leather strap, which held the wooden leg in place, buried deep in the folds of the loose flesh of the man's buttocks.

And so, when the gaunt doctor told me that "for the time being we are not accepting recruits for pilot training who require corrective glasses," I felt almost relieved.

"What about some other job in the Air Force?" I asked hopefully.

"You mean navigator, or gunner? Well, I'm afraid the same rules apply. Mind you, I don't think they will for very long. . . ." he added with a bitter smile.

"And ground personnel?" There was surely some place for me, I thought, some service I could render England and the cause.

"For ground personnel, you'll have to reapply," the doctor said curtly. "I suggest you come back tomorrow morning and ask for Wing Commander Walker."

I nodded soberly and went off to find my clothes, my naked feet cold and damp inside my unlaced shoes. After I had gotten dressed I felt a little better, and returned on foot to the hotel, where I was soon lost in the pages of Tolstoy's *War and Peace*, which had been my mother's farewell present. It was a welcome escape from the grim, sunless town. I read all afternoon, and most of the night, while the wind and the rain beat against the panes of the curtained windows behind my bed.

The next day I went back to the recruiting office, ready to accept whatever menial job was offered me, for I still had a part of my ultimate goal in view, my reunion with Pam in London. But even that hope was soon removed by Wing Commander Walker, a tall man with graying hair and a row of ribbons on his tunic, who explained to me that my German birth would make it impossible for me to be recruited into the Royal Canadian Air Force at all. "Technically you're an American, I suppose," he said politely, "but as you have no proof of your parents' citizenship, I'm afraid we will have to turn down your offer of service."

"I can send for the necessary papers," I said, knowing that I would probably have to wait a year or two before my mother would mail them back to me.

"Well, if you can provide a certificate of citizenship, we'll be glad to review your case," Walker told me. Then, with a false smile, he added: "The army, I believe, is a little less particular . . . even the good regiments."

I had seen a company of the Seaforth Highlanders swinging through the town early that morning, with a dashing subaltern in the lead, and despite the sweaty air of glory of it all, I had felt relieved that I had chosen a less arduous branch of the service. Now I was being diverted to the infantry in spite of my many apprehensions, and I felt fate gripping me by the throat. I smiled bravely and thanked the wing commander for his kindness, glanced covetously at his ribbons, and departed.

I stood hesitating in the doorway of the recruiting office, watching the traffic move slowly through the rain-soaked street in front of me, wondering what to do next. If I went wisely home, it would be an admission of cowardice and defeat. Why had I gotten myself into this impossible predicament? "You're doing something nobody's asking you to do," Riesener had said, and as usual he had turned out to be right. I hailed a taxi and asked the driver to take me to the recruiting office of the Highland Brigade.

It was as if I no longer had any will of my own. There appeared to be no other solution than to go and present myself to the one branch of the service I had always hoped to avoid. The taxi driver was studying me in his rear-view mirror. "You're an American, aren't you?" he asked.

"That's right."

"A lot of your chaps are coming up here to volunteer," the man said. "Most of them go to the Air Force."

"They turned me down."

"They did, eh? You'd think they'd take anyone they can get." He shook his head. "Well, there's not much to choose between them," he added, as if to console me. "The main thing is to come home unharmed and alive." He paused. "I was with the Princess Pats in nineteen-seventeen, and I wouldn't go again if they came looking for me with the Mounties," he said, pulling up in front of an imposing-looking armory a few blocks from where we had started.

I went inside with a quaking heart. The battle honors of the Highland Brigade looked down upon me from a black metal plaque on the wall. Vimy Ridge, Paschendale, the Somme. I had read about all of those places with horror at the folly of man. This was where so many of those who had made "the supreme sacrifice" had signed up for their ultimate mass graves. And with my last ounce of courage almost expended, I pressed on, gave my name to the corporal at the polished wooden desk near the entrance, and was taken up a narrow stairway to the office of a paunchy sergeant major in shirtsleeves, who sat staring up at me with glassy eyes.

"So the Air Force wouldn't take you, son . . . ? Well, what did you expect from that lot?" he said, grinning.

"I was born in Germany," I confessed quickly.

"You don't have to put that down on the form, do you, lad? I mean, once you're in, who's to know where you were born?"

I hesitated. The smell of creosote and sweat was overwhelming. "Let me think about it," I said.

"Sure, you do that, lad. Think about it. Just remember that we're not as fussy here. If you're keen, that's all that matters to us. Not where you were born."

I shook the sergeant major's hand and left the room, hurried down the stairs, and went out past the corporal's desk without even looking up at the plaque on the wall. I wasn't keen; I knew that with a feeling of overwhelming certainty. Not keen enough, anyway.

I went back to the hotel and packed my things, feeling as if I were escaping doom, the meat grinder, my own premature end. That I was ultimately to wind up as an infantryman was something I would never have dreamed possible at that moment.

I loaded my car and headed south, driving all day and most of the night, anxious to leave Canada behind me. I stopped in a motel on the American side of the border and managed to get a few hours' sleep. In the early morning I drove on.

Only many hours later, as the hills and forests and plains I had admired a few days earlier began to slide past my window, did I become aware of the seriousness of my personal failure. All my heroic good-byes had been for nothing. The admiration of my friends, I realized, would soon turn into a well-merited contempt. I had wanted to set an example. Instead, I had merely succeeded in making a fool of myself. I wasn't even looking forward to seeing my parents again. I had caused them so much needless grief. Although I knew they would forgive me, and be glad for a temporary respite from anxiety. Uncle David was gone forever. I, at least, was returning home for a while.

And Pam? How could I explain what had happened. No letter, no matter how long and well written, could alter the basic fact: that my idealism was limited. I was prepared to fight for the cause in a blue uniform, but not in a khaki-colored one. My cowardice had doomed us, she would soon realize, to many years more of separation. Until America became involved in the war . . . and that possibility seemed more remote than ever. And as I drove through the brilliantly colored valleys of eastern Oregon, I knew that by failing to enlist I had lost her finally for good and forever, was leaving her farther behind me with each passing mile.

It would be better to write and bravely say farewell, as I had made up my mind to do several times in the past months; but I hadn't had enough courage for that either. There was nothing I could do, except allow her to recede slowly from view, just as she had done that day a year ago when the freighter had carried her out across the smooth water of the port. Only this time she was departing from the turbulent whirlpool of my brain, gliding off into the depths of my memory. If only I had been a few years older, I thought once again, as I had done a hundred times before, already conscious of a permanent feeling of loss.

There was snow on the summits of the mountains in northern California. Well, at least summer had ended, I thought, summer with its constant, painful reminders of our love.

∾ Six ∽

I DIDN'T SEE Pamela Gordon again for nearly a quarter of a century. By that time I had long ago accomplished two of my earliest ambitions: I had become a writer, and I had been to the wars. Neither one with any *éclat*, but at least I had gotten my feet wet. I had even managed to get to London before the end of the hostilities, and had spent an enjoyable five-day leave in the company of a lieutenant of infantry from Lubbock, Texas, who had been assigned the same billet in the blacked-out town. We had both admired the spirit of the people, their friendliness and courage under attack, for the V2s were still falling on the city. But like most soldiers on leave, we had remained outsiders. This condition I could easily have rectified by getting in touch with the Gordons, who would not have been difficult to find, as he was still a prominent actor in those days. I didn't, though. Too much had happened in the intervening years, and I was unwilling to experiment with my emotions by seeking out a confrontation that I sensed might be painful rather than pleasant.

For I had arrived in England much later than I had planned. Much against my will, I had spent a year in the South Pacific first. My abortive trip to Canada had made me feel that some kind of heroic gesture was demanded of me, and so I had joined the Marine Corps a few months after Pearl Harbor, which, besides curing me of all romanticism about soldiering, caused me to be sent off in the opposite direction from the one in which I had always wanted to go. However, my foolhardy choice of service had had nothing to do with my final estrangement from Pam. The end between us had come long before that fateful decision was ever made.

Because I had fallen in love again . . . with someone my own age, just as Pamela had always prophesied. The girl in question (her name was Lucy) had come into my life in the spring of the year following my dejected return from Edmonton, Alberta. Not quite knowing what to do with myself, I had decided to continue my college career, and was once more attending classes at the extension division. We met at one of the late-afternoon lectures that were still the rule of the department. The course was called an introduction of psychology, and I had chosen it because a minimum of one science was required for entrance into the undergraduate body proper. That was still vaguely my goal then, although I knew there was little chance of my lasting long enough as a student in order to get a degree.

At first meeting I found that her face reminded me of Cynthia's, although I'm not at all certain now that it isn't Lucy's face that comes back to my mind's eye across the gap of the ensuing years. The stronger memory tends to displace the weaker or more distant one. Not that it mattered. The first impression was a strong one, and closer acquaintance confirmed my initial feelings. It turned out that she had enrolled in the extension division because she had felt the need to educate herself, having been forced to leave school at the age of fourteen in order to help support her family during the lean years of the depression. Because she was pretty, and talented enough, she had gone to work as a dancer in one of the local film studios, so that, like Terry, she was a refugee from the chorus at an early age. The resemblance ended there.

So ultimately I was forced to write Pamela the letter I had avoided writing because I had no real reason for doing so. In the back of my mind I had of course known that it would come to just this kind of a situation, but I hadn't been able to take the final step, which I suppose is understandable enough, as I was still clinging to the fading hope of Pam's return, and because I also knew that my lingering sense of loss would change to an even more painful emptiness if I were to cut the cord. Yet, when the time came, I couldn't bring myself to write the truth, couldn't admit to Pam that she had been right about the hopelessness of our relationship from the start. I had argued with her too often, had denied it too vehemently for too many years.

Also, I didn't want to hurt her as deeply as I knew the same kind of letter from her would have hurt me. And so I lied, put the blame on the distance that separated us, the "growing apart," which was real enough but that had finally been brought to a head by factors I was too cowardly to fully reveal. I tried not to sound sentimental, but only partially succeeded, for I resorted in the closing paragraph to a worn, maudlin expression of gratitude "for a time I will never forget." What else was there to say? It was, I found, the only completely honest passage in what I had written, which was why I didn't delete it in the end.

Yet for weeks after I had posted the letter I worried about what she would write in answer to my many lies. I felt certain that I would ultimately have to write her the truth, and I dreaded the task. I kept remembering my many assurances, and all the things I had written and said. But she spared me the embarrassment, for she never replied at all, answered me with an everlasting silence that was far more effective than anything she could have put down on a piece of paper. She had always been able to prove that she was the stronger one of us two by not revealing what she really felt, and she proved her point again, not because she wanted to, but because it was probably easier, under the circumstances, not to say anything at all.

Her lasting silence troubled me, made me feel ill at ease (an introduction to psychology did not provide an answer to my problems), but ultimately, overwhelmed by the surge of emotion that always accompanies a new love, I began to forget Pamela Gordon, or in any case, I found that she did not often intrude upon my thoughts. Only every once in a while, when driving up the coast highway early in the morning, or whenever I happened to see a kid on a bicycle near the beach. Then the past would suddenly return, and memories of other summers would invade my thoughts for a brief time. But even this began to happen less and less, and soon I was amazed to find that when it did happen, there was almost no guilt at all connected to my thoughts of her. Because by then I felt certain the some "good friend" had undoubtedly informed her of what had "happened to me." The world, I had discovered, was not nearly as vast as it is supposed to be.

That it is quite small was proven to me many years later. For one day I was sent to work on a film that was being shot in a remote village in southwestern Mexico. I was a replacement for an elderly scenarist who had succumbed to the disease that is known as Montezuma's Revenge on that sweltering coast. Paul Hévesey turned out to be the director of the movie, quite as determined a captain as Cortez, although he made no attempt to cross the mountains in a coat of mail, and was content to remain behind in a dilapidated fishing village, panting by the sea. All that he wanted me to do, it turned out, was to write a few scenes in order to embellish the part of the young leading lady of the film, whose protector was one of the principal stockholders in the company that was footing the bill for the entire venture. As banal a situation as ever.

"*Plus ça change, plus c'est la même chose*," he explained as we sat hunched over two tepid beers on the terrace of the squalid little hotel that had been turned into the company's headquarters. Late in life he had taken to talking French whenever possible, perhaps because it had been his first language after Hungarian, or perhaps because he thought it made him appear wiser, which indeed he was. He had lost most of his hair, as well as his waistline, and with the sweat running down his meaty jaws onto the blue linen handkerchief that he had knotted around his neck, he looked more like an aging pirate than one of the "masters of celluloid," which was what a recent issue of *Les Cahiers du Cinéma* had called him. "Of course, the story will suffer if we pad this young lady's role," he said. "But if you and I don't do it, two other fellows will. And Daddy needs the bread," he added, smiling with what appeared to be quite recently capped teeth.

I had traveled too many miles to make a gesture of integrity and return home empty-handed, and so I stayed on in the heat and wrote the scenes required. It was one of the least pleasant turns of prostitution I ever did, for not even sleep was possible after the dirty work of the day was done, as the town was inhabited by an extremely large population of dogs and donkeys who barked and brayed throughout the cooler morning hours, taking over once the insistent buzzing of the mosquitoes had finally subsided.

The indigenous citizens of the community—the licensed harlots and taxi drivers, the storekeepers and the fishermen—seemed not to be immune to this early-morning concert either, for once a year, I was told almost proudly, all the stray dogs in the town were rounded up and herded onto a raft, which was then set adrift on the tepid waters of the deep bay. This communal act of extraordinary cruelty appeared to me to sum up the spirit of the place. That and the discovery that the local fishermen, whenever they chanced to catch a large sea turtle, would turn the unfortunate animal on its back in front of their houses, and leave it to die a slow death in the intolerable heat of the day. Perhaps because of these revelations the unspoiled charm of the place was lost on me, although mine was obviously a minority opinion. Hundreds of tourists were already flocking to the village then, mainly Californians and Texans, who seemed delighted to escape the more regulated existence of their own environment. A good many of these "foreigners," I learned, had built expensive villas on the jungle cliffs overlooking the sea, and had thus put the place "on the map."

There was even a beach club, I discovered toward the end of my brief stay, complete with white-jacketed waiters bearing ice-cold Margaritas across a narrow strip of gray sand, always at the beck and call of their *gringo* customers, who spent their days basting in the tropical sun. With my unpleasant job done, and the Mexican airliner on which I had booked my escape due to arrive in the cool of the late evening, I sat in the shade of the spacious Polynesian hut that housed the club bar, content to watch the languid but noisy holidaymakers all around me. These were not "Greeks without brains," I thought nostalgically, these were decadent Romans, happily unconscious of the threat of the barbarian tribes.

My glance wandered around the interior of the bar. At a table in the back of the place I noticed a small group of people who seemed to be holding themselves aloof from the rest of the alcoholic crowd. A close scrutiny revealed that they were British tourists, and not Americans, which explained their not wanting to take part in the fun and games on the sand. One of them looked perplexingly familiar to me. Then, as they all got up to leave, I realized that it was Richard Gordon I had been staring at. He appeared to be in command of the party, was leading them resolutely toward the beach, where a sailor with a dinghy was waiting to row them out to a motor cruiser that lay anchored a few hundred yards offshore.

I had almost failed to recognize Gordon. His hair was a strange reddish color (no doubt the effect of the sun on the chemical hair lotion he used), and he was a good deal stockier than before. But his profile hadn't changed, and it was that which had revealed his identity to me. I watched him as he crossed the beach in his khaki shorts and open flowered shirt, his strong legs covered with hair bleached blond by the sun. For an instant I was tempted to follow him and speak to him, but I decided not to. He might not be all that pleased to see me again, it occurred to me. Then, too, he was busy organizing his group, helping some of the not-very-young ladies into the small boat. It was hardly the time to renew an acquaintance that had, at best, never been too friendly.

I turned back to the bartender. Yes, the Gordons had a house there, he told me, a big villa up in the hills, where they had lived for quite a few years. They had been among the first to discover Puerto. I was just going to ask about "la señora Gordon," when I saw Pam come into the bar. She was dressed in a long vanilla-colored robe of Mexican cotton, embroidered with red, blue, and green flowers. Her hair was gray, and she wore it cut even shorter than in the last photograph she had sent me. I noticed that her eyes and nose were almost unchanged, and her full mouth was as it had always been, well formed and vaguely tantalizing, pouting a little, as had always been her habit whenever she had to enter a crowded room alone.

I experienced a feeling of shock, as if I had suddenly stepped through a glass door into another life. She had stopped being real to me a long time ago. Now it was almost as if the heroine of one of my novels had been made to appear in the flesh. She was still attractive, despite the Mother Hubbard-like dress she wore and the slight broadening of some of her features. She put her hands on her hips, and stopping in the middle of the hut, said, "*Tiens!* Now, that's a surprise. What on earth are you doing here?"

I got up from my place at the bar and went toward her, not sure whether I was expected to kiss her cheeks, which I noticed had not been left unmarked by time and the tropics. And because I was afraid she might pull back, or turn her face away, I somewhat lamely took her hand, as if I were greeting a former nanny or a half-forgotten acquaintance. "I'm working for Paul," I said, which I realized at once was too precise an answer to what had been an exclamation on her part and nothing more.

She looked puzzled. "For Paul?"

"Paul Hévesey. He's making a movie here in Puerto."

"Oh, yes, of course. I did hear that."

"You haven't seen him?"

"No . . . but then we're not involved in that world anymore. And he's very busy, I believe."

There was an awkward pause, during which we both, I suspect, found our minds racing back to our last meeting. The quai in San Pedro. That was where we had said our final good-bye. "It's been a long time," I mumbled idiotically.

"Indeed it has," she replied with a brief smile. "And lots has happened since those days. To both of us. I heard that you were married, and then quite recently someone said that you were getting a divorce."

Was there a note of censure in her voice, or had I imagined it? As if she had always doubted my basic fidelity? "It happens in the best of families," I said with a shrug.

"Yes, but it's not always the best remedy," she replied. There was no trace of bitterness in her voice, and I dismissed my earlier suspicions.

"It's all done," I told her.

"Well, in that case I hope you won't regret it. I didn't go through with mine, thank the Lord, and it all worked out for the best." She smiled briefly, what in retrospect appeared to me to have been a slightly superior smile. "I just hope it won't make you cynical, that's all." She looked off in the direction of the sea, and noticed, as I did, that the dinghy was starting back from the yacht after depositing its first load. "You were always such a romantic young man," she said. "It would be a pity if you were to change." Someone called her name from the beach with a note of urgency that made her raise her arm in a signal of restraint. "It's not easy to discover what you really want," she added. "It takes a long time."

I took her hand. Her grip felt strangely passive, almost limp. I said: "I'm glad you're all right." I don't know what made me say it. It sounded false, and somehow condescending.

"Well, of course I am," she replied testily. "I was never really unhappy." She turned away. I wanted to detain her, just for a few seconds more, in order to explain how important she had been to me, how much she had mattered. But it was too late. She had gone off, rather pointedly, I thought, without saying good-bye.

I watched her cross the narrow strip of gray sand in front of the hut. The afternoon breeze flattened her dress against her body as she picked her way through the groups of spread-eagled sunbathers. The dinghy had arrived in the shallow water near the shore. She lifted her skirt and waded out to meet it, and then stepped unsteadily into the small boat, with Gordon and the sailor helping her. I noticed that she shaded her eyes with one hand and looked back while she was being rowed out to the waiting yacht.

Had I been the only one who had lived in despair all those years, I wondered? She had left me feeling a little bruised, as if my heart had received a not altogether undeserved cuff. But then, what I had said was obviously the one thing that could have wounded her. I hadn't meant to. I was truly glad that she was all right, quite independently of what had happened between us. I was grateful to her, and always would be. Seeing her again had made me realize it more than ever. I decided to leave a note for her with the round-faced bartender. I started to compose it in my mind while he went off for pencil and paper. "You misunderstood me. I'm sorry. I owe you so much. . . . From you I learned that it is better to have loved and lost . . . *Et cetera.*" The bartender returned and I lost heart. If I had written what I had wanted to, it would probably have sounded ridiculous to her, incomprehensible. We were too far apart, really, for a renewal of any kind of contact.

I described the incident to Hévesey that night, before his Mexican chauffeur drove me to the airport. I knew that he was one of the few people in the world who would fully appreciate the story. "I heard they were living near here," he said, grinning, after I had concluded my anecdote. "I think Edwina mentioned it to me the last time I saw her in London. She was quite nasty about her brother, I seem to remember . . . said he fled the country to avoid taxes. But then, she's a duchess now, and very important in her own right."

I said: "I wonder if Pam really doesn't remember, or if she was just putting me in my place."

"Ah, that you'll never know," Paul replied, spreading his hands in a gesture of Hungarian bewilderment. "*C'est comme ça. Tout passe, tout casse, tout se remplace.* . . ." His French sounded more tainted than ever, yet the proverb was well chosen.

I found myself repeating it as I was being driven down the asphalt road that led to the airport, where they left the donkeys that had been killed by the trucks that day for the vultures to devour. And as the airliner rose into the black sky, and I looked down without regret on the jungle I was leaving, I had to admit to myself that it was probably true: Everything breaks, everything passes, and everything is replaced. Our most acute feelings inevitably wind up being sunk without trace. I was not consoled.